Seren Discoveries

A series of translated literature introducing leading authors writing in 'minoirty' langauges ofr from 'peripheral' cultures. It includes work from Albanian, Basque, Welsh, Québécoise, Danish, and Czech, and from The Netherlands, Francophone Haiti, Luxembourg and Bosnia

UKULELE JAM

JAM

Alen Mešković

Translated from the Danish
by Paul Russell Garrett

Seren is the book imprint of
Poetry Wales Press Ltd,
57 Nolton Street, Bridgend, Wales, CF31 3AE

www.serenbooks.com
facebook.com/SerenBooks
Twitter: @SerenBooks

ISBN: 978-1-78172-342-5
Ebook: 978-1-78172-343-2
Mobi: 978-1-78172-344-9

A CIP record for this title is available from the British Library.

The publisher work with the financial assistance of the Welsh Books Council.

DANISH ARTS FOUNDATION

This translation of Ukulele Jam is supported in part by the Danish Arts
Foundation.

The book has been selected to receive fnancial assistance from English PEN's
'PEN Translates!' programme, supported by Arts Council of England. English
PEN exists to promote literature and our understanding of it, to uphold writers'
freedoms around the world, to campaign against the persecution and
imprisonment of writers for stating their views, and to promote the friendly
co-operation of writers and the free exchange of idea. www.englishpen.org

Printed by Bell & Bain, Glasgow

Contents

Cassette 1

PANORAMA BLUES

PLAY

The bus pulled out of the station. Dad scratched behind his ear and coughed:

'He gave us a hundred marks.'

'I saw,' Mum said.

'He's all right, my brother. In spite of everything.'

'I don't even know why the two of you argue. He opened his home to us. He helped as best as he could.'

'Because he does not understand a bloody thing about politics! Besides, we do not argue. We discuss.'

Next to me, behind Dad, the seat was empty. One of our bags was resting there, but still I kept seeing Neno sitting there. I imagined we were still together, he and I, Mister No and Captain Micky.

Neither of us had a clue where the other was any more.

A month earlier, after Mum, Dad and I crossed the Croatian border and left Bosnia behind, Uncle had been waiting for us at that very station. Back then we still had some hope that our hometown would not fall, that the war would soon be over – that Neno and the others would soon be released. Now the ruins of the entire town were in Serbian hands, the front line had been pushed back, and it was clear to everyone that the war was not going to be over in a matter of weeks. My uncle, who had lived abroad for years but had returned to enjoy a retirement by the sea, believed the war would not be over until the summer ended.

'Just wait till their balls start to freeze,' he said. 'Then they'll change their tune.'

'The people giving the orders do not have to sit in the trenches,' Dad said. 'That is the whole point.'

Mum's dark curls and Dad's shiny egg dominated my view the entire trip along the coast. I was still having difficulty turning my head to the right. The pain came and went as I looked out the window.

'Emir?'

'Yeah.'

'Do you remember the time we came here on holiday?'

'No.'

'He doesn't remember a bloody thing,' Dad said. 'He was too little. Little Miki, we called him back then.'

'You were on a donkey. We took a picture of you riding it.'

'Oh, okay. Wow.'

White facades, small stone haciendas, hotels and even more hotels lined the road. Tourists, well aware that the war had not reached *everywhere* in Croatia, were enjoying the hot July day. Their burnt shoulders, inflatable animals and beach balls kept my mind busy for a while. Then he turned up again.

'Dear Mister No. I know you're still alive. No matter what they say, I know that one day you'll come …'

We had added his name to a number of lists, and Dad had contacted acquaintances with varying levels of influence. Everyone wanted money but no-one knew a thing. As of yet, nobody from his group had been exchanged. The politicians talked and talked, the soldiers shot and shot, and no matter where I was, there was a gaping void at my side.

The most optimistic of all the rumours suggested that they had been sent to a concentration camp in the vicinity of Banja Luka. The least optimistic went that the group had been executed the day they were separated from the rest of us.

'People talk,' Dad whispered. 'If you hear anything, tell *me*. Understood? She spends enough time crying as it is.'

Mum cried a lot during our month at Uncle's place. His flat was not particularly big, and I was bored most of the time. A stressed-out blonde at the Red Cross eventually found us a room at the camp in Majbule. None of us had ever heard of the place.

'It's well situated,' she assured us. 'Right by the sea.'

'I don't give a damn about the sea,' Dad said. 'I want to go home.'

According to the map, Majbule was a speck of flyshit about six kilometres south of Vešnja. I found it in Uncle's thick, German atlas. Definitely not the kind of place you just happened to drive past. It was at the tip of a peninsula. The Balkini peninsula, it read.

While I studied the map, Dad and Uncle discussed the war and the time that preceded it.

'The communists lied,' Uncle said. 'Far too much and for far too long.'

'If it weren't for us, there would have been a bloodbath ages ago. If it weren't for the party, half the population wouldn't be able to read or write!'

'You all just marched in step.'

'Yes, and why are you grumbling? You just up and left.'

'Exactly! And then I invited you to join me.'

That was news to me. I closed the atlas:

'Is that true?'

'Yes,' Uncle nodded. 'He sent me a dismissive letter in return. No way was he going to clean toilets for the Germans! And Canada was too far away. He was not going to abandon his colleagues at the factory, his fishing trips, his football club.'

'I was fine where I was,' Dad said.

Uncle shrugged despondently:

'That town's always been a hole!'

We got off the bus in Vešnja. On the local bus to Majbule, Mum and Dad started chatting to an outspoken woman by the name of Ivka. It turned out that she lived in the camp. Her husband worked for the police, and they had a room facing the sea.

'Most of the rooms have a balcony,' she said. 'There's a beautiful peninsula and an island. You're going to love it. Especially if you get a room facing the sea.'

'The sea stinks of rotten eggs,' Dad said. 'What about water and heating? Is there electricity?'

'Plenty. A shower and toilet all to yourselves. Everyone eats at the restaurant. They say it's the best camp in all of Croatia.'

The bus drove through Vešnja at a snail's pace. At one of the stops, two guys dressed like freaks got on. One was wearing a red checked shirt. The other, a purple T-shirt and a pair of cut-offs. They were dressed like Neno, and I picked up the bag from the empty seat and moved it onto my lap. But they walked past and sat at the very back.

Instead a bald guy pushed his way towards the empty spot. He thumped down onto the seat with a snort and nodded at me:

'Hot, eh?'

'Yeah.'

'Really hot!'

He unfolded a paper bag and started munching away on a greasy burek with cheese.

'Mirko,' he introduced himself to the neighbouring brunette, with flakes of puff pastry sprinkling down over his lap.

I tried to block out everyone around me, their gazes, voices and smells. Staring out at me from the leather cover of Mum's backrest was a huge U, written in black felt pen. I closed my eyes and remembered a viaduct in Split, where Dad and I had seen one that was even larger.

'A few years ago, they would send you to jail for doing something like that,' Dad had said. 'Now people brag about being a fascist Ustashe! Democracy? To hell with them and their democracy!'

Majbule was situated on a hill. We were exiting the only

roundabout in town when I spotted the bay and the small peninsula. Before the camp had been established, the bus would terminate here, according to Ivka. Now, twice a day, the bus continued down through the narrow one-way streets to the refugee camp in the bay.

'The camp's seen better days,' Ivka said, 'and it's no wonder: five hundred arses, one thousand feet, and the same number of hands, all in motion twenty-four hours a day – they leave their mark! Greasy fingerprints everywhere. Broken chairs, scratched tables. Beneath the fig trees and behind the bushes, it stinks of piss.'

'Really?' Mum asked in surprise.

'You know our people. Most of them are from the countryside. They piss anywhere they can. On the other hand, the city people make a lot of racket. The children in particular. Recently there was a boy, he must be half-blind, who ran through a glass door five millimetres thick. Dario was his name. A real brat. And what a racket!'

'Was he hurt?'

'Believe it or not: he escaped with only a cut on his forehead. And of course the glass was never replaced.'

'Why not? What did the owner say? Who owns the holiday camp incidentally?'

'Before the war this camp was the reserve of majors, colonels, their wives and lovers. The army federation, trade union, whatever it's called, Serbian, they built it back in the day.'

'Ah, I see.'

'But all the elegant receptionists are long gone now. The former caretakers and cleaning ladies work behind the counter now. They don't lift a finger. Just sort the post, answer the phones and wait for further instructions from those "higher up the system"'.

'Just like the rest of us,' Dad said with a smile.

'Yes. And those "higher up the system" have far more important things to do than discuss the army federation's former holiday camp. The officers, be they Serbian or

Croatian, don't have much time for a holiday these days.'

'No, that's true,' Dad laughed. 'Unfortunately.'

Funny, I thought. Were it not for the YPA, The Yugoslav People's Army, none of us would have seen Majbule or sat on that stinking bus that day. Not just because the YPA had built the camp, but the YPA were also the ones who had driven us out. Since Croatia and Serbia were now independent states and as such 'did not have the best relationship with one another,' as Ivka put it, the ownership of the camp was still unsettled. Exactly who had come up with the idea to house refugees from the independent state of Bosnia-Herzegovina and the independent state of Croatia inside this no man's land, was one of the few things Ivka did not know.

A plump red-headed, and to all appearances, very sleepy receptionist handed us the keys to room 210 in building D1.

We walked across a broad concrete terrace, our movements followed by a group of old women. They were sitting on the benches of the terrace, crocheting in grand style.

'Hello there!'

'Hello!'

'Is this D1?'

'Yes.'

Then up the stairs and down the corridor, where the greyish wall-to-wall carpeting reeked of synthetic material and rubber.

Dad unlocked the door and we went inside. He shook his head at the sight of the table and the three perfectly made beds.

'Look at this! Karadžić has damn well screwed me over,' he said with a wry smile. 'He's forced me to go on holiday!'

Mum peeked inside a couple of drawers and opened the door to the brown, built-in wardrobe. She placed the few rags we managed to bring with us on a shelf and started to cry. Dad signalled to me – 'act like nothing is wrong' – then went into the bathroom.

'It looks good!' he shouted as he rattled the shower hose. 'We've got water. Hot water!'

I stepped out onto the balcony so Mum could cry in peace. Took my first look at the windows and balconies of D2. Then over at the water, the island and the peninsula, which I could just make out from our balcony.

I went back inside, grabbed our red Sanyo cassette player from Neno's bag and unwound the cord. Sanyo is the name of a Japanese company that makes cassette players, and had no connection to the Serbo-Croat verb *sanjati*, to dream. I knew that. I also knew I was not dreaming, even though everything around me seemed rather surreal and distant. It was as though a thin shell of glass had been placed around me and separated me from everything I could smell, hear and see: the smell of laundry from the neighbouring balcony, the yellowed wall socket above the bed, my mum's quiet and fading tears and the immediate, high-pitched sound you hear when you press *play*.

POLITICS

I only had one cassette with me. I had not had time to grab the rest. White Button, best-of. Pretty good. It was in the player the day we had to pack our things and leave.

'Stop!'

In the middle of 'Blues For My Ex', Bregović's solo was interrupted.

'My turn now,' Dad said and grabbed the tape player. 'Now then.'

'Hey, what are you doing, man?'

'I've been in that rumbling wreck of a bus all day, son. I want some peace and quiet now, I don't want to be tormented by your Indians! The news is going to be on in a moment.'

By the door to the corridor, directly across from the bathroom, there was a mirror with a shelf at the bottom. I ran my hand through my hair, checked my teeth and got a proper downer at the sight of my stupid yellow T-shirt. Not very rock'n'roll. All my best clothes were back home. I should have packed myself. Not left it to Mum during the hurried chaos of the day.

'Oww!'

'Now what?'

'My neck. It hurts like hell! It's almost like it's … on backwards.'

'I'm sure it will pass,' Mum said. 'It could have been worse.'

Yeah, I thought. My right ear could have been damaged by the explosion. And *that* would have been a downer. Having to listen to the coolest rock with only one ear.

As I stepped out onto the terrace between D1 and D2, it felt like everyone was staring at me – the old women on the benches and everyone sitting on the balconies. In several places the Croatian flag was draped over the railings, and blasting from one of the open windows in D2 was the year's big hit, 'Čavoglave'. On both the radio and TV, they played it over and over again, so not a living soul avoided getting it in their head. One day at Uncle's flat, sitting in front of the telly, I caught myself humming along: 'Our hand will reach you even in Serbia!'

The terrace between D1 and D2 had the reception building at one end and a long set of stairs at the other. The stairs led down to a paved path that was shaded by a row of twisted pine trees. Beyond and below the trees was the beach, with the white shiny cliffs of the bay and scattered holidaymakers.

I walked down the stairs and turned right. Dry pine needles crunched under my feet. The path led me to a building, which at first glance was identical to the other two, but it appeared completely abandoned. There were beds with mattresses in the rooms on the ground floor, but no duvets or linen. A sign by the entrance read D3.

I turned and strolled back – past D2, D1 and on towards the restaurant, which was a little further down the path and offered a view of the sea. Between the trees I could just make out the flat cliffs and the people lying on them. It was impossible to see which ones were refugees and which ones were tourists. Two woman passed me. One was topless. I noticed it too late.

Below the restaurant's terrace was the only stretch of beach in the entire bay where there were no cliffs. A couple of fat children were playing with the dazzling white rocks. They were speaking German and throwing the rocks in the water, a turquoise green that reminded me of one of Dad's shirts. I took in the smell of resin, rotten seaweed and summer, and suddenly felt like swimming.

At the end of the only pier on the beach I spotted the two long-haired guys from the bus. One of them took a run-up and jumped into the water. The other one sat on the pier with his toes dipped in the water.

'Hey, Samir,' a gangling woman shouted from the point where the beach and the pier met. 'Dad and I are heading back to the room!'

She had a strong Bosnian accent, and the guy with his toes in the water turned and replied in an even stronger one:

'Fine! But why are you telling me? We're staying!'

'Remember dinner's at six, you too Damir!'

'Yeah, yeah!'

I felt like going down and telling them that I was Bosnian too, but I hesitated. Samir got up and jumped into the water. He and his brother started to swim away from the pier, and only then did I notice that they were not alone. There were two girls and a boy swimming with them. One of the girls smacked her palm against the surface of the water and sprayed water over Samir.

I returned to the shade of the path and continued ahead. At the other end of the camp there were two tennis courts, five or six abandoned bungalows and a vandalised basketball pole with no net.

Neno was really good at basketball. Best in the neighbourhood. I threw an imaginary ball towards the basket as I walked past. Nothing but net.

The gate to the camp was wide open. I went for a long walk, stared at the large villas in Majbule and thought back to our departure with Uncle this morning. Sometimes when I thought of Neno, I thought of Uncle too. He and Dad were so different. They were constantly wittering on about war and politics. And about how the Slovenians got off far too lightly with their one-and-a-half-week war. About the fragile ceasefire in Croatia. About Bosnia, which according to Dad had drawn the short straw.

They disagreed about most things. The night before we left, they discussed whether or not the West would intervene.

'Divide and conquer,' Dad said. 'That's their tactic. The Russians support Milošević, and the Germans and everyone else support Tudjman. Just like in the last war. The Chetniks and the Ustashe want to …'

'Come off it,' Uncle interrupted him. 'This isn't the forties any more! The West is only trying to help.'

'It's all exactly like it was back then. The Serbs and the Croats want to divide Bosnia! Now the only thing we're missing is the German and Russian ground forces.'

'No,' Uncle said shaking his head. 'You're confusing things. The UN is different.'

I returned along the same route the bus had taken earlier that day.

Dad was on his back in a half-prone position when I entered the room. His chin was pressed against his chest, and it looked like he had no neck. Our red cassette player was resting on his shoulder, repeating the same phrases like a unicoloured parrot:

'Fierce battles … heroic resistance … heavy enemy losses …'

'Mind the cassette player doesn't attach itself to your ear,' I said while I loosened my shoelaces. 'You haven't moved an inch since I left.'

'Quiet, son. This is important.'

Mum sat out on the balcony staring into space.

I slipped off my shoes.

This place is all right, I thought. There's that guy Samir and his brother. Girls on the beach. It has possibilities.

NOTHING

Dad was not a big fan of Tudjman – Dr Fanjo Tudjman, the Croatian president. Not a single news report was broadcast without his mug appearing on the TV screen. He spoke proudly and at length, and when he was not speaking, he was being quoted. He loved Croatia. The Serbs and us Bosnians, now referred to as Bosniaks though the president still called us Muslims, were not discussed much on TV. When it happened, it was best to be as far from the TV room as possible. The flickering screen was on twenty-four-seven. When there was no news, you could watch videos of patriotic songs, films with big explosions, and programs with wild animals devouring one another.

The day started and ended with the playing of 'Our Beautiful Homeland'. While listening to the familiar melody for the umpteenth time, the silk fabric of the coat of arms with its red-and-white chessboard fluttered in the wind, attached to a sturdy flagpole. No matter where you looked, you were reminded of the fact that you lived in the independent and sovereign republic of Croatia. That this young country had three hundred and sixty-five national days a year.

The radio was not quite as bad. Between the news and the lengthy front-line reports, which kept us up to date with the number of killed, wounded, raped and persecuted, there was room for the latests hits. 'Winds of Change' by the Scorpions for example. I wondered what the song was about. Did it have something to do with life changing? Something about the children of the future, dreaming of this wind?

When the radio hummed about 'those fleeing' and 'those displaced' both Dad and I hissed. There was a distinction of roles in the two terms: Bosnians fled, Croats from Croatia were displaced. There were constant reminders of that fact.

Croats from Bosnia got far better press than us and the Serbs, but still they did not enjoy the same sunshine as Croats from Croatia. Even though they were Croats, they were also referred to as 'those fleeing.'

Dad grumbled about the fact that they looked after their own first. By 'they' he meant the Croatian authorities, but also the companies, whose lorries and buses occasionally stopped in the car park in front of reception. Most people in the camp called the car park the Muscle Market. It was because many of the men from the camp stood out there waiting from the crack of dawn. Even before the bus arrived to pick people up in the morning, they stood out by the market, rocking back and forth like a sloth of impatient bears. They sniffled, coughed, and lit their first cigarettes of the day while looking up towards the bend in the road. For that is where the owners of the villas, vineyards and farms would appear in their cars.

They hoped they would be picked up.

They cut grass, weeded gardens, emptied septic tanks, picked cobs of corn, made mortar, chopped firewood, welded gates, plastered walls, felled trees, tore down old walls.

When they were driven back to the camp they were a few kunas richer.

The old man usually returned from the market crestfallen. He closed the door behind him and said:

'Nothing.'

'Nothing?' Mum asked.

'Nothing,' he repeated.

'Maybe there will be something tomorrow. At least you're on the list.'

'There are a lot more of them than there are us,' he said. 'That's the problem. They have too many of their own on the list!'

'Maybe someone from one of the smaller farms will come tomorrow. The vineyard is not the only work.'

'Yes, but in spite of everything it does offer something more fixed. I'm bloody tired of standing out there every day! It's embarrassing at my age.'

'We should speak to Ivka,' Mum said. 'She knows someone who needs both women and men. They gather hay, pick corn and dig up potatoes.'

'Oh, God no!' Dad shouted. 'I became a welder to get away from hay, cow shit and pitchforks. And now they're running after me. Forty years later!'

The following day he was back out there but was seldom picked up. He once earned forty kunas in a day. He drank most of it and spent the rest on a bag of clementines.

HOW'S YOUR ENGLISH?

Tudjman had a lot of fans in the camp. Bald Mirko from the ground floor of D1 was without a doubt his biggest. As soon as the president appeared on screen, Mirko raised two fingers high in the air. These two fingers, which formed the letter V, he held high above his head the entire time Tudjman's faced filled the screen. Occasionally the news bulletin dragged on for so long that Mirko had to use his left arm as a kind of crutch for his right arm. When the report ended and the newsreader appeared again, he lowered his arm and waited patiently for President Dr Franjo Tudjman to appear again.

Mirko was a queer fish. He was over forty and had never been married. He claimed to suffer from a range of serious ailments, which he combatted in a number of ways. He constantly went on about plants, preparations and tea; nobody in the entire camp was as trying as Mirko Parasite. He was the kind of guy who would always ask people to do something for him. At the restaurant he always ate alone, and he had his laundry done by the older women in the camp, who sooner or later would take pity on him.

Mirko claimed that he had been physically disabled for some time, and for that reason he wore special shoes, which he had received as a gift from a large Italian company via Caritas. But it was one big perpetual lie! Already on my first evening at the camp I saw him in an entirely different light.

I was sitting on our balcony, staring at the stars, when suddenly I heard an inarticulate screaming and shouting from the TV room. It was located right by the entrance to D2, and since the terrace was well lit, I saw plain as day how Mirko Parasite, moving at an admirable pace, sprinted across the terrace towards the entrance to our building.

A down-at-heel clog went flying after him, but missed.

The next day I discovered that he had got into an argument with Igor, a professional Croatian soldier who had just returned from the front. It was Igor's first day of leave in a long time. He had entered the TV room carrying a VCR and a couple of old porn flicks. Seeing as it was quite late, Igor had not expected to see anyone in the TV room. But the grimy remote was lodged in Mirko's hand, and being the devout Catholic that he was, he did not want to miss out on some random programme about some random church in some random location in Croatia. So it ended in an argument, with harsh words and footwear of a rather large calibre flying through the air in Mirko's direction.

Igor told me the story himself. He had turned twenty that summer and spent most of his time at the front lines in Croatia – Bosnia too, he was quick to add. Whether that was the cause of his constant blinking and nervous twitches, he never mentioned.

I met him after lunch the day after his failed attempt to thump Mirko Parasite with a clog. My stomach was filled with macaroni. It was hot outside. On the terrace in front of the restaurant, Igor came dawdling towards me wearing tight Speedos. He burped, and without asking who I was or what my name was, he said:

'Do you want to go out to the end of the peninsula?'

'To the end of the peninsula?'

'Yes, the peninsula. How's your English?'

'Not bad.'

'Good. Come with me!'

We did not take the well-travelled path through the woods, but struggled across the red-hot rocks along the water. That was Igor's idea, or rather his order.

I soon discovered why I needed to fry off the soles of my feet. Halfway to an abandoned concrete bunker that dated from the previous war, Igor spotted a topless babe lying on her back, lapping up the sun.

At Igor's command, we sat down and took a break. We observed her carefully. Igor, I must admit, a little more discreetly than me.

Then he made me a quick and determined signal with his hand:

'Come with me and translate!'

We reached the spot near the water where the girl was lying. She was wearing sunglasses. She was listening to a Walkman and smelt of sun cream.

'Tell her I'd like to speak to her! Now! Tell her!'

I opened my mouth, and the poor girl jerked like she had been stung by a jellyfish. She switched off her Walkman and raised her sunglasses.

'Excuse me. This man want talk to you,' I said with my elegant English accent.

'Oh?'

Unabashed, she sat up. Oh, my God! Only then could we see the true breadth of her … her … Yes, what do you call them?

'So? I'm listening.'

I looked at Igor. Igor looked at her. And blinked.

'What should I say?'

'Ask her … Ask her what music she's listening to!'

'What music you hear?'

'Music? Why?'

'He will know.'

'Well … It's quite different … Let me see … Duran Duran, The Cure, Pet Shop Boys … and so on. But … why?'

'I listen to Filthy Theatre and Gold Coins. Tell her!'

I translated. As best I could.

'Golden Money?' She wrinkled her nose. 'Never heard of it.'

Soon we were sitting next to her, and Igor was well on his way to asking her rather more personal questions. About where she came from, did she like the sea, the climate, and so on. It turned out that she was from Germany, from a city Igor and I had never heard of. She had been here for nearly two weeks, and the following day she was returning home. Igor started to describe his hometown and his childhood, and the entire scene dragged on, until the babe moved her sunglasses down over her eyes again and lay down on her back in the middle of one of his long, meandering sentences.

On the way back to the camp we were both silent, and when we reached the restaurant, Igor turned back to the peninsula and said thoughtfully:

'Damn! I'm sitting there looking at her while you translate, and I get such an urge to fondle her jades. But then I thought: What do I know, maybe she'll get upset! I mean … you never *know*.'

THE FENCE

Igor drank a lot and talked a lot, and he talked even more when he drank. For whatever reason he selected me as his regular listener. Maybe because I would never dream of interrupting people or getting up from the table in the middle of a sentence. But Igor's sentences were very long. It was difficult to leave without interrupting one of them. They merged together and branched out in every possible direction.

The first time I got drunk with Igor – or rather the first time Igor got me drunk – was immediately after he received a monster of a rejection down on the beach. This time, the girl was a local. We had not even made it through the introductory stage when she cut us off:

'Do you see that muscly guy down by the water?'

A tanned bodybuilder with a tiny head stood hugging a towel. His muscles filled a large proportion of the landscape, so his answer was 'Yeah, sure.'

'That's my husband.'

'A handsome fellow,' Igor commented, and we strolled off under the setting sun.

We headed to Wicky, the only bar in Majbule open year-round, which Igor ascribed many superlatives to. On the way, he rambled on about his unassuming physique. It was of great benefit to him on the front line, in his opinion.

'A big hulk like that, that iron-pumping moron just now. It's difficult to miss him!'

'Hmm.'

'There was one guy … man, I'm telling you! Those are the guys that scream the most when they get hit … Hey, have you ever fired a rifle?'

'No.'

'A pistol?'

'No.'

'Tank?'

'No, jeez! I was the target.'

'Target? Hmm. Who was shooting?'

'Our side. Plus Serbian artillery. She had nice legs, that chick on the beach. Firm!'

'How could that happen, your own people shooting at you?'

'Long story. Did you see how …?'

'What did they fire at you?'

'Shells. All sorts.'

'What kind of shells?'

'No idea. Is there more than one kind?'

'Of course! Bloody hell, kid! Have you never seen a shell?'

'No, only fragments. I've never seen a whole one.'

'Some of them are pretty impressive,' Igor said and blinked. 'Almost like tits.'

The road up to Wicky was long and winding. So at Igor's command, we hopped over a newly erected fence.

Before us was the well-travelled path that led up the hill.

'HEY!' someone suddenly shouted behind us. 'WHERE DO YOU TWO THINK YOU'RE GOING? EH?'

We turned around. Standing by the fence was a bearded gnome who looked to be at least sixty. Wearing an unbuttoned shirt and long trousers with holes in them. His two goats were munching on something in the shade of a shrub. He was holding a cane in his hand, demanding an answer.

'We're going up to Wicky,' Igor said.

'Can't you see that this is private property? Didn't you see the fence?'

'Yes.'

'They why the hell did you climb over the fence? I just finished building it!'

'It's a shortcut,' Igor said. 'Everyone goes this way.'

'Everyone *went* this way,' the man said. 'I want to see you gone! Pronto!'

'I didn't fancy arguing with him,' Igor later explained on our detour. 'That old fool! Moron! I'll pummel him next time.'

Then he started to talk about his military service in the YPA and the difference between the uniforms then and now. I was thinking more and more about the man in the unbuttoned shirt, about my first detour, and about Bobi, the first idiot I had ever run into. Igor's voice slowly faded out. Soon all my thoughts led back to the time before Mister No disappeared.

BACK THEN

It was 1984. Bobi was eight, I was six. His house was on the way to Adi's place. I could see the roof of Adi's house when Bobi hopped over his garden gate. He stood in front of me:

'Where do you think you're going?'

'To Adi's place.'

'You're not going past my house! Go a different way.'

'Why?'

'Because I said so. Scram!'

I tried to go around him. Took two steps to the left. But he took two steps in the same direction.

'When I tell you to scram, scram!'

'Leave me alone!'

'Beat it!'

I looked around and hurried across the street. Bobi followed me at the same speed. He spread his arms out.

'What's that in your pockets?'

'Packs.'

'And inside the packs?'

'Nothing.'

'No way. Let me see!'

'No!'

'Give them to me and I'll let you past.'

'They're mine.'

'Then get lost and find a different way to Adi's with your crappy boxes, man! You're never getting past my house again, ever! Beat it!'

I turned around and took a long detour to Adi's place. Was certainly not looking forward to starting school. I would have to go past Bobi's house every day.

School. That was where Mister No came home carrying his

heavy bag. He ate in the kitchen, drank some water and went into his room. Then I heard music inside. Voices, sometimes. Girls' voices, boys' voices. Sudden sniggers. The girls laughed the loudest. Practically shrieked.

When Mum and Dad were out, he smoked cigarettes in his room. I could smell them from out in the hall.

Freezing cold. The hall was either freezing cold or draughty, back then. I liked to play there.

'Neno?'

'Yes?'

'Are we going to go to school together?'

'No.'

'Why not?'

'Because! You're going to primary school, and I'm going to secondary school.'

'Secondary school?'

'Yes. It's a different school. For the big kids. But if you're lucky, you'll be in the same class as Adi. If they'll even take you.'

He laughed:

'If they can even find anything in there. Inside that little noggin!'

Adi and I always walked to school together. We had physical education together. We played football against each other.

'Has anybody done anything to you?' Mister No asked when he picked me up one day.

'No.'

'Let me know if anything happens.'

'Okay.'

'Are you hungry? Should we go see Mum at work?'

The huge department store had magical staircases. We stood still on them and glided upwards. Mum worked on the top floor. Up by the sign that read CHILDREN'S WEAR.

'How was school?' she asked.

Her arms smelled of rose perfume.

'Fine. The teacher, she pulled Jović's ears five times.'
'What did he do?'
'He couldn't recite a poem by heart.'
'Which poem?'
'It was one … about Tito.'
Neno laughed:
'As if there's only one!'
'The one with the partisans.'
'Aha,' Mum said. 'Have you eaten? Or are you going home to eat with Dad?'

Dad worked at the factory. Dad used the word 'factory' every single day. He also used 'party,' 'workers' council,' 'meeting' and 'problem.'
He said:
'Ugh, I can't wait for early retirement!'
Then added:
'Five more years.'
In small, scattered groups in the park in front of the factory hall, workers covered in soot stood smoking cigarettes. They called him 'boss.'
'Boss' once said to me in private:
'Damn those exhaust pipes and damn the guy who invented them! I get ill just looking at them. Do you realise how many pipes I've welded? Thousands! Hundreds of thousands! If not more!'
He thought about it for a moment.
'More, definitely,' he nodded.

One winter Bobi's cousin Rade made me eat snow. We were playing ice hockey on the frozen river. The puck was a dark, flat stone. During the break we had a snowball fight and I nailed him every time.
'Eat, you little shithead, eat!' he shouted over my muffled sobs; there were rubbery bands of saliva hanging from the corners of my mouth.
Not until Mister No came running down the

embankment and thumped him did Bobi's cousin let go, the idiot. Idiot number two. He never touched me again.

'Why don't you defend yourself?' Mister No asked.

'He's stronger than me. And older.'

'That doesn't matter. You can't just let him do that to you. I won't always be here to defend you.'

No, he would not. In 1988, when I started Year 5, he was no longer living at home. His room was half-empty, his door was always closed. I wrote letters to him and badgered Mum and Dad with the same question, over and over again:

'Why don't we just move to Sarajevo with him?'

When they were out, I twisted the door knob and went inside. I felt like a thief. Like a ghost.

His countless cassettes and LPs were arranged in alphabetical order. That made it easier to put them back in the right place. Not once did he discover that I had sat in his rocking chair. That I had been headbanging in the middle of his room, studying all the cool covers and reading the wicked lyrics.

When he came home on holiday, I played dumb:

'Can I borrow White Button's latest album?'

'No.'

'No Smoking's double LP?'

'No.'

'At least let me borrow a Balašević cassette?'

'No.'

'Okay. Just asking.'

Mister No. I called him tight-fisted and Mister No.

'Nedim Pozder, Neno: Mister No.'

'Beat it, before I unscrew your head!'

It had actually been meant as a compliment. Mister No, the legendary pilot Jerry Drake, my biggest hero. The coolest comic they sold at the newsagent's. Mister No lived in the Brazilian city of Manaus, where he flew tourists over the Amazonian rainforests. His Piper was often in for repairs.

His friend Krüger was German – a World War Two veteran, just like him. In every issue the hero met a new girl, but in the end she always left.

Neno did not live in Brazil, but in Sarajevo. He did not read comics, he read books. He knew everything about plants, insects and animals. He was the smartest person in the world.

During the holidays he brought home countless stories. His words made the whole house light up.

Then we would hire a boat and row upriver. There was often heavy traffic. Kayaks, sandolins and hire boats slowly drifted past. We waved at a lot of them, and a lot of them waved back. He told me about Sarajevo, his classmates and Igman Mountain, where they went and had barbecues.

I knew Sarajevo from the TV and from songs. It was a city a lot of people sang about, and a lot of good bands came from there. Our one-horse town only had lousy cover bands, Neno had actually been in one once, until he left the bumbling amateurs behind.

When Neno returned to Sarajevo, the atmosphere in the house fell. Not just because he had left behind an ugly void, but also because more and more of Dad's sentences began to start with 'Back then …' and 'In my younger days …'

Mum yawned. Sighed sometimes. I lay on the sofa next to Dad and listened to the stories of his wild youth.

'… And look at me now … these grey hairs … this bloody life! It's over before it even starts … Remember what I tell you, Emir. Take what you can, *while* you can. Because time goes by so damn quickly. You're what, ten or eleven now, and …'

'Twelve!'

'Right, twelve … and it feels like only yesterday I was your age.'

'When was that?'

'Right after the war. Back then, there were gangs of

Chetniks and Ustashe still holding out in the woods.'

'Ustashe?'

'Yes, all the collaborators, you know – fascists who slaughtered people during the war. Two of them were captured once, a couple of big fish. One of them was the mayor of the city.'

'Hmm.'

'They were hung down by the bridge, and I witnessed it. It's not like in the movies, where they just fall and die. The two of them dangled there for a long time. The one guy, his rope broke twice and there were rumblings that they should release him, it must have been a sign that he was innocent. Supernatural imbeciles! Our people are so stupid. They were then and they are now. Even though the party did everything it could to help them. Innocent? Like hell he was. He was a butcher!'

'Can you tell me about the time the partisans shot the guy with the milk again?'

'Oh right, down by the bog. Back then there were no houses down there, it was all fields and willows.'

'Why?'

'Because back then the city ended at the crossing. The roads weren't paved either. I was letting the cows graze down by the bog that morning. That was in 1944, I remember – a crazy year. The town was changing hands all the time. When you woke up in the morning, you didn't know if the Ustashe, the Chetniks or the Partisans controlled it. The Germans had as good as given up, Mussolini was already finished.'

'Mussolini? Who was that?'

'Hitler's friend.'

'Ah.'

'So! Let's see: all of them were capable of taking the town, but nobody could hold onto it. I was watching the cows and could see a group of partisans guarding a post down by the crossing. Back then there was a bakery on the corner, which also sold milk. An Ustashe – a young one – came driving along in a horse and carriage. Some empty milk cans were rattling in the back. He must have thought his people still controlled the town and that they would want to buy milk.'

'And then what happened?'

'When he saw the Partisans, he tried to turn the cart around. But he didn't get a chance.'

'Did they shoot?'

'No, you know very well that they did not shoot. They threw a grenade. They captured him alive. Then they dragged him down to the bog and shot him there. I saw it. Through the willows.'

'Weren't you scared, Dad?'

'Why should I have been scared? I was only a child. Children were not touched.'

I was under the impression that everything was over. That the good days would never return. That Neno, just like Dad's youth, was gone forever.

By the time he returns home, I thought, it will be 1992. I'll be fourteen, nearly fifteen. That's a long way off. I can't wait that long.

There and then, I wanted to run away to Sarajevo and live closer to him. One day, after Bobi had ruined my day with some self-taught judo moves, the urge was greatest. His Mum shouted from the window:

'Slobodan! What are you doing? Leave the child be!'

But he did not leave me be. He twisted my around my back and shoved me to the ground.

'Slobodan! Let him go! Let him go!'

Finally he obeyed.

I brushed the dirt off my trousers and hopped onto my bike. Raced over the bridge and through the city. I pedalled like a madman and did not stop until I reached the Tempel water tap. 'A Jewish mosque' had once stood here, Dad had told me. A block of stone and the crooked tap were all that was left of the synagogue now. The Ustashe burned it to the ground in 1942.

I washed my face under the cold water and continued walking with my bike. Passed the pedestrian precinct and made it all the way to the other end of the city. At the first crossing before the ring road there was a sign with three arrows. They each pointed in a different direction: Sarajevo 211 km, Zagreb 223 km, Belgrade 229 km.

The cicadas were shrieking. A mown-down cat lay motionless in the gutter. Rumbling lorries and cars faded into the horizon.

I stopped by the sign, my gaze followed the road to Sarajevo. Behind me the church bells began to chime, and the muezzin announced the call to prayers.

I turned around and cycled home to listen to Neno's albums.

WICKY

Wicky, the bar that Igor thought so bloody highly of, was awful. A turquoise fountain was left thirsting in the middle of the room. The bottom half of the walls featured glazed tiling. Mounted in one of the corners was a dusty television set, which showed MTV on mute, instead the music came from a stereo at the bar; lots of pop, lots of electric drums.

We sat out on the terrace, and Igor ordered a beer for himself. Then he nodded to the waiter:

'Get him something too.'

'A Coke, please,' I said.

Later he ordered for both of us, without differentiating between us and without asking what I wanted:

'Two more beers!'

'He's too young,' the waiter said. 'We don't serve minors.'

'He's my brother,' Igor replied. 'He's my responsibility.'

I drank a sip of my beer, and Igor asked me loads of questions. Mostly about the war, technical details. Half of them I could not answer. Igor could though. He told me, among other things, that the mobile vehicles, known as Pragas, had twin 30 mm calibre cannons. How was I supposed to know that? I had only heard them firing.

'Czech quality,' Igor said. 'We use them too.'

Our conversation was not particularly interesting. Honestly, it bored me. But the actual situation and everything surrounding it was quite the experience. Sitting with Igor on the empty terrace of a bar that summer evening was a huge step forward after spending a month at Uncle's, where for the most part I sat alone staring at a wall. Maybe that was why Igor managed to get me to talk, before he got really wasted and started waffling on about everything under the sun.

'Tell me about the shell,' he said. 'The one that fucked up your ear.'

'My neck,' I corrected him. 'My neck, not my ear. The muscles in my neck, to be precise.'

'Exactly.'

'Why?'

'Why not? Is it a secret?'

'No … But … I'm going inside to take a piss first.'

In the toilet I held my cold wet hand to my neck. An old habit. It didn't actually hurt any more.

I looked at myself in the mirror and adjusted my hair. Then I returned to Igor, determined to tell him bugger all.

PAIN IN THE NECK

The shell fell on the first of June, but it all started at the end of March. Mum drew the curtain and opened my window. Perched on the nearest branch of the pear tree in the garden, two or three sparrows were discussing politics.

'Up you get,' Mum said. 'You have to go to school.'

The sitting room smelt of fresh bread and coffee. The radio was playing 'Lily Was Here,' though I did not know it was called that yet, and for that very reason I had dubbed it 'The Song Without Lyrics, With Saxophone and Guitar.' Adi had grown tired of it. I had not. I drank a cup of hot milk and contented myself with a single slice of bread.

Adi stood by the gate waiting for me as usual.

'Fuck was it ever booming yesterday!' he said.

'It's because of the river.'

'Yeah, I know. It amplifies the sound.'

'Were the detonations rattling your windows, too?'

'Yep. Like somebody was knocking on them. Thumping. One blow at a time.'

'And I was sitting right next to it cramming for The Seventh Enemy Offensive! You gotta be kidding me, man!'

'History?'

'Yeah! Do you want to test me?'

'That's the one with Tito and the parachutes. Drvar … 1944?'

'Exactly. Let's see how many of us there are today.'

'There were eight of us yesterday.'

'We had twelve. Novak asked Jović if his dad had dug out his rifle.'

'And what did Jović say?'

'My Dad doesn't own weapons.'

'Yeah, for sure.'

'It was all too funny. We did nothing the entire lesson. Just sat talking. Maja told the class a joke.'

'Right, right. But people in Nedođ are armed to the teeth. I'm telling you. My dad says they were the worst of the Chetniks during the war. That Jović guy is a moron!'

In the playground we bumped into Vanja, who was walking towards us. He was smiling ear to ear:

'No school today!'

'Who says?'

'Nobody. There is *nobody*.'

'What do you mean?'

'Not a soul, man. The door's locked.'

'Shit!' Adi said and pointed at the entrance. 'Look at all the people.'

A group of younger boys were crowded together in front of the stairs. They stood jingling glass marbles. They were playing the guessing game.

'Make way! Come on you lot, move aside!' Adi ordered them energetically.

They obeyed without objection. He was a head taller than all of them.

Adi grabbed the door handle.

'Fuck, man!'

He rattled it.

'It's locked!'

'You don't say,' Vanja gloated.

My hand took over from Adi's on the cool metal. Same result.

'There weren't many teachers yesterday, either,' Adi said.

'No, but I saw Mandić in the corridor,' I answered. 'I've got him for history today. Third and fourth. Ah, man! This is so stupid!'

We stood under the window of the reception area, gave each other a boost and looked inside. I saw the duty desk at the back of the room. There were no lights on and there was nobody inside.

'Not a soul!'

The staff room had sandblasted windows, so we could not see inside. I knocked a couple of times.

No reply.

Nothing.

'Nobody.'

'What are you staring at?' Adi shouted at the snot-nosed kids. 'Go home. Can't you see it's closed?'

'Maybe we should head home, too,' I said.

'Agreed,' Vanja nodded.

'I crammed my arse off yesterday!' I said. 'All day! I know the Seventh Enemy Offensive inside out, man! It's not bloody fair!'

'Don't worry,' Adi said. 'Mandić won't forget.'

He put his hand on my shoulder. His voice went a little hoarse:

'Don't worry. You'll get your test … when all of this calms down a little.'

A few days later Dad and Mum were in the middle of a huge spring clean. The vacuum cleaner was rumbling in the sitting room. The phone lines were down. Everyone was holding their breath and waiting for the moment when 'all of this calms down a little,' and the two of them were waging a war against dust and fluff.

Barricaded in my room, plugging my ear with one finger and the other resting between the greasy pages of the comic book, I reread an old issue of Mister No. It started with the hero picking up Dana from the airport, where he discovered that Dana was a singer and happened to be black. Later he pummelled all the guests at the inn who had disparaged Dana. He leant back and lit a fresh cigarette.

Boom! That's how it's done!

'I'm going down to the river for a bit,' I said to the old folks, who were now in the garden drinking coffee beneath the pergola and the grapes.

'Don't be gone for too long,' Mum said, worried as usual.

The distance from our gate down to the river was no more than fifty metres, that is if you could be bothered to cut through Zaim's garden and deal with his hysterical dog, Roki.

I took a detour. One hundred and forty-five steps, I had once counted. Down the street and to the left. Then continue until you reach the end of the street. Straight ahead to the embankment.

From there, there was a good view of the middle of town on the far side. I climbed the embankment, stopped at the top – froze.

By the stairs leading to the boats, behind a bushy willow, I spotted two men lying on their stomachs. They were facing the river so they could not see me. During the brief moment that I stood behind them, I had time to notice two things:

– they were wearing YPA olive-grey helmets and uniforms,

– one of them handing the other a large pair of binoculars.

I took a couple of steps backwards, turned and slipped away quietly.

As I walked past Marko's cherry plum I was seized by panic. I was ready to bolt. Marko's wife, Zrinka was hosing down the concrete path with a hose. She was bent forward.

Should I tell her? No?

She straightened up. Spotted me. Smiled.

'Zrinka, there are soldiers down by the boats!'

'Where?'

'Down by the boats. Two! I have to get home.'

'Are you sure?'

'I don't know. I have to get home! Don't go down there!'

The gravel crunched beneath my feet as I opened the gate. The hairs on the back of my neck were stood on end.

'Mum! Dad!'

No answer.

I walked around the back of the house. Nobody beneath the grapes. The tray and the ashtray were still there, but the coffees were gone. I glanced over at Zaim's veranda. Tried to see if they were over at his place. One step forward. Quick glance to the left. At the foot of the embankment, behind Zaim's garden, seven or eight men in uniform slinked forward. They were bent over, hurrying towards the spot on the embankment I had just left. They were wearing helmets and rucksacks. They were holding something.

There was nothing in the world I had looked forward to more than that summer – the summer of 1992. Neno was finally going to finish his studies and move home. I was going to complete primary school and start secondary school. Dad was going to enjoy his hard-earned early retirement. Last but not least, Neno had promised to teach me to drive. I looked forward to sitting behind the wheel and impressing Nina.

But then they came with their shovels, their gear and their rifles. They dug in. Had their arses facing us – along the embankment and along the river – and began to shoot towards the other side.

The power was cut. The water, likewise. The surrounding space shrunk.

Our side started shooting at them. Our people were on the other side. We were occupied by Serbs and being shot at by our own people. Without lifting a finger, we suddenly found ourselves in a really bad location.

The frontline was a stone's throw from the houses. The snipers took up their positions. There were streets and alleys it was best not to use. Certain times of the day were better than others.

Near the bridge, where Dad once watched two Ustashe being hung, they shot at each other with Pragas, the mobile, 30 mm cannons. Each night they thundered away. The guided missiles aimed for the middle of the town, which was situated on a hill, and the Catholic church in the pedestrian precinct. They were extremely precise. The clock on the white churchtower stopped. Parts of the tower were charred and crumbling.

I missed having electricity. My old record player with the inscription *Miki '91*, engraved using the point of a compass, was gathering dust.

One day I was sitting in my room; it was unusually quiet. The only sound that could be heard through the half-open window was the cooing of pigeons in the roof gutter. No Smoking, the album with the grey sticker, was resting under the stylus: *While You're Waiting for Dawn with the Devil*. It must have been the last record I played without the use of electricity.

I placed the needle between 'Uncle Sam' and 'The Sunday When Hase Left Us,' pressed my index finger lightly against the record and made it spin. Reaching thirty-three turns per minute was difficult. It was either too fast or too slow, and when I finally got it to sound the way it was supposed to, I lost my concentration. Once again, I spun too fast or too slow and got annoyed at hearing the distorted sounds. Finally, I gave up.

In the sitting room, Dad lay asleep on his back. His mouth was agape, his left hand on his chest. Neno sat on the other sofa reading the local paper. It was the only newspaper in the house, at least two months old. During the deepest bouts of boredom I read it from start to finish on a number of occasions. I knew the obituaries and the colophons by heart.

Neno was not supposed to have been there. Officially he still lived in Sarajevo, finishing off his studies. He protested in the streets and went to peace concerts. All kinds of bands got together and attempted to sing the politicians to their senses. Actors and authors recited poems. Buses drove people to the capital and back, free of charge. People held up photos of Tito and shouted about peace, fraternity and all that.

I watched it on TV and wished I was there. Some of the coolest bands were playing there. Neno called after one of the concerts and his voice was completely gone. He managed to get out of Sarajevo in a car that took him to Banja Luka. There he spent the night with a friend from school – a Serb, in fact it was his dad who had picked them up. When he appeared at the garden gate the following day, we did not know if we should shout for joy or cry. The Serbian army was digging in by the embankment. Right under our noses.

Neno sat on the sofa reading the paper. Mum was outside by the water pump. She said she just had to water her roses and hyacinths.

I sat down by the window between Neno and Dad. He woke up at almost that exact moment.

'News report,' he said. 'What time is it?'

'Ten minutes to.'

The clock hung on the wall above the TV. Our red Sanyo cassette player was on top of Mum's sewing machine by the entrance. The door was closed, as was the door to my room.

Dad pointed at the sewing machine:

'Would you mind grabbing me that?'

'Shouldn't we wait until the hour?' I said. 'We'll be out of batteries soon. I …'

That was as far as I got.

An indescribably loud noise, something no speaker in the world would be able to replicate, passed directly through my head and chest. My brain felt like it had exploded inside my skull. Like the crash had shattered my head and pieced it back together again.

The sitting room instantly smelled of hot metal. Like when a pipe is cut in half or an iron railing is being welded.

The doors to the display cabinet opened.

The stack of plates that Mum had placed inside crashed to the floor.

Through the crack in the entrance door, smoke wafted in.

I looked at Neno and Dad.

That is how I think it happened most of the time. In that order. Other times I remember the smell, the smoke and the sound of the plates reaching me a second *before* the explosion. The crash being slightly delayed.

The house has been hit, I thought, and jumped up. Dad and Neno did the same.

'Get out! Get out!' I heard someone shout, rather faintly.

I wanted to open the entrance door but it was jammed. Shell fragments had struck the keyhole and made the lock stick. In shock, in panic, or whatever it was, I grabbed the handle firmly and tugged several times.

No luck.

Neno took over, planted one foot against the frame and yanked on the handle. The door opened and he tumbled backwards.

In the brief moment that it took me to run out through the entrance, I noticed the pane of glass in the veranda door was broken. I did not see the shards of glass. I ran in front of Neno and Dad.

Mum was staggering in the drive in front of the garage. She was moaning and manically tugging at her black top. Her face was horror-stricken, and she was crying dry tears. I called out to her, but she could not hear me. Her gaze was directed at the roof of our house, and I turned around and looked up.

It was the next-door neighbour's house, not ours, that had been hit. I started to take it all in, while I stood there wondering why I was not wearing any shoes. I had trampled over the broken glass and scattered pieces of roof tiles wearing only a pair of thin, white tennis socks.

My foot was bleeding.

AND THEN WHAT HAPPENED?

Wicky grew busier over the course of the evening. German and English were spoken around us, and Igor complained vociferously about how his leave had passed so 'dryly,' as far as 'groin grinding' went. The next day he was due to return to the front, and every girl that passed our table walked arm in arm with her handsome fellow.

'Driest leave to date,' Igor concluded. 'Went far better last time.'

Before he got drunk and monopolised the conversation, he pressured me to tell him various things. I evaded him for some time, but three quarters of a litre of beer eventually loosened my tongue. The words poured out of me as soon as he asked his favourite question:

'And then what happened?'

After telling the story about the shell I replied:

'Nothing. One night they told us to pack our things and meet at the crossing the next morning. They wanted to evacuate us.'

'Why?'

'Because more intense battles were expected. At least that's what they told us.'

'Civilians are nothing but an inconvenience,' Igor said.

He exhaled smoke through his nose and added:

'You were probably getting in the way of both sides. And then what?'

'Then we were packed inside some old, stinking buses and driven deep into Serbian territory.'

'Where to?'

'Towards Banja Luka. The previous night they had blown up the nearest mosque. With dynamite. I thought our house had been hit. It was a massive explosion!'

Igor shook his head and spat out a single, but emotionally charged sentence. The words 'pussy,' 'mother' and 'Chetnik' formed part of it. Then he took a big swig of beer and said with a hint of indignation:

'That's the kind of thing they do, isn't it?'

'Yes, but our side also destroyed their church.'

'Cool.'

'No … I don't know … Now all the mosques and churches are gone. Not a single one left in town. And one of them – a mosque – it was really old, you know, a few centuries, and there were …'

'Never mind, your people can just build a new one. A bigger one. You can build five of them on the same spot!'

'Yeah, but …'

'These are minor details. It can be rebuilt. And then what happened?'

'Not much. After two full days they divided us into two groups. The women, children and old men were driven off and delivered to the Bosnian army. Any man able to fight was kept back. Dad rang Uncle when we reached …'

'Wait, wait a sec! What happened during those two days?'

'What days?'

'When they held you captive.'

How stupid could I get! Why did I have to say 'after two full days?' That was an insignificant detail.

'Come on. What happened?'

'Nothing. They just drove us around a little.'

'For two days? C'mon, kid. Spit it out! What did they do to you?'

'Nothing,' I smiled and leaned back in the chair. 'They didn't do anything to us.'

I looked at the two large beer mugs on the table between us. Igor's was half-full and I noticed a chip in the rim near the handle. It looked like someone had bitten off a piece of glass. A customer with really good teeth.

'Why did they drive you around for so long?'

'Uh, I dunno. Probably didn't know what to do with us.'

'Like hell they didn't! You don't evacuate people without a plan!'

'There were hundreds of us. Men, women, children, old people … They drove us around a little and …'

'And they were really nice to you? They drove you around and served you coffee?'

'No, they let us off the buses a few times … so we could stretch our legs a little.'

I smiled again and looked at Igor silently. I felt he deserved to know more, but I did not feel like going into detail.

'They made us empty our pockets,' I said, trying to be a smart-arse.

'Oh?'

'Anything that was chafing.'

'Hmph!'

Now Igor was smiling too. He stubbed out his cigarette in the middle of the ashtray. The table shook under the pressure.

'Did they hit you?'

'No, we slept in a primary school the first night. And on the second night in a leaky town hall. In some random village. I slept like a rock.'

'You didn't get beaten?'

'No. They treated us alright.'

'You're lying.'

'No. I just don't feel like talking about it any more.'

Igor did not give up so easily. His muddled gaze wavered a little.

'Come on! I have to know what they did. It's of strategic importance. You have to know your enemy. His methods.'

'Some other time, maybe. I'm tired.'

'And where are the prisoners now? Where's … Neno?'

'I dunno.'

'I've heard that they're mobilising them. Probably fighting your own people.'

That was a provocation. I did not answer straight away. Finished the last sip of my beer.

'He's in a concentration camp. We were told that by a number of people.'

'Are you sure about that? Didn't you just say you didn't know?'

'That's because ... it's not a hundred percent. There are all kinds of rumours. We also heard that they've been killed ... All of them! But then later we heard that they were at a concentration camp.'

Igor hesitated for a moment. He had seemingly given up. Finally, I thought.

He blinked, like a fly had struck him in the eye, the pounded the table and said:

'Don't worry. We're going to fuck their mothers.'

The rest of the time we talked about something else, or rather Igor talked, while I just sat there, simultaneously feeling drained and bottled-up. At one point I considered whether I should just tell him the truth about those two days, now that he was drunk and would probably not remember much afterwards. But at the same time a sea of images crashed inside me and I knew that I could not do it.

On they way back to the camp I was happy I had not told Igor more. He bragged about a list of women he had 'laid,' and laughing, told me about a 'detained Chetnik' who had shat his trousers in terror.

I had a litre of beer in me. I do not think I have ever drunk so much in such a short time. Igor's laugh annoyed me, and those fucking images rolled through my mind again. Even when I was lying down, ready to fall asleep, the same film played over and over again in my head, accompanied by Dad's monotone snoring and Mum's deep, sleepless sigh.

RESTAURANT

The next day I woke up late, sat up in bed at looked at the white scar on my foot.

It happened.

Last night it had felt surreal and incongruous with the bay, the beach and room 210. But it had actually happened. The scar on my left foot testified to that fact. The stray shell landed, and later more landed. We were taken captive and driven into Serbian territory. Mum, Dad and I were transferred to the Bosnian army. Neno was driven in another direction.

Through the wall, the neighbours could be heard arguing. My parents moved about in the room. Mum was mending one of Dad's shirts. The buttons did not match. That was a problem. I followed the small curve of the scar with my index finger then crawled back under the blanket. The weight of last night's conversation still sat in my body. And the two large beers I had drunk. My head felt heavy and tender, vulnerable in some way.

Is this what you call a hangover?

I stood up and stretched my arms. Mum handed the shirt to Dad, and he put it on.

'We're going down for lunch,' he said.

'Fine. I'm coming too.'

'Remember to lock up behind you!'

'Why?' I yawned. 'What's there to steal in here?'

'Quiet, you little philosophiser. Never poke a hungry bear. It could prove dangerous.'

'Yes,' Mum laughed. 'Mind Dad doesn't bite your leg off!'

I looked at her. This was the same woman who a little less than two months ago stood in the drive, lost and panic-stricken, with the cement dust suspended in the air around her. She looked terrified that day – I had never seen her that scared before – and now she stood in front of me joking like it had never happened.

'We're going now.'

Dad had put his arms around her and comforted her that day. With trembling hands. When he led her around the back of the house, his head grazed the drying line in the garden. His glasses and some of the plastic pegs on the drying line flew off. He bent forward and feverishly felt for his glasses on the ground.

The whole thing looked rather comical in the midst of all the chaos surrounding us. They appeared more shaken than Neno and I, and it was strange to see them so confused, scared and awkward all at once.

Now, they never spoke about the shell or the two days in the hands of the Serbs. They talked about war, politics and the news, but never about what we had been through.

I got myself ready and headed downstairs with the key in the pocket of my swimming trunks. Planned on jumping in the water straight after eating.

Down by the pier I observed the outstretched figures of all the women. Their brownish skin glistened in the sun, but I was so lost in my own thoughts that they and the rest of the beach seemed light years away. The surface of the water shimmered, rather unsettled, a breezed toyed with my shoulder-length hair. I stopped in the middle of the path and stared at the surreal panoramic image in front of me. It looked like a film shoot. Altogether different from the one I was starring in.

Last night when Igor and I passed the marina, I had the same feeling at one point. The night had been mild and pleasant, a number of tourists walked past chattering away, and I felt like grabbing them by the arm and shouting into their floppy ears:

'Hey! We're in the middle of a war here, dammit! Stop it! You can't just walk around enjoying yourselves!'

Now, I stood on the path beneath the pines with a small lump in my throat. I envied every single one of them. They were on holiday, a proper holiday, and they were enjoying it. Their thoughts must have completely dissolved in all this heat. Everything around them shouted sand, sex and sun. That can stamp out the worries of most people.

Our table was furthest from the conveyor belt where the food was dished up. I had to navigate through the restaurant holding a plate and cutlery. People were shoving. Everyone was hurrying towards the queue and several people cut in. They acted like they were afraid there would not be enough food.

'Took you long enough, didn't it?' Dad said when I sat down.

'Why didn't you just grab my serving?'

'It's one thing, you sleeping in till noon, young man. It's another thing for your highness to have his own personal waiter. No chance.'

'Listen, you two,' Mum said. 'Can't I just eat in peace?'

The room echoed with creaking chairs and voices. Cutlery falling on the floor, a number of colourful expletives sliced through the air. I looked around. Mashed potato with tripe and onions steamed up in my face.

Sitting at another table, I spotted Samir, Damir and their parents. Were it not for their names and their long hair, you would never guess that they were brothers – let alone twins. Their dad had managed to bribe the office manager to change their year of birth on their ID cards. So officially, they were still under eighteen.

'Who is going to mobilise them here?' my dad had asked him. 'We're from Bosnia.'

'You never know. They could turn them over to our people, if they were asked. I don't trust anyone any more.'

Amar and Ismar were also Bosnian and brothers, though not twins. Amar was my age – born with three thumbs, two on one hand and one on the other. The thumbs were fused at the first joint, so in fact he had eleven nails, not eleven fingers.

He waved at me when I spotted him.

'Eat up,' Mum said. 'Your food's getting cold.'

I had to force myself. She and Dad tucked into the mashed potatoes. They chewed the tough meat with little difficulty, and I thought about the night four years earlier, when Neno had travelled to Sarajevo to study. The three of us sat in the sitting room at home, eating in silence.

I missed him so much back then. It took me countless evenings to get used to seeing the empty chair. Now I could manage without seeing him for years, if need be. Just so long as I knew that he was okay. That would be enough. I didn't care about the shells and the two days in the hands of the Chetniks. I could forget all about that, just like Mum and Dad had done. So long as he was still alive.

Why did I talk about that so much yesterday? I thought. It was no help. Just made me even heavier and more distant from everything around me. 'Heavy as a horse,' like in the song by Electric Orgasm.

On the tablecloth in front of me the sunlight made a small square. I felt like chatting to the topless German again, translating for Igor and staring discreetly at her fine figure. But Igor had already returned to the front, she was back in Germany, and I sat in this echoey restaurant, chewing on rubbery bits of tripe.

My jaw tired.

'My dear boy! Didn't you know cows had such tough stomachs?' Dad joked, now full up and frisky, but his half-witted gems glanced off me.

I felt like escaping from the overcrowded room, jumping into the clear blue water by the pier – to wash away the last few months from my mind. I felt like merging with the surrounding smells, blending in with the happy tourists on the beach – and forgetting all about Igor and our conversation the previous night.

So when Amar came over and asked if I wanted to join

him for a swim, I smiled and said, 'Yes. Definitely, man!' I pushed aside the plate and the previous night, and we went down to check the temperature of the water.

Cassette 2

MIKI'S SCORING SONGS

NINA

Amar picked his nose and talked about women as we strolled up the path after our swim. When we reached the terrace between D1 and D2, a group of beach bums came walking towards us. It was Samir, Damir and some other boys and girls I didn't yet know.

Amar and I spun on our heels and followed them. We swam by the pier for a long time, teasing the girls and drawing attention to ourselves. Then Samir asked if we wanted to swim over to the island.

There was nothing but cliffs, weeds and brushwood there. A couple of immovable nudists lay roasting in the sun. On the other side of the island – the side facing the horizon – the cliffs rose sharply out of the water. I was amazed at how high they were. There was only one spot were the cliff was low enough to climb out of the water after jumping in.

In that very spot Andrea, Samir's girlfriend, was swimming with one of her girlfriends, whose name escapes me. The girls were from Majbule, meaning that they were neither 'those fleeing' or 'those displaced,' but locals, 'the natives.' Samir was older. He knew how things worked. He had scored with Andrea a few days earlier.

Andrea, who was ten times hotter than her girlfriend, jumped in feet first from a cliff that must have been fifteen to twenty metres high. Splashh! I could not believe my eyes. Even for me, born and raised by one of the deepest rivers in Bosnia, who spent summer after summer jumping in from taller and taller willow trees, hers was an extraordinary feat.

Damir jumped in head first from a lower cliff.

Amar and I did the same.

After salvaging the honour of the newcomers – and of the boys for that matter – I swam back. Getting out of the water was not easy. The sea was choppy, and I was afraid the waves would slam me against the cliff.

When I reached the others, Samir was already in full swing, sitting on a rock a few metres away, French kissing Andrea. Stroking her tanned thigh. She had one hand on her lap. Almost motionless.

I immediately thought of Nina.

It began a few weeks before the soldiers arrived. A few chance gazes and smiles during lunch. It developed into a bit of chat at Vanja's birthday. We held each other's hands after leaving the others behind; they had started to play hide-and-seek with an enthusiasm that was unfathomable to us.

On one of those very days, the river carried the sound of the first explosions to us. The windowpanes in our small houses rattled more often and with more intensity from one day to the next. It was a clear warning that the rest of the world existed. That it was best to bear that in mind.

In my mind there was only Nina. Nina and my plan to become familiar with the taste of her lips. Mister No gave me his expert advice. He described to me how he chatted up countless girls during his tense expeditions in the Amazonian rainforests, at the jazz clubs in the city of Manaus and a number of other places. One night, highly motivated, my hair finally behaving itself, Nina and I strolled through the park in an increasingly awkward stillness. She lived two blocks away, and I was walking her home.

We had been to the flicks. Seen *Time of the Gypsies* with Adi and Maja. Laughed when Azra asked Perhan if he could kiss like they did in the movies. At the bridge, Adi and Maja went their separate ways, and at the end of the park, just as my wandering gaze at long last landed on an empty bench, the rain started to pour down. A heavy spring rain pelted the city. Nina and I took cover under a lime tree, its branches were still bare. With my back against the still dry trunk I noticed Nina's shoulder move closer. My heart was going completely bonkers under my drenched shirt.

'Nina! Ni-na!'

Nina straightened up and headed in the direction of her mum's voice, never to return. From her best friend I discovered that she had moved to Ljubljana, where her Dad worked. That she would not be back until 'all of this calms down a little.'

Later, as I sat in our neighbour Zaim's damp and overcrowded basement, while it thundered and boomed outside, I sedated myself with the thought of what it would be like the day the war ended and Nina returned. How I would wait for her at the bus station in our rebuilt town. About how she would press her nose against the window of the bus and wave at me. Her brown hair had grown longer. Her breasts were bigger. I would feel her head resting on my chest, while the darkness and the rain fell on the city. And everything would be like it used to be – with the exception of the lime tree, which would soon be chopped down, and we would soon have to find other hiding places from the rain, Nina's mum and the rest of the world, which was best to bear in mind.

As I stood on the small, deserted, nameless island, dripping wet and out of breath, far from Zaim's basement, the lime tree and Nina, I could not stop staring at Samir and Andrea, whose lips were firmly pressed together. There was no jealousy. Just a desperate need to pull someone close and kiss that person as best I could.

I looked around.

Sanela and Katarina sat with their legs crossed, talking about some band called Guns N' Roses. Andrea's girlfriend asked if we were going home soon. Marina lay on her back with her eyes closed, lapping up the sun.

CELIBACY

That same evening Amar came up to me and asked:

'Hey, how old are you?'

'Almost fifteen.'

'Cool, same here! I've got a job for you.'

'What kind of job?'

'We're going to score some ladies tonight!'

'Ladies?'

'Yep. What do you say to that?'

'I say, why not.'

'Why not, exactly! Dunno about you, but I've had enough of this damn celibacy!'

'You've had enough of what?'

'Celibacy! Cel-i-ba-cy!'

'What's that?'

'Celibacy,' Amar said, 'is when you're not screwing enough!'

MARINA

Elvis was in love with Sanela. He was a friend of Amar's, a gypsy from Bijeljina. Elvis' Dad, Husein, would later become famous thanks to a profound statement, which many of us in the camp would remember for a long time and quote. After hearing about someone's unbridled complaint about everything that person had lost and left at home – the house, the car, the brand new set of cutlery – Husein snorted and responded with his legendary words:

'Yes, that's how it is these days. Now all of you are gypsies too.'

With that he entered himself on the list of the most unforgettable Majbulian gems, on which Igor and his 'What do I know, maybe she'll get upset' had already taken a well-deserved spot.

Elvis was crazy about Sanela, I discovered that night, and the same went for Amar and Katarina.

'Why don't you take Marina,' Amar suggested, and I had nothing against that. She was nothing special, but then again neither was I.

Amar had done the legwork by arranging a group walk. Everything was arranged: the place, the time and the winding route past the normally dark gardens of the villas. Majbule was not exactly Paris, it was safe to say, neither was it LA. Street lighting was a relatively unheard-of phenomenon. If you fancied a stroll in the middle of the night, for the most part you were left to walk in the light of the moon.

The girls were taking their time. A lot of time. Amar, Elvis and I stood on the terrace in front of the restaurant and took turns glancing up the path. Elvis suggested playing a round of marbles on the path while we waited. Amar and I rolled our eyes:

'Take that shit home, man! You weren't seriously thinking of clattering around with those when they get here, were you?'

'You're such an infant, man! What's with you?'

A little later we filled our arms with pilfered grapes and figs on one of the dark side streets that was furthest from the camp. Then we split up – entirely spontaneous – into three pairs and dawdled towards the Adria campsite.

Adria was the largest campsite in the area. It had bungalows, flats and sites for caravans and tenters. There were communal showers and toilets, a kiosk and last but not least, a restaurant with a terrace, where the same band always played the same songs, including 'I'm a joker, I'm a smoker, I'm a midnight toker. I get my lovin' on the run.'

On the way there, I told Marina about the river that runs through my hometown, about my record player and all the records and cassettes I was missing terribly.

She listened attentively.

The next night all six of us went for a stroll, taking more or less the same route. In the middle of Marina's story about her first swim in the Danube, I heard Katarina give Amar a point-blank rejection. That same moment he exclaimed:

'Hey friends! It sure is dark here! Why don't we hold hands!'

I don't know if Katarina held his hand, I don't think so, but Marina grabbed mine.

We strolled around for the rest of the evening, sweaty hand in sweaty hand, and did not dream of letting go. Because what if all of a sudden the other person was no longer scared of the dark?

Not until her knees were sore and my throat was dry did we head back to the camp. In the darkness beneath the pine trees, between the disused tennis court and the bright terrace in front of the restaurant, we both went strangely quiet. Marina's hair was down, and I spotted a couple of pine needles. She looked up at the treetops and smiled. Almost nonchalantly I plucked the needles from her hair, and with my trembling, clammy hand I touched her cheek. It was blazing.

I still do not know who eventually moved whose lips towards the other. I was far too dizzy to be able to remember such details. All I know is that I later convinced myself that it was me. In any case, one thing was certain: We stood there under the pine trees, tentatively jousting with our tongues, and both contributed to something that, with a little good will, could technically speaking be considered a kiss. I had no idea what to do or what order to do it in. First I rubbed my hands up and down her cotton T-shirt, but that began to feel rather stupid. So I moved my hand up and caressed her neck and hair. I did my best to imitate the guys from *Beverly Hills, 90210*. Mouth half-open, fingers stroking the girl's hair, eyes shut. Marina, however, her mouth was open so wide that I froze in disbelief at first. What is *happening* there? Then I pulled myself together, set aside the *Beverly Hills* variant and attempted to follow her lead. But it was no use: her mouth was much larger than mine. Her saliva ran down my chin. Her lips slid over my nose, my eyebrows, my forehead. Soon my entire head was inside her open mouth, and I could feel the vacuum of her windpipe sucking me further and further inside.

THAT'S WOMEN FOR YOU

The next day I asked Marina to open her mouth a little less, and she was very supportive. She was convinced that I had more experience with that sort of thing. She let me nickname her toes. We chewed gum and brushed our teeth from morning to night. I showered two or three times a day. A frontal assault on bad breath and sweat.

I could never get my hair right. I let it grow out. When Marina walked towards me, I studied her slender body closely. When she said hi to me – discreet, conspiratorial – in a way that only I could see – I was in seventh, eight and ninth heaven.

On our sixth day together she did not show up as arranged.

The following day she was quiet and discontent.

By the eighth day it was over.

She explained that she did not fancy having a boyfriend, that she was not ready for it, and last but not least, that she had been in love with someone else for a long time – some guy whose parents had had enough of war and peace and the climes of the former Yugoslavia. He lived in New Zealand now, and she had just received a letter from him.

I moped around for all of twelve hours before I got over the unexpected break-up. Amar commented with words of encouragement, 'Fuck it. You're finally free,' and Elvis added 'I knew it! That's women for you.'

I left the two of them by the entrance to the TV room and headed up to our room. In some strange way I was afraid of running into the witch.

What does a guy say? How crude do you have to be before she understands that I am ICE-COLD and that I DON'T CARE ONE FUCKING BIT!

The light in our room was on. I saw as I walked across the terrace. So I was surprised, to put it mildly, when I bumped into a locked door.

I rubbed my head and knocked.

A few times.

At first the room was completely still, then I heard the squeak of a mattress spring. I heard mumbling inside and someone taking a couple of steps.

'Are you in there?'

'Is that you?'

It was Dad.

'Yes!'

'What do you want?'

'What do you think I want? I want inside!'

'Why do you want to come in here? It's only nine o'clock!'

I was taken aback and spontaneously asked:

'Where's Mum?'

At that moment I caught on. Man, did I ever catch on!

'Go talk to your friends,' Dad said. 'She's sleeping.'

'Are you …?'

'We'll see you later, son. You woke us up.'

I went downstairs again. Decided not to return until they were really asleep.

Hope they're not using my bed, I thought. Hope they bloody well air out the room!

I had absolutely zero interest in seeing them *after*.

MARINA AGAIN

Everything changed swiftly that summer, Marina too. She gained some weight and became incredibly irritating. At least that was my impression right up till one night at Amar's birthday party on the beach. Here she revealed her true reason for dumping me. She had drunk three mouthfuls of beer and opened up like a flower in the rain: I was her first boyfriend, she was inexperienced. She was afraid of disappointing me and eventually she could no longer stand hearing about Nina, the girl I had got on so well with.

With cheeks blazing from the wine and the mesmerising flames of the fire, I kind of admitted that I missed her on occasion. We slipped away from the others, who sat wailing away to an untuned guitar. We found a place where their severely off-key voices could only just be heard. Soon my plucky right hand slipped in under Marina's top. Marina had lost weight. She was speaking sensibly and rationally again. For example, she said, 'Okay. But just a little,' after listening to me repeat 'Just a little, just a little bit,' for ages. She guided my right hand under her top and boldly placed it in the right place.

On that clear summer night, the white moon smiled down on us, Amar's only birthday balloon. Igor was sitting in a trench somewhere on the Slavonic fields, while Marina's left breast filled my entire right hand. Her hard and protruding nipple reminded me of a puppy's nose. For that reason I did not give Igor or Neno much thought for some time.

Not until my arm started to fall asleep and my hand was rather clammy did I think of Igor's legendary words, 'What do I know, maybe she'll get upset.' I tried to let go of her breast, but my moist hand was stuck to it.

I waited. Marina said nothing. She continued kissing, drooling as usual. Then she moved my hand to her neighbouring breast.

We're together again, I thought. That's the only thing this could mean.

'If you tell anyone about this, I'll kill you!' she said when we walked back to join the others.

'Don't worry. I won't say a damn thing. What would I tell them anyway?'

'That you were groping my ... you know.'

'Groping? Groping what?'

'My breasts, dammit! It wasn't my elbows, was it!'

'Oh, that!' I exclaimed, feigning surprise. 'That was nothing special.'

'I was drunk! Do you understand? Drunk! And I still am. Don't go thinking that we're ...'

'That we're what?'

'That we're ... I'd rather not have a boyfriend! Do you understand?'

I reflected for a moment.

'No, actually, I don't understand! Why not? And what do you mean by "rather not?"'

'I don't know.'

'But if you don't know what you want, or what you mean, then that might actually mean ... that you don't actually know ... you know ... what you want!'

It sounded perfectly sensible in my head.

'Maybe we should just ... not think about things and just ...'

'And just what?' she asked.

'Be together! You know ... *properly*.'

She continued forward silently. I waited.

In a moment we'll be together again, I thought. Come on. Say it!

'No,' she said. 'I think we should be just friends.'

FIFTEEN

The lump in my throat made a comeback near the end of August. Once again I grew heavy as a horse. At night, before I went to sleep, I saw his face in front of me, and my heart pounded under the duvet. I was terrified that I would never see him again. Terrified of forgetting what he looked like.

There was less and less news about prisoner exchanges. Soldiers were exchanged before civilians, and he had the disadvantage of being taken captive as a civilian. The powerful Western leaders with their grave expressions and raised index fingers reminded the Bosnian Serbs – and the Croats for that matter – that what they were doing was unacceptable. That it was about time to sit around the negotiating table and find a solution to the conflict in the former Yugoslavia through peaceful means. They continued to explain to us Bosnian Muslims, now called Bosniaks, who kept banging on about military intervention, that we should not entertain any hope that the West would get involved in our conflict. There were ten global hotspots where the situation was far worse. Somalia, for example, was not all roses either, and even if it were – who was going to pick them?

Mum and Dad rarely talked about him in my presence. Still I knew they thought about him all the time. They had both found new friends in the camp. They went to visit them, drained pot after pot of coffee and followed the news. Waiting for something good to happen. For the war to die down so that we could return home. But nothing good happened. Home grew more distant with every day that passed. Our hometown was now deep inside Serbian territory, and nobody was fighting to liberate it. When they evacuated us, practically everything was taken from us. We had virtually no money, and there was no hope of earning any. There were no jobs, not for the local population and not for those driven out of Croatia, not to mention those fleeing from Bosnia.

I wore my only pair of trainers, long since worn-out, Adidas. The stitching on one side kept bursting. Dad stitched them together with a thick thread, for all the good it did. The process of deterioration continued, and it drove both of us batty. Mum washed our clothes by hand. I only had two long-sleeved tops and two pairs of trousers, one of which was from the Red Cross. The trousers had once been blue, but they were so washed-out now that they were nearer grey.

I was embarrassed. Especially in front of the girls. Most of the others had escaped within days of the first shot being fired. They had managed to bring their Levis with them.

To make matters worse, five or six of us had birthdays that summer. Mine was the last in line, and since I went to all the parties, it only made sense that I should have one too. The birthday boy had to provide a case of beer, bags of crisps, peanuts and stuff like that, while the guests brought small, symbolic gifts.

I was already sweating at the thought of my birthday. I knew that Mum and Dad still had the hundred mark note that Uncle had given them, but was afraid they would not agree to break it up under any circumstance. They always said that they would set it aside for 'the bad times.'

I had to get down on my knees.

'But, Emir,' Mum whimpered, 'that's a lot of money. You know we can't even afford to buy fruit now. Even that's a luxury.'

'But how can you not understand? Am I supposed to die of shame? Everyone has celebrated their birthday, everyone! And I have been to every single party, every single one! How the hell am I supposed to explain to them now that I can't afford to buy drinks once a year? How?'

I started to cry. The tears dripped down my chin. I felt

terrible and felt guilty that I was the cause of yet another problem for them.

Mum sat at my side and tried to comfort me. She kept telling me not to cry, that it would be all right, and tears ran down her cheeks too. Dad was tapping his foot restlessly. His brown socks merged with the carpet, the room and my tears.

Saturday was Ismar's birthday, and I was supposed to have mine the following Friday. I walked around the camp despondently. I was ashamed to go to his party. If I could have run away, I would have done so without batting an eyelid. Straight away. Wherever that might take me.

In the end I sat down with Dad on the terrace between D1 and D2. Amar and Ismar walked past. They were carrying a case of beer between them. Stacked on top of the beer were bags of crisps, pretzels and peanuts.

The sight almost made me dizzy.

Then Dad suddenly put his arm around my shoulder and whispered into my ear:

'We'll find a way to make that party of yours happen, even if it ruins us!'

SMOKE

We sat around the fire facing one another. The rekindled fire crackled between us, while a bottle of cheap, acidic red wine went from hand to hand. Samir's Philips boombox was somewhere in the darkness behind me. It had stereo sound and was twice as heavy and twice as big as mine. The sound was enough to drive the neighbours living across, above, and below his flat up the wall, in contrast to my Japanese mono-lightweight that could barely be heard out on the balcony.

Damir was sat next to Samir, and past them were Amar and Ismar. I had also invited Vlado and Robi, who were from Vukovar. Vlado's dad, a civilian, had been executed in the early days of the war. Robi's dad was a first lieutenant in the Croatian army and still out there somewhere on the Slavonic battlefields. Officially, a ceasefire held in this part of the country, but occasionally a death notice was posted on the window of reception: 'It is with deep sorrow and great pain that we must announce...'

Amar and Elvis were discussing the war. They had both escaped before it got too bad, and for that reason they talked mostly about what they saw on TV. I had to turn up the music. Metallica. 'Nothing Else Matters.' Guitar solo. Samir had given me the tape as a present.

It felt strange that evening. My first birthday away from home, the first one without Neno calling to wish me a happy birthday, and the first one where something other than fizzy drinks were served. All day I had been asking myself whether Neno even knew what day it was. Whether he thought about me on my big day.

I sat observing the four brothers on the other side of the fire. I felt like I had done in the spring during the war, when

I looked across the river and wished our house was far away on the other side of the river. Why did *our* side have to be occupied by the Serbs? Of all the places, why did the front line have to pass along that particular embankment, behind Zaim's garage – fifty metres from our house? Why was Neno not sitting beside me on this night?

Earlier that day, on my way to the marina on the other side of the peninsula, Samir managed to cheer me up a little. He gave me a ninety-minute Samsung cassette packed with heavy and thrash metal. He had chosen the playlist and written MIKI'S BIRTHDAY MIX at the top of the tape. In brackets he added: *To Miki from Sama. Majbule, 4.9.92.* This tape would eventually set the scene for my ultimate Iron Maiden trip.

We bought two kilos of sardines from a fisherman for next to nothing and took a little extra bread from the restaurant on the sly. After dinner we lugged beer, wine and Coke through the woods out to the peninsula. There was nothing to burn but pine and cypress. The branches we collected were damp. They gave off loads of smoke and gave the fish an unexpected aroma. The barbecue smelled like my Dad's aftershave.

'Was it bad where you lived?' Amar asked when I handed him another beer.

'I dunno … We had a lot of barbecues in the beginning … No fish though.'

'Why's that?'

I hesitated and snapped a branch.

'The first thing the Serbs did was shut off the power. Within twenty-four hours all the freezers were defrosted. In the entire town.'

'And?'

'And, all the meat defrosted.'

'Ah, so you had to barbecue! Or what?'

'Right. There was smoke everywhere. One big party. People passing steaks, ćevapčići and bread over the fence.'

I tossed the broken branch onto the fire:

'Everything had to be eaten before it went off. It didn't matter whose it was. Everything was shared.'

'And later?'

'Later it was crap.'

'Not so festive?'

'Nope.'

'Cheers!'

'Cheers!'

I quickly moved over with Sanela and Katarina, who were trying to teach each other to blow smoke rings. They were equally bad.

'That's not a ring, man,' I scoffed. 'That's a spiral! A question mark!'

'Wow, you're so poetic!'

Katarina's dad was Serbian. He had stayed home – fought on the other side. That was not looked upon favourably by those at the camp.

'He was forced to,' she told me that night.

I remained silent. Did not comment. Instead I dropped a brick, a theory that names ending with '-ina' were the most feminine and 'hand on heart' – the sexiest.

'You mean, hand on dick?' Amar corrected me, probably trying to mark his territory. He had still not given up, and my interest in the Nina-Marina-Katarina hat trick was far too obvious.

Soon I abandoned my ulterior motives. Katarina and I were talking names. She wished she had a more neutral name.

'Katarina is not that Serbian,' I said.

'Katarina Jovanović! As soon as they hear that they know exactly what I am. Why don't you just call me Kaća? Or Ka?'

'Ka? That's weird. Why not Kata?'

'It's too common! Just call me Kaća, okay?'

'Fine by me. I'm not really bothered. My name is insanely Muslim!'

The wine bottles were empty. The final scraps of grilled

sardines had long since been eaten, and now beer and smokes were passed around the fire. There was plenty for everyone, and everyone said it was the most luxurious party ever.

'And it's not even over yet!' I stressed, not without some pride.

There was one thing that could have been better, everyone agreed: the wine!

'We fucked up,' Samir said. 'Wrong vineyard.'

'You're supposed to mix it with Coke,' Elvis said. 'That's what the locals do.'

'Yeah, they call it *bambus*,' Vlado added. 'They also mix white wine and Fanta.'

'Ew!'

'Yuck!'

'I don't get why they don't just make better wine,' Kaća said.

'I don't get it either.'

'But don't you see the point?' Elvis broke in. 'The wine is homemade. The owner of the vineyard, that old witch, she makes the wine. She sells it in her shop. It's in her best interest for people to buy wine *and* fizzy drinks. She sells cheap wine and then makes it trendy to mix it. Just so she can make a packet.'

'Yeah, Elvis is right,' Samir laughed. 'We're not buying it. We'll keep drinking it straight. Even if it tastes like piss!'

'Yeah!' shouted Elvis, who took Samir's joke seriously. 'She can stick her fizzy drinks you know where, man! And her mineral water!'

We had a hard time keeping the fire lit. We crumpled up newspapers, shook lighters, knelt down, lit and blew. In the end the flames went out, and we sat in the darkness beneath a silent colony of stars and an egg-shaped moon. The light on the boombox continued to glow. The music kept playing. When the final cigarette was passed around, we were wasted, belting out some good old songs and some good new ones for that matter. I knew all the oldies by heart. I impressed Samir by reciting Balašević's 'The Boy Boža' from start to finish. It was the longest song I knew by heart, and I was happy to discover that even though my records and tapes were gone, the lyrics and the tunes were tucked away safely in my memory. I sang, almost rapping, standing in the moonlight, more drunk than sober, and still I remembered every single word. The verse, 'Ladies and gentlemen, he disappeared without a trace, and that gives the entire story a curious ring' stung me a little. The song was from one of Neno's records.

'Why are you always singing Serbian songs?' Robi muttered, when I was finished.

It sounded more like a complaint than criticism. I shrugged and said:

'Balašević opposes the war, and ...'

It's one of my favourite records. He probably writes the best lyrics in the entire world. And he is not a nationalist. That record was one of the first ones I listened to in Neno's room after he moved to Sarajevo.

I felt like telling him all of that. But I was confused by the unexpected question, saw Vlado and fell silent. Vlado was sitting right next to Robi, and it gave me pause. Would he get offended? Was he sitting there thinking about his murdered father? Was that who Robi meant I should take into consideration, or was he referring to something else entirely?

'Balašević is half Croatian,' Sanela chimed in.

'Is he?'

I did not know that.

'Yes, him mum is Croatian.'

'And his dad is Hungarian,' Damir added. 'A little. I think. Not Serbian.'

'I don't care what he is,' Robi said monotonously. 'Can't you sing something else?'

'Sure.'

'Cool.'

'It was just a funny song.'
'Enough with the Ekavian!'
'Okay!'

The Ekavian pronunciation was completely taboo, even though a lot of people from Slavonia had spoken it before the war. From the shelves of the library, books in Cyrillic disappeared without a trace, and a number of comical words from the Croatian Middle Ages replaced Serbian synonyms. They appeared in the newspaper, on the radio and on TV, and the newsreaders had to make an effort not to stumble over them. Even before my arrival at the camp I had started to say *tisuća* instead of *hiljada*, for thousand, and *zrak* instead of *vazduh*, for air, when I spoke to people other than Uncle, Mum and Dad. Just to avoid furrowed brows and smart-arsed comments. At a market stall in Split, a greengrocer played dumb when Dad asked him how much the *paradajz*, tomatoes, cost. From the heights of Mount Everest he replied, 'that' was not something he sold, but *rajčice*, on the other hand, cost such and such.

I was certain Dad would call him an idiot. Or tell him to relax. That's what he would have done back home. He would not be browbeaten by a moron like that. But Dad did not say a word. Not so much as a syllable, until we left the market and the crowds. He was thinking out loud as he muttered into his beard:

'Dear Tito, you've fucked yourself …'

Cassette 3

THRASH & HEAVY

A GOOD COMRADE

The year was 1984. The woman in front of me had a long, pointed nose and a high, wrinkled brow. She had a deep voice and smelt of something that I could not place. She asked me a lot of questions:

'What colour is this?'

'Blue.'

'And this?'

'Red.'

'And this?'

'White.'

'And this?'

'Yellow.'

'And this?'

'Green.'

'And this?'

There was a pack of plasticine on the table. At the bottom of the pack the colours were represented with a series of broad lines.

'He doesn't know,' Neno said.

She looked at him.

'Brown,' I said.

'No.'

'Grey.'

'Purple,' she said and returned the pack to a drawer. 'But that was good.'

I looked at Neno. He gave a grimace that said, 'I'm sure it'll be fine,' 'I'm sure it'll turn out all right,' and the woman with the nose asked:

'Can you draw?'

'Yes.'

'What can you draw?'

'A car.'

'A car?'

'A star,' he said. 'He means a star.'

'Fine. Show me.'

It was a sham. We had practiced. 'Why a star?' I had asked him. 'Because!' he had replied, as though that word alone was explanation enough.

The woman handed me a pen and a piece of graph paper. I drew five red lines on the paper and showed her the result: a near perfect star.

The expression on the woman's face changed, and in the midst of her broad smile I glimpsed a lonely gold tooth.

Everything was going to turn out all right.

Hanging on the wall of the woman's office, there was a picture of a man. An identical one awaited me in the classroom. At night the man often appeared on the television screen. Sometimes he sat in a car waving. Children and women stood alongside the road. Their faces were joyous, and they were throwing red, white and blue flowers into his open limousine.

Later I was told:

– that he was dead.

– that he still lived in all of us.

This man was everywhere. In the music room he sat behind a piano fingering the black and white keys, smiling harmoniously. In the woodwork room he stood assembling a perfect birdhouse. At the library he sat with his feet resting on a plump stool, immersed in some unknown book.

The walls of the school were adorned with profound quotes attributed to him. Under each of them his brief name was written in sloping block letters. My favourite was the one in the history room: 'We must live as though peace will last for a hundred years, and be prepared as though war will start tomorrow.'

I was sad that he was dead. Got tears in my eyes when we sang in music class: 'Joy spreads in every direction. We now walk freely in our country. But the great days, we will remember them. Comrade Tito, we swear it!'

Maybe it was because my grandparents – all four of them – were also dead and gone. Maybe it was because he looked so old and so kind on the framed photographs at school.

My schoolbag was made of a light-brown leather. It was wider than my shoulders, but I persuaded Dad to buy it for me.

The salesperson shook his head and Dad apologised:

'What can I do, the child wants Vučko!'

Vučko – the wolf that served as mascot for the recent Olympics – was my friend. I wanted a bag with a picture of Vučko and the writing, 'Sarajevo '84.'

'It's too big for him,' Mum said when we came home.

'Yes,' Dad said, 'but what can I do, the boy wants Vučko!'

I had to pull the straps down and press my knuckles against my ribs so the bag did not dangle against me as I walked. Mum always made sure I wore plenty of clothes. Way more than necessary. My back was sweaty under the thick leather bag and the extra layer of clothes.

'Look at that idiot,' my tormentor Bobi said to a classmate. 'Look! His bag is bigger than him!'

I did not even try to get by him. As soon as I spotted them I turned around and took the usual detour. Running this time, because I was already late.

When I entered my classroom, my back was drenched in sweat. The teacher was talking about our extra elective. She outlined several possibilities. In my overheated condition I chose 'Down Tito's Revolutionary Paths.' The only image the words evoked in my mind was a chilly, green park with a statue in the middle and two paths that twisted around the statue. The atmosphere was friendly and relaxed. A group of students and their teacher strolled down Tito's revolutionary paths, took photos of one another and had a great time.

I was mistaken. 'Down Tito's Revolutionary Paths' did *not* take place in a chilly green park, but in a run-down classroom with large windows facing the courtyard. We went to class and listened. The teacher read from a brochure, one that a couple years later we would subscribe to and read out loud to each other. The brochure was printed on rough paper, but the front page was smooth and colourful. We read about how the partisans ate grass in the woods. About how Tito's Alsatian, Luks, saved his life during one of the many German air bombardments. Luks threw himself on top of Tito and faithfully took the brunt of the shell fragments. Tito escaped with a wounded arm. Tito thrashed the Germans and became president. Our country was free again. We had Luks to thank for that. Man's best friend.

Like Tito, I liked dogs. I played with our puppy Boni beneath the walnut tree in the garden. I made my voice as deep as possible and shouted 'Boom! Boom!' but Boni never threw himself over me.

'Maybe if there was a real shell,' I said to Dad, who at the time was still a member of the party.

He came towards me carrying a bowl of milk:

'No! It would run for cover before you could say biscuit. Straight to hell!'

'But Luks saved Tito?'

'Yes. Luks. Tito. Right. How should I put it … Maybe that's the way it happened. And maybe that's not *quite* the way it happened.'

One day in November we were assembled in the city's new sports centre. It was on the same street as the garrison, diagonally opposite our school.

The changing room reeked of smelly socks and leather balls. The classes were called out from the dim player's tunnel and gathered on the pitch, where all the year ones in the city were assembled. The audience clapped every time a class was called out. The girls from the older years knotted our red scarves and crowned us with blue partisan hats. The cool silk felt nice around my neck. The star on Adi's cap was not sewn on properly. I scanned for Neno's face amongst the spectators but could not see him. Mum and Dad could not make it. They were working.

We were arranged in rows so that we could see the stage while we swore the oath. Hanging on the wall behind the stage was a picture of the kind man from the classroom, flanked by two large flags – that of the country and the republic. A girls' choir sang about the forests and mountains of our proud homeland, about the paths that should not be strayed from. There was singing and clapping, clapping and singing. Finally, it was quiet. The girls left the stage. An older man wearing a peaked cap and an olive-grey uniform approached the lectern. Under his smoothly shaved chin there was a fuzzy microphone, and the sound from the speakers travelled directly into our protruding seven-year-old chests. Sentence by sentence, it was replaced by our simultaneous roar. There were so many of us shouting so loud, that you could barely hear your own voice. Still I was nervous as hell of making a mistake and getting some of the more difficult words wrong:

TODAY, AS I BECOME A PIONEER, I GIVE MY PIONEER'S WORD OF HONOUR: THAT I SHALL STUDY AND WORK DILIGENTLY AND BE A GOOD COMRADE: THAT I SHALL LOVE OUR HOMELAND, THE SELF-MANAGED SOCIALIST FEDERAL REPUBLIC OF YUGOSLAVIA: THAT I SHALL SPREAD BROTHERHOOD AND UNITY AND THE PRINCIPLES FOR WHICH COMRADE TITO FOUGHT: THAT I SHALL VALUE ALL PEOPLES OF THE WORLD WHO RESPECT FREEDOM AND PEACE.

Back home we celebrated with a layer cake. The tray was yellow and scratched. The whipped cream stuck to my chin. I was still wearing my partisan cap.

'… crisis…'

'...currency...'

'...inflation...'

Mum, Dad and Neno were using some strange words that day. Mum collected the plates and I switched on the telly.

One channel showed a sailing boat sinking in a foreign black-and-white film. Another had *Tom and Jerry* and then *EPP*, The Economic Propaganda Programme, now called for short, *Adverts*.

STAMPS AND SNOT

All that was gone now. The Vučko bag, the partisan cap and the pictures of the kind man from the classroom.

The summer of '92 drew to a close. A new school year had begun. For some earlier than others, and for some not at all. I was among the latter. My school report had gone up in smoke along with the chest of drawers back home. I had no documentation to prove that I had completed primary school.

I explained that to a stressed out secretary one day at the secondary school in Vešnja. She looked at me. I stood there in my sorry, dated, washed-out trousers, worn-out Adidas trainers and tattered T-shirt. I handed her my yellow refugee card and continued to describe my complicated situation. Told her why I wanted to go to secondary school, how I had always got the best marks, and why I had to leave Bosnia.

Just finding the school and the right office was something of an accomplishment, and finally standing there, I was stared at as though I was from another, less advanced planet.

'According to the Republic of Croatia's new laws, all foreign citizens, be they Bosnian or Japanese, must pay for their schooling.'

'No way. How much?'

An amount corresponding to five hundred German marks per annum.

'Five hundred marks! For each year? I … Can't we find another solution?'

The secretary, an older woman with bleached pageboy hair, shook her head and voiced her regret that she could not do anything. I did the same, voiced my regret and said that neither could I. For me and my parents, that was a staggering sum. Five times our combined fortune.

'But why I am only hearing about this now?' I asked. 'I was just here last week. They told me I should come back in a week! Couldn't your colleague have just told me that back then?'

'Young man, here we speak politely to one another!'

'Sorry, but the school year has already started. What am I supposed to do now?'

'Regrettably, it costs what it costs. Those are the rules. Next!'

In the long corridor on the first floor there was a good vibe. It was noisy, people were laughing and calling one another. It was the first day of school, and for normal people the day held special importance. I maintained my mask as best I could and hurried off.

Upon arriving at the school, I had seen GIVE US ANDRIĆ BACK spraypainted on the wall by the main entrance. Now the graffiti was disappearing under a thick layer of paint. An elderly caretaker was flourishing a paintbrush as he spoke to a woman who I assumed was a teacher. I heard her clear opinion about 'those communist brats, running around making a mess of the buildings.'

I was indifferent. Completely. Both regarding the Nobel Prize winner, whose books had evidently been removed from the syllabus, and the entire secondary school as such. As recently as the spring I had been looking forward to saying goodbye to primary school and starting secondary school in my hometown. I had promised Neno I would enrol as soon as possible. Obviously I was going to study the same courses as him. Obviously I was going to follow in his footsteps. But then war came, bringing with it the soldiers and their fucking shells. The buses we were crammed inside, and all the details I did not care to talk about. When you have been put through the mill like that, you do not cry over a single locked door.

They could stuff it.

All of my classmates back home had very concrete dreams. One wanted to be a lorry driver, the other a teacher, the third a mechanic or a director of some reputable company. I was the only one who had no clear goal.

'Musician … maybe,' I once replied when asked.

I knew four chords on the guitar and one popular refrain. Neno had taught me to play, after borrowing a guitar from a friend. I had talent, in his opinion.

But when I told him my plans, he shook his head:

'Forget it. You can't make a living doing that. Not in this hole of a town.'

'What should I do then?'

'What do you want to do?'

'I dunno. When I'm at the hairdresser's, I think about being a hairdresser. When I'm at a restaurant, I think about being a waiter. And so on.'

'If you don't know what you want, then just enrol in secondary school like I did. Then you have four more years to think about it. Otherwise you'll end up like Dad. Working at the factory. Do you know how long he had to slog it out there before they made him manager? Besides,' he added, 'there are lots of girls at secondary school.'

I walked down Zagrebačka Street and ran into Robi and Vlado, who were wrapping their tongues around two tasty-looking ice cream cones, practically in sync.

I explained my problem to them.

'At technical school, they accept everyone,' Vlado said, 'even people without school reports. It doesn't cost a thing. You just have to fill in an application, inform them of your grades and sign a solemn declaration.'

'Really? Is that all?'

'Yes. Until the war calms down and you can get hold of the necessary papers.'

'Wow!' I pretended to be hugely enthusiastic. 'Where is it?'

'Up by the citadel.'

'Thanks.'

Technical school. What was I going to do there? If it's not secondary school, it's all the same to me, I thought.

But then I pictured Mum and Dad. Waiting for me back at the camp. I needed to come home with something.

Of the two possible routes to the school, I chose the wrong one. It cost me more time in the baking sun. My armpits were damp with sweat by the time I found the school.

What a day! From first thing in the morning, it had been all uphill. First Radio Zagreb informed us that our alarm clock was wrong. Dad had set it during the night; he really needed a new pair of glasses. Then I dashed out the door – with no breakfast and no shower. I made it to the bus in the nick of time.

The secretary's office smelt of glue and fresh orange peel. I stammered out a hello and explained my situation with a sincere desire that the meeting would be over quickly. I stunk like a donkey, and my conversation partner was a young and far from ugly woman. Secretary to the headmaster. That was her official title.

'That is not entirely correct,' she said.

I blushed and avoided her gaze as she spoke. *That's* how hot she was.

'Your friends must be Croatian citizens.'

'They are. They're from Vukovar.'

'There you have it. But don't worry. We have a list of students ... of your type. If you inform me of your previous subjects and marks and get your parents to sign a declaration, we can get you on the list and send it to the Red Cross.'

'Why?'

'They're looking for international sponsors.'

'Sponsors?'

'Yes. People who would like to pay for your schooling'

'Ah, I understand,' I said even though I did not. 'That's

fine by me. I'd like that.'

'Really?'

'Yes.'

Mum and Dad were worried. So much so that following my detailed description of the events of the day, they decided to splurge on three bus tickets. They wanted to join me at the meeting between the headmaster and other students 'of my type,' as the secretary to the headmaster had put it.

'What kind of crap is this?' Dad asked rhetorically. 'Are children no longer permitted to go to school? What kind of world are we living in? I was a child during Hitler's war. And I still went to school!'

'I'm not a child any more,' I said.

'No, that's right,' Mum said.

'You're my biggest problem,' Dad grumbled. 'That's what you are.'

'Stop saying such things,' Mum warned him. 'We're on the bus.'

'Small children, small problems. Big children, big problems. It's always been like that.'

We found the school, the floor, and the room. The latter smelt of chalk and sharpened pencils. Hanging above the blank chalkboard, in Tito's old spot, was a picture of the Croatian coat of arms with its red-and-white chess board and blue crown. The bright colours blinded me in the otherwise dull room, where myself and twenty to thirty students 'of my type' were crowded together. Several others also had their parents with them.

For nearly half an hour, nothing happened. A mute fellow with frog-like eyes and an apathetic gaze was picking his nose in the front row. He rolled bogies between his fingers and stuck them to the leg of the desk. He only stopped when the headmaster's secretary entered the classroom. A small man with obscenely thick glasses followed hard on her heels. After a quick hello, the man introduced himself as the headmaster, apologised for the delay and welcomed everyone. He told us about the school and the prospects and, without beating about the bush, explained that the school, the local council or the Red Cross, I cannot remember which one – in any case someone not present in the room – still had not found a solution for all of us.

'It's not proceeding as quickly as we had hoped,' he said. 'But there's progress. Bosnian-Herzegovinian citizens who hold Croatian nationality can immediately enrol on certain courses, if there are still places, mind you. The rest of you must arm yourselves with patience for a little while longer.'

I looked at Dad. It looked like he had not understood either. The headmaster scratched his nose and continued:

'I know it might sound a little strange – and for some perhaps uncomfortable and unpleasant – but the stipulation is that you must enclose a copy of your birth certificate or some other document to confirm your ... nationality. As you are not Croatian citizens, it is necessary to have some form of documentation.'

The final remark gave rise to a sea of murmuring and worried comments. Half the people in the room started to dig into their pockets and bags. When the first birth certificate was carried through the room in the lively, flapping hand of a Croatian, a woman with tidy hair in the back row asked the headmaster:

'Why are we being treated like this? As recently as last year, refugees from Croatia could be enrolled on any course in Bosnia. I can't imagine it's because you're short of chairs!'

The headmaster ignored the laughter that spread through the room, and endeavoured to provide a sensible answer. A year ago Croatia and Bosnia were still not independent states, he explained, and even if they had been, the situation would be the same. At the end of the day, the fact that displaced citizens of Croatia could enrol at educational institutes in Bosnia-Herzegovina last year was and would continue to be a decision for the authorities in Bosnia-Herzegovina, just as this was the current decision by the Croatian authorities. For that reason, despite his best intentions and a desire to help, he could not change the existing rules, which had been made 'further up the system.'

The mood in the room fell. The majority of us were very familiar with not having influence on those 'further up the system.' We packed our things and left the room.

Out by the gates of the school, daylight swept over us. I squinted, and Dad suddenly swore and turned around. A murky sound that revealed a slimy, vibrating activity in his throat split the air. Dad cleared his throat and took a run-up towards the gate. The headmaster and a couple of Croatian parents came walking across the courtyard. The sight of them made Dad stop in his tracks. He took a deep sigh, clenched his teeth and muttered into his beard:

'Bloody ...!'

Then he spun on his heels furiously and walked past without saying a single word. Mum and I followed. She waffled on about trying some other schools. I thought about the green wad of snot, which instead of landing on the school gate, now slid down Dad's throat.

I could almost taste it. Salty and nauseating.

Back at the camp we agreed that in future I would be the one to attend those kinds of meetings. It would cost less. Both in bus fares and nerves. Dad had been cursing between clenched teeth the entire way to the bus station. On the bus Mum had to shove him and whisper:

'Be quiet. People can hear you.'

But he continued:

'Scum! As though we were never part of the same country! As though Tito himself was not Croatian, dammit!'

In principal, the system was not to blame for the entire furore. It was my age. Had I been one year younger, there would have been no issue, and my parents would have been three bus tickets richer. A primary school in Vešnja had created an extra class for Bosnia-Herzegovinian citizens who were not of Croatian nationality. There were lessons in the afternoon, and the students from year seven and eight were in one big class. Amar's little brother, Ismar, was among them.

While Robi, Vlado, Kaća and Marina went to school, the rest of us strolled down to the beach, skipped stones and repeated the same stories. In the autumn, living in Majbule was boring as hell. The tourists were gone, the streets and the beaches were deserted, and you soon grew tired of staring at the same sea view. It was only eventful during a storm, when the waves started to whip against the cliffs of the peninsula, then we would run down there, stand on the flat roof of the bunker and observe the awe-inspiring water. It swelled up in hazy slow-motion and pounded against the cliffs. The foam sprayed into the air, and we bet each other whether the next wave would be higher or lower than the previous one.

In the evenings we met in Damir and Samir's room on the ground floor of D2. Their parents were often visiting others in the camp or were glued to the screen in the TV room. All of us sat there regardless of nationality or school. There we listened to the same mixed tapes, played cards and drank, when there was something to drink. Damir and Samir were mine and Amar's ultimate heroes. They knew about all kinds of music – particularly foreign – and they constantly talked about their great idol, Jim Morrison, who had written 'The End' and died in a bath. Damir and Samir's hair reached their nipples, and they usually spent a lot of time talking about their hair. Very informative. For example, I had never heard that you could get split ends, and that you should cut them regularly. Or that an egg yolk was good for the hair. You just had to massage it into the scalp and let it soak in before rinsing.

DAD'S GLASSES

When Dad was young, he dreamt of being a tailor. He told me that one dreary night after the meeting at the technical school. He had just started to go out on the town and did not own a suit.

It was the early fifties. Tito had just broken with Stalin, self-management would replace the much-despised planned economy. A brighter future was in store, but much had to be done before then. The country had to be developed, modernised. Everyone had to contribute.

At the local 'office for works and education' Dad was informed that they did not need any more tailors that year. Since he had no possibility of moving from home and becoming a tailor in another city, he agreed to be trained as a welder instead.

'We can't get you any closer than that, an elderly office worker told me with a smile on his lips. You're going to tailor iron!'

Dad comforted himself with the fact that after four years as an apprentice he would start to make some money. At the recently opened pipe factory in the industrial zone, the pay was rather good. He would be able to buy all the suits he wanted.

'The years before the country was developed were very difficult,' he continued, with Mum sitting on the bed knitting. 'One day they picked us up in front of the factory and drove us to Zenica in lorries. That was back when they were expanding the iron foundry. For three months we slept in containers, the fleas danced over the powder used to combat them, and we ate … Well, I can't even remember what we ate.'

'You must have been paid well?' I teased him.

'A swan's bollock! That was what we were given. Three months construction work from morning to night – and then back home! But were commended. They patted us on the shoulder and said "Good work! You will all be remembered." Have you ever seen the smokestacks?'

'Yes.'

'Have you seen how tall they are?'

'Yes.'

'Your father built them. All the bricks had to go past me and my comrades. We sifted through tonnes of them. For three months! And here you are complaining that you have to wait to start school. Imagine I sent you away for three months of hard construction work! We did not weld a thing, all we did was load bricks and other materials.'

Not only did Dad become a welder, he also became a communist.

'My football coach was a party member of the old guard. He wanted to enlist me. "What would it mean to become a communist?" I asked him, and he replied: "It means becoming a decent human being. Fighting for the rights of the workers." So I agreed to join the party. Back then it was something. Back then the party was untainted. Without any of these bastards who have recently joined purely for the sake of their own pockets.'

Dad accepted various other offers. Including being sent for further training in order to become a master craftsman and later production manager at one of the factory's many halls. Even back then he had problems with his eyes. The doctors believed that his serious short- sightedness and rapidly deteriorating vision had to be genetic. But Dad always believed another diagnosis:

'It's an occupational injury. I've welded my eyes away, sacrificed my vision for the homeland! And what have I got in return? A swan's bollock!'

'We've had a good life,' Mum said.

'Exactly, *had*! And look at us now! If I only had my pension, I wouldn't have to beg for peanuts at the market.'

'Yes, that would be nice. You also need a new pair of glasses. The ones you have are too old.'

'I know. But that costs money. That will cost a fortune, as the young people say.'

'I'm just going out for a bit,' I said and got up.

The conversation was getting too depressing.

'On the other hand,' Dad continued his elegy, 'what am I going to do with a new pair of glasses? I'm still not going to like what I see.'

WHERE'S YOUR THROAT?

'Do you realise,' Damir said with a yawn, 'that everything White Button produced in the seventies was copied from two other bands?'

'No, which ones?' I asked, tugging at the neck of my top. For the millionth time that evening! It was one Dad had picked out for me at Caritas. It looked new, but the stitching was all wrong. It was tight around the neck and the left shoulder.

'Deep Purple and Led Zeppelin. Anybody can hear that.'

'I've heard of Deep Purple,' I said. '"Smoke on the Water" and all of that.'

'You haven't heard nothing. Not yet. I can lend you some proper music. Then you'll just have to listen. New and old ... Hey, did you know Filthy Theatre copied Dire Straits from the very beginning? Pretty much all of their first two albums! Do you know Dire Straits?'

'Yeah, a little. That video ... But ... they have some cool numbers, Filthy Theatre, don't you think?'

'Oh yeah, it's fine for parties. When you need to soften up the ladies and that sort. But like so much of the shit our bands play, it's a matter of atrocious copies. They just add a few traditional notes, embellish it a little and sell the shit.'

'Hmm.'

'Everything comes from the outside. The big bands. Anyone who knows music can hear that! You're standing at a Red Apple concert one night, for example. Completely sold out. The girls pushing and screaming like mad. The floor is slippery with pussy juice.'

'Heh, heh, heh!'

'Seriously! I've seen it. I was there.'

'Okay!'

'And then they play that song, "I Like This Thing."'

'Right. Cool tune! Or … what? Now what?'

'The tune and every single chord were nicked!'

I looked at him blankly, and Damir waved his arms impatiently:

'Lennon, McCartney, "Twist and Shout," man! The Beatles! You must know that.'

'Yeah, yeah. Obviously.'

'Do you get it now? They're screwing people. That's what they're doing.'

'Then what about No Smoking,' I said , because I knew all their lyrics by heart and wanted to remind Damir of that fact.

'There you're on to something,' he nodded and tossed his hair back. 'There you're on to something. But they listened to a lot of The Clash and Sex Pistols, you know. A lot. Especially The Clash. Especially!'

It was past two o'clock in the morning, and while I tried to remember if I had ever heard The Clash, I saw old Milan emerging from the entrance of D2. He walked towards us with his hands pressed against his lower back.

'Evening,' we said to him.

'Good evening, boys. Don't you have to go to bed? Don't you have school tomorrow?'

'No, not really. We're just chatting.'

'Oh, I see. And you're not tired?'

'A little. We just can't be bothered to sleep. It's nice here.'

'Yeah! Those who can, don't want to, and those who want to … of course …' he muttered and took the stairs down towards the path.

We heard him greeting some people his age who were still strolling around down there. We could only make out their silhouettes, but one of them had to be Jozo from the ground floor of D2. He had walked past us half an hour earlier. Jozo was one of the oldest people at the camp. According to some, he had not shut his eyes since 1942. The closest thing he ever came to sleep, they said, was when he lay down and rested his muscles for a few hours.

'Maybe it's time for us to call it a day,' Damir said and got up. 'Tomorrow I'll tell you how Metallica was formed. Now *that* is a band!'

We flashed each other the sign of the horns and said goodnight. I walked up the stairs of D1 and slipped into our room.

Dad was leading Mum in the 'loudest snoring' discipline. I went into the bathroom, relieved myself and washed my hands. Finally, I could take off the stupid Caritas top.

I had just closed my eyes when Dad turned over and gave me a proper slap.

He lay in the middle of our three beds, which we had slid together the previous day to make room for a coffee table and a chair in the corner by the balcony door. I slept by the wall to the bathroom. With Dad right next to me. He had his back to me when he screamed loudly and swung his arm. He turned, and in the same movement he smacked me right on the nose.

'Ow, you hit me!' I shouted. 'That bloody hurts, man!'

My words were drowned out by his strange moaning. He muttered something in a strange and distant voice that sounded both terrifying and ridiculous. Mum woke up and shook him. He pulled the duvet up, smacked his lips and said:

'Yes. They're coming with knives. Where's your throat?'

MUM'S ATTEMPT

When I woke up, Mum was gone. Dad was writing a letter to a friend who now lived in Austria. The man owed him a small sum of money. It was such a small amount that Dad had long since given up recovering the debt. But now he sat writing a lengthy elegy about how we were in a tight spot, in the hope that his friend would recall his debt and send money.

'I don't think he'll send you anything unless you ask him directly,' I said. 'Where's Mum?'

'She's gone into town.'

'Why?'

'She'll be back soon.'

'What's she doing in town?'

'She'll be back in a bit. Then she can tell you about it.'

'Hmm.'

She returned on the noon bus, which stopped up by the roundabout. She walked the rest of the way in the baking sun. In a way it was kind of touching when I thought about it, but I was not touched. I was angry.

'Where have you been?' I asked her when she came through the door wearing the ugliest dress I had ever seen.

'I've spoken to them.'

'Who?'

'The secretary. I've given her all your details.'

'HAVE YOU BEEN TO THE SCHOOL? IN THAT DRESS?'

'Yes, why?'

'Why? Why didn't you wear the one you had last time? Your best dress?'

'It's in the wash.'

'And you spoke to the secretary? In those clothes! Dammit, Mum!'

I could picture her in front of me. Standing in front of the hottest secretary in the city in that ridiculous summer dress. An old rag that someone had happily rid themselves of at the Red Cross warehouse. At best it looked like a striped, faded nightgown.

'Did you know about this?' I asked Dad.

'Yes.'

'And you let her walk out the door in that?'

'Yes, and what of it? It's a nice dress. Not the most fashionable but ...'

'"A nice dress?" You two have really lowered your standards, haven't you? That is embarrassing!'

'Relax, it's just an older model.'

'Why did you have to speak to the secretary?'

'I explained our situation to her. Asked if we could pay in instalments. Because it can't go on like this any longer. You're missing out on an entire semester.'

'Did you stand there begging for special treatment? Did you moan about how poor we are, or what? Are you mad? Didn't we agree to wait for a sponsor? Like everyone else!'

'Yes, yes, but it's certainly worth a try. The woman was very pleasant. A nice older lady. Sweet ...'

'Older? ... But ... Wait ... Where were you?'

'At the secondary school, of course. Wasn't that what you wanted?'

I was relieved. Luckily I did not have to stand in front of the hottie at the technical school and hear 'Oh yes, your Mum came by the other day.'

'And what did they say?' Dad asked.

Only then did I realise that he had also been in on it. He was trying to scrape together some money, borrow enough for half a semester, or maybe even an entire semester, while she went to check whether the school would agree to be paid in instalments. They were insane. And insanely naive. They would never dream of borrowing money from Uncle. Dad was too proud for that.

'Brilliant!' I clapped my hands. 'And what did they say?'

'They told me to come back next week.'

'Super! Bra-vo! And do you know what they'll tell you next week? To drop by the following week. Just like they told me.'

'Be quiet, boy!' Dad raised his voice. 'She means well. We'll see what happens. We're doing all we can.'

'Drop it! That was a month ago. If they had wanted me, they would have admitted me straight away. I don't care any more.'

'Fine then, I'll go to the technical school tomorrow and see if there's any news.'

'NO! Both of you stop it, now! *I'll* go to the technical school tomorrow and in the future, and I'll crack their skulls together if something doesn't happen soon. And you two should just relax and mind your own business!'

... THAT ENDS WELL

I was allowed to hitchhike to Vešnja. First with Amar and later on my own, I stuck out my thumb, sniffed around the city and looked forward to my meeting with the secretary to the headmaster. She was really pretty. Smooth, aubergine hair. Large, intelligent eyes.

People in the corridors hurried past me. Their hustle and bustle made my life feel even more stagnant.

'There you are,' she smiled and opened a ring binder. 'How are you?'

'Good,' I answered. 'And you?'

'I'm well, thank you. You didn't come yesterday.'

'No, I was busy.'

'Well, it seems there's good news.'

'Is there?'

The matter had been settled at long last. Finally the rest of us could go to school. A sponsor had been located. Even for someone like me.

But – there was a small *but*, as the secretary put it. Not much to choose between. Actually there was only a spot on the mechanical engineering course. Even if people from the other classes were to drop out later, it would be impossible to switch. The semester was already well underway.

'That's not relevant,' I said. 'Mechanical engineering ... That was just what I wanted.'

It was a performance worthy of an Oscar. In my next life I would be a big Hollywood star. A big star with a mansion and an American birth certificate, with several copies.

Shit! Amar and I had hoped for some kind of civil engineering mumbo-jumbo so we could be in the same class as Vlado. We did not know anyone at the school apart from him.

'What did I tell you,' she said. 'All's well that ends well …'

She helped me fill out the necessary forms for enrolment. She stood up from her chair and held out her hand ceremoniously.

'Congratulations,' she said.

'Thank you very much,' I said.

And with that, it ended well.

Mechanical engineer!

Sitting in the car of a chain-smoking electrician on the way back to Majbule, I imagined a situation, me with greasy fingers and a sweaty forehead, struggling with some huge machine, climbing inside its dark insides, searching for the flaw.

The scene switched to a noisy hall in an anonymous factory somewhere: there was dust in the air. My colleagues and I were coughing as we separated and assembled some machine parts with the help of a very detailed drawing. Our greasy fingerprints covered the curled-up paper. The drawing grew more and more difficult to make out. Difficulties and doubt arose. Time got away from us …

All the images left the hint of a smile on my lips. Mechanical engineering did not interest me any more than the culinary preferences of Franjo Tudjman that the newspapers wrote about. Metals and their properties, I couldn't care less about them, and the only two metals I wanted to know more about were *thrash* and *heavy*.

GARLIC IN THE MORNING

'Hello, mechanical engineer,' Amar greeted me.

'Hello, shipbuilder,' I replied. 'Are you happy with your school?'

'Are you mad, man! Not one girl.'

'None at ours either. Is it exciting, apart from that?'

'That shipbuilding nonsense? God, no! What am I going to do with that? I want to be a journalist.'

'Now let's look at things positively,' I said and pulled my monthly bus pass out of my pocket. 'Look at this! Look!'

I waved the card. All the students at the camp no matter their pedigree were given a free bus pass. No more hitchhiking back and forth to school. Now Amar and I could join the others. Unlimited rides, access to the city buses, a certain coolness the moment you pulled out the card and nodded at the inspector – all of that made possible by the Red Cross and our anonymous international sponsors.

The bus that picked us up by the Muscle Market only came in the morning. For that reason it was always packed. It required good elbows and strong ribs to endure the trip.

Every oddball imaginable was on that bus. Kača's downstairs neighbour, a small blonde man by the name of Zvonko, who boasted that he was able to eat an entire bulb of garlic for breakfast, with bread and thinly sliced bacon. Everyone believed him – you were forced to – we were provided with incontestable proof that the nickname we had given him was justified. Clove, we called him.

When Clove was on the bus, half of the passengers sat with their collars pulled up to their eyes, making them look like a group of newly fledged ninjas. He often stood talking to the driver for a long time. The driver cleared his throat. Amar and I feared the worst: that the poor man behind the wheel would take a turn for the worse and drive us all into a stinking death. Anyway, you were not supposed to talk to the driver.

On the way to school Amar and I went into the library in Vešnja. We spent half an hour in there reading what was set for us. The pensioners hung out near us. Rustling their newspapers, snoring, their glasses sliding down their noses.

The news was not particularly good bedtime reading. Lots of pictures of the wounded, the displaced and the dead. Plenty of big fat lies and plenty of hatred. Not a single word about Nedim Pozder Neno. Not a single bit of news about the others from his group.

FABIO AND HORVAT

Concentrating in class was difficult. Sitting on your arse for seven long hours, taking notes. The pace was fast. I had not held a pen for over six months. My hand cramped up, my thoughts raced in every direction.

The teachers gave lectures. Anything they said was the truth itself, you just had to make sure you jotted it down in your notebook. There were no textbooks, and we were never given any photocopies. I did not even have a school bag. I carried my notebooks around in a thick blue plastic bag.

Mum and Dad woke me up at six o'clock in the morning and were usually in the room when I returned around three. At twelve o'clock they would collect my lunch at the restaurant and later heat it up in the microwave at Kaća's mum's place. Otherwise I would not get anything to eat till dinner, which was not until six.

By the time I came home from school I was starving. Breakfast, consisting of a cup of tea and a piece of white bread, kept my hunger at bay until lunchtime. Then I had to ignore the gaping hole in my stomach until the end of period seven. Then hold out for half an hour on the bus to Majbule. Back to the camp, up the stairs and then finally – food!

The final three lessons were really bad. Especially on Monday, because after the set mealtimes on the weekend, my stomach expected nourishment. I had to improvise. I discovered that if I drank a whole bunch of water during my break, my stomach would busy itself by toying with it, forgetting that it had actually been rumbling for food. Later, when I got to know Fabio and Horvat, I started to ask them for a bite of theirs. They crammed all kinds of stuff inside them. They were all right.

'This school isn't for me,' Fabio said.

He was into punk and wore very tight trousers.

'Why not?'

'The teachers smell and they're smart-arses. Four bloody years of this!'

'What are you going to do then?'

'No clue.'

'How did you end up here?' Horvat asked.

He was into metal, had long hair and Reebok Hi-Tops.

'Couldn't get into secondary school.'

'Your marks?'

'No, wrong pedigree. They wanted five hundred German marks a year.'

'A year! Are they insane?'

'That's what I told them: "Now listen here, friends, I'm short a few pfennigs. Can we find some other solution?"'

'And? What happened?'

'Unfortunately not. Five hundred exactly, take it or leave it.'

MINEFIELD

A few days before Christmas Igor showed up. Fourteen days of leave. He looked like crap. Even skinnier than in the summer, he was completely preoccupied for the first few days.

'Hey, Igi! Do you remember our summer boozer?'

'Yeah, kind of. I think.'

'Wow, we were so drunk!'

On the other hand he remembered the topless German babe from the beach perfectly well. He said he had just sorted out one who was her spitting image.

'Her jugs were just bigger,' he claimed.

On Christmas Eve, half of the camp went to the church in Majbule. Igor and I stayed behind, shivering at a table in front of the restaurant. There was a clear sky above us. People came and went while Igor chain-smoked and drank herbal brandy from a small flat bottle. He said he had lost weight on purpose. That the bullets whizzed past his ears but not a single one had grazed him yet.

'It's not simply a matter of manoeuvring between them,' he stressed. 'It's also about your physique, about a soldier's … infrastructure, so to speak.'

A series of war stories followed, in which he usually played the role of the hero. He boasted about how many Chetniks he had 'knocked off' and how the barrel of his Kalashnikov was glowing.

'You could light a fag on it,' he said. 'You know how many of them I smoke.'

To match his gem I told him a story that Dad had just told me. I did it with enthusiasm and without beating around the bush. Not in my wildest dreams did I imagine that I would think back to this situation many times in the future, to this

Christmas Eve, and to Igor's reaction to the story.

'You've got to hear this, it's insane,' I said.

'Give it to me, kid! I love stories.'

The story was about Zijad Pozder Zijo, my dad's cousin who lived in a village further up the river. At the point of the road where the asphalt ended and the dust from the gravel kicked up when you cycled along. I went there a couple of times during the war to get some milk and bring news from the town.

Shortly after we were evacuated, the looting of our house was well underway. The vultures drove around in lorries and emptied the houses of anything that could be sold: TVs, VCRs, sofas, record players – anything. They could not have been familiar with the local conditions, because they simply continued up the main road and entered Zijo's house too. He and several others from the village had stayed behind. The frontline was three kilometres down the river, and Zijo's wife happened to be Serbian. She and the children had gone to join her family, and Zijo had remained to look after the house. He lay hidden in the stable and watched as Serbian soldiers broke into his home and emptied it of anything of value.

That same night he let his cow and dog out and decided to swim across the river. He slipped down to the water, carrying in his pocket a sealed plastic bag with money, his wedding ring and ID. He silently swam front crawl three kilometres downriver, towards the town and the frontline. Shining rockets and bullets flew over the water. A shell hit a poplar tree a hundred metres in front of him, and it caught fire. The flames lit up the surface of the water, and he had to hide by the shore until the shooting held up.

When he had swum past the car park at the beach, not far from our house, there was a large field of grass in front of him. Alongside the lawn was an approach road, and Zijo guessed that the Bosnian trenches were on the other side of the road.

He carefully crawled through the grass, crossed the road and climbed a hill that passed through a decimated section of the town. He went in through the front gate of someone he knew, who would be able to confirm that he was not a Serbian spy or something along those lines. He knocked on the door.

He told Dad all about it when he rang from Varaždin one day. His wife and children had made it out of Bosnia. They lived in a rented room in the city, but could barely afford the rent. They had been staying in a camp, but had to move because of the frequent raids.

'We're sorting out some documents so we can escape the country,' he said. 'Germany, Denmark, The Netherlands! We've applied for visas for every one of them. I'd clean toilets if necessary, as long as they leave me alone. I can't bear this any longer! I go to bed hungry so that the children can eat.'

Igor was listening more attentively than normal. Especially when I added that Zijo had crawled through a minefield by the shore. He had not realised that until he explained to the military personnel how he had suddenly turned up in town. They did not believe him at first. Because what was the likelihood of crawling through a minefield without triggering a single mine?

'It depends on the minefield,' Igor said. 'Obviously there was something wrong with that one. The ones we make,' he added proudly, 'nobody makes it through!'

It was a smug comment. The same old song, Bosnians had no clue about war and did not fight hard enough, while the Croatians were oh-so clever. It stuck with me for a long time.

Just then Amar and Elvis walked past. They were in the midst of a spirited discussion on why the sea was saltier in some places more than others. They kept going. Igor and I hung out a little more. He was drunk and I was sober. He chatted away. I just sat there listening.

At one point I faded out completely. I think he had been talking about the locals' disdain for the president, but got sidetracked in the details about how expensive it was to buy property by the sea. My mind wandered. I mumbled 'Yeah, yeah' and 'Mmm.' I yawned.

Then Igor suddenly paused and looked at me as though he had just said something extremely important. He expected a reaction, an opinion.

To extricate myself from the situation I went on autopilot and shrugged:

'Yeah, that's how it is … That's life.'

Igor narrowed his eyes and pounded his fist on the table:

'YES! BUT LIFE SHOULD BE *LIVED*! NOT FUCKED UP!'

'Yeah, right. Obviously, man … Obviously.'

HAPPY NEW YEAR

Shortly before everything went to rack and ruin, we had a proper party. New Year's Eve only came once a year, war or not, rich or poor. Mum and Dad had to cough up.

On the morning of New Year's Eve, Damir and Vlado paid a deposit at the office. They were given the key to a storeroom in the basement of D1. The rest of the day we spent blowing up balloons and cutting out paper decorations. Robi attended to the music, the girls attended to the decorating. The room had to be aired out, swept and wiped down.

Samir, Amar and I went to do the shopping. It was a historic shop. Our bags were so full, one of them burst. A bottle of red wine shattered against the asphalt.

We were still trying to clean up the shards of glass when Vlado came walking towards us. He held his head in his hands as he informed us that we no longer had a room to hold the party in.

'Damir has been called down to reception. They say someone complained.'

'Who?'

'No clue.'

In the reception room, Damir sat waiting for Sergio, the former caretaker and current receptionist, to finish a phone call. He was by far the grumpiest receptionist at the camp. Severely overweight. Monobrow and hair bristling out of both ears. The man had some strange notion that the inhabitants of the camp had a better life than other people because they did not work and did not have to pay for food or lodgings.

He made us wait.

Finally, he pulled out a handkerchief and emptied his

nostrils with a single loud snort:

'And? Where's the key?'

'Wait a sec. What's the matter?' Damir asked. 'Why can't we have a party?'

'Too much noise. People complained. Where's the key?'

'It was just a sound test. Who complained?'

'None of your business.'

'Yes it is! Now we've got nowhere to have our party.'

'If you had behaved yourselves, you would have done.'

He grabbed the envelope with the deposit from a drawer and threw it on the counter:

'Here's your money. Take it and find somewhere else to run riot. It's not going to be here.'

'Come on, where are we going to find somewhere now?' someone piped up.

'Yeah, obviously people will be queuing up everywhere to offer us a place,' someone else said.

'But we have an agreement with the people at the office,' Damir said. 'We were promised ...'

'Tonight you can consider me in charge of both the office and reception. People complained, there's not going to be any party. Give me the key!'

'Who complained? Tell us who, so we can talk to them.'

'Talk to them?'

'Yes! We want to celebrate New Year's Eve. Everyone has a right to that!'

'No, they don't.'

'What do you mean by "no they don't"?'

'I mean "no." Who has the key?'

'What do you mean "no"? We do live in a democracy!'

'Like hell you do!' he laughed. 'You're too young for that.'

I nudged Damir:

'Parasite must be the one who complained. One hundred percent!'

'The people on the ground floor of D1 are such idiots,' Amar said. 'It could have been any of them.'

Samir tried to explain how much we were looking

forward to the party. He could see that his brother was close to losing his patience, so he tried to smooth things over. But that exasperated Damir even more:

'Drop it, Sama! Leave the moron alone! He's just pissed off that he's working tonight. That's what this is about.'

Sergio did not respond, but he looked at Vlado:

'You there! You've got the key. Bring it here!'

Vlado looked at Samir. Samir nodded. He reached into his back pocket then threw down the key. The metal clattered against the counter.

'That's it. Your money is there. Take it – and get lost!'

'I HOPE YOUR WIFE GIVES BIRTH TO A ROLL OF BARBED WIRE, YOU MORON!'

Damir should not have added that final comment. He was far too close, hunched over, his elbows resting on the counter. He had no chance to defend himself.

Smack! Smack! Smack!

Sergio grabbed him by the hair with one hand and pasted him with the other. Damir staggered backwards and knocked over an ugly potted plant. Dirt scattered across the floor. The plant snapped in half. For a brief moment Damir remained on his back, before attempting to get to his feet. Samir and I helped him up.

'ALL OF YOU, OUT!' the big slowcoach roared. 'OUT! IF I HEAR SO MUCH AS A PEEP OUT OF ANY OF YOU, YOU'RE FINISHED! UNDERSTOOD? I'LL SHOW YOU, YOU SCOUNDRELS!'

We hurried out. It was already dark .We stood by a lamp post and counted the money.

'It's all there.'

'Now what?'

'Nothing. Let's buy some more drinks before they close.'

'Not a word about this,' Damir said. 'I don't want anyone to find out that he hit me. We're not telling anyone. Promise?'

'Promise.'

'And as far as the party is concerned, we'll just go down to the beach. That belongs to everyone, goddammit!'

After dinner we stood under cover of the cliffs below D3. We tried to light a fire but it was no use. Too windy. The fire went out time after time. We stood in a circle and opened a bottle. Our teeth were chattering.

Then Igor and the girls showed up.

'Where's that bottle?'

'Over here, Igi! The party's here. Under the stars!'

'In the open!'

'Have you got more to drink?'

'What do you think?'

'Then follow me.'

'Why?'

'When I tell you to follow me, then follow.'

Igor, our professional Croatian soldier, had saved the day. The Sergio matter was history. Igi made use of his authority as defender of the homeland and managed to conquer nothing less than the TV room! He went over to see Ivka's husband, Ivan, who lived on the first floor of D2. Among other things, Ivan was known for his shameless shagging. Leaving his balcony door open. Half of the camp could hear the shouting coming from his room: 'More! More!' and 'Yes! Yes!' It triggered a multitude of images in our brains. Once he and Ivka even enjoyed themselves in broad daylight. With my own eyes, I watched the old women on the terrace put down their knitting, cross themselves and slip away.

Ivan had a Croatian flag fluttering on his balcony, and he was by no means the kind of person you could just knock on the door and ask them to keep it down a little. At the start of the war he shared a trench and rations with none other than Igor. Now he worked as a police officer in Vešnja and had his own car.

Igor had explained the situation to him and retold the entire Sergio incident, of course with the exception of the part about the thrashing. The two of them immediately went down to reception, where Ivan proceeded to give Sergio a brief lecture:

'They're going to have that party! And how! They've lost everything!'

'But the noise ...'

'They can use the TV room! It's almost directly under my place, and as for the neighbours, I'll speak to them. They're going to have that party!'

Sergio put up a struggle, making reference to his responsibilities, and stated that if there were any more complaints he would have to call the police.

Ivan sent him a wan smile:

'Pull yourself together, man! I *am* the police. Call whoever you like, and send them to my door. I know all of them. However, I think it would be best if you just keep your trap shut! I've had to kill lice and wade through mud so that you could live and work in peace. I've had to – for the sake of your fat arse – bury my best friends!'

The TV room was commandeered around nine. The news had long since finished. The oldies had retreated to their fourteen square metres.

Robi switched off the TV. Amar opened a bottle. Samir went to get his ghetto blaster. Igi was the hero of the day. We kept him going with a steady supply of drinks. The girls sang 'Under the Bridge' and danced in the middle of the room. Marina sent me a look that I did not pick up on, and at that exact moment the lights went out.

'Oh, no!'

'What the hell!'

'It's not coming back on!'

'Of all the nights!'

There was no point in complaining to reception. Even if there had been a normal person behind the counter, they would not have been able to help. It was a holiday, the caretaker was off, and the fuse, or whatever the hell it was, could not be changed until the day after tomorrow.

Then Elvis got an idea. His dad, Huso, who was famous for his legendary words, 'That's how it is these days. Now all of you are gypsies too,' had an old lorry, which the entire family had escaped Bosnia in. The lorry was in an equal state of decay as our former homeland, and so dusty that we never found out what colour it was. According to Huso the vehicle had not been washed since the days the Germans shouted '*Halt!*' and '*Hände hoch!*' in these parts.

The old lorry was soon positioned beneath the window of the TV room. Some extensions were unwound and connected inside the driver's cabin. A speaker was unscrewed and placed in the windowsill. A candle lit up the room, and then the music went off with a bang …

Bottles were opened, sent round the room and emptied. Standing on the imaginary dance floor in the middle of the room, their lips pressed together, was Amar and Sanela, the newest couple. Dancing next to them were Samir and Andrea, and Igor and Kača. Damir and Ismar handed Igor a bottle as they passed. As he took a swig, Kača walked up to me and pinched my arm:

'Marina is waiting for you, you jerk. Talk to her. Go on!'

Midnight approached. The jackets and sweaters came out. In the dim, undecorated TV room, it was getting a little warm, and Marina and I commented on the music and the temperature.

By the time someone put Filthy Theatre on and everyone in the room roared along to 'Nobody could hide their tears like Marina,' the two of us were already standing outside in the dark, snogging our heads off, just as a matter of form. Normally I kissed her rather distantly. I did not want her to think that she was special. But on that night it was different. Mister No's face and images from a party exactly one year earlier pushed their way in between Marina's cotton sweater and my new Caritas shirt. Almost in desperation I grabbed her and held her tightly for a long time. The images faded. We clung to each other, pressed together, and drifted away like two weightless creatures without a past.

YET ANOTHER WAR

It was the coolest party ever. For days afterwards we hung out in front of the TV room discussing who had said what that night. Who had drunk the most and who had got the most wasted. We could hardly wait till the return of spring and summer. The smell of grilled sardines tantalising our senses. The party season would be opened with a bang, under the open sky, this time with the latest chicks from the beach at our side. Plus more bottles and more batteries, so the party would last even longer than the previous one.

We had tasted blood. Forgotten everything that 1992 had taught us. That the rest of the world existed, and that you should always keep that in mind. Either we did not understand, or we did not want to understand, that you really had to rein in your expectations; we did not live in Beverly Hills, but on the Balkini peninsula, where everything good was short-lived.

The idiots were queuing up to spoil the party.

Over the course of the winter, a fragile alliance between Bosnian Croatians and Bosnian Muslims creaked big time. There had long been disagreements and sporadic clashes, but from the outset of 1993 there was talk of certain war. Bosnian Croats and Bosnian Muslims no longer fought Bosnian Serbs, but also one another.

The radio and TV buzzed with information, misinformation, official denials and appeals. It was not easy to figure out what was actually going on. In order to know the truth, or at least get a sense of it, you had to read as many newspapers as possible, listen to as many radio stations as possible and spend hours flicking through the TV channels. Then place all the conflicting statements side by side and try to make heads or tails of the bloody and filthy mess.

Such demanding mental activity was something very few had the nerves for. Newspapers cost money, the only thing to listen to was Radio Sarajevo and Radio Free Europe, on top of the unavoidable Radio Zagreb, while the one TV station was the Croatian channel, HTV. Every single night President Dr Franjo Tudjman would appear on the screen. If not his entire body in motion, then at least a freeze-frame close-up.

The glass windows of the TV room steamed up. People pretended to be clever, debated tactics, made proposals. Everyone and their dog had an opinion on what ought to be done, how the government ought to react. Everyone and their dog was president for the evening. Brief sentences and phrases like 'That won't do, now listen here' were all the rage. The belief that your side was telling the truth was strong and heartfelt, especially when they said that the other side was lying.

We kept our distance from the TV room. For the most part we met in the ground floor of D2, in Damir and Samir's room. In the corridor, the old women gathered, eternally moaning and complaining about the noise we made. They had no comprehension of our daily requirement to lock the door and let ourselves be carried away by the meandering notes of Slash's masterful solos, by Hetfield's deep, dark riffs and by Morrison's lyrics, words we still understood too few of.

In room 210 of building D1, it was more difficult to avoid all that nonsense. Dad listened to Radio Free Europe every night at seven, eight, nine, ten, eleven and twelve o'clock. Transmitted from Prague. Mutli-ethnic editorials.

It did not make for a good night's sleep.

I dreamt about the war, our friends and neighbours – about a certain Kerim, who directly after his return from the YPA described various drills to me and showed me how to march. He told me about an officer who one time, during an alarm in the middle of the night, all keyed up, whispered: 'The enemy is here. Close by. In the woods.' With a barely visible finger he pointed towards a barely visible woods. It was as dark as the inside of an owl's arse, it was two thirty in the morning, and the moon was hidden behind the clouds. There was not a soul within a radius of five kilometres – friends or enemies.

Three years later Kerim was killed by a shell from the very same YPA with whom he had done his military service, never having taken the drills, alarms and brainwashing presentations seriously. Aided by eyewitness descriptions, I dreamt about him a number of times. His face was slashed, his right hand was resting on his left rib. Standing over him, next to me, was Krešimir Tomič, my history teacher from Vešnja, whispering in my ear:

'Forward march!'

I woke up and turned in the bed, determined to put my fingers in my ears the next time Dad went to adjust the black dial on the radio, summoning waves filled with counts of the dead and the missing, the wounded and the raped, the displaced and the persecuted. I did that for one or two nights, but it did not help much. On a purely physiological level, there are limits to how far you can stick your finger in your ear. However little you wanted to hear, you still heard. However little you wanted to feel, you felt. However much you stayed away from the TV room and turned a blind eye to the ugliness and the unsavouriness, the ugliness and unsavouriness did not turn a blind eye to you. It approached by degrees, growing in strength, both in image and in sound. Metallica's hardest songs suddenly seemed pathetic and weak – like they were played on a harp or a ukulele, accompanied by countless tubas and trumpets.

Balcony doors were opened, but not just to let in the early spring sun. *Čavoglave* and *Here Comes the Dawn* thundered away in the opposite direction. Here and there a greeting was absent. Here and there a collectively directed comment burst out –'Go back to Bosnia and laugh that loud there!' – while other, more precise retorts were delivered in person: 'You Muslim piece of shit!'

The latter was dispatched by a giant wearing a CDC

uniform, his arm around his cousin Zdenko from D1, who stopped in front of Samir and I:

'Hey, you there! You with the hair! What are you? A hippie? A junkie? What's your name?'

'Samir,' he replied. 'And yours?'

The guy held out his hand and squeezed.

Samir bent onto one knee in pain.

'Rambo. That's my name. And tomorrow I'm going to shave off all your hair, you Muslim piece of shit! You're firing shells over our heads in Mostar, and we're feeding you here!'

Samir stuttered out something along the lines of 'I have nothing to do with that,' and the impatient Zdenko exclaimed:

'Come on, Ante. Hurry up! Leave the kids alone.'

They swayed off in the direction of a car parked by the Muscle Market. They were drunk, to put it mildly.

For the next week, Samir was looking over his shoulder, expecting to bump into Ante again. He was unbelievably stressed. Luckily for him it turned out the guy was a deserter. Both he and Zdenko had bolted. But how could anyone have known that in the moment he squeezed Samir's hand? And what would have happened if Samir had returned the favour and called a Croat in uniform a piece of shit?

Luckily I did not have to find out, but I know what happened immediately after the Ante incident.

I stood in front of the open TV room listening to the TV with one ear, which sounded the attack at full blast, and with the other I listened to Igor and his hazy theory that all girls were subconsciously attracted to men in uniform.

Then Sanela appeared by the entrance to D2 and said:

'Damir and Samir are leaving.'

'Leaving? Where are they going?'

'Sweden.'

'Shut up!'

'That must be a joke!'

'No, it's not. They're leaving on Saturday. I just spoke to them.'

'Did you?'

I could not believe it. I *would* not believe it!

I asked Sanela where they were, and hurried into D2.

Igor followed me, his flip flops smacking the ground.

We knocked on the door.

The door handle was vibrating. There was music playing inside.

'Come in!'

I opened the door.

Samir stood in the middle of the room, bare-chested, with a tube of toothpaste in one hand. His hair was down.

He just shrugged.

In fact it had been on the cards for some time. None of us saw them. Their parents had always been worried about the two of them. They feared them being mobilised. Samir had told his parents about the Ante incident and about the thrashing Damir got from Sergio in place of a New Year's greetings. That did not exactly comfort them. Returning home was out of the question. The war in Bosnia, and particularly in Herzegovina, was nowhere near ending. On the contrary, it was clearly just beginning.

Sweden beckoned, and they packed their things.

Nothing was the same anymore. We no longer lit fires on the beach and we no longer sat in a circle around it. Sanela's words had divided us into two camps: those who stayed and those who left. Amar and I, disciples of the twins, had let our hair grow out and addressed each other with the familiar 'bro,' now walked around with no purpose. We were very aware of the fact that without them, nothing would be the same, while they kept silent and avoided any discussion of their imminent journey.

The night before leaving, they held a farewell party in their room on the ground floor of D2. It felt like a funeral.

We sat on the floor and had a few brief, superficial conversations. *Riders on the Storm* drifted lazily through the smoke-filled room. It was Damir's favourite song, and we played it over and over again.

Sometime after midnight, by the wall beneath the window, Kača and Damir kissed. For weeks they had been seen walking together on the beach. For weeks he had hesitated, knowing that he would be leaving soon. That night, with everything already lost and nothing to be broken, she seized the opportunity and made the first move. For the rest of the night, those of us in the room, the old women in the corridor, tomorrow, which would separate them for good, none of those things existed. The only thing that existed was a dim, smoke-filled room in one of the army's former holiday camps by the sea, a long-endured hunger and any crumb that could be snapped up.

The next day we stood gathered at the bus station in Vešnja and bid a lengthy farewell. Samir cried. We swapped cassettes and small mementos to remember each other by. Promised we would write. Comforted each other.

'We're going to meet again,' Damir whispered when at long last he gave me a hug.

He boarded the chugging bus and then he was gone.

Two weeks later I experienced a total déjà vu on the terrace between D1 and D2. Sanela walked towards me and wrapped her arms around my neck:

'Amar and Ismar are leaving!'

'Where are they going?'

'Sweden.'

An almost identical storyline followed: depression, the final collective swigs of beer, embraces, tears and waving goodbye at a sunny bus station in Vešnja.

As he boarded the bus, Amar shoved a piece of plastic into my hand. A cassette tape. He raised his double thumb in the air, smiled and said:

'Primo quality!'

I turned the cover and looked down: Metallica. Compilation. First song: 'Am I Evil?'

Amar was gone.

After Amar and Ismar's departure, things happened quickly. There were no farewell parties, waving from the platform or proper bouts of depression. Bosnian friends my age continued to disappear.

Elvis and his family, whose lorry and accumulator saved our New Year's Eve, travelled to Italy via some illegal routes. Sanela, who grieved over Amar like he was dead, moved away to stay with her mum and some distant relations in Split. Her dad was fighting Croatians in the eastern part of Mostar, and everyone in the camp knew it.

Cassette 4

SOLO PASSAGES

GOLDSMITH'S TREASURE

Within weeks of Amar's departure I felt like dropping out of technical school. The teachers were smart-arses, just like Fabio had said. I was growing more and more uncomfortable in my chair. I wanted to get away.

Our history teacher, Krešmir Tomić, a self-declared member of Tudjman's CDC, was a nuisance. We memorised important dates and royal lineages. Occasionally he drew parallels to current historic events. To help us better understand the Middle Ages . We discovered that the struggle for Croatian independence began long before President Dr Franjo Tudjman was in charge of the most recent battle.

One time, as he told us about previous attempts to unite the country, a small discussion ensued. For centuries Vešnja had been subjugated to Venice and later to Italy. In the front row, Jurišić commented just for a laugh that things had probably been better under the Italians than they were under those ruling from Zagreb now. Tomić was seething. He wiped the floor with this fifteen-year-old local patriot, using such vociferous arguments you would think that the opinion of this pimply-faced boy had decisive importance for the fate of the homeland. Jurišić clammed up – what else could he do – but that did not save him from Tomić's snide remarks for the rest of the semester.

'Traitor,' Tomić used to say to him on a regular basis, 'it's your turn at the blackboard!'

Old Lugarić was funny at least. He taught maths.

'And then? It's easy. Add the two figures together, multiply by such and such, divide by four, in brackets …'

We looked at him listlessly. He was red in the face and always looked like he had just got out of bed. One of us was sent to the newsagent, and while we sat wrestling with equations and vectors, Lugarić sat behind his desk reading the paper. Ten minutes before the bell rang, he picked out three boys, listened to their solutions and told them to write the maths and the results up on the board. Always the same three – Blažević, Ivanković and Horvat – because they were the only three who always had the correct results. And Lugarić knew it. The rest of us just stared ahead, doomed to fail.

Were it not for young Tijana Rožac, our Croatian teacher, my descent would have been complete. Once, in the middle of describing the scene where Hector parts with Andromache before the decisive battle, she spotted Fabio's white T-shirt and read: PUNK'S NOT DEAD. She stopped in the middle of a sentence, smiled and said:

'Wake up, boy! It's stone dead. It was already dead when I was in school.'

Another time we had to read *Goldsmith's Treasure*, a thick novel from the nineteenth century, and write an essay about it. I flipped through, skimmed a few pages and put it down. It was too bloody heavy. It did not spark my interest.

'Have you read that crap?' I asked Horvat before the lesson.

'Of course, man. What do you think? I've got Šenoa in the palm of my hand!'

'Tell me, tell me!' I said. 'What's it about?'

It was a love story about two young people whose families had a running feud. The goldsmith's daughter loved this guy, but her father wanted her to marry someone else. In the end the despairing girl committed suicide. Ended up being a victim of the stupidity and lack of flexibility of the adults. That was how I understood it anyway, from Horvat's summary. 'The hatred and pride of the adults destroys the happiness of the young couple. Contradicting the story's happy ending.' I later wrote.

It was a simple assignment. You had to choose a character from the book and write a profile. I went for the main character, the wretched girl, and I wrote, and I rubbed out, and I rewrote: about her love, her innocence and her purity. About the harsh environment that surrounded her, and the idiocy of the adults 'which renders the realisation of her most humble dreams and desires impossible.' It filled more than two pages.

When we were due to have our essays returned to us, I chose not show up to class that day. Fabio, who was into punk, had money on him, so we went down to Zagrebačka Street and played pinball. Fabio raved about a place called Ukulele, the only place in town where heavies, punks, grungers and other freaks could assemble.

'*There*, they play real music,' he said. 'No commercial rubbish. There are no pop dudes, no pop chicks. You should come.'

'I don't have money for shit, man! I'd have to rob a bank to go.'

After the final token and the final flashing message, GAME OVER! GAME OVER! Fabio headed home and I took the bus back to Majbule.

The next morning I discovered that Rožac was so enthusiastic about my essay that she had read it out in class.

'She was praising you to the skies,' Horvat said. 'She wants your body.'

'Shit! She can't have it. Not until I've read that fucking book!'

After school, I roamed the city, studied shop windows and went to the library. I flicked through the pages of greasy atlases and read about the population, geology and climate of Sweden until hunger forced me to take the bus home.

Back at the camp I was met with the empty places where my friends and I had hung out, plenty of wry looks and a cold portion of potatoes that needed re-heating. In town it was possible to disappear in the crowd. My forehead was not stamped: Bosnian, refugee, Muslim. In the camp it was a different story. Everyone knew who and what I was.

I threw down my school bag, filled the gaping hole in my stomach and glided down the stairs to the beach. Normally it was deserted. The fascists kept to the restaurant, the TV room and the terrace between D1 and D2.

I skimmed stones by the pier, annoyed with what was happening. I thought about Neno. The old void that 'the Swedes' had filled for a while had grown. No one could fill it and no one could get my mind off it. The people around me did not resemble him much, but their voices, bodies and clothes did. He was always somewhere, just never all in one piece. I caught myself walking and talking like him, using his expressions, his slang. I sat in his favourite position: hands in pockets and legs partially outstretched. We did not have a single picture of him, not a single recording. Even if we'd had a VHS – where would I have watched it? In the TV room? In front of everyone while the chain-smoking men played cards at the table and the women crocheted with one eye on the screen?

No way. Some underwear, a black jacket with a yellow pack of Čunga Lunga chewing gum in one of the pockets, that was all we had left of him. It was his old Spitfire jacket with a broken zipper on the left sleeve and an orange satin lining. Back when he used to go to football matches, he would turn the jacket inside out.

Folded up inside a plastic bag, the jacket now lay at the very back of the shelf above the clothes rack. Mum had put it there on Dad's express wish.

One day when I had gone to try it on, I discovered it was no longer hanging up.

'Why's it in the bag?' I asked Mum and Dad at dinner.

Mum said it was probably for the best. Dad said nothing. He slurped down the thin broth, scraping the bottom of his plate.

Once in a while I lay on my bed and faced the wall. Pretended to be asleep. Other times I wrote in one of the notebooks I had picked up from Caritas one time. I often wrote about things that happened in the camp, matter-of-factly and chronologically, often in note form. I regularly reread the various passages, preparing myself for the day when Nedim Pozder Neno, my biggest hero, would be released. I looked forward to telling him about everything that had happened in the time he had been away. I wanted that day to come so damn much, and for that very reason I nearly shat myself out of fear it would never happen.

Whenever my daydreaming got the upper hand, I thought about 'the Swedes' and our farfetched dreams for the summer. I was seriously afraid of a new punishment from above.

Okay, God, or fate or whoever is pulling the strings up there. Fine, let him lose both legs, I thought. Fine by me. As long as he comes out of this alive. Or allow him to make it out in one piece and have *me* lose something instead. Let me get run over one of these days or break my nose or get hit by one of the bullets Ivka's husband Ivan fires into the air on the beach every time he gets drunk. I've always wondered what happens to those bullets. Do they make it all the way up to you as intended, or do they turn back and fall into the big, dark sea. Do we have a deal?

No reply.

Nothing.

No letter. No phone call. No speeding car with the accelerator floored as I slowly crossed the street.

SWEDEN

Loads of letters arrived from Sweden. Brimming with optimism and energy. The brothers were doing well, making new friends. The refugee camps were better, the people nicer. Amar's were the most positive:

'Just wait till I get the hang of this weird language! I'll be chatting up Swedish girls like a real James Bond ... And if anyone asks where in Sweden I am, just tell them I'm up by that screw at the top of the globe. All that's missing are the penguins!'

He could not believe it when I wrote that Vlado and Robi kept avoiding me. That they looked away whenever I spoke to them. Samir wrote back, 'Fuck those morons!', went into great detail about his new experiences and sent me the lyrics to my favourite songs. According to Amar, Sweden was total paradise because of something called a music library. You could just go in and borrow any cassette tape. Absolutely free. Everything from the softest pop to the heaviest metal.

'And they've got songbooks for most bands. I'm thinking of getting myself a guitar. Acoustic.'

Music library? Free? Heavy metal, too?

That same day I tried to convince Mum and Dad that we should move to Sweden too.

'Out of the question.'

'Why?'

'It's one thing that you dragged me away from my home,' Dad said. 'Now I'm supposed to move to the ends of the earth?'

Mum elaborated:

'It's not for us. Traipsing around the world at our age. You have to pay for the papers, run all over Zagreb, queue up. Where are we supposed to get all that money from?'

'You could just borrow some from Uncle.'

'Over my dead body,' Dad shouted. 'Never!'

'Why not?'

'I am not going to borrow money from *him*. And certainly not for a trip I don't even want to make.'

'And what would we do there?' Mum said. 'We're old, we don't speak the language or anything.'

They wanted to go back. To the 'hearth and home of our ancestors', as the newsreaders called it on television. Even though they knew perfectly well that it was no longer a hearth and home but a burnt-out ruin, they could not accept losing everything they had worked so hard for their entire lives: the house, the garden, the two-year-old car.

'There are people who have lost far more than us,' I said. 'Is there another reason you won't leave?'

'Easy for you to say,' Dad said. 'When you were born, the house was already standing. We had to save up for each and every brick. We've been building it for years. It's ours!'

'Fine, but what about me? Do I have to return to those ruins, too? Just thinking of that town makes me ill. Have you forgotten what those fascists did to us?'

'If you knew of all the things I've had to put up with in my life, then those two bloody days in the hands of the Chetniks would look very different to you.'

I snapped at him in annoyance:

'Why can't we just leave like everyone else? Besides, you couldn't go home now if you were related to God himself! Maybe the Swedes can help us arrange an exchange for Neno. We can write to their king, to their politicians, to the Red Cross.'

They could only smile. They shook their heads and went on like a broken record: they wanted to go home.

'Listen Emir. We realise you are sad because your friends have left,' Dad said. 'But do not overdo it. You are only a child. You will live with us until you've finished school and get a job. After that, you can do as you like.'

'I hate that school!'

'It is the only one. Once the war is over, there will be plenty to do. Renovating, repairing and that sort of thing. People will return to their homes. You will see.'

'But wouldn't it be better to wait somewhere safe till we can go home, a place where we'll be left alone? At least in Sweden no one would bother us. What difference does it make whether we return home from here or from there. It just means a slightly longer trip.'

'There are good people here, too,' Mum said. 'Ivka, Ivan and Kaća's mother. As for those troublemakers, you have to learn to ignore them. Scoundrels like that, they don't need war as an excuse to give you a hard time. Just keep quiet and mind your own business. This too will pass.'

I kept quiet. What else could I do? Pack my things in secret and run away from Majbule? How? Where would I go? I had no passport, no money and no clue where Neno was. Of all the things needed to make that kind of trip, all I had was the will and the urge to travel. If Neno had been somewhere safe, it would have been a different matter entirely. I could have just called him up and asked for help.

It was a couple of days before Neno's birthday and it was already noticeable in the room. An odd atmosphere of wary silence and deep sighs.

'Oh, well ...' they murmured with distant looks in their eyes, whenever I tried to get a reaction out of them.

One day at lunch, I tried again. I gave them the entire spiel about civilised Sweden, the country where – according to Amar – even neo-Nazis liked Bosnians. Dad did not say a thing, instead he took me aside after lunch.

'I have to tell you something.'

'What? What now? What have I done?'

'Let's just find somewhere to sit down.'

We stood in the middle of the path and looked around. Not a single table was free on the terrace so we headed towards the bungalows to get away from all the people.

'There's something I neglected to tell you,' Dad said.

'Neglected to tell me? When?'

'You know that I call around asking people for news.'

'Yes. About Neno. And the others.'

'Exactly. You remember when I was given confirmation that they were in a concentration camp in Banja Luka.'

'Yes, you told us that.'

'But that was not all. I also heard that Neno was dead.'

'DAD!'

'Take it easy, it was not true! It was just a rumour. There was a mix-up.'

'What did you hear?'

'I'll spare you the details.'

'Tell me.'

'Apparently the Serbs had forced them to crawl into no-man's-land and drag the casualties back to the trenches. They came under fire from the other side and were killed by our own people. Him, Zaim and two others. But it was all just a rumour. It was a mix-up. He and Zaim were not among the dead. But that's not the point. The point is that …'

'What?'

'That I … Do you not realise what it has been like for me? From the time I heard that until I was able to confirm that it was not true? And you sit there talking about Sweden? Do you not grasp what is happening around you?'

That was a real slap in the face. I felt bad. Sweden without Neno? I realised the chances of that were unlikely. That I'd probably never make it there. But it did not keep me from dreaming about it every day.

There was a lot of time for dreaming. Those days, the only person I spoke to other than Kaća was Igor, or rather he spoke to me. But Igor was spending less and less time at the camp. Duty called. The homeland needed its soldiers. When he came 'home' on leave, the first thing he did was lock himself in his room for several days. Then he went out and got drunk, talked incessantly about women and very rarely about music. I started to avoid him when he had been drinking.

Kaća had inherited some of Damir's cassettes and I assumed the role of faithful borrower. I fast-forwarded and rewound the tapes, listening to the songs until I knew them by heart.

'Okay, Kaćenka. Name any track out of all that Nirvana nonsense, and I'll sing it for you!'

She named a song and I began to mimic it, first the tune and then the lyrics. Any words I didn't know, I just made them up.

'Well? What do you think?'

Kaća yawned.

'You're the biggest nerd I've ever met! You'll be a virgin till you're thirty if you go on like this!'

It was on one of these days that I first listened to 'Dark Side of the Moon' and 'The Wall' in their entirety. As soon as Mum and Dad left the room, I threw myself onto the bed, stared up at the yellowed ceiling or at one particular, carefully selected crack in the wall. I practised looking up at the ceiling without blinking. The image grew more and more blurred, but I kept lying there, counting the seconds, holding my eyes open. Until the Japanese mono speaker emitted the dramatic guitar solo that coursed through my body, Gilmour concluded his refrain with the words, 'I have become comfortably numb.'

I had no idea what that meant.

UNCLE'S VISIT

On one of those Pink Floyd days, we received an unexpected phone call. Sergio, the receptionist knocked on the door.

'Telephone!'

That was the most ambiguous word in the whole world. Telephone. Was there news about Neno? Good news? Bad news? Maybe we would finally hear from Aunt Lamija, who had ended up in Sarajevo. Mum worried about her, shed tears for her. Her husband had been wounded at the start of the war.

I went down and picked up the phone.

'Emir, is that you?'

Uncle's voice sounded more serious than usual, asking if he could come round tomorrow. He had something important to tell us.

'About Neno?' I wanted to ask, but did not dare.

We hung up.

I had agreed to meet Kaća but had to cancel. She was meant to trim my hair. But I had other things to worry about now. I had sweaty palms for the rest of the day and I did not go anywhere near my homework.

'Did he mention what he wanted to talk to us about?' Dad asked.

'No. Just that he'll be here tomorrow.'

'All right, let's keep it between the two of us. The only thing Mum needs to know is that he's coming to visit.'

I waited in front of reception for my uncle. He arrived driving his metallic blue Hyundai.

He was not alone.

Sat next to him was an older blonde woman with curly hair, a long face and large dangly earrings. Had it not been for the old cloth bag filled with presents on her lap, it could be argued that she looked one hundred percent chic.

This woman must know something, I thought, as she held out her hand, introducing herself as Ana. I got the impression that she knew *everything*. About Neno, about me, about Mum and Dad and the entire situation.

Uncle and I kissed each other on the cheek, he smelt of cologne. He had recently dyed his hair. It shone black in the sun.

'I hardly recognised you,' he said. 'Your hair's getting long.'

'Yeah, I was actually meant to get a trim today.'

'What are your mum and dad up to?'

'They've gone for a walk on the peninsula. They're foraging for asparagus.'

'Why?'

'Mum chops them up and adds them to scrambled eggs. At the neighbour's. They've got a hot plate.'

'Is the food here that bad?'

'Don't ask. Dad says: "If only I were able to control what passes through my intestines, now that everything else is decided for me."'

'You'd think he'd be happy having food served to him.'

'He was in the beginning. But after fourteen days, the "holiday" was over.'

Instead of going directly up to the room, we set out to find Mum and Dad. It had been a long drive, they told me, and they would like to stretch their legs a bit. They left the cloth bag with presents in the car.

Uncle thought the bay was idyllic but was disgusted with the poor state of the camp.

'In the West,' he said in an almost religious tone, 'the buildings would have been kept up. There, they wouldn't just neglect them.'

Ana smiled. Maybe they were together? He had been married twice in two different countries, but returned home

140

divorced 'on nostalgic grounds'. My uncle was bloody cool. He looked a lot younger than Dad, even though they were almost the same age.

'We're on our way to Ljubljana,' he said. 'That's where Ana's from.'

Ana nodded:

'I'm sure you can tell from my accent.'

Mum and Dad walked towards us carrying a bundle of asparagus. As soon as they finished greeting one another, Dad got right down to business:

'Have you seen what's happening these days?'

'Not politics again,' Mum pleaded.

'Just the other day, a certain Mirko was nearly the death of me!'

'Now what? What's happened now?' Uncle asked.

'He claimed that Bosnian Muslims were just Croats who followed Islam! That the Koran is a plagiarism of the Bible!'

'Old story.'

'I know. I explained to him that it was all the same to me, that I did not know much about God anyway. And do you know what he said?'

'What.'

'"People like you ought to be shot!"'

'Lunatic.'

'"You communists are the worst!"'

'I want to leave but they won't do it,' I said.

'His friends have gone,' Mum explained. 'To Sweden.'

Ana and Uncle nodded.

'Ah! Beautiful country. Proper country.'

'That is of no interest to me,' Dad replied straight away. 'I am too old for that nonsense.'

'Fifty-eight is nothing,' Uncle teased him.

'Rubbish!' Dad said, waving his hands. 'I am not as strong as I used to be. Anyway … Should we find somewhere to sit down and talk?'

My uncle was wearing new shoes. The laces kept coming undone. When it happened again a few metres past the restaurant, I stayed back with him while Mum and Dad chatted with Ana about her background.

Dad was obviously taking Mum into consideration. He did not want to ask Uncle about 'that' until we were in the room. I could not take it any longer. I was about to explode from impatience.

'What's the news?' I asked.

'Wait till we get up to the room.'

'Is it about Neno?'

He straightened up. His face gave nothing away.

'Wait and see.'

I was afraid to ask anything else.

In the room, I stared at my two magazine clippings. They were stuck to either wall in the corner of the room – right above my pillow. Bruce Dickinson wearing a tight-fitting white jumper and holding a microphone. Hetfield, Ulrich, Hammett and Newsted standing on a rock, looking up.

We were given an electric heater as a present. Dad laughed. It was the middle of May, we had managed the entire winter without one. There were also clothes for me: some large T-shirts in colours that were far too bright. I didn't like them and I couldn't focus on them. Don't even remember if I thanked him.

'We can trade in the electric heater at the market,' Dad said when Mum went over to the neighbours to make coffee. 'We need a hot plate.'

'Shame,' Uncle said. 'I'm sure you mentioned you needed an electric heater.'

Neither Uncle nor Ana commented on the room, but Ana's lengthy silence and sad expression made me rather uneasy. I could not tell whether it was because of the few square metres we lived in or because of what Uncle was about to tell us. It really bothered me if she was feeling sorry for us. I almost felt guilty.

'Coffee's ready,' Mum said and set the tray down on the table. 'Hot, Bosnian style!'

She and our guests sat on the bed. Dad and I took the two chairs on the other side of the table.

'News report!' Dad interrupted and reached for the cassette player.

Mum rolled her eyes:

'But we have guests!'

'I just want to hear about the Mostar front. Just two minutes.'

The radio whirred to life. When the programme started and the reporter fired off an arsenal of sentences in his usual dramatic fashion, Dad shook his head and whispered:

'Lies. A pack of lies!'

'Then why do you listen?' Uncle smiled with an ease for which I envied him.

'I have to,' Dad answered. 'You have to keep up with what's happening.'

The conversation ranged from the weather, the war and Slovenia, and Ana took part as well. Several times I got the feeling that Uncle was putting off the task at hand. As soon as one topic died down, he hurried on to the next.

I couldn't take it. Everyone was acting like nothing had happened, chatting about trivial matters, and I just sat there, staring at Bruce, James and the boys – paralysed by fear, powerless and frustrated.

Why is he tormenting me? Why doesn't he say something?

Then he and Ana finished their coffees and set their cups down on the tray almost in sync.

'Now listen,' Uncle said. 'I don't know how to tell you this, so I'm just going to start.'

His voice was so serious that Mum froze. She was about to pour more coffee for them but put the copper pot down and looked at me and Dad.

My gaze drifted around the room and onto the balcony.

'There's a reason we're here ...'

Through the open balcony door I could see Marina and Kaća standing by the entrance to D2 laughing at something. Marina stood with her back to me and only when she let go of what was in her hand could I see what she held: a heart-shaped helium balloon. It shot into the air but was attached to an invisible string. Marina pulled it back down.

'Actually a number of reasons... There's news about Nedim.'

I looked at Uncle and caught his gaze.

Mister No is dead. I'm never going to see him again. He's never going to set foot in this room.

'I received a call from ...'

The rails on the balcony blurred together. I could no longer see Kaća, Marina or the balloon.

Mister No is dead and they're sitting here about to tell me.

'Emir,' Dad said out of the blue, 'why don't you go for a walk?'

'What ... why?'

'Just for a while. I'll tell you everything, don't worry.'

'Let him stay,' Mum said drying her eyes. 'He has a right to hear this.'

Mum's reaction changed everything. Uncle was confused. His gaze shifted between her, Dad and me. Then he burst out:

'No, no! He's not dead. He's missing!'

It was as though he suddenly realised that his beating-around-the-bush-strategy had gone completely wrong. He said it so quickly, you would have thought someone in the room would have dropped dead had he not spat it out in time.

'What?'

'How?'

'Well you see, what happened was ...'

'Come on! Tell us, dammit!' Dad shouted and stood up. 'Why the hell are you mumbling? Is he alive?'

'Sorry, sorry, I'm not used to this kind of situation …'

'Well, is he alive?'

'Yes, we think so!' Ana said suddenly.

'We think so,' Uncle repeated.

It was my first time seeing him totally out of sorts and confused, completely outside his accustomed role. Dad sank back into his chair:

'Where is he?'

'I don't know. He's not in the camp, at any rate. We don't know whether he ran away or what happened.'

'Tell us!'

'I saw a prisoner exchange list in the paper. Adem Hamzalić's name was on it.'

'Adem?' Mum said. 'Has he been exchanged?'

'Yes, last Wednesday. So I called Rifat, Adem's grandfather. You remember, we worked together in Berlin.'

'Yes.'

'Adem said that he'd been at the camp with Nedim right up till January. Then he and a few others were taken to do some work in Banja Luka, at the home of some soldier or guard or whatever. Adem wasn't actually there, but later he heard that Nedim had met a young boy in front of the soldier's farm. Clearly someone he knew. The boy had given him a cigarette. The next day Nedim disappeared. The others received a thrashing because of him. The guards questioned people as to where he was. But nobody knew anything and one of the prisoners – the last one to see him – got a few broken ribs. Adem said people were really upset with Nedim, that he should have realised his actions would have consequences for the others,' he said.

No one said anything for a while. Uncle took a sip of coffee and added:

'That was four months ago, according to Adem.'

'Oh God,' Mum whispered. 'Oh God, oh God, oh God!'

'Do you know who it was he could have spoken to?' Uncle asked.

'In Banja Luka?' Dad said looking at me. 'There's only his

friend from school. His father helped them out of Sarajevo.'

'What's his name?'

'Dado,' I said. 'His real name is Dragan, I think.'

'How can we find him? What's his surname? What's his father's name?'

'We never found out,' Dad said. 'It was just some friend from uni.'

'That's not good. There's nothing but Dragans among the Serbs,' Uncle said. 'Could it have been anyone else?'

'How would I know?' Dad snapped.

The idea that it could be someone else and not Dragan was far too grim. That could mean anything. Even the worst. Uncle tested another possibility:

'What if he managed to get out of Serbian territory, who would he contact then?'

'Hmm.'

'He could write you a letter,' I said. 'He doesn't have your address but he could just write your name and the name of the neighbourhood.'

'The problem is, he has no idea where we are. Or does he?' Dad asked.

'No, unfortunately not. Adem said they didn't know about anything. Not even that you'd been turned over to the Bosnian army.'

'Damn it! If only he were able to contact someone who knew we went to stay with you,' Dad said. 'If he thinks we are still on the other side of the front, then ...'

'Then he might go home,' Mum said.

'There isn't a living soul there. The city has been obliterated. Vacant houses are looted and witnesses killed.'

'Just as long as he's alive,' Mum said. 'I don't care. As long as he's well!'

Ana comforted her. She bit her lip and rested her hand on Mum's shoulder. At that moment, I grew very fond of her. She had absolutely no reason to be there. Why should she care about us and our problems? Outside, the sky was blue and there were far better ways to spend the day.

The visit ended with a little more confusion. We had spent an hour or two trying to come to terms with the big news about Neno, then Uncle dropped another bombshell on us on his way out the door. His daughter had got into some difficulties in Canada. He needed to go over there for a while. For how long, he did not know.

'I'll fill you in on the details over the phone. You've got your own problems to worry about.'

'What happened?'

'Apparently she's fallen into some bad company.'

'How long will you stay?'

'Don't know. Had Ana not been here, I would have left this week. But she's decided to come with me now.'

Dad stopped:

'Are you even coming back?'

'Of course,' Uncle said gravely. 'I just don't know when. To be perfectly honest, I miss Canada. The air, the streets ...'

'See what happens when you don't come *all* the way home,' Dad said, making reference to Uncle buying a flat at the seaside and not in their hometown. 'You need the healing Bosnian air!'

'You mean the stench? Thank God I didn't come home. I would have been hit by the first bullet.'

I gave him a big hug outside of reception. It felt like we were never going to see each other again. Dad was visibly moved as well. Uncle's visit had turned everything on its head.

'No, there's no need,' he protested when Uncle pressed a handful of kunas into his hand. 'I'm working. I'm making money.'

'Please, just buy the hotplate,' Uncle said. 'And keep the electric heater. The war is not going to end before next winter. Maybe even longer. You were right.'

'Fine then,' Dad smiled. 'We'll buy a used one.'

Ana kissed the three of us on the cheeks. She and Uncle climbed into the car and Mum and Dad waved.

'Wait a minute!' I shouted and walked up to the car.
Uncle rolled his window down.

'Can you tell me what comfortably numb means?'

'Sorry?'

'What does comfortably numb mean? In English?'

'Oh!' he smiled. 'Comfortable means pleasant, agreeable.
Numb? I don't really know … can't you look it up in the
dictionary?'

'Don't have one.'

'What about your teachers at school?' Ana teased. 'Don't
they teach you anything?'

'No, they're morons, the whole lot of them! That's why
you have to help me out of this place.'

Uncle laughed and started the car. I realised something
had completely slipped my mind.

Tomorrow's homework.

FULL MOON

Back in the room Mum started to cry again. I kept trying to explain to her that he was still out there somewhere. That he must be in hiding and would try to make his way out of Serbian territory soon.

'It could have been worse. In spite of everything, he's got a fifty-fifty chance.'

I clung to the thought that he had been seen alive so recently.

'No one's seen him dead. That's something …'

The more I spoke, the more hollow my words sounded. I could just as easily have told Mum that he was hanging out in Manaus, Brazil with the real Mister No, the legendary pilot Jerry Drake. That the two of them were flying Mister No's Piper and that one day they would land near the bay. I knew nothing.

We went in circles, agonising over every imaginable scenario and permutation. What could have happened that day? Where could he be? Dad wanted to call Adem to get more details. He wanted to know everything. And, to find out if there was anything we could do.

In the end, I could no longer bear it. My head was bursting, and we kept repeating ourselves. I hurried out the door.

Hovering over the bay was an unusually beautiful full moon. Kaća stood by the pier looking down at the water. I needed to be alone but she latched onto me and started pestering me with a rundown of the latest from some sitcom she had just seen:

'And then he stands there and takes …'

'SHUT YOUR FACE! I DON'T FUCKIN' CARE! DO YOU

UNDERSTAND? I DON'T CARE!'

I turned and walked away. She shouted:

'Hey, what's going on with you?'

I sped up.

'Wait!'

Her feet tramped on the round stones behind me.

January? What was I doing in January?

'Hey!'

Where was I, the day he disappeared?

'Miki!'

Where is he now? Is he looking up at the same fucking moon or …?

'Wait!'

'GO AWAY!' I bawled and came to a stop. 'LEAVE ME ALONE!'

Kaća stopped.

My voice could not hide the fact that I was crying.

I pressed my fist between my front teeth and roared like an animal. Then I turned, walked back and told her about Neno.

KAĆA

We sat on the smooth stones by the pier with our arms wrapped around our legs. I talked and talked. Kaća threw a stone in the water when I was finished. She looked up at the full moon and said:

'Trust me. I know how you're feeling.'

Then she told me about her father, whom she had not seen in almost two years. About all the idiots at the camp making things difficult for her and her mother. The entire camp knew that he had been separated from them by accident. That he was a doctor and for that reason he was not called up by the Serbian army. Even still, people spread all kinds of rumours. Including one that he forcibly drew blood from Croatian prisoners at a hospital in Vukovar.

'What would he do with all that blood?' she said. 'The last thing Serbs want is to have Croatian blood flowing through their veins. That rumour doesn't make *any* sense.'

'Hey, just imagine if they gave it to all of the wounded,' I said. 'You know, the ones who had lost too much blood.'

'Yeah, then they'd be like me. A fifty-fifty mix.'

'Sorry for shouting at you earlier,' I said.

'That's okay. I just didn't know what I'd done wrong.'

'You didn't do anything wrong.'

'Never mind then.'

We headed back around eleven. I was completely wiped when I climbed into bed. All the things I had told Kaća were still swirling round in my head. I went through some particular scenarios, paying attention to different details, but I kept returning to those two bloody days from nearly eleven months ago.

Mum and Dad were asleep, or at least they were

pretending to be. I tried as well, but was unable to. The tears had taken the edge off my desperation. Kaća's story had helped. But the wound that this crazy day had opened, had grown.

I had school the next morning and had not touched my homework.

SWAN'S BOLLOCK

Down by the crossing, not far from Buljina Bog where as a child Dad had seen an Ustashe get shot, there was an old broken-down phone box in the parking lot in front of the shop. I sat leant against the shop window looking at it. The soldiers guarding the crossing post had used it as a toilet. The stench of shit seeped out.

I had to take a dump myself, but I looked at the phone box for another reason.

The previous night, seconds before the mosque went up in smoke, I had dreamt that Dad and I had stood in this very phone box. Dad rang Uncle asking for help.

'You have to get us out of here,' he said. 'Don't you realise what's happening?'

A moment later the dream transported me to a deserted beach on the Adriatic. I was sitting alone, watching the blue of the water and the sky gorge on one another. The seagulls were shrieking. A sailboat drifted silently past.

Then I was awoken by a massive explosion, jumped out of bed and felt an indescribable pain in my neck.

The nearby mosque was gone.

We had to get up and pack.

That morning, the sky was grey as far as the eye could see. Amongst the large crowd that was gathering in the car park, I was able to pick out many faces I had not seen in a long time. Everyone had their suitcases and bags with them. My history teacher Mandić stood with his family, a little ways off, to the right of the phone box. They lived in a block of flats not far from there.

Mandić did not look well. He was unshaven, unshorn and he had large bags under his eyes. Not at all like the

153

confident and stern Mandić from history lessons.

The few people who still had petrol, stood by their cars on the far side of the crossing. The column of cars stretched all the way to the bridge, but the cars were facing the wrong direction. We were not going to be exchanged with the Serbs who lived on the other side of the river, as Adi had hoped. We were being transported further from the front, deeper into Serbian territory.

'Right into the lion's den,' Dad said. 'I'm such an idiot. Never should have listened to any of you.'

He had not wanted to leave. Neno, Mum and I managed to talk him into it at the last moment. He wanted to stay and 'guard the house', like his cousin Zijo, who lived in a village three kilometres upriver. Only after Neno revealed that Zijo had been considering escaping across the river did Dad drop the idea. He smashed a few watering cans and spat on the front of the house.

'Wish I'd never built you!' he said to the house.

The buses were supposed to arrive at nine, but by three o'clock we still had not seen a single one.

'They're waiting for it to get dark,' Dad said. 'I knew it! I told you so. Right into the lion's den.'

The buses arrived around four and the few soldiers guarding the crossing post received reinforcements. One of the new arrivals I will never forget. Not particularly tall but quite well-built. Dark hair. With clear brown eyes and feminine features. They called him Chinaman.

He was the driver of our bus, the first in the column and the fullest. It reeked of people who had not seen running water for a long time.

Dad and I sat together; he took the window seat, I took the aisle. Mum and Neno were in front of us. Neno's hair was unnaturally short. Mum had cut it so as not to 'provoke the army'. I don't remember ever seeing him with such short hair. It was as though a part of him had already disappeared along with his dark curls.

He cleared his throat. From where I sat, I could see him brushing the non-existent locks of hair off his forehead from force of habit.

The bus stopped near the outskirts of Nedođ.

A burly man in camouflage walked behind the bus and entered through the back door.

'Identity check!'

He pushed his way down the aisle carrying a plastic folder and some papers. Everyone pulled out their identity cards, waiting for him to inspect them.

Mum handed him our cards. He stood pressed against my right shoulder. Before his folder and papers obstructed my view, I noticed that he had a moustache and a double chin. He held the papers to the right of my head and his gaze shifted between them and our ID cards.

Without thinking, my gaze settled on the typewritten list on the back page. I only managed to read two names before my neck began to ache: Muharem Sokolović and Osman Hodžić. Osman was active in the Islamic PDA party and a candidate for a place on the town council. Dad had a running feud with him, and because of his surname, always mockingly called him Hodžica, the little imam. He had not been seen since the first shot of the war.

And then: SMACK!

'WHAT ARE YOU STARING AT, NOSE PRINCE? EH?'

Everything was spinning. My left cheek was blazing but I grabbed my neck instead.

I muttered a confused 'Nothing,' and turned to Dad. His eyes shifted between me and Double-chin.

Then his gaze suddenly fell to his knees.

Double-chin shouted 'EYES FRONT' before adding a few rude comments about my 'big-nosed mum'. I was too shaken to react. Everything in front of me blurred. Dad said nothing. What was he waiting for? I blinked rapidly in an effort to hold back the tears.

'Leave him alone. He's just a kid,' Neno said in a gentle

and pleading tone.

'SHUT YOUR MOUTH BEFORE YOU GET SOME TOO! EYES FRONT!'

Neno obeyed.

Double-chin handed the ID cards back to Mum and said in a completely different tone:

'Here you are!'

As though nothing had happened! Like a polite ticket inspector on a completely different bus.

I looked down as Dad's knee accidentally brushed mine. There was a bluish thread resting on his trousers, no more than three centimetres long.

It irritated me to no end, but I did not move it. Instead I moved my knee.

'Why would you look at those papers?' Dad whispered. 'What's the matter with you? Take it easy.'

I did not answer. I just looked at him with my bottom lip between my teeth.

We were held there for quite some time. The stench and the heat were unbearable. It was still heavy and stifling. There were people standing in the aisle, almost on top of each other. Adi's dad dabbed his forehead further up the bus. He and Adi were wearing far too many clothes, clearly they had wanted to take as much with them as possible.

Suddenly the engine stopped rumbling. The front door opened with a snorting noise.

'ALL THE MEN OUTSIDE!'

I recognised Chinaman's voice.

Dad got up and moved past me. Neno slipped past Mum. She turned to me and said:

'Stay here.'

I nodded. Had not even considered going.

When the aisle had thinned out a little, an older woman in the seat across from me began to mutter a prayer. It may have calmed her down, but not me. A searing knot began to form in my stomach as I listened to her whimpering.

Adi gave me a blank look as he moved to a seat next to his mum.

'WHAT ARE YOU WAITING FOR?' Chinaman shouted at him.

Adi straightened up in his seat:

'But ... but I'm only fourteen.'

'I didn't ask how old you were! Outside!'

At the same time he spotted *me* and nodded:

'You too! What are you, men or pussies? Both of you out before I rip off your trousers!'

So this was the summer of '92, the summer that Adi and I had been looking forward to so much. We would be fifteen, finally be finished with primary school and we could start going into town. I was going to learn how to drive, impress Nina with Neno at my side as both passenger and driving instructor. He would finally be back home. Dad was going to enjoy his hard-earned retirement.

Instead, when the summer finally arrived, Dad, Neno, me, Adi, his dad and brother and some twenty others, all stood with our hands behind our backs, our foreheads pressed against a wall, waiting to be shot. The world had shrunk. All that remained of it could be counted on one hand: the cool, damp odour of the wall, the Chetniks' voices several metres behind us and the sight of a triangular piece of mortar hanging from a crack in the wall, right in front of my nose.

The stone surface of the wall grated against my face. The grey rubble of the foundation slipped a little under my feet.

I've only made it to fourteen years and ten months, I thought. We're done for and I haven't even turned fifteen.

My turd had long since hardened inside me. I no longer felt the need to go. I did not feel anything. When they had led us through a few deserted streets towards the wall, I had thought of Mum still sitting on the bus. Now I thought of nothing. There was no past, no future and no one to complain to about anything. I would not even make it to fifteen. That was a fact, nothing more.

We were allowed to turn around and sit on the ground. I fiddled with the hole in my worn-out Adidas trainers, but my index finger was numb.

Adi's dad raised his hand. He asked the soldiers to spare Adi.

'He's only a child,' he said.

One of the soldiers grabbed Adi by the arm and dragged him away.

Dad put his hand up:

'My son is also only fourteen.'

I looked at him and hissed through my teeth:

'What the hell are you doing? I don't want to go!'

Adi and I were placed somewhere between the centre spot and the penalty area, some fifty metres from the low pavilion by the entrance to the football pitch where the others waited. I said nothing to him and he said nothing to me. We sat on the grass, hugging our legs, silent and motionless. Our eyes were glued to the twenty men who stood lined up against the wall of the pavilion. The four or five soldiers who stood in front of the men were not the same as those who had stopped us at the entrance to town. Chinaman and Double-chin were gone.

From this distance we could no longer hear what the soldiers said. They probably carried on with the same speech one of them had given while Adi and I were still sat there. Something about why Serbs and Muslims could no longer live side by side. Something about how everything used to be and how it would be from now on.

The one speaking had not sounded drunk, but several of those around him appeared rather agitated and not entirely sober. The one who had led Adi and I away stank of booze.

We waited for them to shoot. But they did not shoot. They prolonged the séance. Ordered some men to stand up, turn round, then sit down again. Neno was up once, Mandić twice. Actually I had always thought that Mandić was a Serb. Apparently he was a Croat. Otherwise he would have raised his hand and said something long ago.

My back was dripping with sweat. My underwear was wedged between my buttocks. At one point I saw myself walking back and sitting down between Neno and Dad. But I did not budge from the spot.

Behind the goal and the tall wire fencing I spotted a bald, bare-chested man. He turned the tap on in his garden, swatted at a fly and washed his face. Oddly the first thing that passed through my mind was: they've got water here. The next: can he not see a thing? He was no more than thirty metres from the men and the wall but at no point did he look at them.

Then the sound of an engine was heard. The nose of a dusty bus poked out at the bottom of the street that ran alongside the football ground. It was our bus, the first in the column, and again I thought of Mum.

The other buses followed behind and parked along the fenced-in ground. The men began to stand, brushing the dust off their trousers. The soldiers assumed a more informal stance and walked towards the buses. It was like seeing a meeting or a performance end.

Adi stood up. I wanted to say something to him but I did not know what. He nodded towards the men who were walking towards us. I stood up and followed in silence.

We spent that night in a school. The gymnasium and the toilets looked the same as at the school Adi and I went to.

The following day, we waited from morning till night for them to tell us what was going to happen. Mandić, my history teacher, was acting as some kind of negotiator. It had been decided that we were not going to continue towards Banja Luka, but instead turn south. We were all going to be turned over to our people, just not to those in our hometown.

When at long last we boarded the buses and drove from Nedođ, the lousy town was enveloped in the incipient twilight. Even though I still knew nothing of prisoner exchanges, let alone those that took place in the night, it felt like a step forward. Finally something was happening. At least we were on the move now.

In the pitch black, on a road in the middle of nowhere, the bus stopped, and again all the men were ordered off. I stood up with Neno and Dad, but the old man pushed me back into my seat, saying:

'Take care of Mum!'

'But ... I ...'

I should be with the men, I wanted to say, but he would not let me speak:

'Stay here and take care of her!'

The bus engine rumbled away. A woman was wailing, another fainted, the curtains were drawn. There was little light in the bus. On the other side of the glass I could hear footsteps, indistinct shouts and the occasional vehicle.

I leant my forehead against the headrest in front of me. Mum was in the same position. We waited and waited. I locked my eyes shut and in the darkness, yellow circles began to spread like ripples in a pond. I thought I was going to throw up. But nothing came. My stomach just cramped up and I got dizzy.

The engine continued to idle. The voices outside grew alternately louder and quieter as a gentle summer rain began to patter against the windows.

Maybe they're butchering them with knives, I thought. Or are they using silencers? Maybe it's already over.

When the men boarded the bus again, their clothes were wet. They moved slowly and nobody said a word. Their faces were indistinguishable in the darkness.

We were taken to the meeting hall of a village I had never heard of. We were locked inside. I fell asleep quickly but awoke only a few hours later.

In the middle of the room, there was a yawning gap in the crowd of people. The roof was leaking and a puddle had formed there. We had slept on the concrete floor to the left of the entrance – Dad, Mum, Neno and I. Now we sat against the wall, staring across the room, saying nothing. I ate a dry Petit Beurre which Mum had somehow got hold of. As I chewed, I noticed a lack of strength in my jaw.

Adi and his family must have been among the first to come in last night, when we were herded into the meeting hall like cattle. That must be why they slept on the stage, in front of some tall cardboard staging depicting a green forest. Hanging on the wall above the stage, a milky-white banner with glittery writing: HAPPY NEW YEAR 1992. In the corner on the right, there was a Marshall speaker resting on a chair.

'When's the concert starting?' I asked Neno, pointing to the stage.

He turned his head to me and said quietly and dryly, almost lethargically:

'Shut up.'

I got up to go and chat with Adi, but Mum grabbed me by the sleeve:

'Where are you going?'

'To see Adi.'

'Stay here. We must not be separated.'

'Just for a bit.'

'Stay here, my love, do as I tell you.'

I sat back down.

The door handle rattled. A wave of silence descended upon the room. A soldier walked in and kicked Dad's outstretched legs. He stopped where everyone could see him and shouted:

'Milan Mandić! Where is he?'

Mandić got up and raised his hand.

'They want to talk to you!'

Mandić picked up his thin jacket from the floor, said something to his wife and left with the soldier. The door closed and was locked once again.

My gaze caught an old man with white hair to the left of Mandić's wife. He was frail, wearing a beret and a grey suit jacket. As Mandić was moving towards the door, the old man's mug transformed into a funny, ape-like grimace. Nobody around him reacted, and for a brief moment I thought it was just something I had imagined. The grimace continued to mark his face, and his head kept bobbing up and down in short, sharp movements.

It was not until his daughter or daughter-in-law put her arm around his shoulder that I realised the man was crying.

'Look at old monkey-face over there,' I said. 'He's bloody-well done for.'

Dad gave me his death stare:

'What's the matter with you? Was that smack you got yesterday not enough?'

'Yeah.'

And you still wouldn't have raised a finger even if I'd got a thousand, I thought.

When they opened the door again everyone was ordered outside. It was spitting with rain. The gravel in the yard seemed slimy rather than wet as it crunched under our feet.

Some five or six soldiers stood in the middle of the yard. They split us up into groups, motioning sharply and shouting, 'Women to the right, men to the left!' I wanted to give Mum Neno's leather bag, but her hands were already full.

'It's all right,' Dad said to her. 'It's all right.'

Once we were on the left side of the yard, Dad moved between me and Neno. There was an arched metal gate, halfway open, in the two-metre-high wall behind us. Through the gate I could make out a building at the back of the adjoining yard. The buses were parked along the street on the far side of the yard, behind the women. I was confused by that: had we not come in through that gate last night?

As soon as everyone was outside the meeting hall, we

were ordered to empty our pockets. Everything except for our documents was to be placed on the ground.

My pockets were empty. Dad and Neno threw their wallets down.

'Boys under eighteen, over with the women!'

Myself, Adi and several others did as were told. All of the bags were left at the men's feet. The unfurled wallets were scattered around the bags like a flock of dead, black birds.

'It's all right,' I said to Mum when we made eye contact. 'I'm right here.'

In the ensuing minutes I kept my eyes on Dad and Neno, as they watched each other listlessly, motionless. Everything around me faded into the drizzle and the morning fog, and even when they led my history teacher, Mandić, and a handful of other men across the yard, I did not pay much attention. Mandić's face was bruised and one of the men behind him was missing an arm. They lined them up. Only later did I realise that those men had not been with us from the beginning. Nobody had seen them before.

'Men over fifty-five to the left!'

Dad and Neno were separated. The old, white-haired man who had broken down in tears earlier, collapsed. Adi's dad helped him up. He said something along the lines of 'Spare this man, he's old and ill.' One of the soldiers took a short run-up and kicked Adi's dad in the stomach:

'STAY OUT OF IT!'

I scanned for Adi and his mum, but I could not make them out behind a group of wailing and sobbing women.

The yard simmered like a square pot. The soldiers in camouflage and olive-grey uniforms ran around in a frenzy, shouting at the men and the women and at one another. I held Mum by the arm. My face grew moist from the dank drizzle. My gaze shifted between Neno and Dad, now standing in separate rows. A clean-shaven soldier with thick lips checked the older men's identity cards. He shouted out their names and dates of birth. Another, who was at least a head shorter than Baby-face, followed at his heels carrying a thick A4 notebook. The notebook had a hard, brownish cover and the little fellow sneezed as he jotted down the names and dates that were called out.

Dad's name was called out and I woke from my zombielike state. Our surname startled me, as if I had heard it for the first time. Maybe it was because it was said by a total stranger, shouting so loudly in all the chaos that surrounded me. It was like when you dozed off in school and the teacher unexpectedly called out your name.

Around the same time, the men from Neno's group were ordered to carry the bags over to the other side of the yard. Neno set his down in front of Mum and me and stood there, while most of the others slowly walked back.

'Well ... there it is ...'

The ground between us was a little uneven. He stood with his left leg in front, slightly bent at the knee. His hair was wet and fell flat over his forehead. It looked like the limp corner of a star.

'Miki ...' he said.

A soldier grabbed him by the cardigan:

'Back to your line!'

Neno raised his arms in the air as he tried to turn around and keep his balance at the same time. The soldier pulled him back a few metres before letting go. Mum shut her eyes. My gaze shifted between her, Neno and Dad.

When Neno stood in line again, not far from Adi's dad and brother, the final name was announced. The small soldier closed his notebook and waved towards the gate:

'That's everyone!'

Someone shouted something back but I could not make it out. Neno and his group raised their arms in the air and folded their hands behind their heads. Their row turned ninety degrees and advanced towards the gate like a lazy snake. I kept my gaze on Neno's blue cardigan. His left elbow hid his face.

At the end of the line were Mandić and the men none of us knew. Before they disappeared through the gate, I managed to see the last of them breaking into a brisk trot. Just like in training, their heads began to nod in time – then I lost sight of them.

Someone unseen shut the gate from outside. A metallic clang echoed across the yard. A woman wearing a headscarf started sobbing louder than the others. I put my arm around Mum's shoulder and tried to catch Dad's gaze. The woman with the headscarf fell to her knees wailing. Two younger women helped her up. She pounded her fist against her forehead and wailed almost unintelligibly:

'My child … my child … my child!'

The bus was now half empty, with Adi and I the only boys remaining. Dad and his group were left standing in the yard. Mum sniffled and wiped her face. I squeezed her hand and felt how weak my own was.

We were offloaded onto a car park in front of a pink motel. There were a couple of YPA vehicles and a few older soldiers parked there. Some of them were sitting on the steps drinking straight from the bottle. The road behind us was deserted and it terrified me. The slim hope that Neno and Dad's buses had followed ours began to fade.

All shot? All mobilised? The old ones shot, the young ones mobilised?

The permutations swirled round in my head until I heard the rumbling of an engine.

A bus drove towards us. Dad was the first to get out.

'Where's Neno?'

He shrugged.

'Are there any more buses coming?'

'I don't know.'

'Where are we going now?'

'I don't *know*,' he said and gave Mum a hug.

His glasses were steamed up from the rain.

We were followed part way, probably the first few hundred metres. Then the road began to curve around a wooded hill. We had been told to walk straight ahead. A lanky soldier stood by the edge of the road, and as the column passed, he repeated:

'Stay on the road! There are mines on both sides. Stay on the road, if you value your life! Your people are expecting you …'

We stayed on the road. After a while the first scouts appeared. One of them – the first Bosnian soldier I had ever seen – was wearing a thin, dark-green jacket and trainers. A blue and white coat of arms with a diagonal line and three lilies on either side had been hastily sewn onto his cap.

'Continue down the road,' he said. 'Just keep going! It's a long way to the first houses.'

A long way?

That was an understatement. I thought we were never going to see those bloody houses. We trudged ahead for hours. Uphill, downhill, uphill again.

The drizzle had stopped. Through the grey clouds, the midday sun broke through. In the woods at the entrance to the first village, the birds sang like never before. As we came out of the woods, a valley with overgrown fields and scattered farmhouses appeared before us. I had never been to this part of Bosnia and had no idea it was so beautiful.

Dad walked alongside me, telling how he had once driven through these parts. On a business trip with his boss.

I am not sure why his story suddenly annoyed me. Or rather, why he and his way of telling it annoyed me. Adi and his mum were behind us somewhere. Both Adi's dad and his brother were with Neno.

My annoyance with Dad clashed with my feelings of guilt at about being so ungrateful. After all, I still had my dad with me. A deflated rubber ball lay in the dust by the side of the road. I gritted my teeth and took a short run at it. One step, two steps, three – and then I whacked that fucking ball as hard as I possibly could.

It whistled off and rolled down the hill.

I nearly lost my balance from kicking it so hard. A searing pain shot through my neck and I stopped and moved my hand there.

'Hey! What's going on with you?' Mum asked.

I did not answer.

Only when she repeated the question did I say indifferently:

'Nothing.'

But then!

A few houses down the road, something happened to finally relieve my frustration. I was handed a slice of bread, a tomato and a boiled egg by an older peasant woman.

'May God return everything to you,' she said in a thick, rural accent.

I thanked her, continued walking, and ate the bread and the tomato. Mum and Dad were given water by some younger women a little further ahead. The women had come out of their houses with glasses and large pitchers of water, plates full of fruit and vegetables, and anything else they could muster.

The water was ice cold. Dad drank from a red metal cup that had a faded red enamel. While he drank, his teeth quietly ticked against the edge of the cup. I stood staring at the boiled egg in my cupped hand. It was still warm.

'What do you have there?' Dad asked.

I looked up and opened my hand.

'An egg?'

'No,' I said shaking my head and smiling. 'A swan's bollock!'

For the first time in a long while, we both laughed.

LUGARIĆ READS THE PAPER

'What's up?' Fabio said the day after Uncle's visit and my conversation with Kaća. 'Have you studied what you were meant to?'

'Nah, not really. You?'

'Nope. Spent the whole weekend repairing the Puch with my bro. Didn't even have time for a wank, man!'

'I did. If I fall asleep before the break, that's the reason.'

We had problems with Lugarić, the old fool. The end of the school year was approaching, and there were ten or twelve of us who were going to have to resit the exam with him in August. That meant our summer holiday would be spent thinking of Lugarić's red face and flipping through useless notes from his lessons.

He also realised that nearly half the class was going to fail, and at least seven or eight of us would have to repeat the year. And that would not sound particularly good at the parent-teacher meeting or in the ears of the head. For that reason, late in May he announced that there would be 'one final test,' which at the same time meant 'one final chance to avoid re-examination'. Those who already had a passing mark would not need to come to that lesson. The rest of us would be given two hours to solve five tasks.

'We're all going to pass,' Fabio said.

'How?'

He pointed at Horvat.

'You'll see.'

We found a seat in the fourth row, right next to the extra door to the corridor at the back, on that June day when we had to sit the exam. In the past, under the Italians, the building had been used as a hospital, run by Catholic nuns. It had been renovated several times and for that reason there were lots of absurd and superfluous details. The rooms could do with some TLC, but nothing was done about it. With my own two eyes, I saw plaster sprinkling from the ceiling because people on the floor above were stomping around.

The door that Fabio and I were sitting next to was covered in graffiti and had been scratched by countless compasses. At table height there was a small, almost invisible hole. Fabio made it a little bigger.

When Lugarić had written the questions on the board, he sat down behind his desk and opened the newspaper he had brought with him. He held it up and began to read to himself.

It was a clear signal: do whatever you want, copy, share, cheat and disappear, none of you are ever going to make anything of yourselves anyway!

Fabio wrote the problems down on a small piece of paper, made it into a thin roll and shoved it through the hole in the door. Horvat was waiting out in the corridor. With the roll of paper in his pocket, he slipped down to the canteen and solved all five tasks within thirty minutes. Then he discreetly went back upstairs, pushed five small rolls of paper through the hole and disappeared.

For the next half hour, the five pieces of paper flew from desk to desk while Lugarić read the daily lies. In the end we were blatantly calling out to each other:

'Pass me number five! Number four and five! I've got number three!'

Lugarić just sat there and kept reading. Once in a while he rustled his paper and made a few shushes but that was it.

The following week he entered the class smiling. Practically merry. Almost nice.

'There, you see: I knew you could do it! None of you are lacking in intelligence. You're just lazy! You just need a little push.'

It was the last day of school. Not one of us had to re-sit the exam. Standing by the blank board, Lugarić made a speech about the summer, the holidays and the harmful rays of the afternoon sun.

'They are harmful ... those ... ultraviolet ...'

Jurišić, the local patriot and traitor, leaned back and shrugged:

'Yeah, that's life. We're all going to die from something. Sitting in the shade can also be dangerous.'

THE FUTURE

Horvat and Fabio had a future. Not a bright or a safe one, but undoubtedly brighter and safer than mine. They were Croatian citizens. I was not. I was born in Vešnja. Nobody sent them wry looks.

We shared a fag on the playing field after Lugarić's final lesson and talked about 'the future.'

'I'm going to uni,' Horvat said. 'I'm already looking forward to it. Screw Vešnja, I'm moving to Zagreb! The old folks will send me money. Hot babes, cool concerts. It'll be wicked.'

'Screw uni,' Fabio said, 'I'm going to Italy. My uncle is making money there. I'm taking off before they call me up.'

'What, you're not going off to defend the homeland?' I laughed as I handed Horvat the cigarette. 'Get a haircut, wear a uniform. Fabiano, the killer!'

'No thank you! I'm taking off. That's for sure.'

I imagined Fabio in Italy. What was he going to do there? Nothing. He would be a foreigner. He was born in Vešnja after all. Croatia was his homeland.

'What a bunch of nonsense! Homeland is a broad concept, Bosniako. Unfortunately not many people understand that.'

It was strong tobacco. Horvat coughed and thumped his chest with his hand.

'And what about you?' he asked. 'What are you going to do? You're not very popular at the moment, you lot from Bosnia.'

'No shit! I hadn't noticed.'

'Seriously, what are you going to do?'

'I'm bolting for Sweden. I've got friends there. They're scoring big time, riding horses, eating cherries. But I can't get the old ones to go with me. They can't be bothered. They just want to go home. I think I'll take off as soon as I'm finished here. Maybe even before.'

'How the hell are you going to get there?'

'I don't know. Steal a passport maybe. Lugarić and Tomić are killing me.'

'You're not the only one,'Fabio laughed and took a long drag.

Then he told us about a guy who was studying to be an electrician at trade school. The guy was on work experience with a self-employed electrician and was all set to get some paid work, but then he got called up. So Fabio was thinking of registering on the electrician's programme and taking this guy's work experience spot. At trade school you attended three lessons a week and went on work experience the other two days. The employer paid for lunch and occasionally threw in some small change.

'As far as the actual transfer, it's no problem,' Fabio explained. 'Trade school is one step lower than technical school. It's just a matter of applying.'

'Does he have more places?' I asked.

'I'm not sure … Actually, do you know what? He has a colleague. They do business together.'

'Cool!'

'Are you interested or what?'

'Paid lunch sounds good.'

'The two of you are off your head,' Horvat interrupted. 'What kind of idiots am I hanging out with? Are you insane?'

'Why?'

'Because! Only complete losers go to trade school. A bunch of idiots, man, nothing more. You're going to waste the few brain cells you have.'

'I'm wasting them here, too.'

'Yes, but if you go to trade school you can't get in to uni.'

'Right! Uni! Obviously! You have to be a citizen to do that. How the hell am I going to do that? I'm not Croatian.'

'Then put your name down in Bosnia.'

'The only thing your name goes down on in Bosnia is the casualty list, mate. Haven't you been keeping up?'

'Wait till the war's over then.'

'Yeah, yeah, yeah. "Uni, uni." Forget it, man! If it weren't for you today, I'd have failed my first year.'

'Now it's a good thing you remembered that. You owe me a beer. You too, Fabiano.'

'Relax, you go-getter, you'll get your beer,' Fabio answered and turned to me. 'But there is one thing.'

'What sort of thing?'

'That guy, the electrician ...'

'Yeah?'

'I think he's Serbian.'

'But ... you said he would hire me.'

'And he will, I think. But, I mean, does it bother you, or ...?'

'That depends,' I said and thought of Neno, the drizzle, Kaća and the full moon. 'Is he interested in politics?'

'No, only booze. Drinks like a fish.'

'That's fine.'

'He ... Boro, I think he's called ... he's cool. He worked on the Brioni Islands when he was younger. Shook hands with Tito a few times.'

'Wow! Have you got his number?'

'No. But I can get it.'

The old folks were in favour. They liked the idea of a free sandwich twice a week, the prospect of a little income and last but not least, the chance for me to learn a trade.

'It's about time,' Dad said. 'You don't have any skills.'

With an eye to last year's enrolment fiasco he added:

'Make sure you have a firm agreement with the employer before you change schools. And don't mess it up. Otherwise we'll be left high and dry again.'

'Cut it out!' I said. 'Stop talking to me like I'm a child. I'm fifteen years old, man. I know what I'm doing. If he doesn't want me – fine! Then I'll stay where I am, and that's that.'

He did want me. Obviously there were no other candidates. We arranged over the phone for me to drop by so we could 'get to know each other,' as he put it.

A couple of days later I took the bus into town, walked around and found Master Borislav Krivokapić's residence. It was an old four-storey building on the inside of a courtyard. It was covered in ivy, the green filling cracks in the facade. A dog was barking from one of the floors above.

I walked up the stairs cautiously and buzzed. Was slightly tense and nervous. It was an important meeting, after all. I waited for him to open the door. So we could 'get to know each other.' Him, a filthy Serb. Me, a filthy Bosnian. In Croatia, in 1993.

The door was opened by a grey-haired man in his early sixties. Wearing a tight vest and a wide pair of boxers. With small eyes and a dark and hostile look, the man was anything but a pleasant sight. There was no doubt: Master Boro, the doorman to my bright future, was suffering from a bad hangover.

'Yes?'

'Hello. Would you be a Mr Krivokapić? Borislav Krivokapić?'

'Yes, that's me. What do you want?'

'I called you … you said I should drop by … today.'

'A yes. The apprentice! Was that today? Yes, come in, come in! Don't just stand out there.'

The master electrician livened up, and as I walked inside he offered me the only chair in the room. He walked around clumsily searching for his clothes – some on the sofa, some under the table – while I looked around.

The room was dim and stuffy. On the middle of the coffee table was the largest ashtray I had ever seen. Around it was a swarm of cigarette butts, cutlery, bottles, bills – even a greasy cutting board. There were clothes and belongings everywhere, and I could not help but compare the room to our fourteen square metres at the camp.

There was no question: Ours was far less bleak.

The stories that Boro would later tell me were often contradictory. As far as I could figure out, he was orphaned during the previous war. He had grown up at an orphanage in Serbia and had moved to Vešnja after completing his military service. The idea that he had worked on the Brioni Islands and had shaken hands with Tito a few times, must have been something the other apprentice had imagined. Boro never mentioned any of those things to me, even though we talked about Tito and the Brioni Islands on a number of occasions.

His wife had died many years earlier. Behind the dingy glass of a brown display cabinet he kept a framed photo of her. Next to it was a fading photo of the two of them, taken in the seventies at some point, judging by his sideburns and her middle parting.

For a long time I observed their smiling faces while he was in the kitchen, quietly washing his face.

'Okey-dokey!' he said at long last. 'Let's go downstairs!'

The workshop was on the ground floor. The room was at most ten square metres and had a low ceiling. Another image awaited me there – one I had not seen since my last day of school in Bosnia.

Josip Broz Tito. Wearing glasses. Serious.

On the wall above the workbench, the former comrade of the southern Slavs looked out at a pile of random tools, several coils of cable and a German *Playboy* calendar hanging on the opposite wall.

'We'll have to tidy up down here,' the master electrician said.

Meaning I had to tidy up.

'Now?'

'No, no! Not now. After the holidays. When you start your work experience. Now we're going to go and grab ourselves a little something to drink. Okey-dokey?'

'Okay.'

We went to the nearest bistro. Master electrician Boro polished off three glasses of cognac while I contented myself with one large cup of cocoa. Boro seemed to be on friendly terms with the waitress, Lucija, and as she polished wine glasses and emptied ashtrays she nostalgically harked back to her days as a student.

I noticed her cleavage. Hanging from her necklace was a silver crucifix.

THE NEW DISPLACED

When the Bosnians started to go abroad, loads of rooms were left vacant at the camp. A lot of people complained and pressed to get one of them. Especially people with children over the age of fifteen.

Then news arrived that a number of us would have new neighbours.

'The new displaced,' as we called them, moved into the vacant rooms in the middle of June. The campsite near Grozvin, where they had lived, was sold into private hands, and another place had to be found for them to live. They were all Croatian Croats – from Slavonia and the Knin region – so to send them over to us was an obvious move.

At first I was indifferent to the news. There were people my age among the newcomers, but I dared not get my hopes up. The letters from the north were making me rather envious: the brothers were now living in the same city. Amar had learned the language, was working as a newsboy and earning a packet. I listened to Azra, Pearl Jam and the Sex Pistols. My hair was getting long. I could already manage a small ponytail. Kaća and Fabio supplied me with all kinds of cassettes. The threadbare T-shirts that Dad brought home from Caritas, Merhamet and the Red Cross, I sorted through cynically. I only wore black, purple and grey. I was looking more and more like a proper band member. All I was missing was a band.

Kaća and I went around deliberating over all the big topics like a couple of endangered monkeys. For example: is it wise to bring children into the world, considering its wretched state?

Everyone in the camp thought we were going out together.

'The new ones' disappointed us. A bunch of pop guys, all with smart haircuts, bulging muscles and bad taste in music. They stuck together. Worst of all: no girls. Not a single one worth three glances. I was doomed to stare at the ceiling, fast-forwarding and rewinding Kaća's tapes and listening to Dad's moaning.

'The sun is shining, dammit, and you're sitting inside! Go outside for a while. Get some fresh air!'

'Yeah, and what are you going to do while I'm outside, man? Sleep the day away. Lie down listening to the news.'

'I am old and you are young. It is not healthy for you to be inside. You will get milky white skin like some sort of princess. Go outside for a while!'

During the war, when the shells were whizzing past our ears, he refused to make decisions on my behalf. When I asked him for advice, he would always say:

'Do what you like! You are not going to be a child much longer.'

There was no consistency. All he wanted was to be able to listen to the news. I said as much.

'It was different during the war,' he defended himself. 'If I said to you "stay here," and a shell fell on you: my fault! If I sent you somewhere else, and the shell fell there: also my fault! It was unbearable. It's different now.'

I did as he said. Went outside and sat on the terrace in front of the restaurant. Baked in the sun, studied a small pine cone.

Suddenly Vlado and Robi appeared with five or six of 'the new ones'. The entire group sat down at my table and before I even managed to say a word, the conversation turned to the war and the current battles.

One of the new ones, Pero, was from Slavonia, but his grandfather was from Hercegovina. He quoted his grandfather in every other sentence. He repeated non-stop that the Muslims had no chance. That he could hardly wait for 'Francek to loosen the reins a little, so we put an end to that matter.'

Even if I was brave enough to get up and leave, I would not have been able to: they were both to the right of me and to the left.

Then he started:

'Robi, what would you do to a Muslim if you captured him?'

Robi, sat directly opposite me, got a dazed expression on his face from being asked such a direct question.

Luckily for him Pero did not wait for a reply but managed on his own:

'I would tie him to a table and have four or five rats walk on him. So he got so scared that he shat himself!'

One of the others asked if that was supposed to be a punishment; why would anyone be scared of rats.

Pero suggested that he had no idea how hard a rat can bite. He had been bitten by a rat once and had only managed to tear the beast off by a whisker.

And while two or three of his friends laughed at that gem, he looked me directly in the eyes and said:

'Tied to a table with a rat crawling on you! There's no bigger punishment than that, my friend. Isn't that right?'

Everyone went quiet. I looked at him.

'Isn't that right?'

I was not sure whether I should keep my mouth shut or try to lighten things up a little.

I kept my mouth shut. Glanced down towards the beach.

A holidaymaker was waving a piece of fabric, possibly a jumper, while she called her child. Some boys from the camp jumped into the water at the end of the pier. In the middle of the bay a Dutch yacht was dropping anchor.

The whole thing only lasted a handful of seconds, no more. But if felt like minutes. Finally Pero's voice sounded again, repeating the same idiotic sentence:

'Isn't that right?'

No reply.

My heart was pounding, but I held my tongue.

'Are you deaf?'

Zilch.

'DID YOU HEAR WHAT I SAID?'

A man asking such a stupid question should know better than to shout that loud. I was one and a half metres away. Of course I could hear him.

Small drops of his spittle had struck me in the ear and the temple, but I did not dare wipe them away. I just tried to keep a straight face and stick it out.

But I couldn't. I was too embarrassed. And too scared. There were a lot of them.

'I heard you,' I muttered.

'Isn't that right then?'

'HOW IN THE WORLD SHOULD I KNOW?'

Downer.

Total defeat.

My voice was loud, but shaky. Everyone could hear that. Robi got up and said:

'Hey, does anyone want to go in the water with me?'

Vlad and the others slowly followed him.

Pero remained behind.

'Pero, are you coming?' Vlado asked, clearly trying to save my arse.

I looked down at the scored surface of the table in front of me. For a few long seconds I endured his gaze.

'Pussy!' he said and headed for the pier.

I found Dad in the room and started to complain.

'But why are you hanging out with them?'

'Hanging out with them? I just told you, they surrounded me. On purpose!'

'But why were you sitting alone? Why weren't you with someone?'

'Right, and who would *that* be? You were the one who forced me to go outside!'

'Where is Katarina? Or Igor? Why don't you find some new friends? The beach is teeming with young people, and all you do is lie in here listening to music. What the hell is wrong with you?'

'Friends aren't like mussels, you don't just find them on a beach! And do you really think having Kaća there would have changed anything?'

'Fine, then tell me! What do you want from me? Eh? Do you want me to go out and fight them?'

'No ... I just don't know what you're waiting for here. Why don't we leave like all the others? Amar's parents didn't have money either. They borrowed it. Can't we at least move to the barracks in Vešnja?'

It was appalling there. Two families to a room. The food was worse than ours, there were communal toilets and due to a lack of beds many people slept on mattresses on the floor. But only Bosnians lived there, so I tried to argue that it was probably better to live poorly amongst one's own than to live well amongst psychopaths.

Futile.

'Better the devil you know than the devil you don't know.'

Even when the hot water was reduced to twice a week, and dinner was changed to bread, tinned sardines and an overly salty Danish cheese, they did not change their stance.

There was no point discussing it. I just let them listen to their news and wait for the journey home –'to the hearth and home of their ancestors,' as the radio continued to call it.

I went outside. Thought about Neno, who surely would have agreed with my idea. I did not doubt it for a second. Sweden's music libraries – that would be just the thing for him. But first a couple of nights at the camp and an uppercut to the face of that psycho Pero:

Boom!

And then take off to Sweden, just the two of us.

BEADS OF SWEAT AND SWIMMING

The summer holiday, the one we so impatiently awaited in the winter, passed mercilessly. Sunburnt foreign tourists stared up at the balconies of D1 and D2, unable to understand the reason for all the flags and all the ethnic sounds that droned out from unseen speakers. They blew up their air mattresses and rubbed suncream into their skin, while I sauntered past with the strangest ideas in my head. The beaches of the Adriatic, which I dreamt of as a kind of promised land during the war, they no longer meant anything to me. The bay and the sea were only there to remind me of last summer, of the day on the island, when Samir and Andrea swapped spit, of all the parties at the tip of the peninsula, and of Marina, the chubbiest girl in the camp. She was now seeing an older guy from Vešnja. He was at least twenty-two and picked her up in his car on a side street up by the roundabout.

Before the anniversary of our capture and forced departure from Neno, Dad travelled to Zagreb. There he had spoken to a prisoner who had been exchanged, and bribed every Tom, Dick and Harry at the Bosnian embassy. He also got Neno's name on a new list of missing persons. He did not have his birth certificate, and that caused all sorts of fuss.

I spent the majority of those two days alone on the peninsula. A grey-haired nudist with a microscopic member was swimming in my vicinity, keeping an eye on me. I stood on a cliff staring out at the horizon. Did I look like I was about to commit suicide? Or was the old man just a pervert? My fist was bleeding when I left. It was two months after Uncle brought the only news we had of Neno. One year away from home. One year since I had last seen him.

I wondered: what would it be like to steal a Walkman and take it down to the beach? Find a hidden location, lie under the open sky and listen to some really angry tunes? Or something sleep-inducing or melancholic à la 'Us and Them' by Pink Floyd? I imagined a bundle of cables from master electrician Boro Krivokapić's workshop and pictured it extending from the yellowed socket in our room. It rolled across the balcony, down the terrace, the stairs and all the way down to the beach, where I lay on my back listening to my favourites songs over and over again.

When I went swimming, I chose places that were as far from Pero and his crew as possible. Igor was away that entire summer. Kaća and I went swimming from time to time. Then she went to visit family in Koper.

Counting breasts, buttocks and legs became a sport. I fantasised about all the foreign, unconquered flesh. I masturbated spiritually: is there a god? If not, why? Lay on the balcony deep in thought. Listened to Red Hot Chili Peppers and Led Zeppelin. Lazed about. Masturbated for real. Lay with my eyes shut, my mind blank. Wrote long letters and sent them off to Sweden. Waited for 'this too' to pass, for something good to happen, but nothing passed, and nothing good happened.

The sun roasted, the earth cracked, the asphalt glowed. The ultraviolet rays that Lugarić had raved about were lurking on all sides. I was not afraid of them, so I often walked to Majbule and all the way to the road to Vešnja. I stuck out my thumb and waited. Not a penny in my pocket and no plan whatsoever, I trudged through the streets, peered into the shop windows and held my breath when I had to walk past the restaurant tables where tourists with wide smiles were served their ćevapčići. Then I hitched back to the run-down holiday camp in Majbule, where Mum and Dad, two frail and feeble individuals, were sat with their ears pricked up, waiting for a miracle. The radio continued with its favourite lines:

'Fierce battles ... heroic resistance ... heavy enemy losses ...'

Nobody was turning towards home.

On one of my strolls through the city, I felt a proper smack on my shoulder:

'What's up, Bosanchero? What's going on?'

It was Horvat, the future university graduate. He was with one of his friends. They had large towels that looked like ponchos slung over their shoulders.

'Why don't you to come to Belvedere with us?' he asked. 'We're taking the bus.'

I tried to get out of it by saying it as it was: I had no trunks and no money for a ticket. The Red Cross did not give out bus passes during the holidays.

'As if we have tickets! We'll figure it out, obviously.'

We hopped on through the back door of the bus and remained on the step. The bus was packed. Overheated bodies wearing Bermuda shorts and flip flops were pasted against one another. There was no way the driver could see us.

'If the ticket inspector comes, I'll whip him with my towel!' Horvat said. 'And then with my fist!'

'If the ticket inspector comes,' his friend said, 'I'm taking off. You do whatever you like.'

They started talking about some experiences they had shared at Ukulele, as well as a band I had not heard of: Type O Negative.

'Why don't you come to Ukulele?' Horvat asked. 'There's nothing but ladies there. What are you doing in Majbule, man? It's a hole. Total crap.'

'Yeah, I know,' I said and decided not to repeat my previous point about money, or rather the lack thereof.

I had dreamt of going to Ukulele ever since I heard about the place. Fabio had filled my mind with images. But the entrance fee was a little pricey and my pockets were empty.

Life was a stingy arsehole.

The beach was teeming with people. Children wailing,

adults gorging themselves. It was ten times worse than Majbule.

We met up with another of Horvat's friends and continued towards a quieter location. Horvat's friends all had long hair and listened to death metal. The guy from the beach had brought his heavy-girlfriend with him, and they tickled each other and sniggered incessantly, like they were still in year seven.

Out on the cliffs it was a little quieter. We met up with two of the sniggering heavy-chick's girlfriends. One wore a black Slayer T-shirt, a pair of cut-off jeans and Doc Marten boots.

Boots in the middle of the summer, I thought. Jesus Christ!

They got ready for a swim then ran down towards the water. I was the only one left behind. Beads of sweat the size of nuts ran down my forehead and temples. I wiped them off and observed the back of six heads swimming out towards the horizon. They took loads of breaks. Then they split up into three couples. Horvat was clearly chatting up one of the girlfriends and his friend was trying it on with the other. The ladies were first-rate, and I wondered when a go-getter like Horvat had managed to scrape together so much self-confidence.

And what was that he was shooting off about, I thought. Something about whipping the inspector? He was the most chilled guy in our class, absolutely. What sort of nonsense was that?

The sun was glistening off the water. I had no sunglasses, had to squint, regretted I had not even brought them with me.

What the hell am I doing here? If only I had someone with me, it all would have made more sense.

I imagined the five of them questioning Horvat about me, about what I was doing on the beach wearing so much clothing. And why I was not swimming. Could I swim? The general belief was that since Bosnians came from the mountains they were afraid of the water.

What would Horvat tell them? Both he and his friend could see that I was strolling around town like a bum. If I was better at making excuses, I would not be sitting here baking in the afternoon sun now. It was utterly hopeless.

They came back from their swim. Twittering and hopping over the shiny, scorching rocks. They used their towels to dry off, praised the water temperature and lay down on their stomachs. They chattered away about all sorts. When the conversation turned to music, I had lots of things I could say. I had an entire bookcase of songs memorised by heart. I knew a sea of bands. But I just sat there for more than half an hour like the biggest loser and said nothing.

They had long since forgotten about me. The couple were snogging the whole time, Horvat and his friend continued chatting up the two girls, and I sat next to them with a lump in my throat and swallowed my saliva, sweating away.

Why had Horvat even asked me to come? We had not exchanged two words since he set eyes on the hottie.

Eventually they got up to go back in the water. I seized the opportunity and forced a hoarse declaration across my lips:

'I'm heading out now.'

'With us?'

'No, no. Home. I don't have my trunks.'

'But we just got here.'

'Yeah, but I don't have my trunks. And I've got this thing in Majbule. I've got an appointment.'

That was probably the most blatant lie on the entire planet. Everyone knew it.

I didn't care. I just wanted to get away.

'Okay. See you then!'

'See you, man!,' Horvat replied and gave me the sign of the horns. 'Take care of yourself!'

'You too.'

I nodded to the others:

'See you.'

'See ya.'

'See you later!' Horvat's hottie said, completely over the top. She forced a smile and waved goodbye to me, like I was a little child. I responded with some indeterminate movement of my hand.

Never in my life had I felt so despondent and so stupid as the moment I walked away from them.

Cassette 5

NEW NOTES

ASININITY

Fabio and I looked around. Horvat was right: trade school was for losers.

For example Bobić from the Nenadovo district. I could barely understand him. He only spoke in dialect and very rarely showered.

'What the hell, Bobić,' Fabio said to him. 'Do you sleep with goats or what? Why don't you wash?'

Or Honda-Denis, who had failing marks in almost every subject. While the business studies teacher described the relation between principal and interest, he hawked with all his might and spat on the floor. She looked at him in shock:

'You're mad. You are absolutely insane!'

He put on his motorcycle helmet and crossed his arms.

'Out!' she shouted. 'Get out!'

He got up and left. Calmly and quietly.

Martinović, our English teacher, was the only real nuisance. After the fall of Communism he returned to his homeland from England, and of all the cities in Croatia, he had to settle down in Vešnja, and of all the schools in the city, he had to be employed at this particular trade school. The man dressed unfathomably ugly – tie and grey suits – and only spoke English. He taught us English grammar in English, even though there were those in the class whose brains could barely follow even if it had been in Croatian. We were set some senseless dialogues that we had to memorise and perform in front of the class, in pairs.

FABIO: 'Should I put this in front of the fireplace, darling?'

ME: 'No. Please put it by the window, dear.'

Nobody in the class had ever heard Martinović speak Croatian. Apart from me. I set a trap for him once after the lesson. He completely screwed with me.

'What does "numb" mean?' I asked him in English. 'Comfortably Numb. It's a song title.

'I know,' he smiled and mumbled three possible meanings: paralysed, frozen or without feeling.

I loved him for that. The man in the suit knew Pink Floyd!

Back at the camp Mum told me that Dad had got some work. A vineyard near Lovgar was short of manpower. The trip took an entire two hours, because the bus had to pick up muscles in several towns along the way.

Mum was part of a group of women from the camp who knitted gloves, sweaters and caps for a sleazy businessman from Vešnja. It must have been very good business. He drove past the camp every other day to pick up the finished products.

In the evening, when the two of them collapsed on the bed and complained about their sore backs and shoulders, I prodded them:

'What's up, working class! Once upon a time you had the first of May, a good salary, health and social insurance. And now? Dad, you've been thrown back to the age of feudalism, and Mum, to the age of the manufacturer. I'm the only one in the family maintaining the standards!'

'Drop that crap, son!' Dad said. 'I can barely keep my eyes open.'

I 'maintained the standards' by going on work experience with Master Electrician Boro Krivokapić, who paid for my lunch, though still not for my efforts. He taught me how to lay cables and connect electricity in new flats and business premises. We repaired existing wiring as well as a range of home appliances. I unrolled cables, made plaster, connected copper wires and dreamt I was somewhere else, somewhere in Sweden, in the vicinity of Stockholm, where my friends and I chased fit Swedish babes, went to cool concerts and drank from freshly opened bottles.

When there was no work, we drove Boro's old Zastava from one pub to the next. We stood in the bar and waited for someone to mention something about a defective iron or something. The pubs, the bistros and the wine cellars functioned as Boro's private offices. It was there that people went to look for him and left him messages. All his friends and acquaintances spent most of their time there. Some of them were tradesmen themselves, looking for work. Others were unemployed and permanent fixtures. With long faces, they hung out by the bar from morning till night and squawked about the good old days. The stories got better and better with every emptied glass. One of them was a history teacher, now retired, but without a pension. The other: a policeman, Serbian, fired. The third: Croatian, a drunkard, no job. I never saw any of them eat. They just sucked on their bottles and bought each other fresh rounds.

One I remember was Ljumbomir, a retired YPA officer with an aquiline nose and a thin moustache. He once talked about how in the seventies he had been to the opening of the zoo in Vešnja.

'I go inside, stand there and see something: what in the world is that? Is it a sheep or a donkey? Something furry and tall with a long neck and long ears, really long. I move closer to get a better look at the creature. Then God-help-me the shaggy devil spits at my head! Arghhh! My cap flies off, people are dying with laughter, and I'm near dying with shame. Later a colleague says to me: "Ljubo, that was a llama, it's an exotic animal. How could you make such an ass of yourself while in uniform?" But honestly, I'm telling you: the first thing I thought – that's not a sheep or a donkey!'

Then Marijan, Fabio's employer arrived, with an urgent job. He needed to replace the sockets at the home of a diasporan man in Grozvin. The man had built a two-hundred-square-metre villa and had had a range of nice, very fancy Italian sockets installed. Now, six months later, a number of the sockets had stopped working, and the man wanted to replace the lot of them. Marijan had warned him about the poor quality, but the guy had insisted on the pink mussel-shaped sockets. Marijan was not able to make it out there himself.

'No problem. We'll take it,' Boro said. 'Is everything ready?'

'Yep! But be careful. The guy is a real patriot,' Marijan said, then whispered: 'Emigrant from the communist era.'

We knew what that meant.

'Find yourselves some other names,' he added.

Boro dubbed himself Franjo, and me, he called Igor. At the home of the great patriot the wife was there alone, and she served us beer, wine and Slivovitz. 'Franjo' had already had a few, and as usual his pronunciation had started to slip in the Serbian Ekavian direction. He had lived in Vešnja for two thirds of his life, but the Ekavian made an appearance every time he drank.

I had to make toasts and speak far more than usual in order to keep him quiet. The president's namesake spoke sonorous Serbian.

Around six or seven, we drove back. Boro insisted on giving me a lift to the camp, and I was stupid enough to agree. As soon as we left Grozvin, the Zastava began to drive along the white line. Occasionally we were all the way over on the left side.

I was rather tipsy myself, but still I got a chill down my spine every time we approached a bend in the road. Boro sang: 'The snow fell on spring flowers, on fruit.' I prayed to the higher powers: Please don't let anyone come driving in the opposite direction! Please let me survive this trip!

Never before had D2 and the reception building looked as lovely as it did that evening. I stepped out of the car and breathed in the cool air. I was alive. It was beautiful!

I leaned forward to say goodbye. Boro dug into his pockets and unfurled some crumpled notes:

'Here! Take this!'

That was a first.

'Next time, boss. On a bigger job.'

'Do as I tell you, take it! Do you want me to get angry?'

'It's too much,' I said and was just about to add 'and you're drunk, sir.'

He removed two notes and handed me the rest.

I thanked him, slammed the door and headed slowly back to D1.

Reception was quiet and deserted, while the TV room was more crowded and noisy than I had ever seen. The voices intermingled, people were shushing one another and there were vehement discussions.

Still drunk, I did something I had not done for a long time. I went in. Stood at the very back, by the entrance. Pero was sitting on an armchair further ahead. He could not see me. Nobody could see me. Only the TV screen lit up the viewers' faces and shiny heads.

There was news.

The sound was cranked up, but I could not understand what the newsreader was talking about. I stood furthest from the TV, and sitting between me and the speaker was Parasite, Clove and a bunch of others, all talking at once. I listened to their incomplete sentences, the fragments of their theses and theories.

'It must be our people! That was …'

'Are you mad? They were the ones who …'

' … to get the attention of Europe!'

' … force the Americans to intervene!'

I was afraid to ask someone what the commotion was about. I pricked up my ears and tried to isolate the sound of the TV from the bellowing and bleating in the room.

Then Ivan entered, nodded at me and asked what was going on. The man in front of me turned and stated coolly that the old bridge in Mostar had been destroyed, and now they were waiting for Franjo to say something on the matter.

It was the ninth of November, 1993.

THE BASEMENT WINDOW

I walked out of the TV room. Thought of Safet from our street, originally from Mostar. He had married Amila and moved into her dad's house about one hundred metres from ours. Next to them lived Selim, the man with the finest basement in the entire neighbourhood. Selim was a retired carpenter and used the basement as his workshop. For that reason he had it built so that you could stand upright and work there. To let some light in, he had two small windows built in the wall facing the river.

Now, as I dragged myself up the stairs of D1, half drunk, I thought about one of those windows.

There was not a single cloud in the sky that day. It was spring, nearing summer – sunshine, pollen and horny bees in the air. The only object of desire for Adi and me was the curvaceous Lana on Ribarska Street. She was over thirty, married, and had a spoilt eight-year-old.

We sat on the veranda at my place having a melancholy conversation about the girls from our class. We expected to be treated as heroes once the war ended and they returned. I pictured them admiring Adi and I, two tough guys, two experienced lads who were there when it happened, not sitting far away watching it on the telly.

'Definitely!' Adi said ironically. 'They'll put up statues of us in the park. While we're alive!'

'No, down by the boats,' I said. 'Where I saw the two Chetniks.'

'I want to be on a horse!'

'You are the horse. Beneath me.'

'And a cowboy hat!'

'Not serious! I want to have a woman on the horse with

me! Why are there no partisan statues with women? I thought the partisans scored like mad, man.'

Boom!

The first shell fell. I was on the stairs trimming my nails as we spoke. Adi was lying on the floor of the veranda flicking through a comic book, a Captain Micky issue entitled *Bart with the Scar*. He threw it down and shouted as he got up:

'Wow, man! That was close!'

With talons on one hand and an exemplary manicure on the other, I ran after him. We jumped over the fence of Zaim's garden, dashed around behind the house and entered his basement hunched over.

Then number two exploded. Even closer! I could feel the pressure – the sudden gush of air – before Adi managed to shut the metal door.

Half an hour later we heard screaming and wailing from Selim's garden and knew that it was bad. Adi wanted to go over and see the bodies, but his dad threatened to cuff him if he moved an inch.

I had no interest in seeing it. Neno did, and came back. It was the first time I had ever seen him cry.

'Safet, Selim and Drago are dead,' he said when people started to question him.

The three of them had been sharing some tinned sardines in the garden behind Selim's house. Safet had removed his T-shirt and had his back to the hot sun. Drago was smoking half a cigarette.

When the shell fell, they ran into Selim's basement. Shell number two flew in through one of the windows and killed them on the spot.

The window was no larger than forty by sixty centimetres. How big was the shell? What angle was it launched at? What were the odds of something like that even happening?

Had the three of them remained in the garden, they would have been unharmed. Safet still would have spoken with his Mostar accent, Selim's basement would still be packed with neighbours that night, and chain-smoking Drago would have been sucking on his ciggies as usual.

But how could anyone know that the near impossible would happen? That the place that everyone thought was the safest, was in reality the worst place to go?

THROUGH THE GATE

'Maybe you're right after all,' Kaća said.

'About what?'

'Maybe it was the Croatians.'

'Who?'

'In Mostar, you know. The bridge. Maybe they were the ones who did it.'

'Oh, that,' I made a sweeping gesture. 'Fuck it.'

I pointed at the white plastic bag she was holding:

'Is that for me?'

'Yes. And do you know what? They were on sale. This is how much you saved.'

She handed me a roll of notes, and I unfurled them. A little more than thirty kunas. I pinched her on the cheek:

'You're an angel! One of these days you're going to get a big sweetie. Let's see what we've got here.'

I pulled the cardboard box out of the bag and sat down on the bench. I rested the box on my lap.

I could already *smell* them.

'So, how was Trieste?' I asked.

'Noisy and filthy. Mum was utterly impossible.'

'You always say that.'

I removed the lid, and *there* they were, a set of twins covered with a thin piece of rustling paper.

'Forty-ones, right?'

'Relax,' Kaća said. 'They're exactly as you asked. I'm not an idiot.'

I kicked off my worn-out Adidas and dipped my feet into Paradise. I put the laces in and tied them up.

Then I got up and walked back and forth.

'What do you think?' I asked.

'Not bad. Actually they suit you quite well.'

I placed my misshapen and practically disintegrated Adidas in the box. The things I had been through in them! War and Peace. I looked forward to chucking them as soon as I got the chance. Maybe as early as the following morning, out on the peninsula:

Splaashhh!

Dad completely flipped out:

'What? Are those meant to be shoes?'

'Yeah, what's wrong?'

'It's the middle of November! How could you buy such crap? You are not going to make it through the winter in them.'

'They're Converse All Star, man! They're totally cool!'

'They're a pair of socks with laces and soles! That's an out-and-out con!'

'No, they're too cool, and they suit me. Here!'

I took the thirty kunas out of my pocket and handed it to him: 'Here! I'll get you the rest as soon as I'm paid again.'

He had lent me some of his salary from the vineyard. The money Boro had given me barely covered half of what the shoes cost in Trieste.

'I don't want it,' he answered. 'It was not a loan, it was a gift, you are my child. But those are not shoes! Especially not in the winter! You will get ill as soon as a drop of rain falls on them.'

'Then you'll have to find me something better at Caritas or the Red Cross.'

'But you do not want anything I get from there!'

'The stuff you bring, nobody is interested in wearing them.'

'Why? Are they too hot? Is the prince scared his feet are going to get sweaty or what?'

'No, only pop-boys and country bumpkins wear those. Pointed shoes. Find me a pair of army boots, then I'll take a look at them.'

'Find them yourself, good sir! Don't be so posh. Go dig

through the cardboard boxes with the commoners! Why does it always have to be me?'

I chose not to reply. He'd had some problems at work, before the season ended, and he was often short-tempered at home. Several of the employees were newly-arrived Croatian refugees from central Bosnia. They had been persecuted by Muslims, so they spat in his face. To top things off, he had developed a rash on his hands. The grapevines had been sprayed with chemicals and he had forgotten to wear gloves.

Mum placated him with phrases like 'the child is at that age' and 'young people today.' She even suggested knitting me a pair of warm woollen socks, which would compensate for the insufficient thickness of the shoes. She had already knitted two long sweaters – a thick black one and a thin grey one. The former went with my trousers and new shoes. The trousers were still scruffy, washed-out and tight, but I no longer hated them. Since my hair had grown long, it looked like I wore them like that on purpose. Like it was just a part of my heavy style.

They were going to look good with the shoes and the black sweater, I thought. They are going to look cool in the dim lighting at Ukulele.

Kaća did not want to go with me. Or rather, she was desperate to go, but her Mum would not let her. She had just turned fifteen, and they fought all the time.

The day she returned from Trieste was a Sunday. I had all of six days to break in the shoes. I trained indoors and outdoors. Walked back and forth. Sprinkled dirt on them so they did not look way too new.

I counted down the days. Lay in my bed Friday night and thought: twenty-four hours.

Woke up with butterflies in my stomach. No appetite. Sheer joy that the day had finally arrived. And excitement. Loads of excitement.

From noon till evening, Pero, Vlado and a couple of the others hung out on the terrace showing off. I saw them putting chokeholds on each other for a laugh, and discussing press-ups, when I went out on the balcony to see if my T-shirts were dry.

'Sixty-five!'

'Sixty-five?'

'Sixty-five! I swear. I used to be able to do sixty-five.'

At eight o'clock I stood at the roundabout in Majbule, freezing cold. Not my toes, but my upper body. Wearing an extra jumper under the black sweater and dropping the jacket had clearly been a mistake. Sure I looked cool, but fuck was I cold!

A guy in an orange Lada drove past. Then he must have changed his mind because he slammed on the brakes.

I ran up to the car and opened the door.

'Shit, man,' he said. 'I thought you were a girl.'

'Sorry. Can I get a lift anyway?'

He thought about it for a moment, nodded and said:

'Hop in!'

So I hopped in.

Ukulele opened at eight, but there was virtually nobody there before ten. That was what Fabio had told me. I had loads of time.

I passed my school and the town library. Walked past two cinemas showing the same film. Imagined myself as the leading man. Getting the girl in the end. Kept walking.

On one of the streets of the old town there were several restaurants with ćevapčići on the menu. I chose the smallest and the cheapest.

'A small portion, please!'

I was not actually that hungry, I had eaten at the camp. But it was a special night, and I got carried away. Since the start of the war, I had not tasted ćevapčići once.

From the table by the window you could see the street

and watch people as they walked past. Two unshaven guys in boiler suits and sneakers were sitting at the bar. They were smoking and were virtually silent. A guy with glistening wax in his hair was on a date with a blonde. Unfortunately she had her back to me.

My food arrived. The waitress, who had fuzz under her nose and a beauty spot on her serving arm, said 'enjoy' and I thought: Oh no! They serve them with chips and bread here! No pita bread dipped in homemade broth? Chips and dry white bread?

I cut into one of the meat rolls, tried a piece and chewed. It was too salty and rubbery. This was nothing like Bosnian ćevapčići. I had landed in a tourist trap.

What the hell had I been expecting – at that price?

I paid and left. Never managed to see the blonde's face. Tipsy soldiers, beggars, and all sorts walked down the pedestrianised street. One of the soldiers staggered towards me. He was alone. I tried to evade him, but it was too late: we grazed shoulders.

'Sorry,' I hurried to say when he stopped and sent me a scornful look.

'Sorry,' I repeated. 'I didn't see you.'

He turned around and continued walking without saying a word. I left the centre, Vešnja's old town, and headed in the direction of Ukulele. I did not know exactly where it was. Had hoped I would see other people walking there and then just follow them. But all I spotted was a punk wearing a leather jacket entering a block of flats.

A woman in her mid-twenties gave me directions:

'It's on a side street to a side street to the first side street after the crossing. On the left.'

'Are you taking the piss?'

'No, seriously: first you go left, then left again at the end of the street. You'll see a small car park in front of an abandoned building, factory or whatever it used to be. Ukulele is right next to it.'

I heard a roar from inside. That was my first impression. A song and a band I did not recognise. Something hard. Something kick-ass.

The bass was loud, the sound grinding and muddy. A large metal gate was open on one side. Through the entrance I could glimpse part of the terrace and the stage, which was used for concerts in the summer.

Sitting to the right of the gate was a guy with a windcheater zipped up to his chin. A pack of fags, a money box and a pile of tickets on the table in front of him. The guy had dark hair that covered his forehead. My heart was pounding as I handed him a tenner.

'Enjoy!' he said and handed me the change.

'Thanks,' I said and slowly walked inside.

It felt like there were ants crawling up and down my back. I felt like raising my arms in the air and jumping up and down. Like shouting or something.

I was only a few months gone sixteen. With no notion of what it would be like to be with a woman. Wake up with her on a mild summer morning. Feel her gentle hand cupped around my balls, which could suddenly speak – both German and English.

So for a long time I hoped that one fine day, when it finally happened, it would feel like walking through the gates of Ukulele.

BAMBUS

There were not many people inside. The broad concrete terrace was practically deserted. Sitting at one of the many tables along the metal fence were two older heavies, hair down to their arses, laughing. A guy holding a bottle of beer said 'see ya' to a couple of girls and walked over to the table with the heavies.

At the opposite end of the terrace, near a wall ravaged by graffiti, there was a two-storey building with two entrances. One led to the bar, the other to the overlit toilets.

The large building, from where the droning music came, was on my right. It was round and had three entrances. I discovered that when I stepped inside. I actually had to piss, but had to see the dance floor first.

Ukulele must have been a church in the old days or something along those lines. In any case, the large building had a high ceiling. At least eight metres. The speakers, standing in each corner of the dance floor, were over two metres tall.

Damn, the sound when you got inside! My Japanese mono-weakling multiplied by five hundred. At least! It was as though the music went straight through your chest and stomach.

Around the dance floor was a small raised arena with three rows of plastic seats. Behind the back row on one side there was a platform with plastic armchairs along the wall. On the opposite side of the dance floor a couple of stairs led to a smaller stage, from where the DJ launched the fierce, angry tunes.

I walked along the edge of the dance floor and looked up at the DJ – a long-haired guy with glasses and cans. Wearing a long-sleeved sweater similar to mine.

The disco ball spun round, but there was nobody on the dance floor. A couple sat kissing in one of the armchairs at the very back. Two girls went up to the DJ with their tapes and a record under their arms. I nipped to the toilet.

A skinny punk with an aquiline nose wearing a black Dead Kennedys shirt stood next to me. He was clearly having problems getting his penis out of trousers that were far too tight.

I read the words on his top: TOO DRUNK TO FUCK, and recognised them at once. Fabio had a T-shirt exactly like it.

I wonder if Fabiano is coming, I thought. His jaw will drop when he sees me here. Definitely.

The neighbouring bar looked like a normal bar, with its own music, tables and chairs.

I sipped my drink and livened up. Wished 'the Swedes' were here. Sent them a toast in my head. Then I took another sip and went out to the terrace to go for a walk.

I drank bambus, a local mix of home-made red wine and Coke. I could not afford more than one beer, but I could get three glasses of bambus for the same price. My big plan for the night was to buy a bambus every hour and a half and walk around with it.

When I emptied glass number two, people started to pour in. The music grew more familiar, and the dance floor filled with a group of punks who were kicking in every direction to something hardcore. They were replaced by the death, thrash and heavy metal dudes, who swung their hair and looked badass. Finally the repertoire eased towards soft rock and grunge, with a few Croatian and Bosnian hits sprinkled in for good measure.

I sat in the third row, drank bambus and followed the evening's developments. My All Star Hi-Tops felt good on my feet. My hair was perfect. The girls walked past, one more beautiful than the next. I just made note of them and remembered them for another time. Had Fabio been there, we probably would have made a move together. He knew a lot of them as far back as primary school. He was from Vešnja, after all.

Had Fabio been there, we would have headbanged to 'Symphony of Destruction' by Megadeath and 'Two Minutes to Midnight' by Iron Maiden. I knew the lyrics to 'Two Minutes to Midnight' from start to finish, and I got up and sang at the top of my lungs, before I downed my third and final glass.

I did not meet anyone I knew that night. Nobody I could talk to. Some familiar faces from the school and the street, standing out with their clothes or haircuts, walked past and nodded now and again. I got annoyed towards the end of the evening, when the bambus finally started to take effect. It would have been good to have at least one witness. One person to have a drink with. One person to confirm that I had been there. When you don't speak to a single person the entire evening, it all seems strange and surreal in your mind. Maybe I should have rung Fabio and asked him to join me.

Another Lada, I thought, when I hopped into the car. Tonight is the night of Ladas!

This one was white, and it was a different guy driving. With a moustache and shoulder-length hair. He was at least twenty-five, if not older. Sitting next to him was his girlfriend, wife, score, or whoever she was. They were heading to Majbule. Probably to one of the summerhouses, I thought. I had never seen them before.

'Were you at Ukulele?' the guy asked.

That made me really happy.

'Yes!'

I obviously looked the part. A Ukulele guy!

'Us too.'

I thought: they're probably going back for a shag now. Why else would anyone in their right mind drive to Majbule at three o'clock in the morning?

For a moment I wished I was the man behind the wheel. With a lady, a car, music playing and the keys to a summerhouse with clean sheets and the lot.

'Is that Pink Floyd?' I asked uncertainly, and neither of them had spoken in a long time.

'Yeah!' the guy said and cranked up the volume.

We were deep into the song. The solo passages were over, and Waters began to sing: 'Remember when you were young, you shone like the sun.'

'Shine On You Crazy Diamond!' the guy shouted. 'From *Wish You Were Here*.'

Wish You Were Here? The icing on the cake. An unforgettable night. Pink Floyd in a white Lada, sailing through the night.

'I have to check out this album!' I said. 'I don't know it.'

Tomorrow the crap weather would be there again, I thought, and it's probably going to be a long time before Boro's next handout. But never mind. I would recall the details of this night one at a time. For days. And Kaća, she was going to get the full account. Everything from the gate to the dance floor, the songs, the bambus, and right up to the Lada and Pink Floyd. Yes!

Red wine and Coke whipped around in my body. The adrenaline prevented me from hearing the song properly. Everything buzzed around inside my head. I was a beehive of new impressions and new notes.

Would I ever be able to sleep after a night like this? Could I even be bothered? Is there anyone in those ridiculous buildings right now listening to music this good?

When I reached the camp and our room in D1, I silently loosened my laces. Dad was snoring. Mum turned in the bed.

'Lock the door,' she said.

'Aren't you sleeping?'

'Yes. It's late. You should be too.'

Only later did I work it out. One Saturday after another I stood up by the roundabout in Majbule with Boro's financial contribution in my pocket. I stuck out my thumb, strolled through the city and was already hanging out in Ukulele around nine. Sometimes I did not meet anyone at all. Other times Horvat, Fabio and has brother Mauro were there. Plus their friends, who quickly became mine. Plus all kinds of girls.

After the last song I hitched back to Majbule, and each time I snuck into the room, I heard my Mum turn in bed. She never went to sleep until I had returned to D1 safe and sound.

Myself, I feared nothing. Not the drunken soldiers in the narrow streets of Vešnja or the unknown drivers who picked me up.

I knew that the sun could do damage. But sitting in the shade could also be dangerous.

DREAM

I fell asleep and dreamed I was walking through the pedestrian precinct back home. On my way to Ukulele! Standing in the queue in front of me, Samir, Damir, Amar and Ismar were asking where the hell I had got to. I replied that I had had to walk Nina home. Sitting at the folding table to the right was Mister No, selling tickets. He nodded, and we got in for free. Samir handed me a bottle. He patted me on the shoulder, and I woke up just as I was going to take my first sip of the night.

I had drool on my pillow. Out in the corridor I heard doors opening and closing. I could hear footsteps, voices and sporadic coughing.

Someone knocked on the door opposite us. Then on ours. Twice. Three times.

Dad got up and opened the door.

'Good morning!'

'Good morning!'

'ID check!'

Two men in civilian clothing entered. They were both in their thirties. Wearing unbuttoned denim jackets with shirts underneath. I lay motionless on my side and pretended to be asleep. Through my eyelids I could see one of them flipping through a notebook.

Mum opened the drawer to the bedside table and handed them our yellow ID cards. I closed my eyes and took long breaths.

'Is that your child?'

'Yes.'

'Do you have any more?'

'No.'

'Any more people living here?'

'No.'

'HEY!' one of them shouted.

I 'woke up,' rubbed my eyes and looked surprised.

'How old are you, boy?' he asked. The other held our cards and jotted down the details.

'Sixteen,' I replied. 'What time is it?'

Dad cleared his throat and added needlessly:

'Youth these days! Out all night and asleep all day.'

The men did not react to him at all. They did their job. The pencil or the pen – I could not see which – scratched the paper. The writer moved his hand to his mouth and sneezed. Then he handed the cards back to Mum, and without saying a word he closed his notebook.

'Excuse me,' Dad said, when the denim jackets were on their way out, 'are you from Vešnja? From the refugee office?'

The writer's mate stopped and sent Dad a scornful look:

'"Office?" What "office?" Pull yourself together, man!'

Cassette 6

PUNK'S NOT DEAD

FOUR ILLUSIONS

One day in January 1994, two months after the first raid, Dad burst through the door and shouted:

'What on earth is that stench in the corridor?'

'Dunno,' I said.

'Is there a body somewhere, or what?'

'You never know.'

'It almost smells worse. Try standing here!'

I got up from the bed:

'Ugh! Close the door, dammit, before I pass out!'

'Damn!'

'Shut the door!'

That was how it started. With an unforgettable stench that made the eyes sting, in the corridor of the second floor of D1. Who could know that one thing would lead to another, that it would all end with one person dead and one alive, one person departing and one arriving.

I had been to school that day, but only half followed the lesson. It was windy outside, and on my way to the bus stop, I passed a broken-down phone box. The grimy glass door was ajar. On several occasions I had poked my index finger in the cool hole where returned coins on seldom occasions were forgotten.

This time it paid off. Two kunas. I picked up the receiver, bunged the coins in, selected the country code, the local code along with the number: 832-769.

Of course nobody answered. The hysterical dismissive tone beeped away in my ear. The two coins jingled down to the hole. I collected them and put them in my pocket, pleased with myself and with a good conscience. I had done my bit.

Imagine if suddenly there had been a connection. Imagine if it had been re-connected and somebody had answered. *Him*, for example, the one who did not ring or write or appear in the doorway. Him, the one we are still looking for.

As far as I knew, the house was still vacant. The weeds in the garden and the surrounding grass had grown tall. Most of the furniture had long since been stolen. I should be happy that I had not heard a voice in the receiver. Had I done that, it probably would have shouted at me:

'You don't live here any more! Do you get it! This number does not exist! The same goes for the greyish-blue telephone! Generations of Serbian are going to live here!'

I stepped out of the phone box and headed for the bus stop.

At the camp in Majbule, the harsh stench awaited me.

Gogi, also known as Goran, was a Slavonian of Croatian nationality. Those in the camp not from his village doubted it at the beginning. Pero and several others knew him from before. They maligned him and spread all sorts of rumours about his ancestors on his mother's side. Gogi did not care and had contributd to the confusion the day he moved in. When someone from Pero's balcony in D2, for the umpteenth time played *Čavoglave* and its lines like 'Drop a bomb, chase the gang,' Gogi opened his balcony door and responded with Miroslav Ilić or Sinan Sakić's turbo-folky hits.

'The autumn cried with you …', 'When the love dies …' and such.

Ekavian words echoed across the terrace at full blast.

Then Pero's voice was heard from D2:

'Shut that off!'

'Shut yours off first!'

'Shut it off! You should be ashamed of yourself! They've killed scores of your neighbours, and you come here playing that Serbian crap!'

'*You* should be ashamed! Your father was a member of the party, and you're playing Ustashe songs now!'

'Don't you say anything about my father!'

'Don't you say anything about my neighbours!'

'When I tell you to shut it off, shut it off!'

'You shut it off!'

'Shut it off! I'll call the police!'

'Hah! The thieves are going to call the police now? Ha! Ha!'

I sat by the open balcony door and enjoyed every moment of it. Finally *Čavoglave* was faced with an opponent! Finally someone defied that stupid butchering song!

But Gogi – he was just being provocative. He was as much Croatian as President Dr Franjo Tudjman. The homeland was not in any danger.

He had broad shoulders and thin hair and looked closer to thirty than twenty-one. His physique and my friendship with him would get Pero and his crew off my back for good.

'If he bothers you again, just let me know,' he said. 'His father used to steal our apples back home. Later I ran into him on the street and asked him purposely: "Why don't you give me a bite?" And do you know what he said? "You can't tell by eating." Those thieving rats! In the entire village there was no one worse than them, the scoundrels, and now they're being smart-arses here!'

Gogi grafted away at a number of building sites and occasionally came into possession of some money. In rare moments of generosity he took me with him to Wicky. Here he would buy me a mineral water, a cup of coffee or a small glass of Coke. Sometimes we shared a beer. Igor, who blinked as unpredictably as always, came with us sometimes. He predictably returned to his inexhaustible topic, in which members of the opposite sex played a leading role. Then he travelled back to the front without saying when he would be on leave again.

Gogi and I met Zlaja and Fric at Wicky. Gogi needed a light, and soon the two of them sat at our table smoking

Gogi's fags. I knew who they were beforehand; everyone in Majbule knew that.

Zlajo, or Zlatko, as his parents christened him, hung out with some pop boys from Majbule, guys who drove mopeds and chased girls. Then they started to avoid him. He had allegedly felt up one of the guy's younger sisters and fallen out with him. Then he began to hang out with Fric, someone the pop boys already avoided. Not because his parents were from Kosovo, but because he was considered Majbule's greatest and only death metal fan. His real name was Hamid, and how he came by the nickname Fric, even he was no longer able to explain. His hair was black as tar. His genes did not exactly have Germanic origins.

Gogi called them both 'goat-fuckers,' because they were locals, and called me 'neighbour' because we lived on the same floor. I think Gogi made contact with those two for the same reason as he made contact with me. He was curious. Fric's black T-shirts with monsters and skulls on them, Zlaja's torn jeans and my curly mop must have made an impression on him.

Our evenings in Wicky always began in the same way. We sat down at a table and emptied our pockets. Counted up the change, added them together and discussed the possibilities. A small Coke, a cup of coffee or a mineral water? Maybe a local beer for each of us this time?

Gogi called the waitress over. He plonked a handful of coins into her palm. She snorted in obvious irritation – oh, not again! – and spread the coins out on the table.

'No need to count,' Gogi used to say nonchalantly. 'It's the exact amount. Exactly!'

Then she received one of his legendary smiles. Nobody I knew had such a broad and provocative smile as Gogi.

She brought us our order, thus giving us permission to occupy the table for the rest of the evening, listen to their terrible music and look around: would just one girl come in? Would something happen soon?

As a rule, nothing did.

Zlaja was one year older than me. He played the acoustic guitar and taught me 'Knockin' on Heaven's Door' so I could also tell the girls that I 'played the guitar.'

According to Fric, Zlaja was good with the girls. He had a nice face, tanned skin and long, dark hair. He spoke Italian. In addition he occasionally drove his father's corpse of a Yugo, which in this context was not a bad thing. Several times it had actually turned out that chicks 'could certainly be content' with the three things that, 'in spite of everything,' Zlaja owned, Fric told us: good looks, a propensity for spiritual values – guitar, ergo music, ergo art – and last but not least an eye for material possessions – Yugo, ergo technology, ergo comfort. The only thing Zlaja did not have was a driving license. He had still not turned eighteen.

Fric turned twenty that winter and kept saying that it was time for him to be more serious. That was why he later cut his elbow-length hair so short that he could barely manage a ponytail. He described it to us in detail, how three female hairdressers cried as they tried to talk him out of such a drastic step. He had, to the rest of us, some rather strange and unfathomable ideas about life. He claimed that coffee gave energy, and that for that reason athletes drank a lot of coffee. He was the only one I knew who was able to say the phrase 'imagine this' more than a hundred times a day.

'Hey, imagine this, we're old. The year is 2044. Zlaja is still driving his Yugo, the wheels are falling off. Zlaja looks good for his age. His hair is grey, but still long, you know. And then what happens? Then I come by. Me and my band. We are playing in Vešnja. At the stadium. Big concert; I'm working my magic on the drums. They call me the new Dave Lombardo. The concert ends, I hurry to Majbule. There, the three of you are sitting in the car. The Yugo is rocking: loud bass, death metal. Zlaja behind the wheel, Gogi and you in the back, old men, both with beards down to your dicks. And then what? Where do we go? To Wicky, of course. Grab a bottle of … gin … or wine, for example. And then the ladies flock to us. Hey, imagine this, Zlaja! Zlaja with a beard!'

'Look here, Fricko,' Gogi began in a pedagogical tone. 'For one thing: you don't have a band. Second: Zlaja's Yugo will barely make it to next summer. Thirdly: thankfully very few people listen to death metal. Even today! Not to mention what it would be like in fifty years. And at a stadium!'

Fric criticised Gogi's lack of imagination and referred to some serious books and articles he had read in the paper. About how everything 'only existed in our heads,' and how everything around us, including people and animals, was merely 'an illusion' that is born and dies with us.

Two parts of Fric's illusion – Gogi and I – could not agree whether there was something to that or not. I referred to various programmes on HTV, which persuasively claimed that reincarnation was possible. I thought that life after this one was worth hoping for. Especially when it was impossible to turn back the clock and live the old life again.

Gogi was not buying it.

He took a small spray can out of his pocket, kicked off his shoes and sprayed his sweat-plagued toes.

With no warning whatsoever.

JELENA

We rode in Zlaja's Yugo and emptied a bottle of homemade red wine. The music thundered away. Fric was disgruntled. He complained about the smell of Gogi's toes and rolled the window down. Zlaja fast-forwarded and rewound Obituary and imitated the morbid tunes. He kept saying:

'This really swings!'

Gogi moaned:

'I don't get how you two can listen to this. Honestly. I like happy music. Something popular. Or something you can relax to. And this guy, hell … He shouts like a zombie!'

Fric tried in vain to open Gogi up to the qualities of the drummer. He translated individual lines of the lyrics and recurring words like blood, hell, war, desperation and destruction.

'Their album name, Gogi. Do you know what it means?'

'No, and I couldn't care less.'

'Slowly we rot.'

'Speak for yourself, Fricko! I'm in top form.'

'Ha! Ha! Yeah! We can smell that.'

'Ha! Ha! Ha!'

'Cheers!'

'Cheers!'

At Ukulele they played *Master of Puppets*. I could hear the first slow solo while we stood in the queue, and the second fast one as we crossed the terrace. The place was teeming. Inside, on the dance floor, some twenty or thirty people were head-banging away. Zlaja and I moved to the edge of the dance floor and stepped into character.

We were so cool. We did not go full throttle. We observed the other people and nodded to one another.

But something was missing. Something in our hands. Something you could take a sip of. We only had enough for the entrance fee.

'Hey!' I shouted to the guy next to me. 'Can I have a sip?'

'What?'

He could not hear a thing.

'A sip! A sip of your beer!'

'It's empty,' he said and held the bottle up to the light.

'Why are you still holding it then?'

He shrugged and looked away. He did not put it down.

Gogi started to complain that the place was not for him. Saying we should go home soon. They had just started to play loads of hits: 'Everything's Ruined' by Faith No More, 'Bombtrack' and 'Killing in the Name' by Rage Against the Machine. It was one massive party. Fric was totally buzzing. He was head-banging in the middle of the dance floor with his hair over his face holding an air guitar at head height.

'Not now, man! We just got here.'

'We have to celebrate, Gogi! This is wild!'

A bunch of requests came next. 'London Calling' by The Clash, 'Pet Sematary' by the Ramones. Plus a few I did not recognise. Fric's request – Obituary – was rejected out of hand by the DJ.

The switch to a more melodic repertoire drew a bunch of chicks out onto the dance floor. Zlaja and I stepped forward. We pressed up as close to them as possible. Got their long, freshly washed hair in our tough, wicked faces.

'That's alright,' we said in response to their apologies.

Their hair smelled nice. We said as much, asking them what shampoo they each used.

One answered: 'Coconut,' the second: 'Apple' and the third – 'I don't actually know.'

That was how I met her. She stood smiling with her palms in the air:

'No name shampoo.'

Just then the song ended and she had to go home.

Weeks later the camp was paid a visit by a circus caravan. A colourful box van and two cars were parked in front of the restaurant. A group of grown-ups and an infernal mass of children jumped out. Refugee children from a camp in Vešnja, a former YPA barracks. A group of Italian volunteers who lived in their camp, had taught them some tricks and took part in the performance. The caravan had already visited several camps in the area.

The performance was held in the corner of the restaurant in front of twenty onlookers, among them me and Zlaja. The children walked on stilts and rode unicycles. The stilt walkers had to climb off and on the stilts a couple of times, while one of the cyclists – a spotty boy of twelve or thirteen – crashed into a radiator and nearly flew out the window.

We laughed and clapped, clapped and laughed – in the right places too.

Our host for the evening was a girl dressed in black with chestnut brown hair down to her belly, wearing a top hat. Her face was covered in white paint, and it was only halfway through the show that I recognised her. It was her, the one who had answered 'I don't actually know,' that night at Ukulele. The night Zlaja and I ruled the dance floor.

Was she a refugee too? Bosnian, maybe? I had investigate at once.

'Do you recognise that girl over there?' I asked Zlaja. 'No name shampoo.'

'Yes. But she's not my type.'

'I wasn't offering, either. I've got to get her number.'

'Ohhh!'

'We'll hang out by their van afterwards. Okay?'

'Okay. Should I grab my guitar?'

While the participating circus artists loaded their junk into the vans, she spotted the guitar and recognised us. Zlaja called her over. He started to entertain the Italians in their mother tongue, while I plucked the strings and said clever things.

Then I boldly got to the point:

'What should I play for you, Jelena?'

'What can you play?'

The picks were too damn soft. My intro to 'One' was unrecognisable. I made loads of mistakes, also on 'Knockin' on Heaven's Door.' I was super nervous and had a hard time with C major anyway. My fingers always cramped up when I made that stupid chord. But she said, 'Cool!' when I was finished and gave me her telephone number.

'I'll call you one of these days!' I promised when the caravan drove off, accompanied by a series of hideous, loud honks.

'One of these days' was the following day.

SCISSORS

Dad was telling me something very important. His story was contending with Jelena for my headspace. He had received his salary from the vineyard, he told me. On the way back to Majbule, as was the custom, the bus had stopped at a pub. It reeked of an arrangement between the bus driver and the owner of the pub, because it happened every time they got paid. He had made toasts and drank and got rather tipsy.

Back on the bus, he and his boss, Mišo, sat on the back seat singing, 'By the thin shadirvan, where the running water trickles.' An old Bosnian *Sevdalinka*, a traditional song about unrequited love. Mišo was from Vešnja, but had done his military service in our hometown. He and Dad got on well together.

Sitting in the middle of the bus was a group of Croatians from central Bosnia, the ones who had spat at Dad before. One in particular, called Blonde, he had it in for Dad. He would not accept Dad's baskets when he delivered them to the lorry.

Now they all sat in the bus, drunk and overtired. Dad and Mišo continued singing loudly. I could picture Dad stretching out the song's elastic vocals. He was actually a pretty good singer, even when he was drunk.

'STOP THAT CRAPPY MUSLIM SONG!' Blonde bellowed from the middle of the bus.

He was up on his feet, staggering down the aisle. Holding a pair of scissors in his right hand, Dad said.

Silence on the bus. The singing stopped. The bus kept driving; hands slipped inside bags, rustling in chorus. Hands reaching for their own pair of scissors.

'STOP THAT SHIT!' Blonde shouted. 'I don't wanna listen to all that Muslim –'

'YOU STOP IT!' Mišo interrupted him. 'I myself am Croatian, and this is no Muslim song! It's my wife's favourite song! Now go back to your seat! Otherwise I'll have you fired!'

Blonde stopped short, like a boxer who had just taken a shot to the chin but had not realised it yet. His intoxicated head swung a little to one side and then to the other, before Mišo's straightforwards words registered. He muttered something and went back to his seat. Mišo nudged Dad and said:

'Let's take it from the top!'

Dad was buzzing as he described how Mišo handled the matter. He kept tossing around superlatives.

'A great man!' he praised Mišo. 'Truly great!'

'But I don't understand why you don't feel like taking off?' I asked him. 'Just disappear, get far away?'

He waved his hands predictably:

'To Sweden? You and your Sweden!'

'Yes. Away from all the fascists and their scissors. Them and their fucking hate.'

'They already drove me out once!' he said, raising his index finger as if 'they' lived upstairs. 'That's more than enough. I'm not going anywhere. Back to my own people, that's it. I don't give a damn about Germany and Sweden and the West. Bloody capitalists! I just want what's mine. Nothing more. Them and their humanitarian … their … hum … tinned food, dammit!'

'Fine, fine, but what about me? Can I travel by myself since you can't be bothered?'

'When you're eighteen, you can live wherever you want. And wherever you can! The door is open.'

Mum had just entered the room and had heard the end of our conversation. She said:

'What are you babbling about? Are you drunk?'

'No. Why?' Dad said, and wrinkled his forehead in surprise. 'It's perfectly normal. The boy has to learn to stand on his own two feet. Myself, I was not kept on a tight rein. At his age I was …'

I thought about Jelena.

Jelena, Jelena, Jelena …

The most beautiful name in existence.

BELVEDERE REVISITED

I waited for her at the corner of the playground, besieged by the envious looks of her classmates. I was two years older than them, and the sun was shining on me. She was mine. They could just watch. Get turned on by her during the boring lessons. Dream they were walking in my shoes. In my super cool All Stars.

Dream on, guys, I thought, and just remember to blow your snotty noses! Look here, schoolboys!

She came to me with a smile on her lips and the taste of menthol on her tongue. She was a little shy. I removed a lock of hair from her forehead and gave her a proper, seemingly endless kiss. That will teach them, the brats!

We turned on our heels and slowly walked away. She was wearing a pair of tight black jeans, a white Nirvana T-shirt and a long-sleeved top underneath. She had a schoolbag with the words, WE DON'T NEED NO EDUCATION; a rebellious vocabulary and a heartfelt aversion for the terms system, government and nation.

Naturally I spoke against these terms, reasoned on the basis of sixteen years of life experience and scored cheap points in her clear almond eyes.

A few days earlier, at his home in faraway Seattle, Kurt Cobain had been found dead. Really, really dead. He had written a suicide note, loaded a sawed-off shotgun and pulled the trigger. All of a sudden the streets of Vešnja were teeming with all kinds of Nirvana T-shirts. Some wearing them. Others selling them.

We walked past Ukulele and along the boulevard. Away from the centre and towards the sea. We approached her 'home.'

'I'm just going to chuck my bag in,' she said. 'Come in.'

I was not keen on meeting her mum, but she told me her mum was not home. We went in through the gate, across the echoing courtyard and into one of the three buildings of the barracks.

The floor where she and her mother shared a room with another family was damp and dim. The walls were sooty and they were sweating. A young woman was cleaning underwear in two wash boilers on a stove at the end of the corridor. From inside the various rooms all kinds of noises were heard: the wailing of the radio, laughter, a quarrel. At any rate, I heard, 'you whore!' shouted several times.

I waited in the corridor. Two children with holes in their socks, a boy and a girl, ran around kicking a tennis ball. When she came out, they pointed at us, teased us and laughed.

'Let's beat it,' she said.

'Yes, let's.'

As soon as we came outside in the light, I forgot all about the children and the sooty walls. The steam from the simmering boilers, I forgot about that in particular. She laced her fingers into mine, and we swung our arms in a large V. Her hair fell over her shoulders. It covered part of Cobain's confused face. A bit of wind whistled through her hair.

It was windy out by the water too. A group of grungers sat around an extinguished fire plucking at their guitars. The grey sea stirred behind them. They sang: 'Something in the way, mmm … mmm … Something in the way, yeah …' We waved at them and continued.

One kilometre.

One and a half.

Two.

We found a solitary place and lay down.

The warm surface of the cliffs beneath us. A leaden sky above. An entire afternoon in front of us. Maybe more. Maybe the rest of our lives, who knew?

She said something about death amongst idols at the age

of twenty-seven. Then something about death in general. I lay on my side and leaned on my left elbow. With my right hand I caressed her cheek, her shoulder, her arm and thigh.

Then I kissed her on the lips and glanced across the open sea in front of us. From the high cliff we lay on, the turbulent blankets of the sea could be seen melting into the heavy sky on the horizon. It was perfectly still. Only the gentle sound of the waves striking the cliff, a whistling in the treetops up by the road and our steady breathing could be heard.

A minute passed.

Two. Three. Four.

Jelena, it was on the tip of my tongue, I will never forget this day. This sky, this sea.

But I didn't say that. I said nothing. For over half an hour I did not say a single word.

Neither did she.

MAURO DEAL

On the way back we said at most five sentences each. Jelena looked at me as if I had just stepped down from a stage.

The girl is lost in me, I thought as we walked down the boulevard. What did I do right? Is this really happening to me?

We kissed for a long time by the gate to the barracks. Then I took a city bus into the centre, where I had to get off.

My body was quite relaxed, almost dozy from the wind, Jelena's kisses and the rolling sea, which had flickered in front of us for hours. My left thigh felt moist and cold. By all accounts, I had released a drop or two.

At one point I discreetly pulled my T-shirt down over my groin with a sigh. I was surprised there could even be such banal activity down there during such a sublime, romantic moment. On the bus, it was not only the liquid's cool moisture on my skin that I noticed, I could also see the extent of it. The moisture had soaked through the denim and was clearly visible on my heavy outfit.

I was wondering if the guy sitting next to me could see the stain, when Mauro suddenly came rocking through the bus.

'Hey, Miki!'

'Hey, Mauro! What's up, what have you got there?'

'This,' he said and placed a brown guitar case on the seat in front of me, 'is my new sweetheart.'

'What is it?'

'Gibson copy. From 1970, man! One of a kind.'

'Wow, it must have cost a fortune?'

'Not really, but it sure wasn't cheap.'

'Can I have a look?'

'Wait till we get outside.'

'Fair enough. Where are you getting off?'

Mauro was Fabio's big brother. He had once played in a punk rock band. The band was called Shelter and during its brief lifespan had managed to perform two concerts, until the bass player and drummer were called up. Mauro and the lead singer were left with no rhythm section and decided to break the band up.

He joined another band later, one that played something a lá Pantera, just not as well. Oblivion, they called themselves. The lead singer was completely mental. During Mauro's solos he cut himself on the chest with a razor blade. One night he cut one of his nipples, screamed like a pig, blood everywhere. The concert was stopped. A local newspaper made a brief report of the incident, using the doctor's report as a source. It was the peak of their fame, because Mauro left the band the next day. He mentioned the term masochist when talking about the singer, which it turned out did not have anything to do with the Serbo-croat verb *maziti*, to stroke, which Fabio and I had assumed.

Now Mauro was 'ready again,' keeping busy with 'laying the groundwork for a new band,' as he put it. He had just been to the rehearsal room with some guys, and it had gone 'swimmingly.'

'We're still trying a few different combinations,' he said when he got off the bus. 'Now you get to see how beautiful she is, my sweetheart. Check it out!'

He opened the leather case beneath a plane tree by the bus stop. I immediately praised the guitar's design.

'What does that say? Galson?'

'Yeah! Gibson, Galson. Almost the same, right?'

'Yeah, who cares! It looks like the one Slash plays in the "Sweet Child O'Mine" video.'

'Exactly! Except this is a Galson instead of a Gibson. Maybe I'll cover it with a sticker.'

'Fuck that,' I said. 'I don't know anyone who has a genuine Gibson. Actually, I don't know anyone who has an electric guitar!'

'You mean you *didn't* know anyone. Until now!'

'Yeah, until now, man! Thanks!'

'How are you coming along with the lyrics?'

I knew that would come. He had been asking me that question for months. He was good at putting chords together and composing songs, but his English was not great. Fabio had told him about my famous report on *The Goldsmith's Treasure*, and how I knew loads of lyrics by heart. For that reason, Mauro invested a lot of hope in my writing abilities. I was hesitant, even though I was flattered.

'Why don't you just write a first draft?' he asked and closed the case. 'I'm tired of playing covers all the time, man. It's a drag.'

'Alright,' I said. 'If you can get me the lyrics for "Dead Embryonic Cells" by Sepultura and "The Clairvoyant" by Maiden, then I'll look into it. Those two songs have some wicked lyrics.'

'Deal! Anything else?'

'I heard you've got all sorts of tapes.'

'Yes, and records and CDs,' Mauro added with considerable pride. 'Biggest collection in the city.'

'I want to borrow ten original albums!'

'Tapes or records?'

'Tapes, of course. You choose.'

'Cool! Drop by one of these days. Then we'll look into it.'

We said goodbye and I took the next bus to Majbule. An ugly surprise awaited me there.

COVER

'Police!' Mum said. 'They're on the ground floor.'

'Now? At night?'

'I'm pretty sure it's them. Emir, get up! Straighten the duvet a little! Look at this place!'

'Where are our papers?' Dad shouted. 'Where are our cards? Did you get them extended?'

'Yes, I did.'

We had to get our refugee cards extended every three months. That was done at the refugee office in Vešnja, where they were stamped with a new date and a signature in the field, 'Valid until.' I had been there the previous day.

'Then where are they?' Dad was stressed. 'Where did you put them?'

'Aren't they in the drawer?'

'Which drawer?'

'By the bedside table. Where else?'

'There's nothing in here!'

'Not in the cupboard either?' Mum asked.

Then it hit me. I knew exactly where they were. Exactly. I opened my shoebox and looked for a particular tape. It was not there.

'Shit! I gave them to Kaća!'

'What?'

'I forgot them … She borrowed … It doesn't matter. I'll go grab them.'

'Hurry! They'll be here in a bit.'

I slipped on my shoes and raced out the door. They were still warm. I had just taken them off and hopped into bed when Mum shouted from the balcony. I had a hard-on. Lying on your stomach, it does not take much. I was also still wondering about the stain. It confused me, that I had zero interest in doing it with Jelena. That I did not look at her that way, while at the same time, 'my organ for peace and harmony,' as Zlaja referred to his manhood, was raring to go.

Does it have a life of its own? Are love and sex two different things? Or am I just strange?

I never got an answer for that. Was interrupted by the word, *police*. I did up my laces and went into the corridor. Kaća and her mum had moved to D2, a room with a balcony. I raced down the stairs but was forced to slow down again. Near the entrance to D1 there was a guy wearing a denim jacket and black pointed shoes.

Do the police always wear denim when they're in civilian clothing? I wondered. Don't they have any other clothes?

'Where are you going?' he asked when I got closer, out of breath.

'Over to D2.'

'No you're not! We're checking IDs,' he nodded down the corridor of the ground floor, where a couple of doors were open. 'Where do you live?'

'Up on the second floor. That's why I have to go to D2. Our cards are over there.'

He did not seem to understand so I had to repeat myself. He looked exactly like Danny DeVito, only younger. His face was actually quite sympathetic.

'I just extended our cards,' I said, 'but they're over at my friend's place. I have to run over and grab them.'

On the other side of the terrace, near the entrance to D2, one of his colleagues appeared.

'What does he want?' he shouted.

'He wants to come over to your side!'

'Fine!'

I hurried across the terrace.

'What do you want?'

I explained everything once again. This time less convincingly. The guy was suspicious. Luckily Kaća's mum appeared at the entrance holding a shopping bag in each hand.

'Is Kaća upstairs?'

'Yes, why? What's happened?'

'I forgot our cards inside a cassette cover. Kaća borrowed three tapes from me yesterday. Our cards are in one of them.'

'Umm ... okay?'

'I had them extended yesterday and put them inside the cover. If you put them in your pocket, they curl up. I was wearing these tight trousers. Kaća borrowed ...'

And so on, until finally they understood and we were allowed to go upstairs.

'I haven't listened to them yet,' Kaća said. 'You can't have them.'

'Quit joking. Are the cards there?'

'I don't know ... Yes, here! In the Carcass cassette. *Heartwork*, is it good?'

'To hell with Carcass! I have to fly! They're probably waiting at our place by now!'

They were. The door was open. A couple of metres away I saw the back of a well-built man with close-cropped hair. Both our drawers were lying on the bed, and Dad stood there mumbling something incomprehensible. One of the policeman shouted 'Shut your mouth!' and Dad did as instructed.

'Where's the boy?' the man asked Mum. 'When's he coming?'

'I'm here!' I said before she had time to reply. 'The cards are here.'

The other man – the one not shouting, standing closer to the door – turned around and took the three yellow cards.

Dad looked away and sat on the bed. Mum remained standing with her arms crossed, staring directly at the floor.

'Fine,' they said and left.

I took off my shoes and lay down on the bed.

Right! So how am I going to avoid that bloody stain next time?

ISRAEL

Following the raid, Dad was afflicted by what Mum would later call 'Dad's Israeli madness'. He had no idea why there were still raids taking place. Three weeks earlier the presidents of Bosnia and Croatia, Alija Izetbegović and Franjo Tudjman, had signed a ceasefire and confederation agreement. Even though Mum and Dad did not know exactly what kind of confederation it was, the three of us understood it as a clear step forward, because the newspapers, radio and TV all used that phrase when they discussed the two gentleman's signatures and feeble handshakes.

Following the second unannounced visit by the men in denim jackets, it became clear that the so-called step forward could easily become a more or less unnoticed step in an unknown direction for me and Dad. We had heard stories of raids in Savudrija and Varaždin. At the camp in Varaždin the men shot themselves in the foot – literally – to avoid being sent to the front. In Savudrija the police loaded a group of men onto a bus and drove them to Hercegovina. A CDC officer refused to accept them. They slept overnight on the floor of a primary school and the next morning were driven to the other side of the border. A number of them did not have any money on them, so they had to hitchhike hundreds of kilometres back to their camp.

These rumours, as well as the second visit by the police, gave Dad a temporary, but fierce bout of paranoia. He woke up several times a night, walked back and forth in the room and repeated:

'They're looking for something, something in particular! Why would they want to hurt us now? There's no reason for it. All our documents are in order.'

'Fine, then why don't you lie down and go to sleep!'

Mum said. 'At least let the rest of us sleep. We can't get a wink of sleep when you're walking around talking to yourself all the time.'

Then one day he returned from the Red Cross with an ugly windcheater that did not fit any of us, along with some news: he had added all of our names to a list. We were going to Israel!

'What?'

'We are going to Israel. They are taking two hundred people, only two hundred, Bosnian refugees. If all goes well, we leave in two weeks! By plane.'

You could hear a pin drop. Mum put down her romance novel and looked at me.

I looked at Dad. What was going on with him? It was as though some random person had accidentally mixed up our rooms and just barged in.

'Dad, are you okay?'

Of course he was. He had just been thinking that maybe I had been right. Maybe we should go somewhere after all. Just for a while, maybe. We should find out if there was a right to withdraw or something. This will not do any more. You cannot just stand here, putting up with …

'Then you'll be going without me!' Mum said and I hurried to add:

'Same here.'

'Why? Wasn't that what you wanted?'

I was just about to mention Jelena or Neno, but changed my mind.

'I don't want to travel to a country that has been at war for fifty years, when we've only been at war for two! It makes absolutely no sense.'

'It is a big country,' he assured me. 'I cannot imagine there is war everywhere. And they would not send us to war zone, would they?'

'Sweden hasn't been at war since 1814!'

'Is that so,' Dad said and raised his eyebrows. 'Who told you that?'

'Amar.'

This was not about Israel. No matter how many times he repeated that he would leave on his own, write to us and send us money, if we did not want to go with him, both Mum and I were well aware that it was just a supposition. An abortive but necessary diversion from something else. Of course he would never leave us. Especially not now, with Neno's situation still up in the air. He just needed to imagine himself far away from building D1, room 210, where any Tom, Dick and Harry could knock on your door and say 'ID check' and besmirch you. Israel was his Sweden during those days. That was it.

He really had put us on a list and later received confirmation that everything was arranged. That there was room on a plane from Zagreb on Monday at 18.25. But the closer it got to the Monday in question, the less he talked about the journey to the Middle East.

In the end it went just as Mum predicted: he called the office and cancelled the trip. For a number of trying days he sulked around and barely slept. Then he went back down to the Muscle Market and never spoke about the trip to Israel again. It was as though the country had never existed for him.

SCRATCHES AND FLIP-FLOPS

Mum grew calmer but no less concerned. She said she would happily leave now were it not for 'the stuff with Neno.' Even though we had done everything we could to find him, she did not think we could leave the country without him. If a new opportunity arose to do something, or if news about him arrived, she preferred to be nearby and not in some distant, foreign land.

As for me, I was on an entirely different planet. The police visits, like the wailing radio reports about meetings of politicians in Bonn and Brussels, were just noise – background noise, which grew closer – but nothing more. In the foreground I had Jelena and our frequent after-school meetings. I was unable to write the lyrics for Mauro's song, I was unable to do my homework, on the whole, I was unable to do anything but think about her.

One day after receiving a phone call from her and agreeing to meet in Vešnja after school, I went down to the beach below D3. I sat down on a bench and scratched my name into the wood. Gogi must have forgotten his flick knife there. His name was freshly etched into the backrest.

The bench looked ludicrous. There was barely room for more names, and the middle board of the seat was missing. You had to sit on the two outer boards, with your arse bulging towards the ground.

I fiddled with the knife, felt a light breeze in my hair and enjoyed the feeling that everything was going to be all right. Fuck Sweden. I was not going anywhere. I had Jelena, Kaća, Fric, Zlaja, Gogi and Fabio. I had my nights at Ukulele and my red Sanyo cassette recorder.

What do I care about you, Sweden, I thought. You're so far away. What do I care about your music libraries, I can't even get a membership card! What am I going to do with my knowledge of your cities, your climate and your history, I was never going to be able to cross your distant border anyway! And all the parties in the vicinity of Stockholm. What do I care about them! I was not invited.

Then he arrived – Pero's cousin, who had just moved into the camp. A thickset, broad-legged musclehead with a crooked neck, which meant that he always looked a little to the side when he addressed you. It was like he was talking to a parrot on your shoulder.

'WHAT THE HELL ARE YOU DOING?' he shouted from the path.

'Not much. What are you doing?' I shouted a little too boldly back to him.

I did not know him at the time; it was our first encounter. Otherwise I would not have been *that* bold. But I was in a really good mood and could not hide it.

He left the path and flip-flopped quickly towards me:

'WHO GAVE YOU PERMISSION TO SCRATCH YOUR NAME IN THAT BENCH?'

'No-one.'

'DO YOU REALISE THAT IS STATE PROPERTY?'

'No.'

'SO NOW YOU KNOW! DON'T SCRATCH YOUR SHITTY NAME ON THE BENCH!'

'But … there are loads of scratches … names …'

'WHAT'S THAT GOT TO DO WITH YOU! IF I SEE YOU DO THAT ONE MORE TIME, YOUR MUM IS GOING TO PAY! YOU FOLLOW?'

The gate to the nuthouse must have been left wide open last night, I thought. Who the hell let this madman out? I see him for the first time in my life, and here he is, shouting at me like we've known each other for years. What's wrong with him?

Later he turned out not only to be Pero's cousin, but also a family man, and the future night watchman at reception. Bruno was his name. The madman was going to look after us while we lay asleep.

'YOU FOLLOW?'

'Yeah, yeah.'

I did not complain to Dad. I did not complain to anyone. I was not even humiliated. I put the flick knife down and said, 'Sorry. It won't happen again,' and thought: You can't touch me, you moron. I'm seeing Jelena tomorrow. We're going to hang out in the park, on the beach, or up by the citadel, not talk for hours and enjoy the silence. You and the other psychos at this camp will not be there. I won't spare you a single thought. I'll barely spare a thought for Neno. So just keep shouting, you idiot, it's like water off a duck's back!

JELENA LEAVES

She told me over the phone. The booth went quiet and it remained silent for a long time. I could not manage a single word.

Only later, lost in a diffuse monologue, I said:

'Those bloody fascists! Those grey-haired presidents. Why didn't they play war back when they were sixteen?'

'Yes,' she said. 'You're right. But imagine: if there hadn't been war, the two of us would never have met.'

I was already feeling lonely. Who was going to impress me by saying things like that from now on? 'If there hadn't been war, the two of us would never have met.'

'Jelena, you're pretty clever,' I said. 'It's no wonder you met me.'

She let out a fake laugh.

Pero knocked: 'Are you almost finished, you little faggot!'

'You should have told me you were applying for a visa,' I said.

'We didn't think we'd get one. Who's that knocking?'

'Some bumpkin. I'll pound him later. Keep going!'

'I didn't want to scare you off. That's why.'

'Yeah, I know. But still … It's just …'

The moron knocked again. This time louder.

'Is that him again?'

'Yeah, I'm going to have to go. See you tomorrow?'

'Yeah. Same place?'

'Great.'

'Then we can talk things through, if you like.'

'Nah, I don't think it will help,' I said.

'Okay, or we could just leave it. And do what we normally do.'

'That's probably a better idea.'

She travelled to the USA before the school year ended. Our relationship did not even last one and a half months. The spontaneous periods of silence, which taught me to shut out the rest of the world and think of nothing at all, they came to an end. Even as we walked through the city silently for hours, the air was heavy with the knowledge of a certain date in the calendar – the day Jelena would board a plane that would take her out of the country, while I would stand on the pier and stare at the clear, calm water – gloomy and dark inside like Peter Steel vocals that Type O Negative played late into the night.

The old feeling of being unlucky and cursed returned with a vengeance. Of course she's leaving, I thought. Everyone I care about leaves. Everyone that means something to me, in some way dies. How could I forget that?

Our final hours were spent in Parkolio, the famous park in Vešnja that had a nine hundred-year-old olive tree in the middle. I had bunked off school. Jelena gave me the hand-written lyrics to 'Fade to Black' and I gave her a mixed tape with the best of *Powerslave* and *Piece of Mind*. It was my last desperate attempt to change her opinion of Iron Maiden.

'Take care of yourself,' she said down by the bus stop.

'You too,' I replied. 'Say hi to America.'

I kissed her gently on the cheek and got on the bus. With her tear resting on my bottom lip.

The back of the bus stunk of aftershave and farts. I tried to cry but couldn't. My sorrow had withered up inside me.

Through the grimy rear window I saw her for the last time. She stood in her unbuttoned red lumberjack shirt waving at me. Her hair was in a long plait.

She was crying.

For a brief moment it was as though I was the one leaving, and she was staying. But then the bus turned at the first set of lights and continued on its usual course to Majbule.

LIFE SHOULD BE LIVED

Jelena, Jelena, Jelena …

How's it going – on the other side of the globe?

Is there liberty – *And Justice for All* – where you live? Or is it all just one big sham?

Send me more lyrics. Send me a song or two.

Her first letter had a sad ring to it. I tried to reply in a brighter tone, describe the past few weeks to her on one hand, and on the other hand keep my bitterness at bay. I was not particularly successful. I could not string two positive words together in the same sentence. I had to crumple up page after page and chuck them in the bin.

At the entrance to D1, I saw Kaća hurrying towards reception.

'Do you fancy going for a walk?' I asked.

'Can't. I'm going into town.'

She had found a boyfriend in Vešnja. He was in his first year of secondary school and a fan of Ice Cube. A rapper with baggy trousers!

'Oooh, Kaća! Are you going to change your style soon?' I teased her.

She scampered off when she heard the bus coming, and I decided to go for a walk to the end of the peninsula.

It had been raining. The air smelt of wet asphalt and seaweed. Sitting at the far table in front of the restaurant, I saw Gogi smoking a fag. He flicked the butt away with his middle finger and looked up as he heard me kick a dry pine cone. He had a long face.

'What's up, Gogi?' I shouted. 'What's happening, man? Are you ever going to get some, or what?'

'Haven't you heard?'

'Heard what?'

'Bad news, neighbour. Bad news.'

He lit another cigarette and put the lighter in his breast pocket. He blew some smoke through his nose and told me that he had just got back from Vešnja.

'Yeah, and?'

He was hitchhiking and got a lift from Ivan from D2. The guy who shagged shamelessly. Ivan was all cut up. He could barely drive while he told Gogi that Igor – good old Igor – was dead. He had stepped on a landmine somewhere near Vinkovci and died instantly.

Gogi shook his head, swore and repeated that he didn't get it. I pictured Igor walking towards us.

Bare feet, tight black Speedos.

He burped:

'Do you want to go out to the end of the peninsula? … Yes. The peninsula. How's your English?'

Gogi stubbed out the cigarette and lit another. We sat there, confirming to each other how shitty it was. That of all people, Igor had not deserved it.

Then we went for a walk along the peninsula, and I told him about the German girl and Igor's legendary words 'What do I know, maybe she'll get upset.' Gogi believed that Igor had died a virgin. That was why he talked about women so much.

I did not agree. I remembered a slightly mad brunette who stayed in Igor's room for a few days. She was from Split, looked like a squirrel and had run away from home. Igor had picked her up somewhere in Vešnja and hidden her in the camp, until someone blabbed and the police showed up and took her away.

I also told him about the Christmas Eve where Igor pounded his fist on the table and said, 'YES! BUT LIFE SHOULD BE *LIVED*! NOT FUCKED UP!' I described our first trip to Wicky, the man with the goats and the newly erected fence – the bodybuilder whose wife Igor had tried to chat up. I went on and on for as long as I could. Was afraid

I would bawl my eyes out if I stopped.

But when I finally stopped, nothing happened. We just sat on the flat roof of the bunker and looked out at the horizon. Gogi lit his last fag and threw the pack into the water.

'Yeah,' he said. 'Igor was a fine fellow. Dumb as a doorknob, but fine.'

'Dumb? He wasn't that dumb.'

'Going to war for money, that's dumb. Getting killed during a ceasefire – even dumber.'

'Don't talk about him like that!' I said. 'Jesus, Gogi! What's going on with you? I thought you were upset.'

'You don't know shit, Miki. You don't know what that idiot did.'

'What did he do?'

Gogi looked at me in his characteristic manner: provocative, a trace of irony.

'He ran after a pig.'

'A pig?'

'Yeah, he ran after a pig. He was drunk.'

'Drunk?'

'Yes! Him and the pig were blown into the air. Don't tell anyone.'

'Bullshit!' I said and waved my hand. 'That makes no sense. What would he do with a pig?'

'I don't know. Eat it? Fuck it? How should I know?'

'Shut up! You're full of shit, man! I don't believe a word you say!'

'Fine. Let's leave it at that then. I'm full of shit. He stepped on a mine. On patrol! Forget all about the fucking pig!'

PARANOIA

Gogi never mentioned the pig again. We never talked about Igor again either, the two of us. A death notice with a photo, date and everything was posted on the window in reception for a while: 'It is with great sorrow and pain we announce that …' Later it was removed.

Igor was gone. He had left the stage in May that year, and nothing on earth could bring him back. Not even my frequent dreams, where I saw him on the terrace between D1 and D2 – with no legs, in a wheelchair, disabled, but despite everything, alive.

I would get really scared when I woke up in the morning. Not like normal, scared of something specific, more scared that something unexpected would happen. I thought about war, Neno and God. Would there be more? Would more people die? Were we just some small figures at the end of some thin threads, with some *Master of Puppets* tugging on them? There were plenty of facts that testified to that. Was it a coincidence that I was on my way out to the end of the peninsula when I ran into Gogi that day? The first time I met Igor, he asked me to go out there with him. To top it all off, it happened in the exact place where Gogi gave me the bad news.

Even more chilling was the fact that Igor stepped on a mine. That completely knocked me flat. It was one thing that he always talked about evading the bullets, never hinting at the danger of being hit from below. It was another thing altogether, that for a long time I had connected Igor with the story about Dad's cousin, Zijo, who had walked through a minefield. I never forgot Igor's expression when I told him the story. When I asked him the odds of something like that happening, Igor said:

248

'It depends on the minefield. Obviously there was something wrong with that one. The ones we make, nobody makes it through!'

His haughty expression and that final comment, I could not get them out of my thoughts. The peninsula, the place in front of the restaurant and, 'The ones we make nobody makes it through!' Metallica's third album and the cool title track.

There was no doubt: the *Master of Puppets* was up there somewhere.

I started to see the threads everywhere and I was terrified of his next tug.

CASSETTE SWAP

Luckily there were also other threads. There were also cables, cords and strings. There were also cassette tapes.

One day I went to visit Mauro and Fabio with a bag full of cassettes and some song lyrics in my pocket. They lived on the ninth floor of a sixteen-storey building. The lift was broken.

I stopped at the seventh floor. Thought about Jelena and Igor. Thought about Mister No. Thought about everything that could be done differently. Everything that could be done differently to a person. Constantly.

Fabio opened the door and said hello.

'Mauro's in the shower,' he said. 'Probably be done in an hour or two.'

Their room was in a state of emergency: cardboard boxes and dust sheets everywhere. It gave me a bit of a shock when I saw it.

'What's all this? What's happening?'

'Uhh … the parents,' Fabio said. 'They want to paint … I think.'

He did not sound convincing.

'Before you go to Verona?'

'No, when we get back.'

'Hmm.'

I left it alone. It might actually be true.

We went into his room and sat down. I sank into his deep armchair and stretched out my legs.

'Make yourself at home,' Fabio said and put on *Icon* by Paradise Lost. 'I don't need to tell you that.'

'Embers Fire' started. I hummed along and looked at Fabio's new poster on the wall above his bed. Arnold Schwarzenegger. *Last Action Hero*. My arse.

'Is your brother going too?' I asked.

'Yeah, the whole family.'

He leaned back on the bed and started picking at the worn edge of his trousers. He wound bits of fabric around his index finger. He looked away.

'How long are you gone for?'

'Dunno. The folks are driving. Didn't you say something about some tapes?'

'Yep. I've got some for you guys, too. When do you get back?'

'Probably about six weeks from now. What have you got?'

I pulled ten or fifteen tapes out of the bag.

'Bit of everything. But you have to take good care of them,' I said. 'That's practically my entire collection.'

'I didn't think you had that many.'

'That's how I spend my money. That guy Fric I told you about – the one who copies them for me – he gave me a whole bunch.'

'Cool.'

'A few originals, too. I've got the original *Somewhere in Time* now. The Yugoton edition, with the cover and everything. The sound is so clean.'

'Doesn't he want it for himself, or what?'

'Nah, he only listens to death metal now. Everything else is too soft, he says. You should hear him.'

I handed Fabio a couple of cassettes:

'Look at this! King Diamond, Mercyful Fate, Fric thinks they're all too soft. Paradise Lost: too slow. Iron Maiden? "Kid's stuff, I used to listen to that when I was sixteen." He's twenty now, you know, going on strong at me with his grown-up attitude. But I don't care, as long as he keeps me supplied. I've got practically all of Metallica now.'

Fabio had started getting into metal when we changed schools. He'd had enough of punk, but his brother still worshipped it.

'What's does he listen to then, this guy Fric?'

'Obituary, Napalm Death. All that shit, man. Occasionally Slayer.'

'You should play this for him!'

'What is it?'

'Sepultras's latest. Have you seen the video for "Chaos AD"? It kicks ass!'

'Actually the song is called, 'Refuse/Resist,' not Chaos AD. Chaos AD is the name of the album.'

'But they sing, "Chaos AD Tanks on the streets" and … what's this? Helloween?'

'Maiden copy. They're German. You should hear "I Want Out."'

Mauro came in without knocking. His hair was wet. He was wearing a white Psihomodo Pop T-shirt. It depicted Mickey Mouse lying on his stomach in a pool of blood. With an axe stuck in his back and his red tongue hanging out of the corner of his mouth.

'Hey, Miki!'

'Hey! What did you do to my namesake?'

'It wasn't me. It's from the album cover.'

'Ah, okay.'

'Hey, what's your real name anyway?'

He had known me for more than six months and had never asked. I like people like that.

'Eustahije Brzić,' I answered.

'*The Blue Racer*, c'mon.'

'I love that cartoon!'

'Emir,' Fabio said. 'Emir Pozder. Bosnian with a vengeance!'

'Have you got those lyrics for me, Emir Pozder?' Mauro asked.

He was not expecting me to have them. I could tell. For months he had asked the same question and always got the same reply. So his eyes widened when I said:

'Yes, but they're not very good! You have to read it when I'm gone.'

'My arse!' he said and grabbed the piece of paper. 'There's

no time for that. I'm reading it now.'

'What do you mean, "there's no time"?'

He did not answer. I looked at Fabio, who looked at his brother. He was still picking at the edge of his trousers.

Mauro unfolded the paper and read the text a few times. 'THIS, THIS IS TOO COOL, MAN!'

'You think so?'

'Yes! It's wicked!'

'Where did you get "I feel the sweat break on my brow" from?' Fabio asked. 'I don't know that.'

'It's from Maiden, "The Clairvoyant", first line.'

'Oh yeah: "Feel the sweat break on my brow. Is it me or is it shadows that are dancing on the walls?"'

'"Is this a dream or is it now? Is this a vision or normality I see before my eyes?"'

We started to head-bang a little, but Mauro waved the piece of paper and interrupted us:

'Hey, what should we call it? I mean, what do *you* want to call it? There's no title.'

'*Empty song*,' Fabio broke in.

'Predictable! Unsexy!' Mauro branded his suggestion. 'I would call it *Wrong*.'

'Nah, I prefer *Easy Rotting*,' I said. 'Now that's cool.'

'Or *Dreams of Home*,' Fabio said.

'Or *Fear Again*,' I suggested.

'Stop! Stop!' Mauro shouted. 'Maybe we should wait till the music is done. A lot can happen when the tune comes in.'

For a moment I forgot about Igor and Jelena; I was ecstatic. Me, Emir Pozder Miki, songwriter for Mauro Marinelli's future band. I could already see my name in parentheses after the song title. Pozder/Marinelli or Marinelli/Pozder, it would read. Then the scene shifted to various stadiums around the world. Fabio, Mauro and I backstage. Surrounded by groupies – and cases of beer. My role was practical and twofold: songwriter and crew member. Head of the electrical department or something like that. I was in charge of ensuring the lighting was top notch. That the speakers worked. I got my employees to do the heavy lifting so I could write super cool lyrics.

Then Fabio and Mauro's parents came home, and the mood changed. They rustled the shopping bags and asked the boys for help. I politely said hello to them, as usual.

'Do you feel like staying for dinner?' their mum asked with a weary voice.

I saw that her eyes were red and swollen, too. She looked like she had just been crying.

'No, thank you,' I said. 'I should probably head home.'

We went into Mauro's room, and I chose a bunch of tapes from his many drawers. Including some early eighties' Yugo Rock and new wave. I purposely avoided the bands that I had left at home. I could not deal with nostalgia right now.

Fabio walked me to the door and we flashed the sign of the horns.

'See you, old man,' he said. 'Take care of yourself!'

'You too.'

Then something very strange happened. He gave me a hug. The fucking moron gave me a hug!

It caught me completely off guard. We only hugged when we were drunk. Never when we were sober.

I said goodbye from the stairs, heard him lock the door and I started down. Only two floors down I felt like turning back and asking him point-blank.

He did not usually act like this. And he was not in a good mood.

Mauro's "no time" and his mother's red eyes. Cardboard boxes! Fuck, yes!

The bright afternoon sun blinded me when I stepped outside. A guy wearing Bermuda shorts and rubber sandals was checking the front wheel of his freshly washed car. I stopped.

Fabio is leaving. That's what's happening. He just doesn't want to tell me. They're both leaving!

I turned around and ran back inside. Without stopping

once, I raced up the stairs to the ninth floor. I buzzed, my heart in my mouth. I was gasping for air.

Luckily he was the one who opened the door. I must have looked like shit when he saw me.

'What's wrong?' he said. 'What's going on?'

I could not speak. I signalled for him to give me a couple of seconds.

'Did you forget something? ... Or ...'

'No ... Well, yeah ... I forgot to ask you something really important.'

'What?'

'Are you're really coming back?'

'Back?'

He made a face:

'What do you mean?'

'Are you're sure you're not just taking off? ... To Italy ... you know ... That you're going to stay there?'

'Eh?'

His expression alone at that moment made me regret my trip up the stairs. It was so stupid. It was pathetic, panicky, and idiotic!

Of course they're coming back. They're just going on holiday.

'What's going on with you, man?' Fabio said. 'I'll be back next month! I just told you that.'

Mauro and their dad appeared behind him. I hurried to give Fabio an affectionate pat on the shoulder:

'Be sure to come back in good form, old man! And be sure to get that room painted!'

He shook his head, not understanding a thing. I turned and left.

THE MAGICAL PATTRESS BOX

Boro's business went bad that June, but Marijan's did not. One day he picked me up at the Muscle Market with Boro's blessing. I hopped in and we drove out to an old hacienda in the vicinity of Grozvin.

Marijan was chipper as hell that morning. He was annoyed that Fabio had gone on holiday so early, and thanked me for wanting to help.

I was in a terrible state. A strange frailty was lodged in my body and refused to leave.

Sometimes I thought it had to be because I had dreamt something sad, something I could not remember in the morning. Other times I gave myself a merciless diagnosis: chronic sadness. I lay on the bed and practised my new signature – *Sad Micky, Micky the Sad* – page after page. But not even the irony helped.

We reached the old stone house; the interior was wonderfully cool. Outside hell was already beginning to take shape. The cicadas hissed like hidden alarm clocks. Their insistence grew in strength as the sun crawled higher and higher up in the sky.

The owner, a small tubby man with short arms and a shiny crown, showed us around. He breathed heavily and wiped sweat from his brow, as if someone was constantly at his heels. Never in my life have I seen a man so stressed.

The furniture had been moved to the middle of the rooms, covered by transparent dust sheets. In the bedroom I saw a painting of a crying child. I got a slight sinking feeling in my stomach, and Marijan and the man's voices quickly faded out.

We had one like that in our sitting room once. Mum was

crazy about it. Dad could not stand the child's big eyes.

'They're staring at me, like I've done something wrong,' he said. 'It makes me sad!'

He got rid of the painting at the first possible chance and hung a landscape painting on the same nail.

The stressed homeowner suggested a few manageable tasks, complained about the heat and drove off in a metallic green monster of a car. Marijan and I rolled up our sleeves.

The house was going to be renovated. Our task was to swap out the old wiring before the bricklayers set to work in earnest. We started upstairs and took one room each. We clipped the wires and pulled out the old cables. It was easy enough.

When we reached downstairs and I had to take care of a small kitchen niche, I realised that my wire cutters were upstairs. I walked into the sitting room and towards the corridor. Marijan stood whistling an unfamiliar melody while he fiddled with the cover of a pattress box.

'I've …'

I've forgotten my wire cutters upstairs, I was about to say. But then I spotted an extra pair on the coffee table behind him. It was a normal pair, without insulation.

'I've never seen such a stressed-out man,' I said.

'He isn't stressed,' Marijan said. 'He's fat.'

I grabbed the cutters, went back to the kitchen niche and pulled the bundle of wires out of the box. It was quite low in relation to the ceiling. A chair was not even necessary, I could just stand on my toes and stretch my arm a little.

I clipped one wire. Then the second. The third. Fourth...

The last one was a little thicker than the others.

I squeezed.

Light.

A distant light in the bottom of the wall box.

That was what I saw.

It approached through the semi-darkness of the niche like a car careering towards you on a road at night. Just much faster and more than once. It poured over me like a gigantic, flashing signal light. Silently. Like in a dream.

My breathing stopped. My thigh muscles froze. I felt a pressure in my chest, as the current pulled me up. It was as if someone had shaken my hand. As if I stood in a dark hole in the ground and the person in question was helping me out of it.

I don't know why people say that electricity gives you a shock. That it hits you. Strikes. No, it does none of those. It sticks you to the copper wire and pulls you forward. In my case towards the open wall box.

Marijan did not notice anything. I did not utter a sound while the surreal experience lasted. No moaning, no sighing. Only a single thought managed to cross my mind, while I stood with the cutters in the wall socket and my lungs in convulsion:

I'm dying.

Without fear. Without complaint.

This is it.

At the same moment the wire cutters fell out of my hand and onto a roll of old carpets. I took a step back and breathed.

In the sitting room, Marijan was whistling the same tune. I had missed at most one or two notes. He stood with his back to me winding up a cable.

Without saying anything I hurried past him, into the corridor and up the stairs.

'What are you doing with that?' he said when I came downstairs with the toolbox.

'I've got a bad feeling about this,' I answered. 'I'm worried there's electricity in the kitchen.'

'Not in the entire kitchen. Like the fat one said: only in that one box there. In the niche.'

Fuck! Had he said that? I ought to have been paying attention and not just standing there nodding. It must have been that stupid painting in the bedroom. Damn!

'But it's good to be vigilant,' Marijan smiled. 'That's the sign of a good electrician.'

'Yes, obviously man. Thanks!'

Good electrician? My arse.

Before I started pulling the leads out of the wall, I found a plastic cup in the cupboard and drank some water. I stood with the cup in my hand and looked up at that box. I had seen and opened so many of them, but this one was another matter. It was magical in its own way.

The plastic cup was shaking in my right hand. There was no stopping it. I took the insulated cutters out of the toolbox, stood on my toes and simulated a clip. Then I pulled the cable out of the wall with a series of short, determined tugs.

On the drive back to Majbule, Marijan asked if I was okay.

'Yes, I'm fine. Why?'

'You're not saying anything, man. I have to draw the words out of you with a pair of pliers!'

'I slept quite bad last night,' I explained. 'Have to lie down for a bit when I get home.'

Of course that was a huge lie. I had slept like a rock at the bottom of the sea.

I looked out the window and thought about what would have happened if I had not survived. Marijan would have finished whistling his song and discovered that I was lying on the floor. Then called for help. Gone out to the camp and called on my parents. 'Your son is dead,' he would have said. The others would find out later, one by one. Kaća would have cried, Fabio would regret his trip to Italy. Gogi, Zlaja and Fric would all shake their head and repeat that they did not understand. Of all people, I had not deserved it.

I thought about all kinds of things. About everything that still would have been in the world, would have moved and gone wrong and continued like nothing had happened. Just like the rest of us continued as if Igor was not dead. As if we had never experienced war, had shells launched at our heads and seen people die.

The car kept movving. The evening sun reddened in the west. It was gentle and beautiful at that time of the day. It was as round as the magical pattress box in the niche.

Marijan gave me twenty kunas for a whole day's work. Now I know why he suggested picking me up at the camp. He had deducted my bus ticket and multiplied it by four.

But I did not care. I just smiled, said thank you and waved goodbye. Had he played the fool and not given me anything at all, I would not so much have said a word. The only thing I felt like doing was having a shower and lying down in bed. Face the wall and shut my eyes. Hope to wake up in a better mood.

'Hey, Pozder! Pozder!'

I looked up.

It was Sergio, shouting from behind the counter in reception. He had seen me through the window, and now I could see him in the doorway.

He waved for me to come inside.

Oh no, I thought. Not him, not now. It was probably a complaint from the neighbour or something along those lines. Can't I just be allowed to go upstairs and lie down?

The bag with my work clothes bumped against my leg as I dragged myself into reception. Only when I got right up close did I notice him holding the telephone receiver

'It's for you! Take number one!'

'Who is it?'

'How the hell would I know?'

That bastard! One day I'll hook up your chair to the electricity, you fascist!, I would normally have thought when he treated me like that. But now I just walked into booth number one and waited for him to connect me. I did not have the strength to feel offended.

Booth number one, unlike the rest, had a large window facing the Muscle Market. I stood looking at a parked Zastava when the device rang.

The clammy receiver stuck to my hand. It had not seen a cloth in years, and the lower part stunk of bitter saliva and nicotine.

I kicked a couple of cigarette butts aside, coughed and said:

'Yes, hello.'

Nobody answered. It was quiet as a graveyard on the other end.

'Hello!' I repeated a little louder this time and suddenly I heard the most beautiful sentence that anyone has ever spoken in this shitty region or entire world :

'Miki, is that you?'

ACROSS THE TERRACE

It was a shock. Shock number two that day. I stepped out of the booth and did not know what to do with myself. Cry, laugh or run over to Sergio. Go behind the counter and embrace that stupid, ugly oaf. Forgive him for all the rude remarks he had subjected me to over the course of time. Forgive him for all the times he had slapped Damir.

I did none of the above. I just nodded, said thank you very much and let him chew on that while I hurried out.

Nobody knew.

Nobody in the entire world knew yet.

Kaća's mum stood shaking the crumbs off a tea towel on the balcony. Two elderly people, whose names I did not remember were playing chess on the terrace between D1 and D2. The weak-sighted Dario caught a ball. A little girl applauded and called for it.

None of them knew. They just continued as though nothing had happened.

And everything had happened, everything. My war was over. My only soldier had won his battle. Pounding in my chest was a different heart. It counted the first seconds of my new life. Made me into a stronger Miki, *Micky the New*.

I looked up at our balcony. Mum and Dad! The thought of them suddenly made me vulnerable.

The magical pattress box, the flashing light, booth number one and 'Miki, is that you?' – all of it poured down on me. I could neither contain it or push it away. And the two of them sat up there and knew nothing about it. I just had to go up, place two words in a certain order, and their sufferings would be over. They would no longer look so obstinate. Mum would thank God for having heard her prayers. Dad would brighten up and send me to the shop for beer. We would celebrate the news with a small glass after having squeezed into one of the booths together. After taking turns to speak to him – relieved, terrified, happy and confused.

What was I waiting for?

The bag of work clothes dangled from my right shoulder. I raced across the terrace and into building D1. I did not break down when I entered the stairwell. Nor when I flew up the stairs. Not until the door was shut behind me and Dad asked in astonishment what had happened.

LETTER READING

Eight days later a letter arrived. A thick one. The receptionist who handed it to me looked suspicious. The letter was all of sixteen A4 pages.

It was the most beautiful letter anyone had ever written. The handwriting was a bit plump; he wrote some very strange d's. The circle of the stamp could only partially be made out; the date and city were completely smudged. Two perfectly placed stamps had cost five Swedish kroner each. On one of them, a thin, elongated fish swam in bluish water above a brown sea bottom. Along the bottom of the sea it read SVERIGE 5 KR, in the water, *Cobitis Taenia* and above the water, *Nissoga* with two dots above the o. The drawing on the other stamp depicted a powerful, aristocratic woman sitting in an armchair, surrounded by a semi-circle with white stars on a dark-blue background. SVERIGE 5 KR was written along the left edge, while EES-AVTALET 1994 could be read at the bottom under the woman's chair and feet. The sticker on the left side of the envelope was also dark-blue and perfectly matched the colours of the stamp:

PRIORITAIRE
1:a-klassebrev

His address was written on the back of the envelope – he was far from Stockholm, south of Gothenburg – and there were two other words I could not decipher were also written: MILJÖKUVERT, again with two dots above the O – I wonder why they put those dots there? – and LJUNGDAHLS, such a wonderful and difficult word!

And then the paper inside. Swedish! Checked and thick. Primo quality.

That's the Swedes for you. Excepting a few flops like Roxette or Ace of Base, everything that comes from that region, tip-top quality. Just look at Europe, 'The Final Countdown', they are also Swedish. A little too much synthesiser for my taste, but cool riffs, obviously, damn, it is heavy after all!

I read the letter over and over again. I read it to myself. To Mum and Dad. In order to remember the passages by heart.

He wrote very little about the day they split us into two groups – the day they drove them away and let the rest of us walk towards the Bosnian army.

We did not write about where they were driven to, and what happened to them there. He skimmed over the many months he had spent in the camp. 'All kinds of things happened,' 'It's nothing to write about' and 'One day you'll get the whole story' were some of the recurring sentences. One I would never forget went like this: 'We got a little food, a lot of thrashings, and we worked from morning to night.'

They slaved away for long periods out in the fields, I later found out. When Serbian farmers from the region arrived in their tractors, the prisoners were lined up in a row in the courtyard. The farmers chose the ones with the biggest muscles and drove them into the fields or to their homes. The prisoners were supervised by at least three to four armed soldiers, while they gathered hay, chopped firewood or did various other jobs.

I tried to imagine him collecting hay – and laughed. It was an impossible combination.

Going out to work with a farmer had certain advantages. The farmers' wives made good food, and you got a lot more than at the camp.

The farmers did not beat them either. The guards and the soldiers who had to go to the front did. On occasion the army's lorries stopped outside in the night, the door opened, and the brave Serbian heroes stormed in, kicking and stomping away. Then the engine was switched on again, and the lorries drove off in the direction of the front, now with a battle-ready crew devoid of nerves.

The last part he told me during our second phone conversation. Even though he kept repeating that I asked too many questions, and that he would rather talk about anything else, I kept at it. In the end he had no more call time on his card.

Most of the first letter described how he had got away from the camp and made it to Sweden. He obviously preferred to write about that. Parts of the story I knew in advance – that was what he told me after 'Miki, is that you?' – but I re-read every single word and sucked it all in anyway.

It started one day when he was chopping firewood at the farm of a younger prison guard. His old schoolmate from Banja Luka, Dragan, whose dad had got them out of Sarajevo back then, happened to walk past the gate. Neno said hi to him. The friend saw him, but did not reply. Not because he wanted to ignore him or anything, he simply did not recognise him. At that point Neno had lost over twenty kilos. He was unshaven and wearing clothes that were so used and filthy that they would fall to pieces if you pulled on them.

This friend and his dad would be the cause of two of Neno's favourite phrases in his first letter. One made Dad suspicious of the so-called Stockholm syndrome. While the other even Dad agreed with:

'Not all Serbs are alike,' and 'Money makes holes where drills can't.'

Now it was just a matter of earning enough money to pay them back.

'There's something fishy about it,' Dad muttered, when I managed to finish the letter. 'Why doesn't he say who he borrowed the money from?'

'Of course! You always have to look for the hair in the ointment,' Mum said. 'Can't you just be happy?'

I sat alone in the room that day and re-read his letter several times. I mulled it over incessantly. Sweden, fate, basements and minefields filled my thoughts, while the bass boomed from one of the lower balconies.

What was it with me and this faraway country? I had hardly heard of it before Samir and Damir had to go there. And now they're there, as well as Amar, Ismar and Neno. Now I have to sit and read that greasy atlas in Vešnja's library again. Dream of saying goodbye to the old folks and taking off north, as soon as I was finished with school – upwards of a year from now. Hope that one day he gets the papers and passport and comes to visit us in the camp. Imagine showing him around. Tell him that I had a friend named Igor, and a girlfriend named Jelena.

'Igor is dead now, and Jelena is living in Ohio, USA. I got an electric shock from a kitchen niche the day you called. I don't know if that was what it took. I had tried all kinds of things … Maybe all that with Igor, Jelena and the electricity, that was heaven's preferred payment, and not my arms and legs and whatever else I offered. Maybe I had been completely mistaken. Attempted to trade with unwanted currency.'

Immersed in Neno's plump handwriting, I sat playing homespun philosopher for hours that day. I got up, put on some music, changed tracks, walked back and forth, lay on my bed, cried and read the letter over and over again.

Can it really be true? Is it really him? Am I dreaming, or will I be woken up by Dad's howling radio soon? The holiday has just started. Why am I not celebrating, looking forward to it? Has superstition placed a rock on my shoulders? Do I dare not hope for a good summer at last? Is the third time not lucky? Neno is alive, dammit, he is living somewhere safe! The sky is blue, and waiting down by the pier are your friends. Now go down and let loose, man! Stop mulling over it so much! Life is too short for this shit; it should be lived and not fucked up!

I put the letter down, opened the brown, built-in

wardrobe and pulled Neno's Spitfire jacket out of the bag. I found the yellow pack of Čunga Lunga chewing gum in one of the pockets and sniffed it.

Then I bawled a little more, blew my nose, walked out the door and let the summer begin.

Cassette 7

BIG HITS OF SUMMER

TEJI AND DENI

Zlaja threw the towel over his shoulder and put his sunglasses in place. He handed me a piece of chewing gum.

'Do you know what?' he said.

'No, what?'

'The two of us, we freaking rule this place.'

I knew he would say that! Sooner or later. He said it at least once an hour that summer.

'What do you mean?' I asked.

'I mean, the two of us: two dangerous dudes, two heavies. Two shaggy animals! Eh? What do you say to that?'

'Yeah, maybe. That depends on who is looking.'

It was late July. The ground and the asphalt were glowing. We jumped from one tuft of grass to the next.

'Seriously,' Zlaja continued, 'what do you think? Are we not the coolest in the entire bay?'

'Yeah, that depends. It's all just …'

'An illusion!'

'To a degree. "We are one another's illusions,"' I quoted Fric. 'And check out those two illusions there. Take a look at those two hot illusions there!'

Zlaja glanced down at the beach and saw: two wonderful young bodies stretched out in the sun. Two bodies we had neither seen nor noticed before. Meaning two bodies that must have just arrived at our keenly observed bay.

One was lying on her stomach reading a book. The other on her back, with a blue top covering her face.

'I know them,' Zlaja said.

'Bullshit! They just got here.'

'Nix. I saw them yesterday.'

'Okay. Whereabouts?'

'At Wicky. Sat with them last night drinking beer.'

'Already? You told me nothing! Who are they? What happened?'

'One of them is Slovenian, the other one … probably Slovenian too. I think. But they're from Italy. They came and sat down at the table next to Gogi and I. Then Pero and Robi came and threw themselves all over them in the most uncool manner. You should have seen it. Utterly hopeless. Something like "Do you have the time?" and "Haven't we met before?" Jesus-fucking-Christ! You should have seen how cold those chicks were.'

'No way, If only I'd been there! Fuck-all happened at Ukulele yesterday.'

'Nothing?'

'No. It was half empty. People are partying on the beaches. It's cheaper. Anyway. What happened next?'

'Yeah, what do you think? They started to look to daddy-o here, you know. They asked for help.'

'And?'

'I switched to Italian, and they didn't give the idiots a second look.'

'Boom!'

'Robi tried showing off with his English, but they were ice-cold. They changed tables.'

'Ah, how cool, man!'

'Let's go down and say hi to them. One of them is sweet on me. Are you ready?'

'Yep, two secs.'

I took off my sunglasses. Caught a glimpse of myself in the reflection: dangerous dude! Shaggy and cool.

Winked at Zlaja:

'Now I am!'

He winked back:

'Okay. And now: on the prowl! Now something is going to bloody happen.'

Danijela, the girl with the book, was a little better looking than Mateja, but they both seemed really sweet. I assumed that it was Danijela who was sweet on Zlaja, so I concentrated on Mateja. She had a pointed nose and a cheeky little mouth: a reverse Marina. On the outside of her left thigh I noticed a white birthmark, a pale island surrounded by tanned skin.

They offered us crisps and orange juice, and we chomped away and talked about U2, Danijela's favourite band. Here I launched a small arsenal of discreet compliments. They happened at relatively brief intervals, but the compliments were well disguised with general comments about good taste in music, nice T-shirts and the like. At this point of the summer it flowed quite naturally. Zlaja and I had ruled the beach for over a month, and our routine was to be tangible.

I had just had my 'fingering' debut as the guitarist Zlaja called it. A certain Stefanie from Graz introduced me to the practical side of petting after Zlaja's, Gogi's and not least, Fric's craziest theories and talks on the subject. Fric claimed that the term *petting* only applied in the instances you used all five fingers, since *pet* meant five in all of the south Slavic languages: Slovenian, Croatian, Bosnian, Serbian and Macedonian. While he outlined the languages, respectively his thumb, index, middle, ring and little finger shot up at me.

'Do you follow me?' he said and pointed at his open hand. 'Five. Right? Five! Five fingers, five languages. Petting!'

'Ah, I don't bloody know, Fric. Serbian, Croatian and Bosnian are one and the same language. And then there is Montenegrin, which you didn't even mention.'

'That's because Montenegrins don't do petting! They're too lazy for that sort of thing! Everyone knows that!'

Typical Fric. He tried to make me believe all sorts. Including there being a difference between onanism and masturbation. That it was a matter of two different techniques. Good old Fric.

The best thing about Stefanie and other tourist girls was that you did not have to fall in love with them. It was all very simple: they hung out in the bay for a week or two, they were out to have fun, and they talked openly about which day and what time they were going home. No reason to fear them suddenly informing you that they were going to Ohio, USA or something.

'Teji' and 'Deni,' the nams our new acquaintances called each other, were a class above, not only Stefanie from Graz, but also most other girls we had met up till now. Danijela had an absolutely perfect body, dark hair down to her chin and thick, full lips. At first I felt more like touching them than kissing them.

She and Mateja asked loads of questions. Especially about the area and opportunities to get away from the wailing brats and snoring old folks, who farted in their sleep into the bargain. One of them let loose while we were having a conversation about U2.

Just as we were about to go in the water and swim across to the island, Zlaja grabbed my upper arm firmly:

'What the hell are you doing?'

'What?'

'Chatting up my girl.'

'Her?' I asked in amazement. '"Teji?" Is *she* sweet on you?'

'Yes!'

'I thought … Oh! … But … No, forget it! I'll just take the other one. Better looking too.'

On the way over to the island Danijela got the usual spiel. About how electrical installation was the most dangerous trade mankind has ever engaged in. About how us electricians make a maximum of one mistake in our hazardous career. That's all we get. I told her that I had five brothers in Sweden, but that I would rather stay in Majbule, because the bay was so beautiful, and you met new people all the time. I fired off all sorts of crap.

She had just finished secondary school and was going to

study at uni. Either journalism or archaeology.

'Archaeology?' I said. 'In other words, you want to dig up the bones of our ancestors.'

'Yes, I love history.'

'Get other people to do it! Physical work hurts.'

She laughed.

'Are you crazy?! Spend four years at uni, get a degree and then still have to dig up the earth and sweat like crazy. That is completely absurd!'

She had a very ambitious mother, who sent her to a chosen few summer schools in Vienna and London. Her dream was to go to New York. She was crazy about that city, especially Brooklyn, Manhattan and Skyline.

Hm, I thought. And here we are counting loose change at Wicky. This is going to be an uphill battle, this is.

ON FORM

The island was its old self. It was small and deserted – with an excess of rocks in relation to underbrush. The gulls shrieked in the sky, and Danijela said:

'Wow! It's beautiful here.'

On the other side – the side facing the horizon – we positioned ourselves in the spot where Samir and Andrea had sat slobbering over each other two years ago. The spot where I stood thinking about Nina and feeling like I had a lot of catching up to do.

'I don't think you'll win today,' Zlaja said.

'Yes, I will,' I said. 'I can feel it. I was just thinking about taking the highest one.'

'The highest? Are you mad?'

'Just wait and see!'

We had a competition going that summer. We jumped from gradually higher and higher cliffs and moved up towards the spot from where Andrea at once jumped out feet-first. I had made it up to a cliff that was two metres blow that one. Zlaja couldn't believe his ears: the stupid Bosnian was about to beat him on his home turf.

'I'm taking the highest one today!' I said. 'I don't care.'

'Relax, Miki. Then you'll have a long life.'

'No! I can feel it. I'm ready. Just have to take some of the lower ones first. Just have to warm up a little!'

'What's going on?' Mateja asked.

Zlaja answered in Italian, and the three of them laughed.

'What did he say?' I asked.

'He said you want to jump head-first from that cliff,' Mateja answered.

That provoked me.

'That's right,' I said. 'And I'm going to wank at the same

time. With both hands!'

They did not catch that. I winked at Zlaja and hurried off. Took a couple of jumpos from some lower cliffs.

Zlaja was content with one. He was good at doing 'the swallow,' keeping his legs together and his arms stretched out nicely. But this was my day. I could feel it. I had bigger cojones than him.

Mateja and Danijela walked down to the water, threw themselves in and commented on some yacht that sailed past.

'I'm bloody doing it,' I said to Zlaja. 'I'm doing it now.'

'Hey,' he said and whispered, 'just jump feet first. That alone is crazy. It's more than fifteen metres.'

'I'll assess the situation from up there.'

I stood on the tallest cliff on the nameless island across the bay from Majbule. I pushed my hair behind my ears and looked across the horizon. Italy, I thought. Somewhere out there is Italy: Fabio, Mauro, Toto Cutugno and Pope John Paul II. Then I turned and looked at the peninsula, the bay, and the coastline that stretched towards Vešnja. Small cutters, large yachts and a few inflatable boats. The camp. The sun. And an endless blue sky. I was going to jump. This was it. This was my day. My island. My jump.

Zlaja and the girls sat on a cliff a little further down whispering to one another. I gathered my thoughts. Shut the three of them out of my head. Breathed deeply.

Then I stretched out my arms and focussed on an invisible point in the air. It was chest height. I imagined launching myself out and hitting it with my chest. I told myself that everything was going to be fine. That it was just a taller cliff, nothing more. 'The principal is the same, everything else is a nuance,' like in the song by Balašević. Just remain calm, don't change anything during the jump. The hands should be outstretched. Just bring them together before you hit the water. Otherwise your head will split open like a pumpkin.

But that would not happen. I could feel it. I had calmed myself. Had imagined several times, hitting the point in the air with my chest, keeping my arms outstretched and pulling them together quickly before the splash.

Now it was just a matter of doing it.

I'll never forget the moment my feet tore away from the cliff. The moment I threw myself into the air with outstretched arms and was blinded by the sun and the void around me.

The flight down had sometimes felt long. The cliffs, especially those from the last couple of jumps, had been rather high. But never before had it felt like the water failed to appear. As though it was keeping its distance. And continued to keep its distance.

Splaaash, I heard at long last at long last, and then it was perfectly still.

My body slipped deep down through the thick water. My speed decreased.

I put my legs together, straightened up and started to swim towards the surface. I needed air badly.

Now the air was keeping its distance.

I was further down than I had thought.

Come on, come on!

Aaah!

Air and light at long last. Applause from the cliff. I could see my audience stand up and clap.

Zlaja shouted:

'Are you okay?'

'Yeah. Why wouldn't I be?'

'Just asking.'

'How did it look?'

'Not bad. But a little frog-like. You bent your knees at the end.'

'Shut your face, man! It was absolutely perfect!'

We went back to the bay, dried off and relaxed. Zlaja threw out a few pearls and told a few jokes, but he was nowhere near my level of activity. I was completely buzzing. The adrenaline whipped around in my body. I caught myself fencing with my arms. Only now did it dawn on me what I had accomplished. How far-fetched the entire project had been. That was the jump of a century. Shame there weren't more people who had seen it. A couple of journalists and photographers from the national newspapers, for example. That was front page material, it definitley was.

'Hey, why don't we meet up tonight?' I asked the girls. 'Throw a little party. Light a fire. Celebrate my jump. Drink a few beers. Just the four of us.'

No, they had to get up early, they said. They were going to Grozvin for a few days. They would wait for a third friend and return to Majbule with her on Friday. Mateja's aunt lived in a house not far from the camp.

I looked at Danijela while she explained this, and I *really* felt like licking the salt off her slender upper arm. It was white and fine as dust.

Then I realised what she had just said, and I thought: what the hell! Here I thought that this was my day. My big moment. And then everything gets so difficult: they're leaving, coming back, Friday, maybe. What the hell kind of crap is this?

'What do you say to that?' I asked Zlaja.

I expected full back-up. A couple of strong arguments – something that could make them change their mind. But Zlaja said:

'No, let's just say Friday. We can arrange a time.'

What?

'What's going on with you, man?' I shouted when we had said goodbye to the chicks. 'Have you got plans for tonight, or what?'

'No, I'm doing the same as you. Nothing. Shit!'

'Why didn't you back me up then? We've spent the entire day doing the preliminary work. I put my fucking life on the line.'

'Easy. You can be a little *too* cool some times. They like us, and they'll be back soon.'

'They say!'

'They say, and they will. You'll see. You just have to relax and not look so overstrung. You were completely sold, man! They could see that. You laid it on a little too thick.'

'Thick? You were the one who set the scene, that loads would happen. And then you're just sitting there saying next to nothing! Is it because your Dutch chicks are coming soon, or what?'

'You've still got a lot to learn, Miki. You're only sixteen. Talk – that's just a small part of it. Didn't you see the way Danijela was looking at you?'

'No. And I don't bloody care.'

'And that's how you came off. You were just going on and on. Instead of smiling back at her, communicating, charming her, being cool. And as far as Miraja and her friends are concerned, they aren't coming for another two weeks. Take it easy. And remember: Don't ever push that hard again.! Ever!'

'But … They were secondary school girls,' I said. 'Archaeologists. Do you really think we'll see them again?'

TWO WORLDS

The day Mateja and Danijela were meant to return, I got up early. Boro had rung and asked me to help him and Marijan. They were installing electricity at a new build in the vicinity of the trade school.

I played hard to get. I was not obliged to do work experience during the holidays. But when he said that it was urgent, that it was a matter of a full day's work, and last but not least, that I could earn a fifty-note, I was ready.

A German tourist from Adria picked me up. He was on his way to Zagreb – very much against his will. The previous night there had been a break-in at the office of the campsite. The unknown burglar had looted all the passports of the registered guests. So he was now on his way to the German embassy to be issued the necessary papers. Otherwise he and his wife could not return home.

It would take an entire day of his holiday, he said – and a hot one at that, because it was roasting in Zagreb, almost as much as it was here. There were crowds in the streets and queues in front of the embassies.

'But what are they going to do with all those passports?' I wondered. 'I would understand if they stole money. But what in the world are they going to do with all those passports? It's ridiculous.'

'Well, you should know,' the German behind the wheel smiled. 'You are a refugee from Bosnia.'

The police were clearly of the same understanding. When I returned later that afternoon, Mum and Dad told me that there had been another raid. The cops had knocked on all the selected doors. Everyone had to prove their identity.

At our place, they opened cupboards and drawers. Lifted

the mattresses.

'They asked about you,' Mum said, clearly worried.

'Me? What would they want with me? The only thing I steal are grapes and figs.'

'And you should stop that!' Dad said. 'You shouldn't do that either.'

'They asked where you were,' Mum said. 'It's probably best if you go to reception and show yourself.'

'But what do the people in reception have to do with the police?'

'Just go down there and ask if there is any post for us. Or something. Just so they can see that you're still here.'

'Okay, okay! Then I can also ask them if we're getting water today. I have to shower. And wash my hair!'

The water was not coming on for a few hours , so I lay down and slept one of them away.

Dad woke me by switching on the radio.

'Is the war over?' I asked.

'What?'

'You listen to the radio bulletins every single hour, man! Do you really think the war is going to end in the meantime?'

'Be quiet, boy,' he said and adjusted the small knob. 'I have to know what is happening. What else am I going to bloody well do?'

I had to have a cold shower. It was Friday, and we only got hot water on Wednesdays and Sundays. My nose was running while I dried myself. My snot was brown: pure cement dust. It was like that every time after work.

I put on my new Diesel trousers. They were Zlaja's old pair, which he couldn't fit any more. I said, 'Thank you vry much, Mother Teresa' and cut them off below the knee. People weren't going to bloody see me wearing Zlaja's old trousers.

At a market in Vešnja, I bought a black Iron Maiden

T-shirt, where Eddie stood on a battlefield in uniform, with a sword in one hand and a tattered English flag in the other. It was a copy of an original T-shirt for the song 'The Trooper', and I fell for the interplay between the black and red.

Buried in the right pocket of my trousers was the fifty kuna note. It was folded into a small square, and I could not stop thinking about my hidden treasure. I was a rich man. I was a winner. The world was the land of opportunities and I was its hospitable owner.

Bring on the evening.

Outside a storm was brewing. A couple of thunderclaps rumbled in the distance, and there was a warm and pleasant wind. While I walked down the steps, the light on the terrace went out. People on the balconies complained, and some good old-fashioned grumbling and juicy swear words rsounded across the terrace.

Gogi, Zlaja and the girls sat under shelter in front of the restaurant smoking fags. Gogi had had a couple of shots after finishing work. He was talking a lot and entertaining Mateja, Danijela and a third girl, who in the darkness introduced herself as Isabella. Zlaja had to translate. Isabella could not speak a word of Croatian.

When the rain stopped, I suggested we go to Adria and order something in the bar. But Zlaja did not feel like staring at the cheek-dancing tourists, who stepped on each other's toes and pretended like nothing happened. The band, consisting of old, balding hippies, was not a particularly uplifting sight either. They did not look like they enjoyed it – at all. But once in a while there was a nice guitar solo or a song like 'Black Magic Woman' – and then Miki's night was saved.

'Let's go to Wicky,' Gogi said and whispered to me:
'I'm buying.'
'How much have you got?'
'Fifty.'
'Same here.'

'It's going to be glorious.'
'It's going to be fucking beautiful!'

At Wicky, Dr Alban was playing at full blast. I wanted him dead on the spot, but not until we had ordered did I ask the waitress to turn it down a little. We got a whole bottle of white wine, ice cubes and a pitcher of water, so we could make *bevanda*. When the bottle was gone, I ordered a pitcher of the house red and a large Coke. Never before had I paid so much for one and a half litres of bambus. Never before had I ordered one and a half litres.

'You've really rolling in the notes, eh?' the waitress said. 'Now I know why it's raining.'

I shrugged:

'First coins, then notes. Next time we'll bring cheques and gold bars.'

She laughed.

'Were you flirting with her?' Danijela asked when the waitress shifted her arse away.

'No. I wouldn't know how to do that.'

'Yes, he would!' Gogi shouted and smacked me on the back so hard that it really fucking hurt. 'He's very mature, despite his young age. Experienced!'

He cocked his head at Isabella, who he had been having some kind of conversation with:

'Do you understand "mature?" Ma-ture?'

'She understands that you're getting super-drunk,' Zlaja laughed. 'More water, Gogi. Less wine.'

'Water? No, that's where we're going in later,' Gogi raised his index finger. 'Have you heard of midnight dips?'

The girls took a collective trip to the toilet. Danijela grazed my shoulder when she went past. I lit one of Gogi's fags in satisfaction.

Was that a hint? Or am I just too young?

Zlaja leaned back and stretched his neck like a boxer getting ready to fight.

'Those are some really sweet ladies,' he said. 'Really sweet! Imagine, they can turn a blind eye to *your* bad breath and *your* rotten toes! Gogi, they actually think you're nice!'

Gogi did not get it:

'My toes are fine.'

'Better,' I said. 'Seawater and sun have really helped.'

'And wind, the wind in particular!' Gogi emphasised with a smile on his lips.

Just then Pero and his cousin Bruno walked through the door. Pero was wearing a military T-shirt and a pair of worn Bermuda shorts. His cousin was dragging his feet in the only pair of flip-flops he owned. I had never seen him wearing anything other than flip-flops, and you could not exactly call them smart.

They sat up by the bar – about four to five metres away from us – and Bruno took off his green tracksuit top. He nodded at Gogi and said:

'Oh, big drinking session, eh? What do you know!'

'Just wait till you see the ladies!' Gogi answered.

'The ladies? Well, we're waiting!'

That was stupid. Really stupid. The man was an idiot, and Danijela and Mateja had already rejected Pero. Now the two of them would keep an eye on our table and do their best to ruin it for us. I wished Gogi could keep his mouth shut.

'Relax,' I whispered to him while the two ordered.

'What? I'm more relaxed than you, man.'

'And more drunk. Just try to chill a little.'

Bruno turned around. He started to tease Gogi with jokes like "You old ladykiller, where have you hidden the passports?' and 'Are you flying across the border soon, or what?' I regretted that I had not insisted on going to Adria, but then good old fate sent an unexpected greeting – a much needed shot in the arm.

Suddenly they played 4 Non Blondes, 'What's Up,' a cool song! The place was mine again. I leaned back and hummed along to the song, while I observed the two in the bar.

Pero and Bruno. The cousins. They were still after me. Back home they were called Bobi and Rade. Now they were just older, more crass, more muscular. Pero and Bruno. So stereotypical. All biceps and triceps and whatever else. In the camp they were something. They had their flag on the balcony and their big mouths full of patriotic piss. But up here, at Wicky, among tourists, plastic palm trees and 'I say hey yeah yeah, hey yeah yeah! I said hey, what's going on?' they seemed like two completely out of place wretches.

Military T-shirt, flip-flops and worn-out tracksuit? On a Friday night? Jesus-fucking-Christ, how could you have so little in common?

I did not get them. We spoke the same language and lived in the same camp. But they did not head-bang and never requested a song at Ukulele. They would never be able to become a part of my band. I would never be able to become a part of theirs. Because they subscribed to *Croatian Soldier* and talked about fighter planes and Schwarzenegger, while I would rather spend my money on a couple of cassette tapes or nice shoes.

I got up and went to the toilet. Did not feel like listening to their smartass comments when the girls returned. Gogi was going to have to get us out of this mess.

I urinated, washed my hands and looked in the mirror. I was not actually that ugly. My hair looked good. My eyes seemed clear, if not a little nervous.

Maybe I should not have left the table, I thought. Maybe the two of them have already squeezed into my spot.

They had! Almost.

Bruno stood right up against our table. He spread out his arms and babbled about something or other, I couldn't hear because of the music. Gogi got up and looked alternately down at his lap and at Bruno. He shook his head and smiled ironically, while Pero approached from the bar. I could already see where the first blow would come from. I was about to shout: 'Gogi, watch out!' But it was just my massive paranoia.

The music stopped. A male waiter got involved, there were some reproving words, holding a cloth. Isabella was picking up a water glass that had been knocked over, and Zlaja put the cigarette butts back in the ashtray.

'Sorry, sorry!' I heard Bruno's stupid sarcastic voice. 'It was an accident, man!'

Gogi swept out his hands and wiped off his trousers with the cloth. Pero dragged Bruno away by the arm, and they went out on the covered terrace. They sat there and plagued my view for nearly half an hour. They disappeared as suddenly as they had arrived.

'Cheers!' I said and sponged a cigarette from Mateja.

I took a proper drag and breathed a smoke of relief diagonally upwards.

Maybe it will be a good night after all.

MIDNIGHT SWIM

'These are rubbish, they're not even ripe,' I said on the way down to the bay, 'because I fancy some now.'

'Grapes?'

'Yes, dammit.'

'I think we should go for that swim!' Gogi said. 'I need to freshen up a little.'

'What do the girls say?'

The girls were singing 'Two dinara, mate' by Bora Čorba. Mateja said she was crazy about him, and I didn't have the heart to tell her that the old rock'n'roller who had written some super cool lyrics, was now one of the worst nationalists in Belgrade. I just said that *Dead Nature* was one of my favourite albums.

Bora Čorba: a massive disappointment! He had betrayed everything rock stands for.

The Slovenian Italian trio slipped past Mateja's aunt to grab towels and put on their bikinis – 'No, it's called a midnight dip, not skinny dipping!' – and I grabbed my swim trunks in the meantime. Zlaja and Gogi were going to swim in their white underpants. Not even they dared to swim naked.

Down by the pier we carefully stepped over the round, slimy rocks. The moon was gone. The only thing that lit up the glassy water were the few lamps from up on the path. The water felt unusually warm.

'It's because of the air temperature,' Zlaja enlightened us. 'It falls quicker than the water temperature.'

'Back home,' I said, 'when we lie on the beach and the storm comes, we jump in the water straight away. It's totally cool. You only got cold when you stood up.'

Mateja and Danijela began to splash water at Zlaja and

me. I threw myself forward, dove down and raced into a forest of women's legs. I tickled a couple of them, heard a sharp scream pierce the air above the water – and then came the blow:

Boom!

Right in my face.

Right in the jaw.

The legs were thrashing about and I grabbed my mouth: 'Fuck, man!'

My front teeth were on the seabed. I was in no doubt.

'Sorry, sorry, sorry!' Danijela shouted.

Damn, she kicked hard!

'It's okay,' I said. 'It'll be fine!'

'It wasn't on purpose! It was a ... reflex!'

'Yeah, yeah, I know that! It's all right. My teeth are just a little loose.'

I carefully checked with my tongue. Blood. The teeth were apparently all there, but there was a hole on the inside of my upper lip. I rinsed my mouth with some seawater, and the salt made the wound sting.

'Are they loose?' Zlaja asked.

'No. But I'm afraid I'm going to have a double upper lip! It's going to swell up.'

Gogi lay down in the low water snorting like a rhinoceros.

'I'll stay here,' he said.

He was twenty-one years old, born and raised by the Danube, Europe's largest river, and still he could not swim.

The three mermaids, Zlaja and I swam out towards a log raft that was an anchored further out. Danijela was older than me. All of two years. It held me back. A few more signs that she did not think I was too young – that was what I was waiting for. No move until then, I promised myself. Not because I was scared of rejection as such. Fabio and I had picked up an entire collection of rejections at Ukulele. I just thought that the night was really cool, and didn't feel like spoiling it for myself. I shouted:

'GOGI, GOGI, GO-GI!'

'Ye-es?'

'YOU'RE A LITTLE GRO-GGY!'

Danijela laughed.

Zlaja cautioned me: a yacht and several sailboats had dropped anchor close to us. People were asleep in them, Zlaja thought.

That completely pissed me off:

'Jeez, man! Do you have to go to open sea to be able to shout a little? Why in the world are these people even sleeping? They're on holiday! They can sleep when they get home! I'm not even shouting that loud!'

'Not so negative,' Zlaja whispered. 'It's going so well now. Women hate that stuff.'

I dove down headfirst and back up again. I threw my hair back:

'All that shit from your mum's magazines, man. I don't understand how you can be bothered to read all that shit!'

Isabella helped Mateja onto the raft. Zlaja and the two of them hopped on the spot to keep warm. I wanted to go back in the water straight away, but Danijela asked:

'How's it going with your lip?'

'Bad,' I said. 'I think I'll have to go to the doctor.'

'Don't say that.'

'It's swollen.'

'Can't I take a look?'

'Mmmmm-no!'

She did it anyway. Her fingers touched my cheek.

'It's not that bad,' she said and stroked me. 'It just needs a little ciggy.'

Pause. One heartbeat. Two. Five.

'Have you got any?'

She laughed:

'Not here.'

Shit. It was completely maternal, her stroking.

CODE

Gogi was wrapped in my towel when we got out of the water. He was smoking a fag and complaining about how fucking cold he was now.

'Not so negative!' I returned Zlaja's critique. 'Not so negative, Gogi!'

My teeth started to chatter when I was changing into my trousers.

'What about nabbing a room in D3?' Zlaja said.

'D3?' Mateja wondered. 'What's D3?'

'A code!' I laughed. 'We can only speak in code for the rest of the night. *Hey, U2? UB40 in D3?*'

While Zlaja explained to the girls what D3 was, Gogi told me that Fric and him had recently broken into one of the rooms on the ground floor. On the other side of the building – the one not facing D2 – there was a gravel path down the incline. You could easily jump over the narrow drain between the path and the balcony and crawl over the railing.

'Broke in is maybe going too far,' Gogi whispered. 'I opened the balcony door from inside. Sergio and I had to find a bedside table for my mum. Fric needed the room.'

'Oh! What did he do in there?'

'Slept.'

'With who?'

'Nobody. The shit at home again.'

'Hm.'

'The old man was going to kill him.'

I banged my shins on this and that while I searched for a pillow in vain. You couldn't see a fucking finger in the dark.

The two beds in the room were pushed together, and we

threw ourselves onto the bare mattresses. On the other side of the gravel path was a small private campsite. The guests and people who walked past were the only ones who would be able to hear us. I was afraid of the latter, mostly. If there was one thing I did not need, it was to be caught doing something illegal by that psychopath Bruno. On the other hand there was a seventy percent chance that the madman was not out patrolling, but sleeping behind the counter. That was what he was did most of the times I walked past.

'Draw the curtains,' I said to Zlaja.

'It's already dark in here,' he whispered. 'Relax. He won't come, he's sleeping.'

There was not room for all six of us on the beds. Someone would have to lie on the floor, and that ended up being Gogi and Isabella. Mateja lay on Danijela's right, exactly where I would have preferred to lie. When she got up to search for her lighter, I asked:

'Is this spot free?'

'Of course,' Danijela replied.

We shared the last cigarettes. Zlaja, Mateja, Danijela and I lay partially leant up against the wall, with our hips close to one another. I did not know what to do with my left arm. The silhouettes of the objects in the room gradually became clearer.

We talked very little and with increasingly longer pauses. Most of the words came out of Gogi's mouth. He told us about the time he was in the military in Slovenia. It was during the ten-day-war three summers ago.

He was stationed in Nova Gorica and did not care much for the city:

It was either rainy or sunny. It was enough to drive you crazy.

After the retreat he was discharged and sent home. He was given papers stating that he was unfit. Of course he did not mention it that night.

'Why?' I had once asked him.

'I don't know,' he said. 'Something about the psyche.'

He had screamed and shouted 'I want to go home, I want to go home' one night in the dormitory. The way he explained it, he had done it on purpose. As if he was screwing with them. In reality it was the other way round. The YPA were screwing him. When he got home, a new war was waiting for him. A bigger one. One where he was the enemy.

Now he threw Slovenian phrases about to impress the ladies. Zlaja yawned and answered 'M-mm … m-mm' to Mateja's whispering. Danijela took a proper drag and handed a dying fag to Mateja. At that very moment my fingers settled on Danijela's bare elbow. Entirely of their own accord. They slowly began to caress her forearm.

The others in the room had no idea what was going on, and it turned me on like crazy. Almost more than our whispering and the silence and the fact that it was forbidden to be where we were. It was a little like stealing grapes and figs, just with a far bigger added adrenaline kick. Bruno was asleep behind the counter and had no idea that we were here enjoying ourselves.

Danijela pretended like nothing had happened. She continued to participate in the conversation with the others, and I did the same.

If she moves her arm, I thought, I'll die on the spot. If she does not respond – the same thing.

She did not move it, she twisted it.

I stroked the inside of her arm and continued down towards her fingers.

Yes!

Her hand in mine.

Micky the happy. Micky loves the world, I thought, nearly suffocated by the pounding of my own heart. Micky wants more. And more and more and more!

Danijela placed her head on my chest and let her hand crawl up under my T-shirt. Ten centimetres from the spot where it really mattered! I guided our interweaved fingers away from my groin. I was sold. Naked and erect underneath the cut-off Diesels. The rough denim helped. The drop was on its way out. Gogi burped and excused himself. Everyone laughed.

'Your heart is pounding like mad,' she whispered in my ear.

'Guess why,' I whispered back.

Her lips felt softer than I had believed possible. Her tongue was small and fat. It was no bigger than a ripe strawberry, but it just tasted completely different.

Stimulated by a mixture of peppermint, nicotine and the scent of hair conditioner; I stuck my nose into her moist hair and inhaled loudly through it.

Goodbye, you stupid and uncomfortable rocks, lonely park benches and city steps. A special day has arrived. Now I'm finally kissing indoors! Between four walls, on an actual bed. One day it will be with pillows, duvets and covers. Take that, Ukulele's orange plastic armchair. You've been surpassed.

The closest thing to indoor furniture I have ever managed was with Jelena at Ukulele. She kept an eye on her digital watch while we tried to beat our old record. Kissing marathon, she called it.

Now I lay on my side on a mattress that was not exactly freshly aired out, feeling up Danijela's bare thigh. Was it the very same leg she had kicked me with? She had prickly hairs. .

Zlaja, the shaggy beast, no longer spoke. Even Gogi kept his mouth shut. I wished that they and their girls would take off somewhere. Or that Danijela and I could. But outside it was getting light. The door to the corridor was closed and locked. All the empty rooms on the ground floor were so close and yet so bloody far away. All the beds behind closed doors. All the locks.

If D3 really had been a code, it probably would have meant 'a bitter place to be for *Micky full of lust*!'

CHURCH TOWER

Still frustrated, I swayed home with Gogi. At the entrance to D1, after a long period of silence, he let out a muffled and squeaking sound:

'I have a hard-on the size of a church tower!'

'Same here.'

We reached the second floor.

'No,' he said, 'it must be different for you. A mosque tower … or no … what's it called again?'

'A minaret,' I laughed. 'Damn are you ever crude!'

'Remember to check!'

'You're mad!'

'Good night, neighbour.'

'Good night, Gogi.'

Mum and Dad were already awake. They sat out on the balcony drinking their morning coffee. Masturbating was out.

The same for onanism.

GERMAN AND ENGLISH

Radivoje Radisavljević, the popular actor from Belgrade, nicknamed Raša, made his career in a series of partisan films in the sixties and seventies. As a rule he played a young, brave partisan who shoots Germans in masses, was very rarely overpowered, and killed in the most cowardly way. In the eighties he did advertisements for shaving foam, was a guest on various TV series and hosted a children's programme, *House, House, Small House*, which I was a big fan of. Once I got the days of the week wrong and was so inconsolable afterwards, that Dad had to ring the TV station to find out if they could re-broadcast the episode in question.

I knew that Raša's villa was in the vicinity of Zlaja's house. And like so many other Serbian properties by the sea, that it was uninhabited. But I had no idea that Zlaja's mum looked after it, aired it out and tended the garden. Not until Zlaja told me about Miraja, his Dutch chick with the strange name. Miraja had taken Zlaja's virginity in Raša's villa the previous summer.

For that reason I felt a little rush in my stomach the day after the D3 incident when he pulled out a bunch of keys from his pocket and started to rattle them in front of my nose. I knew what he was hinting at. I could figure out his plan.

We sat at the tip of the peninsula, drinking cans of beer and wine from two one-and-a-half litre Fanta bottles. A freckled guy by the name of Martin was partying with us that evening. Thanks to him I had my first Heineken. He was Miraja's cousin or something along those lines, and Zlaja knew him from the previous summer. As far as I could understand, he had a friend stationed as a UN soldier somewhere near Goražde or Žepa.

Martin studied history at uni and wanted to write an

essay about the former Yugoslavia. But he had been forced to abandon it. It was too complicated. He zapped between Ustashe, Chetniks, the Kosovo Field, Ottomans, Tito, Austria- Hungary, north, south, east and west, all the while shaking his head and repeating what turned out to be his favourite phrase:

'Complicated.'

I got exhausted from listening to him. He obviously thought I knew more about it than Zlaja. I was the only one he looked at.

Then he asked how the war started in my hometown.

I gave him the shortest version. But that too was difficult. I got mixed up in loads of long, complicated English sentences about how our own people fired at us, while the Serbs shot at their own, since both one and the other lived on either side of the front. He said, 'complicated' yet again and asked:

'And how did you manage to escape from Bosnia?'

'Aargh, it's a long story.'

'Why?'

'I don't know. We were evacuated.'

'To Croatia?'

'No. To a Serbian town.'

'What happened then?'

'Many things happened. We were in prison … and hungry.'

'In a concentration camp?'

'No, in prison. They took young men in a camp. Later. But it is a long story.'

'What happened then?'

'Nothing. They drived … drove men away and give us to Bosnian army. It is very long story. Very complicated … and long.'

I had not even given all the details to Kaća. So why should I give them to you, mate, I thought. I may be drinking your beer, and you seem very nice, but I do not enjoy talking about it.

Martin rustled his bag and handed me another Heineken. I had a knot in my stomach and which continued for several hours after. It was going to take a lot of cans of Dutch lager to wash that muck away.

Raša's villa was situated on a hill. The view was probably beautiful from the balcony, but we did not get to see it that night, when the lock opened and we snuck in. Zlaja stressed that we should not open the windows or switch on the big lights. Preferably no sign of life should be visible.

'No big deal, I just can't be bothered to discuss it with the old lady.'

'Ah, so you nicked the keys?'

'My present to you.'

'Can I sleep in Raša's bed?'

'You can do whatever you like in it.'

Apart from Zlaja and I, the three Slovenian mermaids, Martin and Fric were also there. None of us could find Gogi that day, and Isabella seemed a little moody at first.

'Wow!'

Mateja was fired up about being in Raša's villa. It was something.

I took a curved wooden sword down from the wall above the mantelpiece and started to wave the loathsome souvenir.

Fric responded with some karate kicks, but accidentally stumbled over an island of cow hides. The rug, which lay in the middle of the room's parquet floor, was uneven at the edge.

'Mooooo!' I scorned him.

He got up and tried again.

Zlaja asked us to be a little more grown-up.

I fenced with the curved sword a little more. Waved it around like a tipsy musketeer. But the dark thoughts would not disappear. They continued to buzz in my drunken head.

It was Martin's fault. When we put out the fire and headed towards Raša's villa, he continued where he let off. I don't know what he was fishing for. Personally I had never been very interested in any one of the same sex. The best thing about Zlaja, Fric and Gogi was precisely the fact that they never asked those kinds of questions. If there was one thing we did not talk about, then it was war. But Martin was indefatigable:

'Are you Catholic or Muslim?'

'No, no, I'm a pioneer.'

'A pioneer?'

'Yeah.'

'A pioneer of what?'

'Of Tito.'

Or when I told him that the Serbs locked us inside a gymnasium the first day after the evacuation:

'And what happened then?'

'Nothing. We slept well. Very well. And in the morning they took all young boys out. From ten to fifteen years.'

'Really?'

'Yeah, I was there too. I was fourteen.'

'Oh! And what did they do?'

'They put us into buses, two buses, and drove us to a big wood. Big green wood with trees and flowers and the water! And then …'

Pause.

I took a small sip of beer. I waited.

'And then?' he said. 'What happened then?'

'And then they gave us a ukulele each!'

'WHAT?'

'Yeah, so we could jam a little.'

Not even that made him stop. No matter how much I took the piss out of him, he just laughed along, took a break, spoke to the others and then returned with brand new questions. He got up every time I clocked him one.

Maybe he was still working on that essay, who knows. Maybe I had misunderstood him. No matter what, then he was well on his way to fucking up my night. All kinds of thoughts whizzed through my brain. All kinds of images followed:

Mister No in a tight blue cardigan. The bag with his clothes at my feet. Chinaman and Double-chin. Drizzle. The wailing woman wearing the headscarf. Mandić's battered face. The soldier who grabbed Mister No and dragged him away, away, away …

I kept waving the sword, I laughed and talked a lot. I would not let go of the sword. But one image led to another, and the film I had no desire to see continued to play in my mind's eye. Even the large sitting room in Raša's white villa with the fancy furniture and peculiar things on the walls began to remind me of 'the good old days.' I thought about how obsessed I was with growing up back when I followed Raša's programme. How I never wanted to be one of the children he called comrades, but *him*. How I could hardly wait to start secondary school, Mister No's school, which I had heard so much about.

Now Raša's programme, the car, the gymnasium and Neno were far away, and I stood in Raša's villa in Majbule of all places, wishing I could blend in with the smell of the room's fancy furniture. I wanted to lose myself in the bloody here and now just like the previous night, out there in the water and on the mattress in D3.

How could I be so far away from that now? That had happened no more than twenty-hours ago. How could a couple of questions in fluent English have forced me away from a super-cozy evening?

I shouted to Zlaja:

'Hey, where's the wine?'

He had found a small radio in the kitchen and was looking for a certain station with the sound at full blast.

'Not Radio Zagreb, man!' I protested. 'They only play shit. And then there's the news.'

'No, you got to listen to this.'

He found a local station with a night programme and a host who was not too crazy. He also threw in pop between the good old rock classics, but not the worst shit like Dr Alban and Ace of Base and other commercial shit with synthesisers, digital drums and infantile lyrics sung by money-grubbing adults.

'Welcome to the Hotel California, tant-ranta-tan-ta-ta ...' they played, and Danijela and I danced to the final two choruses. Plus the solo. Plus the next number. I drank more. I laughed more. I felt like dancing, dancing, dancing! I dropped to one knee in front of Danijela and asked her for one more dance. She told me I was the strangest guy she had ever met. I told her she was mean. I told her she was beautiful. I told her not to go home and leave Majbule.

Then came the hourly chime and the local news, and we sat back down on the cool leather of the sofa.

'Humidity: seventy-four percent ...'

I lit another cigarette. Poured a little more wine in Danijela's plastic cup. She drank from hers and I drank from mine. The music programme continued. We stood up and danced again. Zlaja danced with both Mateja and Isabella. Fric with Isabella, Danijela and me.

Finally, we settled in on Raša's corner sofa. Zlaja regretted not having his guitar with him. We talked about the film *The Doors* and the language of the Netherlands. Martin said a few phrases at that point so we could hear how it sounded. He explained that in a way it was a mix of German and English. He called it *Dutch*.

'I thought you spoke Hollandish,' I said.

'No, man, in English it's Dutch. In Dutch we call it ...'

He mumbled something that neither Isabella, Fric nor I could repeat.

'Do you then speak both English and German?' Fric asked.

'Not very well. But many Dutch people do. Yes, yes.'

He took a sip of his beer, stifled a burp in its infancy and said:

'Serbian and Croatian are almost the same language, aren't they?'

'Not any more,' Zlaja said.

'How come?'

'Come?' Zlaja wrinkled his forehead and looked at the door. 'Who come? Where?'

'I mean, how come? How can it be?'

'Oh! That is quite complicated,' Zlaja said. 'In our country, things change.'

'Yeah. I know,' Martin nodded, oddly distressed.

Fric started a new sentence with 'Imagine one day you ...' while I nibbled on Danijela's earlobe:

'Why don't we look around a little?'

'Later,' she said and burped softly.

ELECTRIC SOCKET

Wow, was I ever wasted when I stood up! Lovely, lovely drunk!

In the bathroom I splashed water on my burning face and pissed into Raša's pink toilet bowl.

He must have sat here and had a proper dump, I thought. Or read those 'adults only' magazines far away from the shrieking brats and the exhausting TV recordings.

We looked around upstairs, switching lights on and off.

'They should have placed this lamp a little higher,' I said. 'And look here! The two electric sockets that aren't at the same height. Amateurs, man! Pure bungling.'

Danijela said nothing. She just smiled. The sound of laughter exploded down in the sitting room.

'I would have placed a double switch here, so you could turn the balcony light on both there and here.'

She nodded. Grabbed a magazine that was on the bedside table. Quickly put it back.

'It probably would have cost a little more. You would have to run a cable from here. Here!'

She looked up and smiled. A little ironically. Enigmatic.

'Now it's really stupid. You have to go to the other end of the room to switch on the light when you come in from the balcony. It would really be worth it to pay a little extra. I remember the time Boro – that's my boss, he's Serbian but that doesn't matter – once when he and I were ...'

'Switch off the light!'

'What? Nobody can see us ... There are heavy curtains and ...'

'Switch off the light and come here! Here!'

She tugged my lower arm. I just managed to switch the button, making us both disappear. Had it not been for a small gap between the two curtains at the window, we would not have been able to see anything at all.

Danijela wrapped me around her. I played along and voluntarily toppled over onto the velvet blanket on the bed. She threw herself on top of me like in a play fight. She gathered my hands above my head, held them there with one hand and played a harmonica solo on my ribs with the other one. I couldn't help but giggle, dammit, it tickled:

'No, stop!'

She laughed:

'Shhhh!'

And pulled up my T-shirt.

Her kisses jumped around on my stomach like small, moist frogs. It tickled like hell. I held my breath and bit my tongue, until she enveloped my left thumb with her soft lips. Instinctively I moved it and scraped the base of my finger against her front teeth. My entire left side was tingling, even my bones.

I discreetly wiped off the one finger with the other four, while in almost a single, tug she pulled off my trousers and underwear. I helped her the rest of the way.

Danijela straightened up and pulled her T-shirt over her head.

'Mmaaghr!' I said a little later, if not even less articulate.

I had no idea where I was when she lowered herself onto me. I just noticed that the bed moved in time with her movements. It was a double bed with a velvet blanket stretched over the mattress. Still no sheets.

REVENGE

I woke up with one of Danijela's knees pressed against my ribs. It was *not* a dream.

From downstairs Zlaja and Isabella's voices could be heard, they were calling each other and rustling around,, but I had no desire to go downstairs yet. I closed my eyes and remained still.

Danijela was breathing heavily. She was more than two years older than me. She could have chosen anyone at all, but she chose me. And it was *not* a dream, I kept thinking.

When I finally got up, dizzy from the hangover, and stumbled onto the balcony, everything seemed a little different. A little kinder and closer. An aeroplane with a banner fluttering behind it crossed the bay. A red transport ship out on the horizon beyond the island. It was the world and not the bed that had moved. And it had moved – in my direction.

I ignored Zlaja's instruction and remained standing on the balcony. The warm marble felt nice under my bare feet. I wished for nothing at all. I felt light and free, was completely present and relaxed.

'Dear Mister No, I wish you were here. You still think I am just a little boy. But I am much older than you think. I can do lots of things by myself. Now I can manage without your help.'

Danijela slept with her mouth half-open. I woke her up with a gentle stroke behind the ear and a kiss on her dry, full lips.

She had killer breath.

Down in the sitting room, the hangovers dominated just as much. Mateja and Isabella had collected the rubbish in two large bags. Now they sat drinking water from Zlaja's plastic cups. He stood by the kitchen tap and gave out rounds of water. Martin and Fric were gone.

'And?' Zlaja shoved me when we went outside to throw out the rubbish. 'Did you?'

I tried to conceal my smug smile.

'Boom!' he shouted and raised his arm. 'I need all the details! Tell, tell! What have I taught you? What have I taught you?'

'No, let's meet by the pier later. Then we can talk about it. What about you and Mateja?'

He made a face and shrugged.

'What? Didn't she want to, or what?'

It was a rhetorical question. Is there anyone that would not want Zlaja, the number one scoring king of the bay? No way. That could never be the case.

'No, no,' he shrugged again. 'It was me, I couldn't be bothered.'

'Why?'

'I don't know.'

He jumped over the fence and put the rubbish in the round bin of the neighbouring villa:

'She looks like an iron.'

'What?'

'She looks like an iron.'

'What the hell do you mean by that?'

'I don't know. That nose … And then that guy Martin was there too. He was staring like crazy!'

'Ohhh! Now I'm with you.'

Zlaja jumped over the fence. He was in Raša's garden again:

'Wait till you see Miraja, man! She is … She is *completely* wild! I'm telling you. Just wait till you've seen her.'

The abandoned bungalows were where they always were, but looked a little cosier than they ever had before. The three girls and I were on our way home, when the fascist Pero came walking towards us. Danijela and I were holding hands, Isabella and Mateja were walking further back.

I had loose, uncombed hair and was wearing a pair of Lennon sunglasses. Our gazes could not meet.

He was wearing his new orange shirt. He was probably headed to Vešnja or something. The colour of the shirt really stood out from the surroundings and the rest of his clothes. He risked having someone pour a bucket of water over him. Wrap him up in a blanket. Ring the fire service.

'Hi,' he managed to mumble when we passed.

It must be Danijela who had nodded to him. I completely ignored him.

When he was behind us, Mateja broke out sniggering: 'The new fashion!'

All four of us laughed with all our hearts. Mine was dancing a jig.

The moron turned around and mumbled something. But I didn't care. Revenge was so sweet.

That's what it takes, I thought. Three girls and a clear indication that you have not slept at home. From now on I was going to score like a madman, stand here and wait for Pero and the other fascists to walk past. Those snotty brats, man! They don't score shit!

The next morning Danijela, Mateja and Isabella set course for Italy. Zlaja and I wandered down to the beach, played shaggy beasts and came into contact with two Czech grungers named Barbora and Tereza. Barbora had bigger breasts than Tereza, but the unpredictable Zlaja graciously left her to me.

'There's more to life than a pair of good breasts,' he rambled on profoundly on the terrace at Adria, where the band still played the same songs, mostly that one, 'Oh Carol, I am but a fool. Darling, I love you though you treat me cruel.'

Afterwards he took Tereza with him down to the beach, where she surrendered without much fumbling, while I was not given permission by Barbora to unbutton her torn Levis. She grabbed my wrist discreetly and said, 'No!' somewhere between a vague plea and a firm order.

Later she wrote letters in terribly bad English about how it was also baking in Karlovy Vary. About how we should be happy that we live by the sea and could just jump in.

I did not reply to her. Zlaja's Dutch girls had arrived at Adria, and again he had luck on his side. He repeated his success with Miraja – whose name was actually Mariah – while Fric, Goi and I drew the short straws.

One of the girlfriends had a guy back home, the second had brought hers along on the trip, and the third – according to Gogi – 'was not capable of winning his heart.'

Cassette 8

HARD TURD MACHINE

WHAT ELSE HAPPENED?

July turned to August. Zlaja and I ruled the beach, Fabio and I ruled Ukulele. The summer had already lived up to expectations, and it continued to surprise me with its generosity. It was not merely an unforgettable summer, it was *the* summer. I did not think it would come to an end. Everything that '92 and '93 had cheated me out of, '94 gave back. Just in another shape and surrounded by other people.

The thieves who stole the tourists' passports in Adria were never caught. The police did not even sniff around any more.

The war in Bosnia continued tirelessly. The Bosnian muslims, now called Bosniaks, no longer fought against only Serbs and Croats, but also against each other. The businessman Fikret Abdić and his supporters in the Bosanka Krajina region had declared independence and had jumped over to the Serbian side. Agreements were made and rejected The radio and the TV fed people with fear and indigestible amounts of bad music. I was part of an entirely different film. I idolised Bruce Dickinson's solo album that he made after the break with Iron Maiden. *Balls to Picasso*, it was called. It kicked arse! Pantera: *Cowboys from Hell, Vulgar Display of Power*. Suicidal Tendencies: *The Art of Rebellion*. My red cassette player glowed with thrash when Mum and Dad were out.

When I woke up, I immediately thought of Neno. With the same fear as before. Then it struck me: Oh, no, he is in Sweden, all's well, nothing to be scared of. I hopped out of bed and launched myself into the new day, relieved and grateful that he was in safety.

Then a letter suddenly arrived from Adi.

'What's up, Nose-prince? ... Are there Chetniks with

you? Punish those you can, man, and those you can't – Allah will take care of! … One day we will return and make minced meat out of them! … You and I, the great heroes … Do you remember the good old days? … We played Germans and partisans …'

And all in a kind of suspicious tone with a mixture of gravity and irony, nostalgia and hate.

He included his address and telephone number. I considered calling him straight away. Ask him if he was drunk when he wrote that, or had eaten mushrooms over in Slovenia?

But for some reason or other I did not. I also hesitated in replying to his letter. My mind was swimming for the rest of the day.

Not until that night in Wicky, where Fric came up with a fantastic gem, did I manage to shake off Adi's strange letter.

'What's up, Fric? How are you doing?' I asked him when he came in.

'Like an arse without buttocks,' he replied.

'What the hell does that mean?'

'Exactly! You caught on right away.'

'What do you mean?'

'Precisely! That's precisely what I mean. Do you understand?'

Slavko, the camp's self-appointed mayor, was responsible for another unforgettable gem. It was the middle of August, two to three weeks before the last weekend of the holidays. Everything was shit during those days. Literally. The soil pipes dripped and rattled and you could hear grandiose tunes between the thin walls of the toilets.

White-haired Slavko made a speech on the terrace between D1 and D2, while I sat on the balcony. It was not as long as some of the president's, but I had neither the strength nor the time to hear the end.

He started by reeling off all the sufferings that we – which later became I – had experienced since arriving at the camp, 'back when pictures of Serbian generals still hung on the walls.' He reminded the audience about back when we still had Serbian cooks at the restaurant, and who knows how that might have turned out, had he and some others, not reacted in time.

'And now this!' he concluded. 'This! Yes!'

A tin of liver paté hung from the small flap that you pull to open the lid. He held it between his thumb and index finger, like it was the tail of a dead mouse.

Then it came. The theory that, 'French liver paté like this' could be to blame for the food poisoning and the collective intestinal drainage taking place in the camp. The French were known to be Serbian allies. Mitterrand supported Milošević!

I don't know if the liver paté really was French, or if it just had something written in French on the tin: Mum had binned the one we had. But it was not the culprit. Shortly after Slavko's interminable speech, a couple of inspectors from the food hygiene department came by. They conducted an investigation and wrote a report. The liver paté was completely exonerated. Disinfectant had been sprayed in the kitchen the day before the first – and the worst – diarrhoea day. The inspectors took tests and came to the conclusion that the spray, which was meant to be used to exterminate the kitchen's many moths, which had accidentally landed on an open bag of macaroni.

It was a regrettable mistake. Nobody was fired. The war on moths could continue. Tirelessly and without fear of further victims.

BLOOD AND SOUP

The most sensational event of the summer was Mirko's dramatic departure from the camp. For a long time afterwards, people shook their head when they talked about Mirko Parasite – the man who briskly strolled around and doggedly insisted that he was disabled, who idolised the president and the pope and always wore a rosary around his thick neck. But by then it was too late. The damage was done and blood had been spilled.

Every day after lunch, Mirko had the habit of opening the French windows on his balcony on the ground floor of D1. Here he placed various fruits – apples, pears, oranges and bananas – and tucked into them with undivided delight. The passers-by who presumed to ignore him, were verbally challenged, just watch Mirko 'vitaminizing himself.'

Next to his colourful fruit he usually placed a framed photo, which everyone in the camp knew all about. It was a photo taken by a professional photographer from Vešnja, whom Mirko had hired and paid for a single, yet unforgettable shot.

In the spring of 1994 the first rumours had emerged that President Doctor Franjo Tudjman was going to pay a brief visit to the city of Vešnja. Tudjman wanted to pass through the city, it was proudly whispered, and on foot even! It gave Mirko the brilliant idea to force his way through the passionate crowd of people, step in front of 'the president of all Croats' and hold out his hands towards him like some kind of supernatural figure. At the same time it had to be done spontaneously and *sincerely*, as though he was his equal, or a member of the family that you had not seen in a long time.

At least that was how it looked in the photo: Tudjman

smiling too. His right hand was open and outstretched. It was as though he was emphasising: this is a hand. In the background stood one of the president's corpulent body guards, suspiciously dissecting Mirko with his piercing and cool gaze. As Kaća put it: the gorilla nearly managed to ruin everything. His presence alone dragged the photo down a little, from the supernatural to the earthly.

Mirko tormented us for a long time with his unique photo. He walked around with it in his inside pocket and showed it to everyone regardless of sex, age or nationality. When he was no longer both annoying and ridiculous, but just annoying, and when people began to avoid him and his photo, he had it enlarged, framed, and at regular intervals exhibited on his balcony next to his 'vitamins.' In that way he raised himself up above the rest of us, who, for one thing, had never been photographed in the company of the president, and for another, could not afford to improve our vitamin deficient diet.

One day, while he stood eating a banana, he was teasing two boys, two brothers around ten or eleven, who were playing beneath his window. They responded by throwing pebbles at him. He told them to stop, and they replied that they would only do that if he gave them a banana.

Mirko replied with an obscenity about another banana that they could get a little of, and a voice from the balcony above also found it incredibly amusing. When Mirko's laughter started echoing between D1 and D2, the brothers started to throw bigger rocks at him. One of them hit the framed photo of the grandiose meeting between Mirko and Tudjman. The picture fell down, and the frame broke.

When Mirko came running out of the building, the children were already sprinting down the path. Their mother, a widow from the region of Osijek, was just passing the restaurant. Her children hid behind her, and she stepped forward.

The folk, who encountered Mirko on the path, later described him as being completely red in the face. That he was out of breath and literally moaning with anger. He started to shout that the children had shattered his photo, that it was an attack against the president, and that she – if she were a true Croat – would immediately give the children a proper hiding. Otherwise, Mirko would 'take matters into his own hands.'

The mother replied rather calmly that nobody in the world was going to hit her children. Least not him. That he should just relax and mind himself and not go round deciding who was a true Croat and who was not. Especially when he himself was not 'the Croatian Croat' but 'the Bosnian.' And then she called him a sycophant.

Mirko did not reply, but grabbed her by the hair and started to pound his fist into her face. The children hid behind a fig tree near the path, crying and screaming and shouting for help.

To make matters worse, Mirko was wearing a watch with a metal band, which cut the woman on the forehead and the face. The band sprung open, and the watch flew off. The woman fainted and Mirko let go.

With blood on his shirt he ran into the restaurant. A handful of the old people who witnessed the incident were in shock and moved out of his way, while those who saw it all from the corner balconies of D1 were already on the way down towards reception to call the police.

At the restaurant, Mirko ran straight into the kitchen, where he shouted something inarticulate about the bad food and the lack of salt. He demanded to speak to the chef immediately. The female cooks walked backwards and crossed themselves at the sight of the bloody man babbing away.

The chef demanded that Mirko leave at once. Access to the kitchen was reserved for employees. They started to argue, and Mirko insisted on his portion of food being brought to his room in future. His torrent of words was interrupted by the chef, who grabbed the handles of a large pot of soup and threw the contents over Mirko. Luckily for the Parasite, the soup – with carrots, parsley and letter-shaped pasta – had long since cooled down.

He turned on his heels and ran. First out of the restaurant and then past the tennis court and the disused bungalows.

For half an hour he ran around Majbule, and then he showed up on the terrace by the corner of D1. With dried blood and soup on his shirt he slipped into the building and locked himself in his room.

At the other end of the terrace, between the TV room and the entrance to D2, half of the camp had gathered. Everyone was waiting for the police to arrive. The woman was driven to the hospital, where they patched her up. She later returned with her face wrapped in white gauze. She looked like a mummy and said that Mirko should thank God that her husband had been killed in the war. Had he been alive, he would have made sure he really was disabled.

When she returned, Parasite no longer lived in the camp. Directly after he had locked himself in his room and drawn the curtains, the authorities pounded on his door. The cops asked him to open up and promised they would not harm him. One of them came out of D1 and went down the stairs towards the path. He stopped beneath Mirko's window, where the photo of the president was still lying. He picked up a couple of pebbles and threw them at the window, while he shouted and called Mirko. The rest of us did not utter a peep. Not even a whisper could be heard in the crowd.

Finally, Mirko let the cops in, and a few long minutes later, they lead him across the terrace towards their car by the Muscle Market. The crowd split in two so they could get past. Suddenly a sea of accusations, taunts and condemnatory curses were heard. Mirko swung away in handcuffs. He was perfectly calm. He looked down at the ground. The dried pieces of letter-shaped pasta still clung to his green Hawaiian shirt. I clearly saw a V and an O on his left shoulder.

PHONE CALL

Some things are better remembered than others. For example, I am still in doubt as to which day the police collected Mirko Parasite. The same goes for the day his belongings were collected. On the other hand, I clearly remember that it was Friday morning of the same week that I received a letter.

It was a rectangular envelope and difficult to bend, but the letter itself did not take up much room. Two lousy pages.

'Congratulations … You're almost grown-up now … Behave yourself …'

Included were two hundred Swedish kroner, folded up in silver paper.

He was clever, that Mister No. He did as he was taught. A letter from abroad, addressed to a refugee camp was a rather easy target. As soon as the people in the post office spotted it, they knew what was in it. Time after time we heard about post that never arrived. On the radio they went on about transport issues, about a few mail sacks that were drenched with rain. But they could not fool me. Except for the hourly chime, by now everything you heard on the radio was a lie. Not even the weather forecast did I trust. You always had to prick up your ears, break the codes, read between the lines. 'Clear with a few showers' for example meant that it would either piss down or remain dry and cloudy.

'Oh, already!' Mum said when I came in.

'Yes. Rather two days early than two days late.'

'The post doesn't come on Sundays, either, does it.'

'No, he couldn't get me on the day.'

I handed her the letter:

'Why doesn't he send a picture soon? I would like to see him. It's been over two years.'

'I don't know,' Mum sighed. 'Maybe it's expensive to get them developed up there.'

'There's something fishy about it,' Dad said. '*Very* fishy.'

'Yes, you've said that,' I snapped. 'How's Uncle doing? Did you call him back?'

'Yes. He said to say hello. He complained about an uneven footpath.'

'Why?'

'Heh, heh! He tripped over it yesterday. Kissed the asphalt and hurt himself. Right outside his flat.'

'Two days after his return?' Mum asked. 'How unlucky! How is he doing?'

'Good. But imagine! He's seen so much of the world and still can't figure out how to walk. How come *I* don't trip? Why does that never happen to me?'

'Stop it,' Mum laughed.

'That's how it is when your feet get used to the even, Canadian asphalt. You grow inattentive.'

'Maybe,' I said. 'But better that than walk on this all your life. You always have to stare at the ground here! You can never relax.'

'Yeah, the tanks have also destroyed it in a few places. But still! Why do *I* never trip? Why does it never happen to *me*?'

I went down to reception to exchange the money. Sergio sent me to the shop, and the shopkeeper looked at the daily newspaper lying on the counter.

'Exchange rate?'

He nodded.

'It's not every day people come here with Swedish currency. Who have you got up there?'

'Five brothers! I'd like some coins, please. Do you know how much it costs to call Sweden?'

'No. I never ring abroad.'

They had finally cleaned the two booths in reception. It

smelled of spirits in number one, and the receiver was dry and smooth. I dialled the number, but it was busy. I tried several times, went out, waited a little and tried once more.

No result.

Then I remembered him once saying that a lot of people shared the phone.

'People hang onto the receiver all day long,' he had complained, 'even though it costs a fortune. It's better to write letters.'

I went out and sat down on the step in front of reception. Old Jozo from D2, who suffered from insomnia, had fallen into the deepest sleep of them all. Mum had told me that same morning. Now they carried his corpse past me out to the ambulance at the Muscle Market. The situation became more awkward for me than necessary. His daughter and two ambulance workers spotted me while I sat scratching my balls. I got up awkwardly, looked away and hurried into reception.

This time I was in luck. A woman answered the phone and said that she knew Neno – they were neighbours – but that she had not seen him for several days.

'There are a lot of us in this camp,' she said. 'Can I get him to call back when I see him?'

'Yes. Where could he be?'

'I don't know. But I'll give him your message.'

'Okay. Thanks.'

I remained there, hungry. The stupid situation with the balls and Jozo's corpse made me think of Adi. He scratched himself down there all the time. Especially after he had got hold of a Jackie Collins novel during the war. For a number of days he constantly talked about 'Jackie' and the detailed depictions of sex in the book. He let me read several select passages.

I went up to the room, found Adi's number and gave him a ring. The phone rang and rang but nobody picked up.

Maybe it's for the best, I thought. Maybe he should not even have written to me.

OUT THE DOOR

The following day was a Saturday, and Saturday was known as Ukulele day. I slept in as long as I possibly could. Woke up alone in the room and lay there. No erection. Over from D2 I heard the intro to 'Oh Croatian mothers, don't mourn. Call, just call. All falcons will give their lives for you.'

I listened closely to 'Peace Frog', 'The Rime of the Ancient Mariner' as well as the A-side of *Vulgar Display of Power*. My Sanyo cassette player was by Dad's pillow, within reach. I turned it up all the way. The patriotic chorus only bothered me during the silence between the songs.

Then I got up. The sky was full of small white clouds when I opened the balcony door. My purple T-shirt had been left to soak, when I finally found it, and the toilet seat felt lovely and cool.

The shit refused to die. It really was irrepressible. I had to empty the cistern several times before at long last it accepted its fate.

It also surprised me that my toothpaste spit was more red than usual. My gums were apparently not what they once had been. When I checked them with my tongue, they felt tender and soft on one side.

Despite that, I was not dissatisfied with the start of the day. For some reason I was rather chipper. Maybe it was because I was going out to celebrate my seventeenth birthday that night. Maybe because the music, Pantera in particular, worked me up.

Sometimes you are just happy. You wake up and can feel it, and that's just how it is.

It was quarter past twelve when I grabbed our orange plastic bowl and went out. The door to Gogi's room was wide open.

It reeked of oil inside. Gogi's grandfather stood bare-chested by the electric hob flipping a pancake with a single, constant movement of his hand.

Outside, hot air poured over me. Red-haired Ljubica, who I always found 'hot for her age,' was painting her toenails on the balcony of D1.

At the restaurant I saw neither Pero nor Bruno. That alone, that they were neither in front of me nor behind me in the queue, made the news about the daily special bearable.

Rice with liver gravy for lunch. Tinned sardines for dinner. Bread.

'No fruit today?'

'None.'

'No yoghurt?'

'None.'

After eating I did not manage to find either Zlaja or Fric at home. Fric was slaving away in Vešnja, while Zlaja had driven to Grozvin with his dad. I stood picking figs somewhere on my way back when a car came driving towards me. I let go of the branch and stuffed the figs discreetly into the pocket of my swim trunks.

I could already see the headlines of tomorrow's paper: 'A young man, who happened to turn seventeen today, was imprisoned for stealing fruit in Majbule.' And further down in the story: 'The underage EP … bla bla bla … is previously unknown to the police. The theft is exclusively down to his dietary awareness, he explained to the police and the assembled press.'

They tasted good, the figs. I wolfed them down on my way past the abandoned bungalows. Thought back to the summer of '92. Marina, Elvis Amar … The dry pine needles … The same gentle smell of suncream and resin.

Kaća was lying by the pier in Adria. I sat down next to her, and we lazed about for a couple of hours.

'What time are you going to Ukulele?' she asked.

'I don't know. What about you?'

'That depends on Silvija. It's her party.'

'You have to come before it's over.'

'Yes, and what time is it over?'

'Five bands, half an hour each, plus sound check … they'll probably be finished before twelve. I don't think they can play later than that. It is outdoors.'

We only went swimming once. I held out my hand and helped her up. Was completely gobsmacked when she stood up. It struck me that Kaća had grown beautiful. She had really developed in the time I had known her. Especially this summer, something had happened. She had gained a little weight, and the longer hair suited her better than the messy short hair.

'Kaća,' I said. 'It's a damn shame that you're so ugly!'

'What?'

'Otherwise I would have made my move a long time ago.'

She ducked her head underwater and let her right hand remain above. Her middle finger pointed directly up at the sky. I laughed. Kaća flung her hair back:

'I'll never get married. Men are such pigs. And you're not very sweet today either! What kind of shit is that you're spouting?'

Some things you remember better than others. For example, I am still in doubt as to whether Mum and Dad came home from the beach *while* I took a shower, or if they did directly *after* I was finished. Nor do I remember if I shaved the few soft hairs I had south of my nose, or if I trimmed them with nail clippers. On the other hand I remember clearly that the label on the shampoo bottle was green, that the contents of the bottle were thin and barely foamed up. Apple. Almost no smell. I remember the strangest things.

Dad was lying down reading the paper, while I put on my checked shirt. I did not button it up, had my Maiden

T-shirt underneath. It had got muggy over the course of the afternoon, and I had forced myself into a pair of tight jeans. You have to suffer for the sake of being cool.

The trousers came from the Red Cross warehouse, but they were tip top. Thin and dark-blue, with spacious pockets. I imagined their previous owner, a tough heavy dude, a drummer who had grown out of them. Then a crazy hot chick, who just had to have a new pair.

The latter was my preferred version. The thought that the girl had had her groin right where I now had mine was the icing on the cake. I wondered what she might look like. I wondered about the likelihood of us meeting tonight. For her to point at my tightly packed groin and say: 'Those are my old trousers!'

Would that actually be cool? Would she ridicule me in front of the whole gang or laugh excitedly about how small and wonderful the world was?

'You can have them back, if you like,' I heard myself say.

'No, that's alright,' was her reply. 'But I would like to try them on. Just one more time. Just to see if they still fit.'

'Fair enough! Here?'

'No! He-he! I know a *much* better place.'

Dot, dot, dot … And so on … And all that.

Mum stood on the balcony hanging up the washing when I put on my good old All Stars. I waved goodbye to her and said, 'see you' to Dad. He nodded. Without looking up or putting the paper down. His lips moved as he read.

'Take care of yourself,' Mum said. 'And don't drink too much.'

'Alright, alright! Take it easy,' I replied and went out.

I came out the door the same way I had done so many times before. Without stopping or turning around. I forgot all about Mum and Dad before I even grabbed the door handle. I was on my way to Ukulele. In my mind, I was already outside and far away.

But sometimes, when I think back, I wish that I had

stopped at the bloody door, had turned around and taken one last look at the room and the two of them. That I had told them not to worry if I didn't come home that night. That maybe I would sleep at a friend's in Vešnja.

Sometimes it is Saturday night again, and I stop at that same door, nearly seventeen years old. I hold onto the door handle and observe Mum and Dad and everything around them. Time stands still. I am a ghost and don't say a single word. I just stand there and dwell on the smell of our laundry, the sight of the orange plastic bowl with cold liver gravy and the faint, almost sleep-inducing sound of Dad rustling the newspaper that is packed with lies.

Then I depart from room 210 in building D1.

UP AT THE CITADEL

I hitch a ride into town. It was the last weekend of the holidays, and my monthly pass was not valid yet. School was going to start two days later, and Zlaja was already jealous. He was looking for work. There was nothing. He considered pretending to be insane in order to avoid military service. He didn't want to 'lose his hide' as he put it.

'You don't need to pretend,' I joked. 'Just act normal, then they'll probably send you home.'

Fric was hired as a 'server.' That is the bricklayers' assistant at various building sites. He mixed cement, sand and water and served the mortar to the officious masters. Gogi had got him the job. Gogi spread his legendary smile and raised his eyebrows while he told me in detail about how the bricklayers took the piss out of Fric and his 'Imagine this.' I could picture it all in front of me: the master bricklayers sitting on the scaffolding smoking their fags, Fric wiping his brow, and the sun baking everything and everyone at a building site covered in cement dust.

'Herr Fritz,' one of the masters said. 'This mortar is too thin! Imagine this, that you add less water! So do it! Hurry!'

'Ha! Ha! Ha!'

'"Herr Fritz!" Ha! Ha!'

Myself, I had to tackle the third and final year of trade school. The door to my bright future was about to open for me. I could already glimpse what awaited me on the other side of the crappy doorstep: a goodbye and a thank you from Boro, who did not have enough work or could afford to employ me, then a regular spot at the Muscle Market and best case, periodic employments at one of the building sites where the Turbo-folk king Gogi and the death metal prince Fric honourably earned their daily bread.

Beep! Beep-beeeeeep!

A column of cars passed me in Vešnja. A wedding party. A true orgy of kitsch and loathsome sounds.

I hated car horns. I hated trumpets. And most of all, I hated people in suits and ties.

At the head of the column, an older guy with slicked-back hair stuck his head out the window. He was singing something inarticulately and energetically waving a Croatian flag that was already fluttering. Several windows were open, and several people stuck their heads out and hollered in excitement. The problem was that you couldn't hear a thing because of their car horns.

Beep! Beep-beeeeep!

I turned down a narrow street that led towards the marketplace. A new record shop had opened at the end of the street. I wanted to check it out, even if it was after closing time.

It was a small shop with a nicely arranged display window. *Angel Dust* by Faith No More and a best-of The Smiths hung from a nylon thread at the same height. I still did not know The Smiths, but immediately fell for the low-key cover, with a woman sitting in a bar smoking a cigarette.

Then my eyes rested on the bottom of the display window.

Wow! They had all six White Button cassettes! The first six albums!

It was Yugoton, now called Croatia Records, who had re-released them with Bregović's consent. I discovered that later. I just stood there, breathing on the glass and feeling my heart press against my throat. It grew. It wanted out.

The tapes were spread across the bottom of the display window. It was strange to stand there and look at the cool covers again, after such a long time, through the glass, and in such a small format. Apart from *A Lullabye for Radmila M*

I had all the other albums as LPs back home.

It is a good thing that not everything is lost, I thought. It is a good thing that records can be re-released! On tape, at least.

I decided to buy all the tapes as soon as possible. I had to have them. I could just save on something else. Celebrate tonight, assess the finances tomorrow and go from there. Or ask Boro for a small advance.

A few riffs, melodies and solos washed over me. Soon I had the craziest ex-Yugo-retro-trip, without even knowing what that meant. I hummed various verses on the way through the packed marketplace, where the were wasps buzzing and the juicy watermelon slices were tempting.

The good old White Button records! My old record player! My room! All the issues of *Džuboks*, which Mister No subscribed to, and all the old posters! It felt like two hundred years ago.

'Six litres of bambus and some plastic cups, please. No, not the jug. Can I get four bottles of Coke instead? And then that small one there … What is that? Rum? Okay. Good! A small bottle of rum, too, please!'

I dragged two heavy bags out of the wine cellar and past my old school. Thought about all the water I drank in the school toilet. Of the go-getter, Horvat, who was going to come that night. Of that moron, Tomić, who did not teach me anything except to hate him.

Up by the citadel I quickly assumed our usual spot, sat there waiting for the others. We had some warming up to do before our trip to Ukulele. I had invited every Tom, Dick and Harry: Fabio, Daco, Endi, Glava, Bego, Neven, Role, Tonči, Kreja, Brale, Horvat, Anastasije … Everyone said they would come and bring friends with them.

The citadel was a well-preserved medieval fortification, where you had to pay to get in, look around and climb the lookout tower. Beneath one of the walls of the fortification – the one facing the harbour – there was a plateau with a few slender trees, green bushes and scattered building remains from the time of the Romans. The excavations had long since stopped and were overgrown. They were one and a half metres deep, and there were bottles and condoms in most of them. I never understood why nothing more was done with this place. It had the best view in the city.

Our spot was between the furthest blocks of stone and the security fence. Through the fence and across the bushes on the slope you could see across the dense city centre and the large cranes by the harbour.

Twilight. The first lights were being switched on. I opened a chilled bottle of bambus and took the first sip. Below, the city was buzzing with summer and life. The vehicles rumbled away, quietly but constantly – as if there were only a single unseen car. A ship's horn blew hollowly on the horizon beyoind the harbour, and I suddenly felt very happy. The sky was quite clear. Ready to reveal the stars.

I thought about Mauro, and about how everything was going to go that night. He and his new band, Hard Turd Machine, had not had much time to practice. I wondered if it was stupid of them to sign up. They could have just waited until next month. There was talk that the Open Stage events would become a tradition at Ukulele. The place wanted to support young talent and bla, bla, bla. Mauro hoped there would be producers and managers there, that he would be discovered that night. So did I. The only problem was that I still hadn't heard the band play. They acted like divas and banned any form of visit to the rehearsal room. They needed to 'work in peace.'

Fabio and four others arrived five or ten minutes later. I did not even get a chance to think of the two Ukulele girls I had talked to last time. Further behind me others groups had gathered. I knew almost none of them, only a guy with the nickname Vampi. He was the only one in Ukulele who wore a long vampire-like leather coat. He was lean and had thin dark hair. He actually looked like Nick Cave, now that I think about it. Don't know if he knew Nick Cave back then.

I didn't, at any rate.

Fabio and the others wished me a happy birthday, hugged and kissed me, as custom dictated.

'It's not until tomorrow,' I protested.

'Yes, and you won't get your present until Monday,' Fabio said.

'What is it?'

'It's a surprise.'

'By twelve we'll already be wasted,' Endi said. 'Let's see what you've got in the bag!'

I remember the two or three hours of hanging out at the citadel. I remember several conversations, jokes and funny stories. The Satanist Brale rambled about Tolkien and *The Hobbit*, which he had read several times. Fabio talked about a tame concert he had been to at Ukulele – a concert that I had missed because I had been broke. Horvat, who arrived later dragging several of my good school friends with him, was in an unusually good mood. He drank quickly and told good jokes. I remember the one about a man sitting on the bus. The inspector arrives and wants to check his ticket. 'Ticket!' the inspector says. 'Yellow,' the man says. 'What?' 'Yellow,' he says. The inspector repeats himself: 'May I see your ticket please?' 'Yellow,' the man repeats. 'What do you mean yellow?' 'Yeah, what do you mean "ticket"?'

I responded with one I had heard on the radio. The Free Europe reporter from Geneva had said about the peace negotiations reminded him of a joke, where a man walks into a church and prays to God that he will win the lottery. He prays week after week and simply does not understand why he doesn't win. One day he hears a deep and annoyed voice from up on the altar: 'Then why don't you buy a ticket for once!'

At one point I realised that I didn't feel like leaving. I was sitting on a warm block of stone from the Roman times, surrounded by friends and their friends, observing the city and passing around more and more fresh bottles. It's probably called something like melting into the situation or the moment, but I didn't feel like I was melting into anything at all. I was still completely myself. I was just not in a hurry to move on, had no idea what time it was, and did not think about what might be happening at Ukulele at that point.

Later, when I started to feel the bambus a little more, I walked a few metres away from the others and sent a stream of piss down through the fence. I stood alone in the dark and was raised above the city and its sparse quantity of lights. Wafting from behind me came the sweet smell of burnt corn silk, a girl sniggering stupidly several times, and I stood there with my manhood in my hands and felt content and powerful. I wished I had more piss in me. I could have stood there for an eternity. Just stood there pissing. And be almost seventeen and almost drunk for the rest of my life.

I shook myself off and walked back to my guests. The sweet smell was here too. Fabio and Horvat were arguing over what it was.

'Hash!' Horvat said.

'Grass!' Fabio said.

'No, it's hash!'

'No, it is grass!'

'It is hash! I know what I'm bloody talking about!'

'Boys,' I broke in a slightly pedagogical tone, 'why don't we just say that it's both?'

Then I told them about Boro's friend Ljubomir and his 'neither sheep nor donkey' story. Everyone laughed, and I laughed too. We drank everything in the bags, apart from the small bottle of rum, which only Jurišič, the local patriot, tried. He grimaced and shoved the bottle back into my hands: 'Yuck!'

I took one sip with my nose closed and stuffed the bottle into my back pocket.

Then we slowly walked down the path, towards the city.

SEVENTEEN

On the tall foundation of the terrace, to the left of the gate, some provo had written in large letters: UKULELE IS JUST A SMALL GUITAR. Horvat was dying with laughter. They had in fact put up a new neon sign up by the entrance. The graffiti ended up being right under the sign, and Horvat and I proclaimed it as the new slogan for the place.

While we stood in the queue, I remembered the bottle of rum. I hurried down the street, placed the bottle in the grass behind a bush and hurried back.

The others were talking to Mauro and a powerfully built and totally dangerous, pierced chick. She was at least twenty. She had ripped tights, a leather skirt and a short-sleeved pink shirt. The colour of the shirt reminded me of the icing on wedding cakes I had seen on TV, but had never tasted.

'There he is! The birthday boy!'

'Our songwriter!'

'The Ukulele beast!'

'Mi-ki!'

The girl's name was Renata, and to everyone's surprise Mauro introduced her as the new lead singer of the band.

'Wow! Did you know anything about this?' I asked Fabio.

'Yes, but I wasn't allowed to say anything.'

'Yeah,' Mauro said. 'We alternate between male and female vocals. It establishes tension in ... how should we put it ... the repertoire. Wait and see!'

'As long as you don't sing a duet, like some musical,' I said, 'then I'm happy.'

I didn't dare ask him how far they had got with 'my' song.

Mauro and Renata walked ahead to have 'an internal meeting' before they went on stage. The rest of us finally got in.

The band that we could hear from outside, and which was still pounding away on stage, was from Split. They were playing their arses off. The lead singer's T-shirt was drenched in sweat. He poured a glass of beer over his face between songs. He was so ugly, he was almost beautiful.

'They remind me of The Exploited,' Fabio said, and I nodded:

'Agreed. All punk sounds like The Exploited!'

The terrace was pretty full, but there were not as many people as on a normal Saturday night. I searched for Kaća and her girlfriends, but found Dejo, the bass player in Mauro's band. He stood at the base of one of the two spotlight constructions placed at either end of the terrace. The lights pointed at the stage and the OPEN STAGE SATURDAY banner behind it.

In front of the stage, a group of punks were dancing the craziest slam dance. Kicking military boots flashed in every direction. A guy with no top on climbed onto the stage. He wanted to stage dive, but changed his mind when he saw how few people there were at the very front of the stage. He contented himself with jumping off the stage feet-first and continuing to slam dance, as if nothing had happened.

I studied the equipment and the instruments. They were cool. The bass guitar was massive. The bass player – small and round-cheeked. The background vocals were sung by the drummer, who could barely be seen behind his busy cymbals. He was pounding away.

Dejo downed his beer and lit another cigarette. He looked impressively calm.

'What time are you guys on?' I asked.

'In an hour. This is fucking boring. They're just droning on.'

'Yeah, but they bloody mean it! Do you want to come with me? I'm buying.'

'No, you don't have to do that. I can afford it tonight.'

'Come on! It is *my* birthday after all!'

We squeezed through the crowd and went into the bar. I

said hi to Komar, Ukulele legend number one. The man was twenty-five years old. Famous for being only one of three guys from Vešnja who had been to the Pink Floyd concert in Vienna that summer. Stood twenty metres from Gilmour, he had said. Had drunk Vodka Red Bull on the way to the concert grounds. I was close to bursting with pride because I knew the man. He had the wickedest sideburns. I looked forward to the day I would be able to pull something like that off.

'Do you want to go backstage with me?' Dejo asked when we took the first sip.

'Backstage? Where's that?'

'Upstairs.'

'Cool! I'm in.'

He laughed:

'No, I'm taking the piss!'

'Oh, fuck you, man! It could be true.'

'Easy, man! Who do you think we are? The Beatles?'

'No,' I said. 'I hate The Beatles. You know that.'

A little later I cruised around and maintained my calm state of drunkenness. Two really hard bands played after the punks, and I stood with Fabio head-banging a little. They were very bleak and vicious. Especially band number two. They used keyboards in several of their songs and sounded a lot like Mercyful Fate and King Diamond. Something with deep organ notes in the intros and a lead singer who could really hit her falsetto.

When they were finished and the name Hard Turd Machine was blasted out of the speakers, I stood in the toilet taking a piss. The heavy stench of ammonia already hit me several metres from the large entrance. In its own way, it was a brilliant smell, the smell of Ukulele.

Mauro and the others stood on the stage fiddling with the equipment and their instruments when I came out. There was a brief pause. I moved over next to Renata, who stood to the left of the stage with Fabio and Gabrijela. She had long since declared that she only wanted to be friends with Fabio, but he had not given up.

'How come I've never seen you before?' I asked Renata, when Fabio and Gabi left.

'You must have been blind, and now you see.'

'Good answer!'

'I'm from Lovgar. I'm Dejan's cousin.'

'A-ha! And how many numbers are you going to play for us, Dejan's cousin?'

'Seven. Sorry, boy! You seem very nice and all that, but I'm up now.'

'Boy?' I said and looked around. 'Who are you talking to? I'm the only one here.'

She disappeared behind the stage and popped up on the side where Dejo was sipping a beer. They exchanged a few remarks, and she remained standing there, to the left of the drums. People were hooting and whistling impatiently. Mauro fiddled with an amp and stepped on his two pedals. Dejo got people to laugh when he put his sunglasses on, while Baja tested the bass drum and adjusted his chair.

Then an uncontrolled and far, far, far too loud sound roared out of Mauro's Marshall. It sounded like a Lipizzan horse whose back leg had ended up in a gigantic meat grinder. It was a hideous sound, full of suffering and confusion. You could almost see the froth dripping out of the horse's mouth, as it desperately attempted to get away.

'What the hell are they doing?'

Dejo jumped aside in shock. Mauro looked surprised, as he restlessly grabbed his Gibson copy and stomped on the various pedals. He tried to tame the equipment and at the same time make it look intentional.

He succeeded. The drummer came to his aid by making a drum roll and a quick break. Dejo made a single 'bop-bop' on the bass, and then it went quiet. Mauro adjusted his microphone and said:

'Good evening!'

The crowd roared. A few murmured a greeting in return.

'We're called Hard Turd Machine, and what you just

heard was our latest number … "The Wild Horse Symphony"!'

People applauded. So did I. Nice save! Just in the nick of time.

Mauro unbuttoned his shirt. He had nothing underneath, apart from a chain with two devil's heads made of carved stone and plastic. He was already sweating.

'Yeah!' he shouted. 'The next number is *not* instrumental. We call it 'The Physical Act of Love!''

Then he played the first riff. He knelt down a little and started to hammer away. Four quarter notes! His left knee poked out through the tear in his ripped trousers. When Dejo and Baja followed, Mauro started to head-bang like a madman. The machine was driving!

Ramones, I thought. Stolen riff, but to hell with it: the audience was clearly up for it. After the hard, wicked boys and lyrics with death, blood, war and pain in every other verse, the more melodic punk rock hit was a godsend. The atmosphere grew festive. Mauro stepped to the side and left the centre of the stage to Renata. We responded with a massive roar.

She stepped forward and grabbed the mic. She looked insanely good with her jet black hair, the piercing in her nose and the bright pink shirt. She stood almost motionless on the stage, her eyes closed and her lower arms hanging by the microphone stand. Her voice was alluring and sexy. It caught me completely off guard, that such a special voice could come from the same girl I had just stood talking to.

'She's so cool!' Horvat said.

Unfortunately we could not hear half the words she sang. The sound of the guitar was far too loud and drowned out parts of the vocals. I heard only the chorus in its entirety – 'The physical act of love, man! The physical act of love, yeah! The physical act of love, man! That's what I need, yeah! That's what I neeeeed!' – and then there was a brief modulation and a thumping guitar solo. Mauro went down on his knee again and proved his worth. They were sizzling!

The next four numbers were sung in Croatian. Mauro sang backing for the first one, then lead on the next, with Renata singing the second chorus. He was right. It actually worked really well, the interplay. And Renata's charisma was in a class of its own. It looked really promising. Hard Turd Machine! If they didn't make it, I don't know what would.

But there was also room for improvement. Mauro's lyrics lacked a little wildness, at least the ones I could hear. There were far too many repetitions. A lot of rock cliches. I could easily see myself giving the lyrics an affectionate hand. Throw in some more vitamins and minerals. Mix them around a little. Fine tune the stanzas to new heights.

After playing 'We Want the Airwaves,' a Ramones cover – yes, it was all right! I knew it! I have a nose for that sort of thing! – Mauro took off his shirt and wiped his face with it. He threw the shirt aside and looked at his watch.

'We're about to wrap up!'

'Noooo,' we roared, and Fabio, Glava and I clinked glasses and took a sip of our beers.

Mauro smiled:

'It's almost twelve o'clock, and we're going to play one last song for you.'

'Boo-ooo!' Fabio bleated. 'Crap band!'

'This song,' Mauro said, 'really means a lot to me.'

'Boo-ooo!'

He suddenly got serious:

'As many of you already know … it hasn't been much of a secret … that I've been through a major artistic crisis.'

Silence. A couple of claps. People didn't really understand.

'That's how it is in this industry …'

Fabio and I looked at each other:

'What the hell is this he's spouting off?'

'It's been a difficult time. Not least because … when you live and breath to write and play music … and …'

'He's high!' Horvat said.

'I've had several highs and lows in my career ... several bands and fans ... But now we've found each other, the four of us ...'

He pointed at the others, and people clapped. Renata got the biggest applause and lots of whistles when she was introduced.

'And then there's a fifth ... band member, we could almost call him. This is the man who saved me ... to put it mildly ... There is a man who helped me through the difficult time thanks to some lyrics, which showed me the way, opened new horizons, started a new creative process!'

'Pope John Paul II!' someone in front of us shouted, and those who could hear him laughed loudly.

'No, not Polly! Polly is a fine fellow, but ... no, this is a man, who is actually here with us tonight. He has ...'

Mauro looked at his watch:

'He has already been seventeen years old for three minutes. It is ...'

Nobody understood a thing apart from me and my birthday guests. The reactions – our sporadic *yeahs* – came from the various places we stood.

Mauro played the first notes of 'Happy Birthday to You' and stopped.

'Yeah! His name is Miki! I call him Micky the Beast. This is the man who knows all the lyrics in the history of rock by heart. Miki, would you please come up here?'

No, I did not fancy that at all, but Fabio pushed me towards the stage and to the stairs on the right. Renata had already got people to clap in time, when Eli, the DJ, who functioned as MC on the night, moved some cables aside in front of my feet. I thanked him and walked past.

The spotlight blinded me.

Standing on that stage was nothing new to me – we normally hung out there on Friday and Saturday – but the spotlight and all the eyes directed at me made me a little uncertain and awkward.

People were clapping. Mauro started to play 'Happy

Birthday to You' again. Renata sang the four sugary-sweet lines to me. I didn't know what to do with my hands, so I lifted them up and began to conduct. Finally, before the final note, I went over to Mauro's microphone and shouted in it:

'... to meeeeee!!!'

I was holding a lit cigarette between my fingers, and the smoke stung my eyes while I held the mic. It was insanely weird to hear your own voice across the terrace. I was nearly frightened by it.

'Thank you! Thank you very much.'

Mauro gave me a hug. I waved at the other three and bowed on my way off the stage. Eli said happy birthday. Fabio hugged me. We remained by the stairs behind the speakers, because Baja was already starting to beat the rhythm – one, two, three! – and the song began.

It was a ballad. E-minor, D- and C-major. Those were the three chords I could see Mauro play – but there were more! The tempo was relatively slow, but at the same time you could sense that it would not be like that throughout the song. Harder riffs were on the way, the lurking disquiet in Mauro's phrases hinted. Something was brewing.

The song's build-up reminded me a little of Metallica's old ballads – 'One,' 'Sanitarium,' 'Fade to Black' – but mostly of 'Civil War' by Guns N'Roses, one of their few songs I could still put up with. It was a rock'n'roll song. There was not much metal and no punk at all.

After the second refrain Mauro stepped on one of his pedals and turned towards me. He nodded with a smile and played a brilliant, melodic solo. Then he turned to the audience again. There was an instrumental break. Mauro played the same chords and the same melody as during the pieces, now just as riffs with a shaggy distortion included. The crowd roared, I felt a tingling down my back.

When Renata started to sing an extra piece, which Mauro had added himself, people went completely amok. He had figured out my method and used it. Taken various phrases and verses from the different songs and pieced them together. He even took two band names and stuck them together: Sick of It All and Rage Against the Machine became 'I'm sick of it all, I feel a strange rage against the TV, this hard turd machine that poisons my eyes.'

Wow, I thought. He named my lyrics after the name of the band, or the other way round, the band according to the lyrics, the majority of I had written. That is too cool, man! It's like Iron Maiden and their first album, where the band, the album and the song have the same name! And Maiden always plays that one at the end, too, just like Hard Turd Machine now!

I got tears in my eyes. I stood there behind the speakers and looked across the crowd as they head-banged in time. They liked it. It looked insane with all the outstretched arms and crazy signs of the horn and devil heads, that just swung at the same tempo.

I was gobsmacked. The thought that several of them would soon swap their air guitars for a proper AK-47 and be shoved into another kind of machine, did not cross my mind at a single point. I had completely forgotten that there even was something called war. That I came from somewhere else. That maybe one day I would leave this city and travel somewhere.

I put out the cigarette and hurried down to see how everything looked from the crowd's perspective. Got the same feeling as up at the citadel, when I stood pissing and looking across the city. Fabio and I mixed in with the audience and head-banged to the rest of the song.

When the band retired, there was a wild roar from the audience. It was the biggest applause of the night, no doubt about it. The applause went on and on and on. I raised my arms high in the air and checked: the ceiling of heaven was right above my head. I felt its hard, cool surface and pressed my palms against it.

No, you couldn't get any higher. Simple as that. It would never get better, I thought, and almost immediately, I discovered that I was wrong. Heaven's ceiling was raised again, straight away. My hands just swinging in the air again. There was at least a metre between my hands and the ceiling.

Because in that moment I spotted Suzi.

SEA SALT

Suzi! The blonde curly-haired Suzi with a colony of freckles on her face and a constant cheerful attitude. I had exchanged a couple of words with her one night when she had to go home. It was a long time ago. Then I met her again on the street one day, where she stood twirling a tuft of hair around her finger. I was just about to suggest a cold lemonade at the confectioner's or something along those lines, when she informed me that she was waiting for a girlfriend. They were going to play table tennis.

Now she stood talking to Anastasije. I told him that Glava was looking for him, which actually was true. Just that it was an hour ago.

He took off.

Suzi hugged me and wished me a happy birthday.

'So! You're getting pretty famous, eh?'

'Oh, that,' I shrugged, 'that's nothing special. How's it going?'

'Good, good.'

'Hey, do you know this one: a blind man meets a cripple. The blind man asks: "How's it going?" and the cripple replies: "Well, as you can see …" Do you know that one?'

'Yes. Everyone does.'

'Ah, okay!'

Quick change in subject. Slightly frenetic:

'What about the table tennis bats? Is that what you've got in your bag?'

Table tennis was the only thing I had to work with. She only had a small backpack with her. Not exactly a widespread phenomenon Saturday night at Ukulele.

'No, just a towel. We were out swimming. Larisa, Tanja and I.'

'Cool!'

'We just came from there. I've got salt everywhere.'

Just what I was waiting for! A quick forehand:

'Salt is fine with me. Where should I start?'

She hit me on my arm:

'Really!'

'Really, what?'

'A couple seconds on the stage, and then he thinks he can just, that he can ...'

'No, really it's got nothing to do with that,' I said while I dug into my pockets and emptied them of coins. 'Let's share a beer.'

'I don't have a penny,' she said. 'Tanja paid for my entrance.'

'Hey, that's not what I meant. I've got enough. Actually a little more than enough. It will be the last one of the night. Anyway ...'

'Yes?'

'Do you remember the last time we saw each other?'

'Obviously. In the pedestrian precinct.'

'I was just about to invite you for a glass of lemonade. And cake and ice cream and the whole caboodle!'

I did not run into Kaća that night at Ukulele. Nor Zlaja or Fric, who I had expected would come. The only one I did not expect to see was Gogi. His cousin had died, and the funeral was in Karlovac.

Suzi and I sat on the recently installed folding seats near the entrance. We shared a half litre of beer, and I told her excitedly about some of the bands that she had missed out on. Instruments and equipment were packed away and pushed away from the stage. Inside Eli was whipping up a party. In half an hour there would be free entrance, and people stood on the other side of the gate, drinking bambus they had brought with them, waiting.

Mauro and Baja walked past at one point. They wanted to know if Suzi and I wanted to go outside with them to drink Baja's Slivovitz. I was not interested. I was fine. I was exactly where I wanted to be. Suzi put up with my terrible jokes, and that was a good sign.

I bummed a fag off Mauro. He and Baja took off, and Suzi and I continued drinking and talking with bigger and bigger pauses. Another good sign. There was no need to jabber away. We could be content with commenting on what happened on the terrace in front of us. Share the hops and maintain some form of *we* in relation to the rest of the crowd.

Tanja went past and was content with a wave. If Suzi was not interested, Tanja would at least have come over to us. Another good sign.

Things moved in my direction. The night was mine, and it continued to prove it.

Then the plump half-litre bottle was empty. I rolled it aside and asked:

'Why don't we go for a walk and see what's happening?'

I actually wanted to go ask Eli if he would play 'Hallowed Be Thy Name', the *Live After Death* version – not the relatively slower album version. He definitely would have, it was my birthday after all, but Suzi said:

'No. Do you know what I feel like doing?'

'What?'

'Teasing your hair.'

'Teasing what?'

'Teasing,' she said and found a small strange comb at the bottom of her rucksack. The comb had very few teeth, but they were long. It was far longer than it was wide. An oddball comb. A comb freak.

'I can make you look totally cool!'

'Can you?' I said, noticing a bit of nerves. Because now she was going to sit there and touch me.

'Teasing! Why have I never heard of that before?'

Her fingers felt cool on my neck and scalp. The comb made some dry and bristling sounds, while Eli played The Cure, 'Doing the Unstuck'. I had long since grown tired of that song, but Suzi's enthusiasm rubbed off on me.

'I'm making you into Robert Smith!'

'Are you a fan?'

'Obviously.'

'Then go ahead.'

Eli had obviously gone over to the softer tunes, so I dropped the idea of my request entirely.

'Should we go for that walk then, m'lady?' I said and gallantly offered Suzi my right arm.

'Let's go, monsieur,' she replied and took me by the arm.

She was studying to be a chef and French was a mandatory subject.

'What is ćevapčići called in French?' I asked.

'I don't know,' she said. 'I don't eat meat.'

We went for a walk. Then another. Then more. People looked. I didn't know whether it was because of my brief appearance on stage or because of my hair. One ruled out the other in a way. So it had to be the hair. It was airy and massive. My head looked like a king-sized candy floss.

Near the entrance to the toilets we passed Vampi and one of his friends. They looked pretty stoned. When they spotted me, they broke down in laughter. They stopped, pointed at my hair and grabbed their stomachs. They could not control their laughing fit.

'Fuck am I ever high, man!' Vampi shouted. 'Do you see what I see?'

'Fuck, man!' the other moaned.

'It's grass,' I told Suzi. 'Or hash. Soft drugs.'

'He should eat more, that guy,' Suzi said. 'Man, he looks more zombie-like than you!'

The more walks we went for, the less we talked. I did not actually feel that drunk, by no means tired, in any case. We looked at each other a couple of times along the way and a smile flickered across her face. Suzi had large calf-like eyes and a crooked lower front tooth. She was the perfect height for me, and I caught myself thinking that we were actually a really good couple.

When we walked out the gate, helped along by three bouncers, who were impatiently cleareing the terrace of people, I finally spotted Fabio and Gabrijela. Fabio was going to walk Gabi home. It looked like they were holding hands, but I wasn't certain.

We banged fists and gave each other the sign of the devil. Agreed that the night was 'better than sex.' That Mauro and Renata had fooled all of us.

On the way towards the boulevard I said goodbye to a few people and reminded Kreja that he was going to have to find my *The Art of Rebellion* cassette soon.

'Otherwise I'm going to file a fucking compensation claim! You can count on it!'

I found my small bottle of rum completely unscathed in its hiding spot. We drank a little before we parted, and Fabio and Gabrijela disappeared down the deserted footpath.

'Where do you live?' I asked Suzi, who didn't want any rum.

It was rather far away, actually in the exact opposite end of the city. In the exact opposite direction I had to go. I knew that if I did not take my usual position soon and thumb a ride, it would be difficult to get a lift to Majbule before the early hours of morning.

But I did not care. I felt a lurking sadness that the evening was already drawing to an end. I wasn't tired and wanted to postpone its conclusion.

Suzi was still holding my arm, but I swapped sides and grabbed her hand. I could have kissed her already there on the boulevard, where our paths would part. I could have asked for her phone number and thanked her for the evening. I could have surprised her with a kiss in the middle of her synopsis of a film she thought I should see at the cinema. I could have stopped and pulled her close to me at the spot in the pedestrian precinct where we had met that day she was going to play table tennis with Tanja. I had loads of possibilities. I could also have gone back to Majbule early and in so doing avoid everything that was going to happen. But everything that was going to happen, obviously was *going* to happen. So it was not until much later that I kissed her, when we stopped to take a break in her neighbourhood.

In front of something resembling a hospital, but probably wasn't, we sat on a damp bench, surrounded by bushes, trees and paths of cracked cement. Suzi put her legs on top of mine. We sat across the boards and weaved our tongues together.

Ten metres from us, a gigantic popular hero from Tito's war stared at us. He watched over us with a tarnished machine gun, which, just like him, was made of bronze. The park was named after him, and his statue still stood in the middle. Even though unknown suspects had attempted to remove it. Even though the newspapers were abound with reader's letters for and against – with discussions about whether the man was a Croatian national hero or a communist war criminal. As often was the case with many things, it was a subtle line.

Both of Suzi's earlobes tasted of salt, the left more than the right. She smelt of summer, night and sea, and she kept adjusting my hair.

I played harmonica on her bare thigh.

'That tickles.'

'Of course it tickles.'

At the foot of the hill leading up to her block of flats, she said told me I didn't need to walk with her any more.

'You have to get home, too.'

'Yes, I have to get to Majbule.'

We agreed to meet Monday at one, in front of her school. We were not expecting to have many lessons. It was only the first day of the school year.

'If it drags out, then I'll just sneak out and wait for you,' I said.

'Already?'

'Yes.'

'Are you sure?'

I nodded:

'Sure as shooting. Good night!'

'You too.'

'And remember to dream about Miki!'

She laughed. Took a couple of steps back and stood up on her toes. I closed my eyes and got an extra kiss. She ruffled my hair with both hands.

'See you, cutie!'

'See you!'

The ceiling of heaven lowered. Or was I growing? I could sense it right above my head. Every twentieth step, when I checked if it was still there, it hung there and reminded me of what a fantastic night it had been. About how fantastic the night still was.

The vast majority of the city was asleep. Only a few cars drove past. The silence around me and the sound of my footsteps sounded good together. The pavement was there for me alone. I was the world's happiest man and full of strength.

Seventeen, I thought. I am seventeen, man! How crazy is that!

It had to be celebrated. It had to be celebrated a little more. I took the small bottle of rum out of my pocket and drank. The bottle was half-full, and I was full of energy. I could easily have walked straight up to the citadel and done the whole trip once more. I could have drunk and danced and walked Suzi home over and over again. It was no problem, no matter for *Micky the Beast*, the fifth member of the famous band, Hard Turd Machine. He could do anything. He knew every street in the city by heart. He could walk to his usual hitchhiking spot with his eyes shut. Show the tourists around in the meantime, if need be.

QUIET AND DARK

I drank the last drop of rum and threw away the bottle. I opened the car door. It was Toni who had recognised me and had stopped. Toni was one of Zlaja's old friends, one of Majbule's ultimate pop boys. I normally did not trust him, but was really happy to see him. I had waited for nearly an hour.

Toni's car was a rumbling bunker of sound: 2 Unlimited with 'No Limit.' Damn I hated that song. Sitting in the front seat was a skinny guy staring into the darkness. He had a flat nose and wore a cap. He did not introduce himself and did not say a word the entire trip.

Toni asked:

'What happened to your hair?'

And I replied:

'I got an electric shock at work!'

That's as much as I remember of that trip.

The last two kilometres I had to manage on foot. Toni lived in the centre of Majbule. When I climbed out of the car, I rrealised that I was not drunk. I was blotto. The rum had hit me rather hard.

The streets were deserted. I don't remember meeting anyone at all on the road. I remember it was dark. Very dark. The clouds had swarmed together in the sky, had covered it completely.

I walked past the roundabout and sang: 'And behind a cloud my moon has hidden, it has hidden my paths. Your struggling is in vain, fiddler. The other one gets the yellow quinces.'

Filthy Theatre! Good old Filthy Theatre. They too had become great patriots. They too had sold out, just like Bora

Čorba, the fool! 'Stamp your heels and say, 'Everything for Croatia'? The shittiest title on an album in the history of rock!

But they still made good ballads, I had to give them that. Cool refrains!

I approached the camp. The details of the night struggled for my attention. I had a hard time keeping my thoughts on just one. The pre-party at the citadel, Suzi's salty earlobes, six White Button cassettes in a display window, bambus, the massive head-banging seen from the very back of the stage.

I zapped from one high point to the next. Felt ultimate joy all over my body. What a summer! What a night! What a birthday! And Suzi, the chick was completely undefinable. She had a bloody good sense of humour. Just the thought of our meeting on Monday made my entire being tremble.

The note with Suzi's telephone number was in my right pocket, and I made sure it was still there when I suddenly spotted a car. It was an old Renault 4, I remember. It stopped about fifty metres away from the Muscle Market. The car's lights were out, and it was parked almost in the middle of the road. There was no indication that it had been in an accident or anything like that. It was also completely empty.

As I passed the reception building, I saw the faint lamplight behind the counter. It must be the desk lamp the psychopath normally left on. A pair of flip-flops, one on top of the other, were on the floor in front of the worn, rectangular sofa. I could glimpse his bare shoulder and a little of his back in the gleam of the light. He was wearing a sleeveless jumper.

Down from the beach, I heard a couple of distant shouts, and I estimated them to be coming from the D3 side. There was a good place to light a fire, and straight away I felt like going down there. I still felt full of energy and convinced that there was a party down there.

A fire down by the beach, I thought, a fag and a little more partying would be a perfect continuation – a perfect bonus track on top of this brilliant concert evening.

When I went past the reception and turned towards the terrace and its excessive amount of lights, I bumped into a man I had never seen before. He came from the terrace, but was already standing in the shadows when we barged into each other.

I have often later wondered about that, that I of all people ran into him. That we literally bumped into each other. Had I taken another route towards the camp from Majbule, I probably would have avoided him. Because then I would have gone in through the gate by the bungalows or through the side entrance by D1. But I took the other way, because it was shorter.

We apologised to each other, and said almost at the same time, don't worry about it. I could not see the man's face, but from his accent I could hear straight away that he was a gypsy, and Serbian at that. He had a distinct Ekavian accent, and only later did I wonder why I was not more puzzled by it. That it did not make me more cautious.

It also surprised me that he just opened up with such a strong Serbian accent. Of course he could not know where I was from. I could just as well have been a high-ranking Croat with strong family ties to the president or his inner circle.

'Problem,' he said. He was lost, and now his car had also run out of 'soup.' He needed help. Was there a phone box in the area. He had coins. He just had to ring someone who could come and bring him a can of 'soup.'

'Obviously, man, of course, it's right here.'

I led him five metres back in the direction he came from, and pointed at the other entrance to the reception – the one facing the terrace.

'Here! Look here,' I said really excited that I was able to help him.

I don't remember if I did, but it would not surprise me if I patted him kindly on the shoulder and said that everything was going to be okay. What the hell was I thinking?

The psychopath got up and opened after numerous knocks on the door. He looked more sad than upset when he switched on the main light. He moved incredibly slowly.

'What is it?'

The man, who turned out to be around forty, told him that he needed petrol. He had to ring someone in Lovgar. He spoke very energetically and apologetically, and the waking night watchman was clearly struggling to follow.

'Come in,' he said in the end.

I got the impression that he did not recognise me at all. He did not deign to take a single look at me.

The man went inside and Bruno closed the door on my face.

I turned around and walked across the terrace, happy to have been able to help the man.

All the balcony lights in D1 were out, including ours on the second floor. I took it for granted that Mum and Dad were asleep. That I could just go down to the beach and prolong this night by an extra hour or two. I had long since lost track of time, but it must have been getting on five.

On the way towards the stairs leading down towards the path, I heard voices again. This time right down on the staircase. Someone going up them.

Zlaja and Fric!

'Hey, man!'

We threw our arms around one another.

They wished me a happy birthday, and Fric grabbed my hand, as if we were going to arm wrestle:

'Shit man, now that is a hairstyle!'

Zlaja said:

'Cool, man! What's going on? You look like a zombie.'

'Where did you get to?' I pretended to be disappointed and asked Zlaja for a fag.

'Sorry, sorry, sorry!' he said. 'That was the plan, believe me. There was nothing we would rather do. But then we met the craziest group of chicks from Hungary and ...'

'Yes, in Adria,' Fric nodded. 'It's unbelievable. They top

everything I have seen.'

Zlaja lit my cigarette:

'It took time and …'

'Okay, okay! It's all right,' I said. 'It's a good excuse. Actually the only one I can accept. You guys know that. And I love you guys, dammit. You know that. I love you!'

They laughed:

'Shhhhh! Not so loud!'

'Damn are you ever drunk!'

'What have you been drinking?'

'A bit of rum,' I said. 'Just a little bit.'

'One of the girls is just the thing for you,' Zlaja said. 'Trust me. There are nine. We just nab three of the best.'

'Nine? Wow! An entire flock.'

'A fucking volleyball club, man! On an excursion! Sixteen, seventeen years old, the entire lot.'

I thought about Suzi. She was also seventeen.

'No, forget it,' I said. 'I've got a date on Monday.'

The moment I said Monday, I heard the reception door open.

I stood with my back to the door, and when I turned around, I saw Bruno approaching at a brisk pace. It completely caught me off guard. That all of a sudden he was anything but sleepy and slow moving.

He came racing out in bare feet. Still wearing an undershirt and Bermuda shorts. The sound of his bare soles on the terrace's cement made a dull but loud echo.

'You two,' he said to Zlaja and Fric. 'Go home! Get lost!'

'Why?'

'You don't live here. You don't have anything to do with this place. Get lost!'

'What?'

'We were actually on our way home,' Fric said.

'No, let's go down to the beach,' I said. 'There's a party!'

'No, you're not going anywhere!' Bruno hissed.

'What?' I said and looked at him.

'There's nobody on the beach,' Zlaja said.

'*You* are not going anywhere!'

'Why not?'

'Why not? "Why not?"' he said in a spastic voice, trying to impersonate me s.

'Why did you drag that gypsy into the camp?'

'Drag in? No, he was already ...'

'He was wasted, man! Just like you! You can't be dragging all the scum of the earth in here! Children live here! Families! Do you follow?'

He did not shove me. He barely nudged me. Kind of pedagogical. Didactic. With an open hand. Nothing special and nothing I would not have been able to handle on a normal day. But I was anything but sober, and he caught me off balance. I stumbled backwards a couple of steps, tripped over Zlaja's feet and fell over.

'Dammit.'

I leant on my right elbow:

'He was ...'

He was already in the camp, I wanted to say, but went quiet. The sight of the fascist and Zlaja and Fric from my frog's perspective made a strange impression on me. I did not like the position at all.

I got up quickly and immediately got dizzy. I stood right by the top of the staircase, lost my balance and fell down. Luckily I went down at an angle, so that I immediately hit the railing with my left arm. I instinctively grabbed one of the iron uprights and the rest of my body slipped four or five steps down.

It was idiotic. It must have looked very strange.

Zlaja took a few steps down to help me, but I got up and twisted my arm free.

'I'll be fine.'

I got really angry, but pushed the anger aside. My towering mood did not lay in ruins yet. I felt that I could easily endure this one humiliation. Kick the fascist out of this night. Remember everything else, all the cool stuff. If he turned and left, I would easily be able to forget him and what had happened.

But he did not do that. He stood up there and let out a series of muffled 'Ha! Ha's.' I hurried up the stairs despite a thumping pain in my one knee.

'Tsk, tsk, tsk! Look at yourself, boy,' he said. 'You look like a scarecrow. A shaggy shit!'

I finally stepped onto the terrace.

'Leave us alone,' I said. 'There's no problems here. We're minding our own business.'

'Oh, are you?'

'Yes. And that man was already in the camp. He was standing right here.'

'Don't lie to me, you little faggot! I saw you walking together!'

The last sentence shook me so much that I froze. He said it with such boldness, that at first I really doubted myself.

'What?'

Zlaja and Fric did not have a clue what we were talking about.

'You came here walking together! Down the road!'

I saw the image of his flip-flops and his shoulder. The picture I had seen through the glass door of the reception.

The doubt disappeared:

'You must have dreamt that!'

'What did you say?'

'That you must have dreamt that!' I repeated with more irritation, because in the meantime his 'you little faggot' had reached my dying brain cells.

He shoved me again.

'Are you saying I'm lying?'

The two falls, the pain in my knee, and what he had said about my hair – all of that I could put up with. But this was too much. To make fun of me in front of my friends and make me think that what I had experienced had not happened – was simply too much. Still I tried one last time to ward him off, to dodge him before he got really aggressive.

'No … I don't know,' I said. 'You have your truth and I have mine … Fair enough?'

What the hell else was I going to say? He had already grabbed me by my shirt.

Zlaja attempted to get between us, but was shoved aside. Fric stood looking in shock.

'Are you saying I'm lying?' he repeated, as if he had not heard what I just said. 'Are you saying I'm lying?'

I did not answer.

A tuft of hair fell over my face and covered part of my view but I did not move it. I just looked at him.

'Eh?' he said, and gave me a limp slap.

The blood rushed to my head. I was so provoked by the way he slapped me. At half strength. The arrogance. It was as though I was not even worth the effort.

I completely lost control, and like a genuine llama I spat in his face:

'YOU YOKEL! DO YOU THINK I'M SCARED OF YOU?'

He let go of me with one hand and wiped his eyes with the back of his hand. I think he was surprised.

'Miki, come on, we're taking off!' Fric shouted but I did not move.

'WHY CAN'T YOU JUST LEAVE ME IN PEACE! I HAVEN'T DONE ANYTHING TO YOU!' I stood shouting instead of either landing one on him or taking off.

'Shut your trap! People are sleeping!'

'YES, AND YOU WERE TOO. THE MAN WAS INSIDE THE CAMP AND YOU WERE SLEEPING! I …'

I did not see it coming. I just felt a rock hit my right temple. It pushed me to the side, and the pain announced itself after a delay.

The blow was hard, but much to my own surprise I remained standing. Zlaja and Fric shouted at the moron, and suddenly, like some kind of ghost, my Dad appeared between Bruno and I.

'Leave my child alone!' I heard him say.

His presence confused me. I managed to notice that he

was half naked and not wearing his glasses, before the moron punched him.

Dad groaned: 'Ow-oww!' and fell. I swung my right arm as hard as I could. I wanted to hit the fascist in the face – that stupid, unshaven face – but he blocked. He twisted my arm around my back and pushed me away.

Everything happened bloody quick after that. The psychopath raced towards me. He started with a series of blows, both from the right and the left. I waved my arms and evaded as best as I could but I had no chance. He had got hold of my shirt again, and I could not tear myself loose. At one point I stood bent over at hip height, while he held my hair and dragged me aside.

Zlaja, Fric and Dad's voices, and words like 'Leave him alone!' and 'Hey, hey!' only seeped in faintly. Everything began to flicker in front of me. My right side was burning the most. The psycho was left-handed. He spouted a lot of shit while he hit me, but the words seemed strangely foreign to me. They could just as well have been spoken in German, English or Swedish for that matter. He blabbered and bickered and flooded me with groaning syllables.

If I could just hit him once, I thought. If he would just shut his trap.

But he didn't. He went on and on and on. I don't know why he had to talk so much while he beat me. Or whether it was the twinkling stars I saw after his last blow, or if it was just light on the balconies of D2 that were switched on here and there. I heard new and more distant voices echo in my head – maybe someone complained about the noise in the late hours – and then it went quiet. Quiet and dark.

FAST FORWARD STOP

I did not come to until I was a little ways outside the camp. At the side of the road diagonally across from D1. Zlaja, Fric and Dad had dragged me there. There were too many eyes on the terrace, and two of them were probably Pero's. Who else would have shouted 'Hit him again! Give him one for me!' while they dragged me away. Only one of the fascists in the camp could have screamed 'A new fashion!' in that situation.

I sat on a white, square block of stone near a fig tree, where the locals occasionally gathered. My neck hurt like hell when I moved it. The right side of my face was swollen, but I was not bleeding. They were straight cuffs to the ear that the psychopath had landed on me.

'Are you okay?' Zlaja, Fric and Dad kept asking.

I nodded, but said nothing. I had withdrawn. Dad, Zlaja and Fric's presence bothered me. I just wished that they were not there! That they had not seen all that.

'What did you do to him?' Dad asked.

I looked at his shoes. His feet were bare.

'Not many people saw,' he said. 'We'll talk to him tomorrow. No matter what you did, then ...'

I raised my eyes.

He understands nothing. He never has. He was never going to.

The moment I thought that, the disappointment disappeared, and I felt bad for the old man. So bad that I felt like hitting him, deleting him, removing him from my sight.

'Go upstairs and take care of Mum!' I said. 'I'll be there in a bit.'

'Come with me.'

'No,' I growled. 'I'll be there in a bit!'

He placed a hand on my shoulder:

'Let me see your face.'

I removed his hand. Zlaja and Fric looked on. But I did not care.

'Go inside now,' I said and looked at him one last time.

He turned and left.

The light from the terrace lit up his back. He rubbed his temple, while he cautiously walked behind a pine tree. Short-sighted and without his glasses, he held up his left hand against the front of D1. He was afraid of tripping.

Then he disappeared around the corner of the building.

Fric coughed. We sat in silence for a moment.

'Where is he?' I asked.

'Reception,' Zlaja said. 'He's gone inside.'

'I'll kill him,' Fric shouted. 'He ought to be fucking locked up!'

'I'm going in to get some sleep,' I said and looked at the ground. 'I'm tired.'

'Are you sure?'

I nodded.

'Sure you don't want to come over to my place?' Zlaja asked.

I shook my head. Tried to stand. They helped me up.

My head hurt like hell. I was a little dizzy and felt nauseous.

'It'll be alright,' I said and walked across the road. 'Just let go of me.'

'I'll come by tomorrow,' Fric said. 'We'll make a plan. We'll pound him, dammit! We'll tear his brains out!'

'Yes. Obviously, man. It's settled. See you!'

'See you!'

I walked along the wall and out on the terrace. Went through the same entrance that Mirko Parasite took the time he returned to the camp with blood on his Hawaiian shirt. The lights in reception and on a few balconies of D1 and D2 were still lit, but I saw nobody anywhere. On our balcony and in our room the lights were out.

Mum. Had she seen it? Was she standing on the balcony while the whole thing unfolded?

I went into the building and noticed the familiar smell of synthetic material and rubber – a smell that had never disappeared from the stairwell. In a way it was the smell of D1.

I walked up the carpeted stairs, slowly and absent-mindedly, and the more steps I took, the heavier my feet got.

A few steps before the second floor it happened. I started to think about what kind of night it had been. A brief summary of the evening's events rolled through my mind's eye – Mauro, the citadel, Suzi, Ukulele – and I abandoned the last step and stopped.

Seventeen.

It's my birthday today.

It was quiet in the stairwell. The light I had switched on was still lit. I was three, four, five steps from the second floor and could hear a coughing from one of the rooms on the first floor. I could see that someone had spilled gravy on the floor and had not cleaned up after themselves.

Seventeen.

Of all the days of the year it had to be this exact one he had chosen to give me a thrashing. Could he not have picked another one, that fool? Now he is connected to this night for good.

The light went out.

The electrical socket glowed in the dark in front of me.

The thought of going up to the second floor and laying down next to Dad seemed impossible to me. It was as though a glass wall had risen between me and the next step. I could *not* simply go up, lie down, sleep and wake up in the morning as though nothing had happened, as Dad obviously intended to do.

How was I going to get through the next day? I thought. What was I going to tell people? What was I going to do when I saw that idiot, that ox, that stupid fascist again?

I stepped onto the next step with one foot, but quickly

moved it back. I turned around. For a brief moment I remained on the same step, now with my back to the second floor and room 210 and Mum and Dad.

Something yielded, quivered and lumped together in my stomach. I was both angry and confused and had no idea what to do. The only thing that was clear to me was that I could not go the rest of the way to room 210 and lie down and sleep. Because then that moron in reception had won.

I took one step down the stairs.

Then another.

A third …

Before I really realised what I was doing, I was standing outside the entrance to D1 again.

Still nobody on the terrace.

Still a light on in reception.

He's awake, that fool. There's a shift change in an hour. It has to look like he was awake the whole time, the parasite!

Behind the fig tree and the stone block by D1 there was a private fence with red and white wooden paling. I remembered that several of the stakes were loose. A couple were even missing.

I hurried across the road and grabbed the first stake but it wouldn't budge. I tried the next one, and the next.

My neck was still hurting and I could feel a heat stinging my scalp. But the hate and the anger made it hurt less. I already pictured myself walking to reception, standing over the moron with a stake in my hand, while he lies down and pleads for mercy.

But just like one of the two roads to the camp I had chosen in Majbule, and the gypsy who had run into me of all people, again something happened that led me in another direction. Just like back then with the war, the birth certificate and the secondary school. Just like back then with Nina and the shell fragments and all kinds of major and minor things that had led me to Majbule and this fence and this stupid far-out situation, again something happened that changed everything.

I raced along the fence with my face smashed in and murderous thoughts and tugged at a number of stakes, which to my great surprise all turned out to have been repaired and nailed to their stable, horizontal boards. The owner had at long last got his act together and nailed them in place, and this small everyday detail, this incontrovertible fact, that became clearer and clearer to me, as I raced along the fence and tugged on it like a madman, muddled my plan and led me away from the reception. And when I reached the end of the fence, I continued walking and checked the neighbour's fence, which was made made of metal. The next one was a wire fence, so I skipped that one, while the fourth one was just as stable as the first.

'AAARGH!' I shouted and jabbed with my arms and was close to crying, but clenched my teeth and spun on my heels.

I took a couple of instinctive steps towards the camp, but stopped restlessly and turned around again.

The roofs of the houses and the trees in the gardens could now be seen. The sky seemed a little brighter out by the peninsula. Before long the dawn would cut into my birthday for good, and I stood there and had no clue what to do.

I wiped the tears off my face and looked back. The street curved ahead, and I could no longer see the reception, only the corner balconies of D1.

It felt good to establish this. It was my first positive thought since the attack. The forty or fifty metres, or however many there were now between me and the camp, meant that I felt a little better.

I slowly walked forward a few metres. Thought one last time about finding a syake or an iron pole, but stowed that thought for good. Mum and Dad sat up there waiting for me, but that no longer played any role for me. They could just wait, for all I cared. They were very good at that.

I kept walking. Passed the gate to the complex by the bungalows. Passed the bungalows too.

I had no intention of going anywhere specific. It just felt nice to walk, look back and establish that neither D1, D2 nor

D3 were pursuing me. That reception remained where it had always been. That there was greater and greater distance between me and the camp.

It felt good to know that the night was not over. That the final word had not been spoken.

No, there will never be such a cool night at Ukulele again, I thought. I'll never turn seventeen again. The psychopath has ruined this night once and for all. He has placed his filthy hand on an unforgettable summer, and nobody can wash it clean again.

But I am the one who will have the final word. I am still the one who decides. And that is the most important thing.

The restlessness and the confusion were decreasing. I grew calmer and continued to walk. I had no plan, and still I felt that I was doing the right thing: taking one step at a time and not looking back. I stopped under a cypress tree by the marina. The spot where Samir and I had bought sardines for my fifteenth birthday party an unfathomably long time ago. Once more I saw myself standing and explaining to Mum and Dad what had happened. I stowed the thought away once more.

It's not going to happen. I'm not going back. Not tonight!

Fabio! I thought. I'll nip over to his place. He is the only one who has heard about the psychopath. He'll understand everything.

A defiant resolution filled me while I walked past the roundabout and on towards Vešnja. It was a little brighter. I started to think what I would do, who I should ring from Fabio's phone, when the headlamps of a green Fiat appeared.

I stuck out my thumb, but the car just whizzed past.

The hair, dammit! I do look like a zombie – a zombie that has been beaten to top it all off.

I searched for a hairband in my pockets, but only found some coins and the note with Suzi's phone number on it. Should I cancel our date on Monday? Yes? No? Maybe? Aargh, I could not make a decision about that right now!

I gathered my hair and tried to straighten it with my fingers, so it did not look so crazy and airy. I unbuttoned my checked shirt, pushed my hair behind my left ear and let if fall down over the swollen right cheek.

The evening at Ukulele was definitively over.

I had already left Majbule and realised I was going to Vešnja, when a car stopped. The man behind the wheel had grey hair and a grey beard, and I recognised him at once. It was an older guy who ran a souvenir stand with small paintings of local beaches and other junk in Adria.

I was a little unsure whether he recognised me. He asked:

'Where are you going?'

'How far are *you* going?'

'I'm going to Grozvin.'

'Great. Me too.'

How and why those words came out of my mouth, I had no clue. I said it with such brashness so naturally it caught me offguard. But it felt good. I felt a defiant, masochistic joy. Pure enjoyment at doing something completely stupid.

The inside of the car smelled of cold ashtrays, and I made myself comfortable in the back seat. I did not want him to see my tender, swollen right side. That was where it hurt most. The moron was left-handed. That was why I could not see the first blow coming. Not just because I was drunk.

I leaned back. Felt strong and free. I felt like I was the one making the decisions.

Thought: I'm not bloody well going to Grozvin! I'll hop out at the ring road in Vešnja. What the hell am I going to do in Grozvin? I know nobody there. I'll go to Fabio's. He's probably sleeping now, but I'll wake him up.

So Vešnja it was, and that was fine by me. But when we reached the crossing by the ring road, where the old man should turn right and I had to get out, once again I got enjoyment from not doing as planned.

I said nothing. I just let him keep driving.

Leave, dammit! I thought. Let's go to Grozvin! Let me see

what happens!

I leaned my temple against the cold window and looked out. The old man drove in silence, luckily. He must have smelt that I had been drinking, maybe even noticed my swollen cheek. But he asked no questions, did not say a word, and I loved him for that.

The car glided quietly and calmly along the coastal stretch towards Grozvin. The surface of the Adriatic reflected the nascent sunlight, which forced through the hovering greyish-blue clouds.

'They're calling for rain,' my driver said.

'Yes, I heard,' I answered, even though I had not. We drove through the village where I got an electric shock, the day Neno rang. The day I was equally happy and equally sad as during the past twenty-four hours, just in the opposite order.

The first raindrops hit the windscreen when we passed the stadium in Grozvin.

'Where should I let you out?' the old man asked.

'It's not important. What's your final destination?'

'To the post office. I'm actually going to Zagreb, but not for another hour. Right now I'm going to ...' he said and continued with a story about his daughter, but I was no longer paying attention.

Zagreb! I thought. Of course!

The new idea really got me going. I stepped out of the car, breathed in the fresh air and waved goodbye to the nice man behind the wheel.

Zagreb! I'll go to Zagreb, find the Swedish embassy and show them all the swelling and bruises. Tell them all about what happened. Tell them all about the bros I have up there. About everything I know about their country. All about the population and the lakes and the average temperatures. Everything I have read up on at Vešnja's library. Tell them that I know that parties are called *kalas* and beautiful girls *vackra flickor*. That I very much agree with their ideas, especially about music libraries. It is no surprise that both Ace of Base and Roxette are Swedes. Yeah, they're not to my taste, but okay, what do I know, I'm just a stupid little Bosnian and simply declare: They are, after all, international bands!

'Mr Pozder, tell me, what do you want, sir?'

'Sorry, Mr Nilsson! Sorry to come barging in here like this, but there are some first-class psychos living in that camp in Majbule! There are a lot of them and they don't like me. I know that sitting in the shade can also be dangerous, that you can't really be safe anywhere. They are dangerous, the ultraviolet rays, and all basements have a door, if not a window or very thin and fragile walls. But can't you help me all the same? I can't go on like nothing happened. I can't just say, 'Yellow!' or sit waiting for the war to end, or pray to God to win the lottery. I have no ticket, this isn't serious, I have to do something myself, I have to get away, you have to help me!'

'It's difficult to follow you when you speak so quickly and wave your arms about, Mr Pozder. Calm down a little and be more specific?'

'Yes, sorry! Sorry! Well ... I was born by a river, and some psychopaths, some different ones, not the ones from Majbule, chose to establish a front line there. The shells fell. The space around us closed in ... But ... had I lived a little further away ... or many, many kilometres away ... like some ... yes ... But I lived there, and so did my friend Adi! Adi was a nice guy for the most part ... I don't know what he's like now ... We were crammed into buses one day, the army's buses, and you see Mr Nilsson: I have never liked riding on buses! Nor has my father. He is ...'

One dark sentence replaced the next. I fantasised about this visit to the embassy, went to town, and amused myself with it, while I walked towards the main road that led out of town.

'... And when you have finally got a little air ... a little bit of calm ... when you finally think that you are on the other side of the minefield, then they arrive ... the psychopaths ...

They tip over and smash things … and you live side by side with them and you keep your mouth shut and tread carefully and try to ignore them, and the most you get out of it is a cool night at Ukulele, unless of course they come and destroy that too … these are the conditions here, Mr Nilsson, and look at my friend Igor, for example… Look!'

Igor lay dead in the Slavonic fields and Gogi was snoring and dreaming about nothing and Zlaja and Fric were dreaming but did not sleep. I strolled down an uneven pavement in Grozvin, trudged along in worsening rain talking to myself.

To Zagreb or not? Zagreb. Definitely. Where can I find the road that leads to that city? A good spot to hitchhike? A female driver? Preferably!

Goodbye, Fabio! Goodbye, Kaća! I'll return one day. With a big band, I promise. You can come backstage, no, dammit – on the stage! You can play with me. You can tour with me. We'll see the world, tour entire continents. Show all those fascists our worth! We are going to …'

Smack!

The pavement was uneven, and I struck it with my chin. My hands saved my nose and forehead, but my chin pounded into the asphalt. I got up quickly, as quickly as I possibly could, and checked. There was a cut on my chin, it was bleeding and it stung. The rain ran down my back. I stood for a while, completely motionless, with soaking hair, dirty clothes, a swollen face and a soul in tatters.

To hell with Zagreb and the Swedish embassy! To hell with it all! All I want is for it to stop raining.

It was one of the city's main roads, four lanes. There were a lot of cars, even though it was Sunday.

I sloshed ahead in my soaked All Stars, towards the traffic lights thirty metres ahead. On the other side of the road was a phone box with a smashed, half-open glass door.

The first person I thought of calling was Mister No. Second, Mum and Dad. The moron was no longer on duty, and they must be up by now. I thought about calling them and saying that under *no* circumstances would I return to the camp. That they had to pack our things at once, meet me in Vešnja or here in Grozvin. I didn't care. We had to find somewhere else to live.

But soon that thought also shrivelled up, this final belief that the two of them could be dislodged from Majbule. My chin stung like hell. I felt the coins in my pocket and wiped the blood off my neck. I knew who to call!

The cars sprayed water everywhere. They heavy raindrops hit the asphalt like solid-coloured marbles, like shotgun pellets.

I was leant up against the iron post of the traffic lights and stared at the light and the crooked STOP sign on the other side. It continued to rain. The cars roared past.

When I finally realised that the traffic light was broken – that it simply refused to change from red to green – I had enough of it all and stepped onto the road.

One honk.

Two honks.

Three …

'Hello!'

'Hi, Uncle! Miki here.'

'Hi, Emir! What's happened?'

'Where is the Swedish embassy?'

'What?'

'The Swedish embassy. In Zagreb. Where is it?'

'I don't understand … Are you guys in Zagreb?'

'No, we're not. But I'm heading there now. Can you get me a passport as quick as possible?' I said and slid my final coins in the slot.